PRAISE FOR TAHOE CHASE

PRAISE FOR TAHOE TRAP

"A FASCINATING STORY WITH FIRST CLASS WRITING and, of course, my favorite character, Spot, a Great Dane that steals most of the scenes."

- Mary Lignor, Feathered Quill Book Reviews

"SUPER CLEVER... More twists in the plot toward the end of the book turn the mystery into an even more suspenseful thriller."

-Harvee Lau, Book Dilettante

"AN EXCITING MURDER MYSTERY... I watch for the ongoing developments of Jack Reacher, Joanna Brady, Dismas Hardy, Peter and Rina Decker, and Alex Cross to name a few. But these days I look forward most to the next installment of Owen McKenna."

- China Gorman blog

PRAISE FOR TAHOE HIJACK

"BEGINNING TO READ TAHOE HIJACK IS LIKE FLOOR-BOARDING A RACE CAR... RATING: A+"

- Cathy Cole, Kittling Books

"A THRILLING READ... any reader will find the pages of his thrillers impossible to stop turning"

- Caleb Cage, The Nevada Review

"THE BOOK CLIMAXES WITH A TWIST THE READER DOESN'T SEE COMING, WORTHY OF MICHAEL CONNELLY"

- Heather Gould, Tahoe Mountain News

"I HAD TO HOLD MY BREATH DURING THE LAST PART OF THIS FAST-PACED THRILLER"

- Harvee Lau, Book Dilettante

PRAISE FOR TAHOE HEAT

"IN TAHOE HEAT, BORG MASTERFULLY WRITES A SEQUENCE OF EVENTS SO INTENSE THAT IT BELONGS IN AN EARLY TOM CLANCY NOVEL"

- Caleb Cage, Nevada Review

"TAHOE HEAT IS A RIVETING THRILLER"

- John Burroughs, Midwest Book Review

PRAISE FOR TAHOE SILENCE

WINNER, BEN FRANKLIN AWARD, BEST MYSTERY OF THE YEAR!

"A HEART-WRENCHING MYSTERY THAT IS ALSO ONE OF THE BEST NOVELS WRITTEN ABOUT AUTISM"
STARRED REVIEW - Jo Ann Vicarel, Library Journal

CHOSEN BY LIBRARY JOURNAL AS ONE OF THE FIVE BEST MYSTERIES OF THE YEAR

"THIS IS ONE ENGROSSING NOVEL...IT IS SUPERB"
- Gayle Wedgwood, Mystery News

"ANOTHER EXCITING ENTRY INTO THIS TOO-LITTLE-KNOWN SERIES"
- Mary Frances Wilkens, Booklist

PRAISE FOR TAHOE KILLSHOT

"BORG BELONGS ON THE BESTSELLER LISTS with Parker, Paretsky and Coben"
- Merry Cutler, Annie's Book Stop, Sharon, Massachusetts
"A GREAT READ!"
-Shelley Glodowski, Midwest Book Review

"A WONDERFUL BOOK"
- Gayle Wedgwood, Mystery News

PRAISE FOR TAHOE ICE GRAVE

"BAFFLING CLUES...CONSISTENTLY ENTERTAINS"
- Kirkus Reviews

"A CLEVER PLOT... RECOMMEND THIS MYSTERY"
- John Rowen, Booklist

"A BIG THUMBS UP... MR. BORG'S PLOTS ARE SUPER-TWISTERS"
- Shelley Glodowski, Midwest Book Review

TAHOE GHOST BOAT

by

Todd Borg

THRILLER PRESS

Thriller Press First Edition, August 2014

TAHOE GHOST BOAT
Copyright © 2014 by Todd Borg

Library of Congress Control Number: 2014938250

ISBN: 978-1-931296-22-9

Cover design and map by Keith Carlson

Manufactured in the United States of America

For Kit

ACKNOWLEDGMENTS

Anyone can write a book. But only someone as lucky as me can get editing help from Liz Johnston, Eric Berglund, Christel Hall, and Kit Night. Good editing makes the difference between a presentation that distracts the reader and a presentation that allows the reader to pay attention to the story. I have fantastic editors who make me look much more professional than I am, and for that I'm eternally grateful.

The same thing applies to a book's cover. I'm always after a cover that screams, "Excitement, Mystery, and Intrigue inside!" I'm incredibly lucky to have the magic of artist Keith Carlson, who each year creates another cover that communicates this message and yet makes the cover fit in with all of my other covers in perfect series fashion. This year, I hoped for something that would communicate a "Ghost Boat" version of excitement, mystery, and intrigue, and I was wowed by the result!

Heartfelt thanks to all of them!

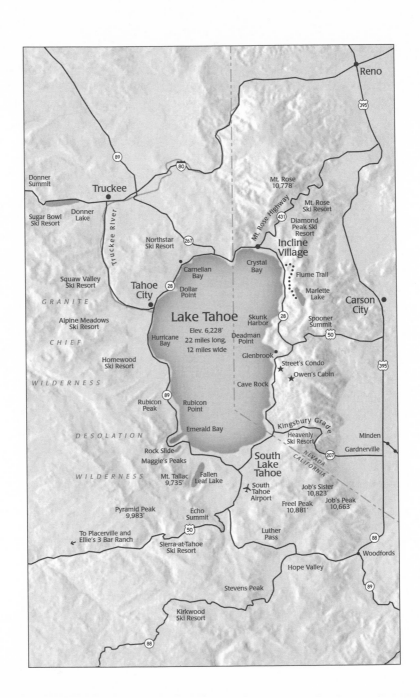

PROLOGUE

The wind and waves of the winter storm were ferocious. The skipper wrestled with the wheel of the restored Gar Wood wooden boat. He had left his dock on Hurricane Bay on the West Shore of Lake Tahoe and headed east-southeast, toward Glenbrook, twelve miles away on the far side of the mountain lake. He'd barely gone one hundred yards from shore before he thought his mission was crazy. He shouted at the wind while he drove the troughs of the five-foot winter swell.

"Nobody kicks Ian Lassitor! Nobody!" He took his right hand off the wheel just long enough to pull his flask out of the cup holder that dangled on a gimbal mount beneath the cockpit dash. He swigged enough Jim Beam to spread warmth down to his frozen toes, jammed the flask back into the holder, and grabbed onto the wheel again.

The man angled downwind at the same rate as the waves rolled south. He steered between the wave crests. Now and then, the swells became uneven. The waves didn't line up. A wave trough ended like a little box canyon. The skipper had no choice but to drive the little wooden boat directly up a wave that loomed above him like a small mountain.

The Gar Wood was a 1947 Ensign, its lines designed for cutting small chop at high speed, not for coping with deep-water swell. The boat teetered at the crest of the wave then tipped down the other side, nearly swamping.

The howling winter wind on Lake Tahoe created conditions more like those on the arctic ocean than those on a lake, even a very large one. With Tahoe's great depth and size, the cold, north wind created a swell that grew large and mean as it rolled 22 miles from the North Shore to the South Shore.

After coming close to capsizing the woodie, the man was

desperate not to allow his little boat to be forced up another one of the big waves.

Shouting at the wind helped him control his emotions.

"The Lassitors are hard-ass mariners! Nothing can break us!"

The swells on Lake Tahoe were inconsistent. But by steering hard and revving the small inboard engine here and there, the man angled from one swell to another and mostly stayed down in the liquid valleys. It made the ride a bit less dangerous. It also kept his little boat almost out of sight.

As the Gar Wood's skipper struggled with another swell, he heard a sudden roar to the starboard. He jerked his head to see the source. The hull of an approaching craft blasted over the wave top to his side. The wave thrust the bow of the onrushing boat up into the air.

There was no time to react. But in the single second before the other boat struck his, the skipper realized that the approaching vessel had been downwind, its low profile blocked by the big waves and its sound masked by the constant howl of the wind and the crash of whitecaps.

The woodie's skipper gasped as the other craft shot off the big wave and loomed above the woodie's starboard gunnel. The skipper cranked his head around, watching horrified as the other boat crashed down onto the Gar Wood's engine housing just behind where he sat. The blow was too much for the woodie's hull structure to withstand.

The man held the Gar Wood's steering wheel with one hand and grabbed the cockpit dashboard with the other as the woodie's sides cracked and shattered.

A large section of the boat's side broke into several pieces. One swung forward and hit the back of the skipper's head, slamming his face against the wheel. Another piece split into a sharp shard and stabbed through the man's hand, nailing it to the cockpit panel.

The man screamed. Blood spurted from his nose. His fingers clenched onto the dashboard like claws as blood gushed from the wound made by the wooden spear.

The other boat was an aluminum fishing boat. Its hull

snapped and then folded as it crashed down onto the woodie's engine housing, the center supported on the housing, the bow and stern down.

The woodie pilot tried to turn, tried to see the skipper of the fishing boat. But his hand, attached to the cockpit dash, locked him in place and prevented him from turning around.

He jerked his head the other way and watched as the next wave from the north crashed onto the lowered bow of the fishing boat, filling it with water.

The two boats immediately began to sink, broken and folded into each other.

The Gar Wood cracked in two. Now disconnected, the rear portion of the woodie came free from the more buoyant bow. The heavy engine and drive shaft pulled the stern down into the depths with a single unceremonious burp of escaping air.

The skipper's terror paralyzed him. He gritted his teeth as the bow section slowly lowered into the ice water. A garbled howl rose through clenched teeth, but it was soft against the roar of wind and waves.

The broken bow of the woodie had enough buoyancy to float just beneath the waves. The man's head was barely above water. But after just two minutes, the relentless waves of 32-degree water drove the voice from his throat and the sharp edge of terror from his brain. In another minute, hypothermia sapped his ability to hold his head above the water. His head slumped, and the cold water filled his lungs.

ONE

"One more ride?" Street Casey said as she brushed snow off her jacket. She had that wild, demonic look in her eyes that meant she would once again try the feint-left-and-lean-right trick on the toboggan, sending me tumbling off into the deep snow while she continued down the slope with Spot, my Harlequin Great Dane, chasing her.

"Okay, but it's my turn on the rear," I said. Because the last person on a toboggan has the steering advantage, I could maybe get the upper hand against Street's superior strategy.

We walked back up the slope, me hauling the toboggan, staying on the windblown ridge where the snow was packed enough to support our boots without snowshoes.

At the top of the slope, we pointed the toboggan toward fresh powder. In the distance, 1200 feet below us, lay Lake Tahoe, a startling indigo backdrop that distracted all winter playground participants. Closer to us, a mere 800 feet down, we could make out the buildings on Kingsbury Grade where I had my office and Street had her bug lab.

Street sat at the front of the toboggan, holding onto the curved wood, while I lay on the rear, my legs hanging off the end. I pushed off. We accelerated down the steep slope on the shoulder of the mountain where Heavenly Resort's ski runs sprawled above. Powder snow flew up over us. Street shrieked as she started leaning and pulling on the wood, trying to make me lose my grip and tumble off. I held the rope lines at the edge of the toboggan and used them to resist or add to Street's leaning. By dragging my feet one way or the other, I could also manipulate how the toboggan turned.

We slalomed down the mountain, out of control, laughing, each trying to throw the other off. Street started to lean right. I thought it was another feint. Then she leaned even harder to the right, so much so that the toboggan carved a sharp turn. I didn't see it coming. I went off the left side. But I held onto the rope line as I was dragged into the snow. The toboggan and Street flipped over onto me. The front dove into deep snow, and we all turned end-over-end and came to a fast stop. Street was lying on top of me. She giggled, kissed me, then dumped a handful of snow onto my face.

"Payback!" she shouted, referring to an earlier run when I'd managed to dump her. She pushed off me, jumped back on the toboggan and took off without me, laughing all the way.

Because the snow in most places was too deep for Spot to run in, he had stayed over on the windswept ridge, running down, keeping pace with us as we made our toboggan descent. Now, as Street raced down the rest of the slope, he sped up to meet her at the bottom, leaving me alone.

I lounged in the deep snow for a bit, listening to Street's laughter get more distant and then be joined by Spot's bark.

It was a glorious end to a perfect morning.

When I finally slogged down to join them, Street made the evil grin again and said, "What took you so long? Getting old or just out of shape?"

"Both older and outta-shaper." As I said it, the compressed snow beneath my boots gave way and I sank down a foot. Street was now standing above me.

"Do I need to find a more youthful model?" she asked as she jumped onto me, wrapping her legs around my waist. With her small additional weight, we sank farther. I lost my balance, and we fell sideways into the snow. Spot jumped onto us, and we became a snow-caked pile of bodies, laughing and barking.

Life doesn't get more delightful.

An hour later, Spot and I walked into my office building. We were still damp from rolling in the snow, but that wasn't an excuse to play hooky from work. And with my own coffee maker, a desk made of actual wood – albeit cracked and older than my grandfather – and a window which, if you looked carefully through the trees, gave a filtered view of Lake Tahoe, my digs were practically guaranteed to impress a potential client. In a nod to modernity, I'd gotten rid of the old desktop computer with the curved screen. When I set out my laptop and my new smart phone, no one could doubt my tech cred. Unless, that is, they asked me to do more than make a phone call or write a business letter. The only thing missing was a client.

The phone rang as I was pouring water into the Mr. Coffee. I didn't want to seem too eager, so I let the machine get it.

A woman started leaving a message. She sounded scared. I never could ignore a damsel in distress.

I picked up the phone.

"This is Owen McKenna," I interrupted. "I'm here."

"Mr. McKenna, I need help," she said in a shaky voice.

"Who's calling, please?" I said.

"My name is Nadia Lassitor. I'm... Hold on!"

I heard noises in the background. A high screech like squealing tires. The woman made a choking cry.

"Nadia, are you there?"

Another cry. "Help! A man is chasing me! I've been watching him in the mirror. But I almost swerved off the road."

"Who's the man chasing you?"

"I don't know! He's behind me. Two cars back. No, three."

"Where are you?" I asked.

"I'm coming down Echo Summit toward the South Shore."

"Has the person following you done anything to you?"

"No. But he's been behind me for hours!"

"How do you know it's the same man?" I asked.

"I just know! Can you do something?"

"Maybe. Keep driving. Take a deep breath. Stay calm." I paused. "Have there been any specific signs that this person is a threat?"

The woman made no response except for audible worried breathing.

"Because if there is a threat," I said, "I can call nine-one-one and have the police intercept you."

"No! You can't call the police."

"Nadia, if you're in danger, we should call them."

"No. Just tell me where to go so you can help me. Hurry!"

I thought about it. "What kind of car are you driving?" I asked.

"Dark blue BMW."

"Can you tell what kind of car the person following you is driving?"

"No. An SUV. Darker than mine. Maybe black."

"Do you know where the Heavenly Gondola is?" I asked.

Another pause.

"On Highway Fifty at Heavenly Village?" I added.

"Oh, right. Yes, of course."

"There's a bus stop pullover as you get close to the gondola's base station. Pull in there. Get out of your car and run up past the gondola and back to the parking ramp. Go inside the ramp and keep going as if you're going to walk out the other side."

"Then what?"

"If your pursuer is serious, he will stop and follow you. I'll be in the ramp to intercept."

"Okay." The phone disconnected.

I hung up and turned to Spot who was sprawled on his side. At seven feet from nose to tail-tip, he took up most of the available real estate in my office. His eyes were shut. We'd only been in the office a few minutes. I didn't think that anyone, man or beast, could fall asleep that fast. But we'd burned a lot of calories during our morning snow play, so it made sense.

"Hey, largeness," I said.

He opened a single droopy, unfocused eye.

"We're in a hurry, Spot. Wanna go for another ride?"

Outside of eating and, maybe, tobogganing, it was his favorite activity. He rolled onto his elbows, pushed up to a sitting position, and then, grunting, stood. At only 45 pounds less than my 215, it was work to get his bulk up from the floor. But another head-out-the-window rush beckoned.

We went back down the stairs and out the door of the office building. The entry was much improved since the remodeling contractor trucked away the last of the scaffolding that had collapsed the month before.

Spot jumped into the Jeep.

I started the engine and rolled down the rear window. Spot stuck his head out and looked around with excitement as if he hadn't seen the area hundreds of times before.

I took the Jeep down Kingsbury Grade and turned left at the highway. We drove past the casino hotels, crossed the state line into California, parked in the ramp behind Heavenly Village, and walked out onto the pedestrian plaza just far enough to see the bus stop a short distance beyond.

Dozens of people in bright-colored sports clothes carried their skis and snowboards through six inches of new snow to the gondola base station. The gray gondola cars emerged from the station at regular intervals, each making a short swing as the machinery clamped them onto the fast-moving cable to be rushed two miles and 3000 vertical feet up the mountain.

Ten minutes later, a dark blue BMW jerked out of the right lane and came to a halt in the bus stop lane. A woman in a dark pantsuit the same blue as the car got out carrying a small dark blue purse. She slammed the car door and did a girly, high-heels run around the Beemer, one hand held out, palm down, doing an exaggerated back-and-forth wave. She stepped over the slushy berm at the side of the road, then hurried across the open area near the gondola. She was a match for the Beemer. Stylish, sleek, and she looked fast even if she didn't move with speed. But her two-inch heels weren't good in snow. On her fifth or sixth step, she slipped on an icy patch and fell on her butt. I wanted to go help, but I didn't want my presence to discourage any pursuer.

She got up fast, brushed off her pants, and continued on, limping across the snowy plaza, her hand rubbing her butt. She'd have a large bruise, but she'd be okay.

Out on the boulevard, a black Buick SUV pulled in behind the BMW, its bumper almost touching the Beemer's, and a short, very thin guy with longish black hair got out. The man wore skinny black jeans and a turtleneck and over it a shiny black leather jacket, unzipped.

The guy put his right hand on the hood of the Buick and did

a little vault over the point where the two vehicles kissed.

I jogged back into the dark parking ramp and told Spot to sit-stay on one side. He hesitated, no doubt wondering why I'd make him sit on cold concrete in a dark garage when the winter sun was hot out on the plaza. I told him again, and he slowly sat. I walked over to the other side and stood in the dark. Spot looked at me, his ears perked up. I raised a finger to my lips. I saw his muscles tense.

"Stay!" I said again, holding up my hand, palm out.

I looked over the parked vehicles toward the ramp entrance.

The skinny guy in the black leather jacket trotted after Nadia Lassitor, his hiking boots much better suited for snow than her dress-up footgear. Without running, he moved three times as fast as she did, and I worried that he'd get to her before she even came into the garage.

But she made it first. I made a soft whistle and waved to get her attention. I pointed to the other exit.

"Go right on through the garage and back outside," I said in a loud whisper. I stepped back behind a parked Suburban.

Nadia did as told. Spot watched her come and go. Miraculously, he stayed sitting, a performance so impressive it suggested that he thought there was a steak reward waiting for stellar behavior.

The guy came in at a trot and saw Nadia hurrying out the other side. He sped up. I couldn't see what he looked like in the darkness of the garage. Squatting a bit so that the man couldn't see me, but in full view of Spot, I waved at Spot.

Spot stood up, wagging. The man stopped, alarmed. He turned and faced Spot, hesitant. Now that he was momentarily still, he looked thin to the point of being tiny. I quietly stepped behind him.

Without touching him, I said, "Looking for the woman you're following?" I said.

As he spun, his hand went to his shoulder holster under the unzipped leather jacket. I was ready and grabbed his hand before it got the gun. I pulled down and twisted. He grimaced and grunted in pain, but it was the high-pitched cry of a woman.

TWO

The woman reaching for the gun was strong and put up serious resistance for a diminutive female as I cranked one hand up behind her back, held the other at her side, and marched her over to the wall, her face to the concrete.

"We could have had a simple chat," I said, "if you hadn't reached for your weapon. Never think you can best someone who gets the drop on you. It will get you killed."

Out past the garage entrance, Nadia had turned around to watch. I sensed her movements in my peripheral vision.

When she saw me grab her pursuer, she did a sideways skitter like a water drop on a hot skillet. She continued sideways until she hit the ticket dispenser. She seemed to slam into it, which made a loud noise. She cried out in pain.

At that moment, the woman I was holding stomped the top of my left foot. She twisted 90 degrees and tried to knee me in the crotch. The foot hurt, but she missed my crotch. She lurched to the side and tried to run.

I held firm and twisted her back against the concrete wall.

"You okay?" I said to Nadia.

"I just hit... I'm sorry. Yes, I'm fine."

I pulled back on the other arm of the woman in black and hitched it over the first so that I could hold both of her slender hard wrists with one hand and keep her immobilized. I kept enough upward pressure on her wrists that her shoulder and elbow joints would be screaming and she wouldn't be able to even think about kicking back or slamming her head back into my chest.

She made no sound. Impressive.

With my free hand, I reached around and pulled the weapon from her holster. It was one of the pocket Glocks, Model 26, a small but serious 9-millimeter weapon. It had a round chambered, common for those who concealed-carry. I gently slid it into my front pocket.

"Gonna pat you down," I said, assuming this woman would have experience. I continued to hold her arms with one hand as I reached down and around and satisfied myself that she didn't have a back-up weapon more significant than a fingernail clipper. She squirmed, but I held her in a firm grip. I found a cell phone and car keys, and a leather wallet that was connected by a chain to her belt. I slipped the phone into my other pocket. I couldn't get the wallet chain unhooked with one hand, so I reached around and unhooked her belt. I pulled the belt off and tossed it on the concrete some distance away. I caught the wallet and chain before it fell to the ground. I let go of her arms and stepped back.

The woman turned around, rubbing her left shoulder.

Up close, it was hard to imagine that I'd mistaken her for a man. But she had narrow hips for a woman, and her leather coat hung straight, disguising the curves beneath. She moved like a man, a hard, straight walk with no hip swing.

She had thick, shiny, black hair cut off like broom bristles just below her earlobes. She glanced right and left, her hair swinging, a feral look in narrowed eyes. It was a look I knew well from my past life on the San Francisco PD. It said that she would try anything regardless of the bodily risk to her except for one condition. That condition was if she realized that she had no chance of escape.

Without turning from the woman, I said, "Spot, c'mere." I clicked my fingers and patted my thigh. He appeared at my side.

I pointed at the woman and said, "Watch her."

He looked at her then looked up at me.

"I know, I've never told you to watch a skinny woman before. But trust me, she's a bad guy."

Spot wagged, but he watched the woman.

"I've seen some hard women, but you're not like most of them," I said.

"Yeah, I don't go for girls," she said.

"A straight girl who kicks butt," I said. "Who woulda thunk?"

"Screw you," she said.

Without taking my eyes off the woman, I pulled her Glock from my pocket, released the magazine, and pulled the slide back to eject the round. I put the pieces back in my pocket.

"What do you want with Nadia?" I said.

"Who's Nadia?"

"The woman you're following," I said.

"Not your business," the woman said.

"Yeah, it is. If you don't want to talk, I'll call Commander Mallory at the South Lake Tahoe PD and explain that I've got you and your sidearm, which I imagine will not be registered to you. What about a concealed carry permit? You got one of those?" I gestured out toward the highway and her Buick SUV. "Sweet ride, too. You must do well to afford that. Or did you borrow it?"

She stared at me, her face unmoving.

"Not good," I said. "It won't be hard to find your parole officer. You'll be back inside as soon as they do the paperwork."

She thought about it, making a dismissive head-shake.

"Nadia," I called over my shoulder. "You better get your car before it gets towed. Call me later."

I heard the click of her heels as she hurried back out toward the gondola and the street beyond.

I flipped open the woman's wallet and pulled out the driver's license. It was a California issue and said her name was Amanda Horner. The birth date put her age at 32.

"Pretty good ID," I said. "The photo is clear, but the bar code looks like it's got Vaseline on it. And the stock isn't stiff enough. Your boss needs to upgrade his provider." I closed the wallet and put it in my pocket. "What's your job?"

She looked at me, thinking. If Spot weren't at my side, I would have taken a step back to prepare for a surprise move. As it was, I stayed close, which maybe made my height more intimidating. But she seemed a hard case. Maybe nothing intimidated her outside of giant dogs with large teeth.

"I was just supposed to follow her and report the time and her location," she said. "I didn't break no law. You give me my gear and let me go, I won't tell my boss. You take my stuff, he's gonna come after you."

It sounded like a calculated answer. But it could be true.

"Consider me warned. Who do you work for?" I asked.

She didn't speak.

"Answer my question or I call Mallory," I said.

She gave me the hard look of someone who'd grown up in juvie.

"I don't know his name," she said.

"How do you get assigned your jobs?"

She hesitated. "Email."

"What's the address it comes from?"

"A Hotmail account. Some letters and numbers. I could never remember it."

"How do you report your progress?"

"Email."

"How do you get paid?"

"Cash drop on designated days," she said. No hesitation now. "Three in the morning. Location changes each time."

"Where?"

"Sacramento."

"How does it work?"

"He puts my pay in trash cans. I wear old clothes, make like I'm homeless. Dig it out."

I pulled out the woman's phone. "I can call your friends. Someone will know how to reach him."

"It's got a pass-code lock," she said.

"That's no problem for law enforcement," I lied. "The carriers give them a universal digital key. He's probably called you. After we unlock it, I'll try getting him on callback."

"You don't want to do that," she said. "He'll kill me. You too." Her voice betrayed fear.

"You say it like you believe it," I said. "How would you know that? You said you don't know who your boss is."

"I been around. I can tell he's connected."

"You mean the Mob?"

She didn't answer. Her eyes flicked left and right. I wondered if she had a comrade sneaking up on me. I stepped to the side, put my back to the wall next to her. Spot was still in front of her.

"If you don't know him, how did he find you in the first place?"

"I've worked for him in the past. Way back. A guy he knew contacted a guy I knew. I do easy jobs for him. No laws to break. He pays regular. It went on from there. I haven't broken any laws."

"Including the piece without the permit?"

"Except that," she said. "Anyway, I'm from Nevada."

"What's that got to do with it? You think carrying is a residency requirement for Nevada? Even for ex-cons with California licenses?"

"Practically," she said.

A jacked-up pickup pulled into the garage and came near us. Loud music with a booming bass beat came from open windows and throbbed in the confines of the parking garage.

"HELP ME!" Amanda shouted. "RAPE!"

The truck jerked to a stop. Both doors opened and two young men, thick with muscles under tight T-shirts, got out. They looked eager to be heroes. They looked at Spot, glanced over at the woman and me, looked back at Spot.

"Easy," I said as both guys came close to me and the woman. Their arms hung out from their sides, pushed there by bulging beef. "I'm Detective Owen McKenna. I'm apprehending a sus..."

The woman bolted so fast that dirt shot back from her shoes as she sprinted away.

One of the guys took a step forward so that he could grab me if I chased her.

I thought of sending Spot after her, but that would be excessive.

"Interfering with a law officer is a crime," I said.

"You want us to believe she's some kind of bad-ass? She's just a girl."

"Git," I said, "before I call backup."

Moving slowly, they got back into their pickup and drove up the ramp.

I walked to the opening that led to the plaza. Down on the boulevard, a flatbed tow truck was just pulling out with the woman's Buick SUV on it. The woman who pretended to be, or maybe even was, Amanda Horner was nowhere to be seen. Maybe I could sprint around, check the women's restrooms, ask passersby if they'd seen her. But my experience suggested that I wouldn't find her. She'd probably had a lot of experience evading cops.

THREE

I took Spot out of the parking garage and over to a bench near the gondola. A small patch of low winter sun came through. Spot stood broadside to the hot sun, and looked at me. His faux diamond ear stud sparkled. I sat on a bench. People in ski suits stopped to hug him. Mostly women. They didn't hug me.

I turned on Amanda's phone and looked at the pass-code screen. It looked very locked.

I turned it off. Spot looked at me, his brow furrowed.

"What?" I said.

He shook his head, jowls flapping. Saliva flew. A woman who'd just hugged him wiped her cheek.

Spot shifted next to the end of the bench where I was sitting and leaned against my side. A woman with huge purple goggles over her eyes was heading toward the gondola. She stopped a safe distance away, pointed, and said, "Did he hurt his foot?"

"What do you mean?" I said.

"He's leaning on you."

"Oh. Danes do that."

She stared some more, then headed into the gondola.

I stared again at Amanda's phone, wishing I knew a twenty-year-old geek who could hack it, when it rang.

The display said the number was blocked. But there was an answer button. Apparently, you could receive calls even when the phone was locked. I tapped the button.

"Hello?" I said.

There was no response from the other end. Maybe I heard faint breathing.

Spot leaned harder. Why carry your entire weight when you can get someone else to support part of the burden.

I spoke into the silent cell phone. "I picked up Amanda Horner while she was following Nadia Lassitor. Amanda's pretty good, so don't blame her for getting caught. She told me all about her jobs and your pay system in Sacramento trash cans. Are you the pay master?"

There was no response. Maybe I could provoke one.

"Pretty stupid, hiring a tail who is sloppy. Not only do I have her phone, I have her wallet and ID and keys. Oh yeah, she had this neat little pocket Glock that is now mine. Of course, I'll give all this to Commander Mallory, SLT PD."

The phone still had an open-air sound in my ear. The person on the other end hadn't yet hung up.

"If you want to meet, I'd be willing to sell this phone back to you," I said. Still no response. "Of course, it won't be cheap. If you don't want to meet, I turn Amanda in along with this phone and the Glock. Incidentally, you should know that they're pretty good these days with cell phone forensics. If you don't talk to me, maybe you can look forward to a visit from the FBI or whatever law agency you'd like to ignore you."

"You're gonna die, McKenna," a man with a deep voice mumbled, then hung up.

It was a pompous statement, but that didn't make it untrue. It corroborated what Amanda already said. The fact that the caller knew my name was McKenna when I hadn't told him gave his threat some gravitas. Not that there was much I could do about it. It was unlikely that I could find her without a lot of work. It was also unlikely that her real name was Amanda Horner. It would be more difficult to find the man who called. His voice had some kind of accent that I couldn't place.

I had seen the name of the local company that towed her vehicle. I gave them a call.

"I saw one of your guys tow a black Buick SUV at Heavenly Village a few minutes ago," I said to the guy who answered. "I've got a friend with a car like that. I tried to reach her to ask if it was hers, but haven't been able to get through. I wonder if you can tell me the plate. I'll recognize the number if it's hers. It'll speed up the recovery time, and you'll get paid faster."

"Hold on," he said. I waited. He came back and read off the number. I wrote it down.

"Thanks," I said. "I'll call my friend and double check."

"Tell her it'll be at the city impound lot out by the airport. Tell her to bring some bank 'cause the fees have gone up."

We hung up. I dialed SLT PD and asked for Commander Mallory. He was unavailable.

"Maybe you can help me," I said to the woman who answered. "This is Owen McKenna."

"The private cop." The woman said it with a judgmental tone.

"I'm at Heavenly Village," I said. "A woman just pulled a Glock Twenty-six on me. I relieved her of it. Her driver's license says Amanda Horner. She doesn't have a carry permit, her ID looks fake, and the gun is probably stolen. She got out of a black Buick SUV that was just towed out of the bus stop. I have the plate for you. My guess is it's stolen. I'm hoping you can check on that." I read off the plate number.

"Hold on," the woman said.

I waited on hold for five minutes. From all directions, skiers streamed toward the gondola station. When people stopped to pet Spot, he sniffed at their backpacks, no doubt determining what kind of lunch they carried. Periodically, he wagged. I'm pretty sure that meant roast beef.

The phone line clicked.

"McKenna? Mallory. Just got in. Edith said you gave her the plate off a Buick? It was taken at a gas station in San Rafael last evening."

"Like I figured," I said. "I'll swing by and turn in the thief's sidearm and fake ID."

"Maybe turn in the thief, too?"

"Wish I could. She saw an opportunity to claim I was assaulting her, and two young guys intervened, allowing her to run away."

"She," he said, his voice flat.

"ID says Amanda Horner," I said. "I assume it isn't her real name."

"You let a woman get away."

"I could have sent Spot after her, but he's reluctant to chase down women."

"Obviously takes after you," Mallory said. "Then again, maybe you figured you weren't fast enough to catch her."

"Probably true," I said.

"I'll be here if you swing by soon."

Ten minutes later, I parked at the police department on Johnson. I told Spot to be good, walked in, and asked for Mallory. He came out holding a can of Coke, switched it to his left hand so he could give me the shake that could crush river cobbles. He took me to his office. I gave him the gun, its magazine, the cell phone, and the woman's ID. He set them all on his desk, then pointed to the gun.

"Did you check this for prints?"

"I was kinda busy removing it from the wannabe shooter. She wasn't wearing gloves, so it probably has prints. But they'll be mostly covered up by mine."

Mallory picked up Amanda's driver's license.

"Photo look like her?"

"Yeah," I said.

"She certainly doesn't look like most car thieves," he said. "You got any idea if this woman is working solo or if she hires out?"

"The woman said she has a boss and that messing with him was going to get her and me both killed. After she ran, the phone rang. I talked awhile with no reply. Eventually, a guy spoke, and he knew my name. He mumbled and had a bit of an accent. I've been trying to think of where it was from. It seemed like Russian mixed with the way they talked in the movie "Fargo." He repeated what Amanda Horner said. That I was gonna get dead."

"You think it was bluster?" Mallory asked.

"Hard to say. The woman also said that she thought her boss was connected."

"The Russian Mob has moved to Fargo?" Mallory said. "I've heard stranger. Either way, he might be serious about killing you."

"I'll try to stay alert," I said.

"How'd you get involved in this gig?"

I told him about the call from Nadia Lassitor, how she said she was being followed, and how she led her tail to me in the Heavenly Village ramp.

Mallory sipped the last of his Coke, making a slurping noise. With his left hand, he tossed the empty can into a waste basket as he reached his right hand into a mini fridge and pulled out another and popped the top.

"You're like a smoker who lights a new cig off an old butt."

"All that new info about sugar being bad," he said, "makes me crave it that much more. This lady you're working for, do you know about her husband?"

I shook my head. "No."

"That's the name of the guy who drowned in Hurricane Bay last week," Mallory said. "His name is Ian Lassitor."

I thought about it. "Hurricane Bay is West Shore, right?"

"It's the one that isn't on most maps. The first bay south of the one with the Sunnyside restaurant."

"This guy was swimming?" I said, trying but failing to pull up a memory.

"Boating. He was wearing all his clothes along with a flotation vest. He was attached, more or less, to the front half of his boat. The rear part was missing. From what Sergeant Santiago of Placer County told me, it looks like he was struck by another boat. But that boat is nowhere to be found. Maybe it sank. There were no witnesses." Mallory drank Coke and then pointed at the pocket Glock. "You gonna pursue this thing with Lassitor's wife? Because I'd like to be in the loop on anything that connects all this to South Lake Tahoe."

"If I sense that something's going down in your happy hamlet, you'll be the first to know."

"Check with Santiago. He handled the Lassitor drowning." Mallory picked up the gun, turned it over, hefted it in his hand. "Wimpy, but nice size for a woman."

Back in the Jeep, I called Street.

"You had lunch, yet?" I asked when she answered.

"I figured that hauling a toboggan would make you hungry, but I didn't know if you would still be speaking to me after losing so badly."

"Ah. Well, I learned as a kid that real sportsmanship is embracing the winning team after you get trounced. And then stealing their technique so you can kick their ass next time around."

"I'll be careful what I say over cheeseburgers."

We met at the Mott Canyon Grill on Lower Kingsbury. Diamond Martinez was pulling up as we got out of our cars.

"Sergeant," I said. "We were just going to discuss tobogganing humiliation rules over lunch. Want to join us?"

"Who got humiliated?"

"Me."

He smiled. "I'm in," he said.

So we three ate, and we didn't talk tobogganing. But I did tell them about Nadia, the woman being tailed, and Amanda, the Glock-packing tail, and the number of skiers who delayed their trip up the gondola in order to hug Spot and make him feel that I was a huge disappointment in how I dispensed my affection.

After lunch, I took Street's half-burger leftovers in a doggie bag to the doggie in the Jeep. I let him out onto the parking lot.

Spot did the drool-anticipation thing followed by the black hole-devours-burger demonstration.

"Drool-flood's impressive," Diamond said. "But you know we have rules about unregulated run-off in the Tahoe Basin."

"I'll start carrying sandbags in my Jeep."

Street headed back to her bug lab where she was working on a new honeybee study, Diamond went back to the wide-ranging Douglas County trails to keep them safe from bad guys, and my hound and I went back to the office where we would likely take a nap.

FOUR

The phone was ringing as Spot and I climbed up the stairs. I tried to hurry, which made me fumble the key in the door and take twice as long to get in.

Like before, it was Nadia Lassitor leaving a message on the machine. I picked it up and said my name.

"I can't believe it was a woman following me!" she said.

"It happens."

"Did you arrest her?"

"No. I'm a private cop, not an official cop. I can't arrest people in the usual way. And it's no crime to follow someone if you're not threatening them."

"But she had a gun!"

I ignored the comment. "We should talk. You could come to my office."

She hesitated. "I don't know where it is."

"Turn up Kingsbury Grade. On the right. It's the building with the nice new front entry." I gave her the address.

I watched out the window. Several minutes later, the dark blue BMW pulled into the office lot. No one followed her that I could see. Nadia opened her door and got out. She stood between the open door and the vehicle and looked around, studying the territory, ready to jump back into the safety of the car if necessary.

Satisfied, she shut the door. I saw the Beemer's lights flash as she hit the key fob lock button. She trotted to the office building's entrance, doing that bent-knee stride peculiar to women in heels. Probably, there wasn't another woman in all of Tahoe currently wearing heels outside of a bedroom or a showroom stage.

I opened my door and waited. She came up the stairs and down the hall. After she was in my office, I shut the door and turned the deadbolt with force so that it made a click loud enough to reassure her.

Spot's tail wag was dialed up to medium high, the standard rate for women he's seeing for the second time. He lifted his nose to sniff Nadia's chin. She backed up until she hit the wall next to the door, her arms tucked behind her.

"My God, he's huge. I saw him in the ramp, but up close, he's..."

"If you give him a single pet, he'll be happy. His name is Spot."

The woman slowly reached out and patted the top of his head. Then she quickly wiped her hand on her pant leg.

"Spot, c'mere and sit."

I took hold of his collar and pulled him back behind my desk.

"What's with the ear stud?" she asked.

"He's hip."

The woman frowned at me, then looked at her palm. She looked down at her thigh. "Your dog sheds. There's little white hairs on my clothes."

"Yes, dogs do that. But it's minor. Nothing like some dogs."

Nadia reached into her little purse and pulled out a miniature sticky roller. She rolled it over her pant leg where she'd rubbed her hand after petting Spot. Her sculpted fingernails were large and dramatic, long blue arcs sparkling from glitter embedded in the varnish. Her skin was the color of a deep, permanent tan but so smooth that it suggested several layers of base paint, each one sanded before the next was applied. Assuming the resulting color was close to her natural color, and looking at Nadia's face shape, I guessed her to be native Hawaiian.

Her pressed suit was the same blue as her nails and the blue leather purse. She wore a heavy coat of blue eye-shadow, more than needed to emphasize dramatic, wide-set eyes with arched eyebrows, plucked-thin. Her hair was black and shiny with a thick wave that made it undulate when she turned her head. A strong perfume wafted through the room. It smelled vaguely like pineapple on a Hawaiian breeze with an overlay of rubbing alcohol.

Although pretty, Nadia wasn't a spectacular beauty. Yet it seemed that she thought it was achievable with enough cosmetics and expensive clothes. Everything about her had too much color, too much polish, and too much burnishing. She reminded me of a country music star in thick stage makeup, all of her features visible at 50 yards.

"I grew up with a German shepherd," she said as she worked the lint roller. "In Honolulu. He shed enough every month to stuff a pillow." It was the first sentence she'd uttered that didn't radiate tension and fear.

"I bet he was smart, right?" I said, thinking it would be good to keep her on a more relaxing subject for a bit.

"Oh, Lord, his name was Señor Inteligente."

"Spanish for Mr. Smart?"

"You speak Español?"

I shook my head. "You just heard twenty-five percent of my Spanish."

"When we didn't want Mr. Smart to know what we were saying, we started spelling the words, like walk in Spanish." She glanced at Spot. "But Señor Inteligente learned what that meant. So then we mouthed the words without any volume. But Mr. Smart also learned to read our lips. After that, we had to hold up our hand to block his view of our mouths." Nadia held her hand to the side of her mouth and turned her head slightly, away from Spot, blocking his view of her mouth. He looked at her, did a slow wag, knowing, probably, that she was playing some game about keeping him from knowing what she said.

"But that didn't work, either," she continued, "because whenever he saw us hold up our hands, he knew we were talking about something that would get him excited." She looked at Spot, then back at me. "Does your dog read lips?"

"Spot's pretty smart," I said, "but not like most German shepherds. Spot's got some street smarts, but they're mixed with low work ethic. Shepherds have classroom smarts and major work ethic. Even if Spot could learn to read lips, he'd think it was too much work."

The woman was more relaxed now that we were talking about dogs. She'd finished with the roller and put it back in her purse. She sat down in one of my chairs. I sat down behind my desk.

"Why do you think the woman was following you?" I said.

Instant change of mood. Eyes darkened. The fear came back.

"I'm being blackmailed. I need you to catch him and put him in jail. I can pay you whatever you charge." She looked down. It wasn't about looking at her lap. It was about avoiding my eyes. "It might take a while. But money is no object once I get my insurance settlement. My husband died ten days ago." She paused. "I assume your fee is reasonable."

I explained my per diem and other expenses. She waved her hand in the air like it was nothing.

"Tell me about the blackmail," I said.

"I got an email. I can't remember the exact words, but it said something like, 'We know about your husband's life insurance policy. We know who you are and where you live.'

"Then it said, 'If you want to live, you will pay us the money your husband owes us. Two million dollars. We will contact you with payment instructions. Commit them to memory because our emails are self-deleting.' Then the email vanished. I went back to my inbox, and it wasn't there."

"Do you remember the sender?"

"No. I just saw the subject line. It said something like, 'Your future is in our hands.' I opened it and had just enough time to read it before it vanished."

"Tell me about your deceased husband."

She nodded. "Ian Lassitor. He drowned. They found his body out in the lake. His boat was broken in two with only the front part still floating, and he was on that. He had on a life vest, but it couldn't protect him from the cold water."

"Did he tell you he was going out on the lake?"

"No. But Ian was impulsive. He had a restored woodie, and he liked to do bold things like take it out in a winter storm."

"Pardon my saying this, but you don't seem very upset," I said.

"I was very upset when it happened. But what you're really asking is if we were close. And the answer is no. We were cordial and accommodating and respectful of each other. We had appreciation for each other's efforts. But we weren't close or especially caring. Not romantic at all."

"Have you been married a long time?"

"Four years. Long enough for us to realize that our initial attraction was more about hopes than reality. You know how it is. Some people really like each other at some deep level. They actually like to talk and be together. Other people never find that. They just get the thrill of initial attraction. Next thing you know, you've planned a big wedding. But after you're married, you realize that you put more planning into the wedding than the marriage. Then you find out you've married a jerk."

"Ouch," I said.

"Well, it's true. Ian could be a real bastard. I won't deny it. He was often rude to me, to his employees, to his customers. Even so, having him die was very traumatic."

"Right. He was thoughtful to leave you with a hefty life insurance policy," I said.

"Yes. The payout is two million, just like the email mentioned. I wonder if the blackmailer killed Ian to make the insurance company pay out."

"Always a possibility," I said, wondering if she could have done so herself.

"When they called me up to identify the body, the cop I talked to said it looked like he'd been in a collision with another boat. How else could his boat have broken in two? Maybe it was an accident. Or maybe it was on purpose. Either way, there was no sign of the other boat. They said he drowned. But I've heard that Tahoe water is so cold even in the summer that it can kill you. So wearing a life vest did him no good."

I nodded. "That's true."

She looked at me, over-painted eyes holding a slow and steady gaze but imbued with something like sadness. But I couldn't tell if it was the genuine kind or the manufactured kind.

"Do you have a picture of Ian?"

She nodded, reached into her little purse and pulled out a tiny wallet. From it she pulled out a small newspaper picture of Ian. It was so small that it was hard to see much.

"What kind of business was Ian in?" I asked.

"Tech stuff. Down in Silicon Valley."

"Hardware or software?" I asked.

"I think software, mostly. He was writing some program about facial recognition. And he was involved in patents. Patents for inventions about the Internet. That's all I really know. He would rarely talk about work, but when he did, the words would just go through my head. None of it makes sense to me. It's like lawyer talk. I understand real stuff. Like clothes. And cars. And iPhones. I use my computer for shopping. But the behind-the-scenes computer stuff, the Internet stuff, I don't get it. I don't even know what a patent does."

"Who'd Ian work for?"

"His own company. Symphony TechNation."

"The company produced software?" I asked.

"Like I said, I don't really know. I actually think that most of the money Ian made was from lawsuits."

"I don't understand. He sued people?"

"Companies, I think. A few times that I know. Maybe lots. Something about patent infringement."

"You mean, he invented stuff, patented it, and then sued someone who illegally used his invention?"

Nadia frowned. "I don't think he ever patented anything. If he did, he would have bragged about that. He was pretty insecure, and that made him boastful. I'm not sure how it worked, but I think he bought a bunch of patents on the cheap when a company was going out of business. Then he got lawyers to sue companies for infringement about really complex stuff. I think the companies usually thought that it was cheaper to pay him than fight the lawsuit. I know that sounds really bad."

"It sounds like a kind of legal extortion."

Nadia nodded. "Yeah. I'm sorry to say it. He said someone once called him a patent troll. I don't know what that means, but it's obviously not good. So maybe the blackmailer was one of the companies he sued, and they had to pay him, and now they want their money back."

Nadia blinked one eye as if a piece of dust had gotten in it. She reached up her little finger and, with surgical precision, used the point of the nail to get the dust.

"Ian wasn't your typical tech guy who just wrote software," she said. "He grew up in the poor part of San Jose like me. We went to the same high school but never were friends. Years later, after I divorced my first husband, we found out how similar we were. That we had ambition. That we'd always looked at the rich kids and thought it wasn't fair that they got all the breaks."

"Ian's ambition was to be a software engineer?" I said.

"Not so much software, although he was good at it. Mostly, he just wanted money."

"What was your ambition?"

"Me?" Nadia looked surprised. Maybe no one had ever asked her before. As she hesitated, I thought that maybe she didn't know.

"My ambition was to pull myself out of poverty, to make money, to live a good life and not be trapped. Kind of like Ian."

"What kind of career did you want?"

More hesitation. "Well, my ambition wasn't about a career so much as a quality of life."

She stopped at that as if satisfied that it provided a good example of ambition.

"Was Ian ever combative? Did he make enemies?"

"Of course. He had to force his way in the world. No one ever made it easy. He was like me that way. If no one will give you a break, then sometimes you have to push people aside. I'm sure that some of them would have become enemies."

"The people he sued," I said.

"Well, yeah. But Ian always pointed out that it's just business. He wasn't suing them personally. He was just suing them as a... as a prudent business move."

I thought about people who might be destroyed by a lawsuit against them. It might not just take them down financially, but emotionally, too.

"When you first called," I said, "you said that I shouldn't call the cops. Why?"

"Didn't I tell you? The email said that if I went to the cops, I would die."

"Did your husband have any other family?"

"Just his brother William who died when he was in middle school. Some kind of infection, I guess."

"Do you have family? Or anyone you're close to?"

"My parents died a few years ago. I was an only child. The people who are closest to me are my friends. I do have some cousins back in Hawaii. And my neighbor lady in Los Altos who is very dear. Oh! I also have a daughter."

"A daughter. And she's not at the top of your list of people you're close to?"

"Well, she lives with her father, my ex. They're in Sacramento. That's a long way from my world. Even though I drive through there on the way to Tahoe, I've never visited them there. And she's... She's very different from me. She doesn't like what I like. She doesn't even like me. She's pretty much told me she doesn't want me in her life. We never bonded. Even when she was a baby, she wouldn't nurse. It's like from point A, she was telling me that she didn't care for me."

"This was her decision, not a reaction to anything you did."

"Of course! I just told you. My daughter rejected me. I've been suffering ever since."

"And she rejected you from the time she was a helpless baby."

"That's what I just said."

"Sorry," I said. "I thought that parents of newborn babies were in charge. Not the other way around."

Nadia squinted her eyes at me as if I'd suddenly become her enemy.

"I guess I never had a good family experience," she said. "My mother was mean. She never missed a chance to tell me that I was homely. Two or three times when I was a kid and I put on something nice and did my hair and tried some makeup, my mother said, 'What's the point? You could never make yourself look good. Why bother trying?' One time, she even told me I was ugly."

"So you've been trying to make up for those slights ever since," I said.

"Yeah." Nadia seemed to look inward. "For most of my life, I believed what my mother said. I had self-contempt. I would wear ratty clothes and not comb my hair. In high school, the other kids would taunt me. Especially the kids who had new clothes and their own cars. They were the worst."

"And now you are beautiful and you have a great car, right? So you can move past that."

FIVE

Nadia stared at me.

"What's your daughter's name?" I finally asked.

"We named her Gertrude. You know how old-fashioned names are back in style. Merrill, my ex, calls her Gertie, but I call her Trudy."

"Is Trudy your only child?" I asked.

"Yes. I have visitation rights. But Trudy doesn't want me to come." The woman used a pleading tone in her little speech, but it felt flat to me.

"It doesn't sound to me like you ever liked your daughter."

"What do you mean?!" Nadia said. "I love her dearly!"

"She was last on your list of people who are close to you. Maybe the truth is she's just the victim of two parents who don't care about her."

Nadia squinted at me. Her cheeks colored a shade of burgundy. "Merrill and Ian weren't the only bastards I have to deal with."

"Were they bastards for the same reason I am? Because they made you face your real feelings about your daughter?"

Nadia's eyes moistened. Tears thickened and spilled over her lower lids. She cried soft at first, then harder. Eventually, her lungs heaved as if she couldn't get enough air.

She reached into her purse and pulled out a tiny designer handkerchief that had a stitched logo and wouldn't be sufficient to blot the tears of a distraught parakeet. She used it on her eyes, but tears escaped and fell onto her pantsuit.

Spot was worried. He looked at her, turned to me as if to see if I was going to do something, then turned back to Nadia.

I reached a box of tissues off the little sidebar that held the coffee maker and handed it to her.

Nadia reached her fingers into the box and pulled out most

of the tissues in a bunch. She held them against her eyes.

In time, she calmed a bit, sniffled, blew her nose.

Spot and I waited a long time.

When she could breathe well enough to talk, she said, "Do you have a powder room?"

I wondered how much of her reaction was sincere and how much was for dramatic effect. "In this building, we just have restrooms. Even the ones for women are just restrooms. Bad light. Tiny mirror."

She stood up. Even though she held the tissues in front of her face, I could see that her makeup had smeared. The pretty eyes were now more Halloween than beauty queen.

"May I use your window for light?" she said, a little catch in her voice.

"Certainly." The only window in my office was behind my desk. Spot and I were blocking it. I stood, pushed my chair to the side, took hold of Spot's collar, and took him to stand by the door with me.

Nadia walked behind my desk, pulled a little makeup case out of her purse, and flipped open the mirror. She stood at an angle to the window, looked in the tiny mirror, and made a gasp.

Eventually, she focused. She patted and blotted with the tissues. She found a cotton ball in her purse and rubbed it around her eyes. She used a miniature brush to draw with blue pigment. Then she pulled out a little tin and an applicator to dab at what looked like light chocolate parfait. She rubbed it on her cheeks and under her eyes. The cotton swab came out once again for touch-up. Then came a Q-tip for fine tuning. She blinked hard. Blotted some more. It was a long time before she put her tools back in her purse.

I'd once had two rusted fenders repaired and the entire Jeep repainted with less work.

Nadia went back to the chair and sat down, her back to Spot and me where we were still standing at the door.

I let go of Spot and went back to my desk chair. Spot tried to sniff Nadia's face. She held her hand up and ducked.

"Spot, c'mere." I patted my thigh.

He didn't even look at me.

"C'mere," I said again.

Spot glanced at me, then looked back at Nadia. His head was taller than hers when she was sitting. She kept her hand up as a barrier.

Spot walked over to the rug by the door, turned one and a half circles, lay down, and sighed, no doubt wondering why people put on strange-smelling stuff and then didn't even let him smell it.

"I'm a bad mother," Nadia said. "I know that. But Trudy has been a difficult child to love. She's hard in every way. Hard acting, hard personality, even hard looking."

"What does that mean, hard looking?"

Nadia closed her eyes and took a deep breath as if to calm herself. She let it out and said, "Trudy was born with a cleft lip. They did surgery, of course. But it didn't turn out very well. The scar kind of pulls at her lip. I've suggested several times that she could get it fixed. She could have pretty lips. If she got braces, she could have pretty teeth, too. But she won't hear of it."

"How old is Trudy?" I asked.

"She's fifteen. Plenty old enough to know how important it is to look good."

"You mean, look good on your terms, like you," I said.

"What does that mean?"

"Perfect skin, perfect hair, perfect makeup. What you like. Maybe Trudy looks just fine according to what she likes."

"With a scar on her lip? How could that ever be fine?"

"There are some famous actresses with scars or at least some imperfections. Most people think they look great."

"They're famous." she said. "And they're beautiful otherwise."

"They achieved in spite of their scars," I said. "They can afford to get surgery, but they decide that their marks are part of who they are."

"But Trudy is young," Nadia said. "She needs all the help she can get. She's got her entire life in front of her. And she's never going to be famous. She's weird. Normal girls play with dolls.

Trudy likes to make videos of weird stuff. Normal girls practice singing along with popular songs. Trudy recites rap lyrics. And she plays softball. She's not very athletic, yet she wants to be a softball pitcher. How could I ever connect with a girl like that?"

"I don't know, Nadia. You said Trudy lives with her father?"

"Yes. In Sacramento."

"What's Merrill's last name?"

"O'Leary."

"What's Merrill like?"

Nadia looked down at her lap. "He's pretty rough on the outside, especially when you first meet him. But he can be a nice guy. At least, he was when I first met him. I was at a sports bar and he was next to me. He was the first guy who didn't try to use a stupid pickup line on me. Instead, we just watched the game. And we discovered that we liked the same teams. So we started going to some games. Pretty soon we got married. He promised me he'd take me to Hawaii for our honeymoon. But when we got married, Merrill's probation officer wouldn't let him go."

"What was Merrill's crime?"

"Assault. He's a big guy, and, you know, sometimes fighting just comes natural to big guys."

"Why did you and Merrill get divorced?"

"What does this have to do with me getting blackmailed?"

"Everything about you and your life and the people closest to you matters because somewhere in your world is some bit of information that might lead us to the blackmailer."

She took a big breath and let it out. "The reason we got divorced is that Merrill's kind of a loser. No ambition. No drive to improve himself. I suspected that when I married him. But I believed all that stuff about how money doesn't buy happiness. I stayed married to him for ten years. I gave him and Trudy my best years, but I couldn't take it anymore. And because of Trudy, which we didn't plan, we couldn't afford a new car or even new clothes. We couldn't eat out. We couldn't travel. And Merrill never even applied for promotions when they came available at work. I'm a girl on my way up. I've got big plans. Merrill is never going up. Level or down is his direction."

"What's he do?"

"He drives a forklift in a warehouse. He says it's fun and that it's useful work. Imagine that. What could possibly be fun about driving a forklift?"

Nadia held out her hand, palm down, fingers outstretched. Maybe she was admiring her nails.

"We lived in Reno all ten years we were married. After we split, he took Trudy to Sacramento."

"When was that?"

"Our divorce was finalized six years ago. He asked for custody of Trudy, but I think it was more about spite for me than wanting to care for Trudy. So I gave it to him."

"Custody," I said.

"Yeah." She nodded.

"Did you give him custody just to spite him back? Or because you didn't want to care for Trudy, either?"

I thought she'd get mad, but she was reflective for a bit.

"Probably both," she said. "The truth is that I'm shallow. I admit it. I care about presentation more than I should. Merrill is a regular guy. He likes sports and blow-'em-up movies, and he drinks Budweiser. Too much Budweiser."

"You liked sports, too. That's how you met Merrill."

"Yeah, but not anymore. Big guys slamming into each other. That's like – I don't know – like those ancient guys with horses and buggies and trying to throw the losers to the lions. I forget what they're called."

"Gladiators."

"Yeah. That's what Merrill likes. He's more into the violence of sports than the skills involved. He's pretty primitive."

I nodded. "And you like opera and intellectual films, and you drink red wine."

Nadia's eyes looked afire. "You're making fun of me."

"Am I wrong?"

She paused "No. Well, sort of. I don't like opera, but I like musicals. Grease and Lion King are my favorites. I mostly watch rom-coms."

"What's that mean?"

"Romantic comedy movies. The only real intellectual film I've seen is Forrest Gump. That one really made me think. The lines he says are so profound. And yes, I like wine. Sitting around with a bunch of Monday-Night-Football fans drinking beer and yelling at the TV is the last place I want to be."

"Is Merrill a handsome guy?" I asked.

"What does that have to do with anything?"

"Curious, that's all."

Nadia looked at me with suspicion. "No, he's not. And he's overweight. Real overweight. It's not like it's a genetic thing because his brother Ellison is normal weight. I'm convinced that if Merrill didn't chow down constantly, he'd be like Ellison. He'd be handsomer, too."

The way she said it was wistful. "Handsome like Ellison," I said.

"Well, yeah, not that I care about that, of course. And if you're wondering if Merrill being overweight had something to do with my leaving, the answer is no. And when I say that Trudy isn't attractive, either, that doesn't mean I don't love her. She just doesn't love me back."

Her answer sounded sincere, but I had no doubt that Trudy was aware of her shortcomings in her mother's eyes.

"You said that Trudy doesn't want you to visit. Do you think Merrill has manipulated Trudy's feelings?"

"To be fair, no, not in any significant way. I don't think he says bad things about me. But he doesn't try to convince her that she should spend time with me, either. The truth is that I managed to ruin my relationship with my daughter all by myself. See, I'm willing to admit that. I don't think I'm all that great."

"Has Merrill been in any other trouble besides assault?"

"No. And anyway, that was a long time ago. Years before we were married. And it wasn't his fault, either. The other guy attacked him. He was just defending himself. But because he won the fight, he was the one who got charged." Nadia stared at me. "You're a really suspicious man, aren't you?"

"Part of my job."

"You think Merrill might be the blackmailer?" she asked.

SIX

"I'm just wondering. He could be the blackmailer and a murderer."

Nadia made a short, quiet inhalation.

"He lost you because he wasn't flashy enough," I said. "You said he was on the down track and you were going up. With two million, he could buy a large amount of flash."

"I find that insulting." Nadia flared her nostrils.

"Is it untrue?" I asked.

She looked as if she were about to stand up and leave. "Yes, it's untrue. I know Merrill. He would never blackmail me."

"Do you think that the blackmailer's threat could mean that Trudy is at risk?"

"Trudy?" She sounded shocked.

I waited.

"The blackmailer threatened me, not Merrill and Trudy. And that... that would be pure evil to threaten a child," she said. "But even if the blackmailer were that evil," she continued, "no one in my world even knows that Merrill and Trudy exist."

"Two million is a big reward for effort. It's not that hard to poke around and look for ways to pressure you."

"I just can't see it," she said.

"Would you respond to a threat to them?"

Nadia paused, then said, "Of course! I couldn't let anything happen to them. They're my family. Like Ian. Well, not like Ian. But I still care."

"Would you pay the blackmailer's demand if he threatened Merrill and Trudy?"

"Oh, that's what you meant. No way. That would be like negotiating with terrorists. That's morally wrong. I won't pay it because of the threat to me, either."

"You are a woman of high ethical standards," I said. I tried not to sound sarcastic, but this woman made it difficult.

"Of course. Good morals are the only way to have a worthwhile life. You must know that, working in law enforcement."

We were silent a moment.

"Where does Merrill work?" I asked. "Do you have the phone number?"

"I don't know where he works."

"Do you have his home address?"

She nodded. "I've never been there, but I have it in my purse." She reached into the small bag, pulled out a tiny book, flipped through the pages. She wrote on a Post-it and handed it to me.

Nadia suddenly frowned. "You're not going to go there."

"I don't know."

"Please don't. Merrill is kind of a privacy nut. If you tell him about my problem, he'll be angry."

"Why?"

"Because he wants the world to leave him alone. He's ornery. He would think that my problem was forcing him to deal with the world. He wouldn't like that."

I wondered if Nadia didn't want me to visit him for reasons of her own. "Ornery doesn't give him a pass regarding his responsibilities. Being in charge of Trudy means he has to accommodate any kind of threat that might touch her."

Nadia seemed to ponder the thought. "If you go, I'll come with you."

"That's not a good idea. I may just talk to him on the phone. Either way, I don't want to interject the tensions between you and your ex into the situation. Better if I just talk to him. It will keep things calmer."

"Then I should prepare Merrill for your visit."

"No, it's best that I approach him independently, not as an emissary from you."

"What does that mean?"

"If he thinks of me as your representative, his response will be different than if he thinks of me as a law enforcement officer warning him of a threat."

SEVEN

I ushered Nadia out. She'd given me a job to do, and I was happy to have the work. But I didn't want to spend any more time in her self-focused world than necessary.

I took Spot with me and drove over the summit heading west. The sky was a dramatic mix of fast-moving, dark gray clouds. The sun stabbed through in short bursts like stage lights going on and off in a theater. Snow showers of hard, little pellets pinged on the windshield. When I turned on the wipers, the snow stopped, and the sun hit the windshield making the wipers squeak. Off with the wipers, and the snow fell again as if I could control the weather with the wiper switch.

Traffic was mild, and I was in Sacramento in two hours.

I found my exit off the freeway and navigated multiple turns through the Oak Park neighborhood before I drove by a small bungalow with the house number Nadia had given me. I found a parking spot down the block and walked back.

The house was a narrow, rectangular box on a narrow lot. There was a short wire fence of the type to suggest property boundaries to a pet, but it was not substantial enough to restrain an arthritic Chihuahua. I opened the little gate, walked up a short stretch of broken concrete sidewalk, and knocked on a white door, my knuckles breaking off little chips of peeling paint that had maybe never been subjected to knuckles. The door was old and had panels like a thin interior door, not like a secure, exterior door. There was no deadbolt lock.

If this house had visitors, they weren't frequent.

After a minute, the door opened, and a roundish girl with a messy mop of red hair looked up at me. She made me think of a Raggedy Ann doll. But despite the soft exterior, she looked strong underneath. She had three large silver rings in her right ear. They weren't the smooth silver of jewelry but tarnished gray rings like the rims of very old nickels. Her left ear was plain. Barely hanging from her lips, looking about to fall, was a cigarette. It distracted from the cleft lip scar that so irritated her mother.

In the girl's left arm, she cradled a small dog with long, wiry gray hair and intelligent eyes. The dog stared at me, panting. In the girl's right hand, she held an iPhone.

With a single deft thumb, she pressed several buttons, then pocketed the phone. The girl took a drag on the cigarette then plucked it from her lips with the first and second fingers of her right hand. She lifted her arm up so that her hand rested against the door frame. The cigarette ash was a quarter inch long, and it wavered next to the door frame molding. Her fingers were callused and looked strong, and her skin was tan in color, no doubt inherited from her mother. It was a startling contrast to her red hair and blue eyes.

The girl exhaled smoke and said, "Sorry, my dad's at work. You could probably catch him on his afternoon break."

"Hi," I said. "My name is Owen McKenna. I was sent here by Nadia. Are you Trudy?"

The girl's nostrils flared, and it seemed that a shadow went across her face like a sudden squall across a pond.

"I'm Gertie!" she said. "And she knows it. Everyone – my friends, my teachers – they all call me Gertie. Only my mom calls me Trudy!" The girl's cheeks reddened just as her mother's had in my office. "It's like... It's like she lives in an alien world. She's oblivious to anything that I want. Everything I want."

"Your dad calls you Gertie, too?" I said.

"Of course! That's my name! My uncle Ellison calls me Gertie. Everyone does except mom!"

"Got it, Gertie," I said. "Any idea what time your dad takes his afternoon break?"

"Three p.m. I can never call then. If I visited, they'd put me in a locker until the break was over. It's a union thing. The place could be on fire, they'd still take their break."

"Should I come back here to talk to him this evening?"

"No. You should go find him at work. At least he'll be sober there."

"Your mother said he works at a warehouse?"

"STSV. Shipping The Sacramento Valley. He drives fork for them."

"Wouldn't most kids be in school right now?"

"What, you moonlight as a school narc?"

"Maybe."

"Well, school got out fifteen minutes ago, mister school policeman. And I didn't leave homeroom until the bell. You can check with Ms. Casales. And she's tight with Mr. Torres who's, like, the hall monitor when he isn't teaching stupid geometry. Between the two of them, you can probably establish my cred."

"Cred," I repeated. "What's with the cig? Is that part of your cred?"

"Life experience requirement for teenagers," Gertie said. "I'm fifteen. The rules say I have to try grownup stuff." She said the lines like she'd rehearsed them.

"Cigarettes make you look pretty cool," I said. I assumed that she would know I wasn't being sincere.

"Of course. Why else would so many adults smoke? It's not like they go, Hey, these are great for my health, so I better make sure I squeeze in my minimum daily requirement."

"Good to choose behaviors carefully, if you pick adults as role models. We're a pretty flawed group," I said.

"It didn't hurt James Dean's career," she said.

"What didn't?"

"Smokes." Gertie lifted her hand off the door frame, flicked the ash onto the ground, then took another long drag. She blew a smoke plume past the side of my head.

"Yeah, they gave him a certain look," I said. "But it was dying early that really helped make him famous."

"Duh. It's practically the only way to guarantee that your work is remembered."

"Doesn't mean you should emulate that behavior."

"Well, I might not quit the smokes, no matter how bad it is. My coach is practically begging me to stop, but her constant preaching has, like, the opposite effect of what she wants."

"You're into sports?"

She nodded. "I'm right up there with the best third-string, fast-pitch pitchers in the tenth grade. You'd have to search a block or more in this city to find someone better."

"You're a softball pitcher?"

"What, you don't believe me?"

"No. I mean, yes. I'm just surprised," I said, immediately realizing that I reacted wrong.

"Why do you doubt me?" she said. "You think I'm just a pudgy girl with bad posture, so how could I be an athlete?"

"I wasn't thinking that," I said. "I just... When you first started talking about smoking, the athlete vibe didn't come through."

"Vibe? Aren't you hip for an old guy."

"Whatever I am, it ain't hip."

"Me neither," she said.

"So you pitch. I'm impressed."

"Wanna see?" she said in that innocent kid manner that was touching.

"I'd love to."

Gertie took a last drag on the cig, then stubbed it out on the siding of the house. She stuck the cigarette butt into the mail box, then set her dog down. "Careful of my watchdog. He's cute, but he's vicious." The little dog sniffed my ankles, wagging his tail at high speed.

Gertie walked over to a stainless steel waste bucket that was near the corner of the house. She stepped her toe onto the pedal. The lid rose, and she reached in with both hands and pulled out three softballs.

She walked over to the narrow driveway and set two of the balls down on the broken asphalt.

"See this chalk line?" She pointed at the asphalt.

Any line that had once been there was so faded that it was invisible to me.

"This is my pitching mark," she said. "See the net at the end of the driveway? That's home plate, forty feet away. The small net within the bigger net is the strike zone. Okay, let's see how I do."

She stepped up behind the invisible mark, got into position, and paused. She brought her arm forward a bit, swung it back into a deep back swing, then came forward in an under-handed arc and brought the ball up around in a full circle. She released the ball near the bottom of her swing. The ball shot out, seemed to hesitate, then began to rise a little as it shot into the strike-zone net.

"Wow!" I said. "Congrats. I'm impressed." I clapped my hands.

She picked up the second ball and fired it into the net, this time with no rise, but even more speed. Then came a third.

"Strike three," she said. "But that was a little weak."

"You're a softball maestro and self-deprecating too, eh?" I said. "What's your pitching specialty?"

"Probably my fastball," she said.

"You're obviously very good at putting it exactly where you want it. How did you get so good?"

"It's 'cause I made a plan. About how to get good. I've noticed that everybody who gets really good at something has a plan."

"And your plan was to pitch well," I said.

"Yeah. My plan was simple, really. I imagine the ball, the strike zone, the windup, and the release. In fact, the more I imagine my pitching, the better my accuracy when I actually throw the ball. I do it in bed at night. So you're into softball?"

"We have some girl teams in my area that can kick butt. Sometimes my girlfriend and I watch their games."

"Where's your area?"

"I live in Tahoe."

"Oh. I was there once. Like, it was a quick stop on the way from Reno to Sacramento. I begged my parents to go to the beach or swim or ride one of the cable cars up the mountain or anything, but they never let me."

Gertie walked back to the front door, opened it, and grabbed a pack of cigarettes off a table just inside the door. She shook one out, lit it with a lighter, took a drag and looked at me through smoke. "I've also got a changeup that makes 'em swing too early every time," she said. "And I'm working on a rise ball to rival

Jennie Finch's."

"Who's that?" I said.

Gertie looked shocked. "You're into softball and you don't know Jennie Finch? She's only the most famous softballer of all time. Finch led the US team to a gold medal in the Athens Olympics. She pitched lots of perfect games over her career. She's even struck out a bunch of major league ballplayers in exhibitions. It's like, they're big, macho, famous guys who think the idea of a girl pitching to them is a joke. And softball, too. It's the easiest thing in the world to hit a big softball, right? But they can't touch her rise ball. They just throw out their shoulders swinging at air because the ball is never where they think it's gonna be. Finch is a goddess. Talk about having a plan."

"You think she planned it all out from the beginning? How to become the best softball pitcher?"

"Of course."

"And you are going to follow the same path? Plan and all?"

Gertie shook her head. "My coach says I have the skill set but I lack the hunger. She says that winning pitchers are dominant on the mound. Dominance is her big thing. How many times have I heard her say that she can teach pitching but she can't teach dominance? Talk about making me feel worthless."

"A coach should never make you feel worthless."

Gertie puffed out her cheeks then blew the air out. "She wanted me to hit a batter once."

"That can't be ethical. Or am I just naive?" I said.

"What's naive?"

"Innocent and unaware."

"You're naive," Gertie said. "The whole sports code thing is about not doing bad stuff. But it happens. And coaches sometimes encourage it. My coach said it would prove whether or not I had the fire."

"So you hit the batter on purpose?" I said.

"No. And that proved to my coach that I'd never be dominant. And she's right. I'm a head wimp. My arm can throw the ball, but my head doesn't have the fire. Never will. That's why I'm thinking of quitting and running away."

"That doesn't seem right. No kid should quit sports because of a coach who pressures her to do unethical things. Maybe if you quit the cigs, she'll see you differently."

"Maybe not." She glanced over her shoulder to the wall just inside the open front door.

It was hard to see in the relative darkness, but I could make out some large movie posters. One was a portrait of Marlene Dietrich looking very haughty as smoke curled up around her face from a cigarette that hung from her lips. Another showed James Dean leaning against a doorjamb much the way Gertie did, a cig in his fingers. A third poster was Cary Grant from "North By Northwest," no cigarette that I could see.

"You're into old films?" I said.

"Classic films," she said. "Most old films suck just like most new ones. But the classics are here to stay."

"Are there any softball films you like?"

"Not really. I've seen a few, but they're pretty gaggy. The writers and directors are suckers for sentimentality. It's like, the down-on-their-luck team with hand-me-down shoes finally gets to the championship and wins against enormous odds. Anyway, you sure try hard to keep me talking," she said. "What's your job? How is it you know my mom?"

"I'm a private investigator."

Gertie stared at me. "A detective?" she said. "Like in the movies?"

"Kinda. But movie detectives have more exciting lives than real detectives."

"My mom came to you to investigate something? She always was melodramatic. What's her worry this time?"

"Someone is following her. She's worried."

"And I'm all alone after school," Gertie said. "So you came to... what? Protect me?"

"Are you? Alone every day?"

Gertie nodded. "I'm the unwanted child, the dreaded surprise. Mom didn't even fight dad when he wanted custody. But he only wanted me in concept, not in reality. It was more about denying her. He never comes home until just before dinner or even bedtime. I make all the dinners, and half the time I eat alone. Sometimes I just give up the whole dinner concept and have peanut butter on toast and a Coke. And my cigs, of course. Best part of dinner."

"Your dad likes being out with the guys, huh?"

Gertie shook her head. "One time I got his permission to go to this girl Emily's house after school and then stay overnight for a slumber party. I found out that dad came home early from work that day. The one day I'm gone, he thinks, great, now I won't have to talk to Gertie. There were lots of beer bottles to clean up the following day. And leftover pizza on the table in front of the TV. It's like he was celebrating that he could be in the house by himself. Having me around makes him have to interact. Actually talk. Wouldn't want that, would we? I used to think that dad and mom will change their attitude about me when I run away. But I don't think they are changeable. Now if Uncle Ellison was my dad, that would be different. He's fun and nice. Not an old sour-puss like my dad. Ellison likes me way better than my parents."

"You do stuff with Ellison?"

"Not very often. But when he comes over, he talks to me while my dad just watches TV."

"What's Ellison do?"

"I don't really know. Certainly nothing boring like driving fork, I can tell you that. It has something to do with business deals. He's always got something exciting going on. And he drives a classic old Corvette Stingray. He's given me a ride in it a few times. That's a wow experience. Compared to my dad in his old Ford Taurus? Ellison knows how to live. Dad just barely gets by."

"You like Ellison a lot?"

"He's only my favorite person in the whole world," Gertie said.

"You said earlier that you're planning to run away?"

"'Course. It's the only reasonable way to deal with a childhood like mine. And don't tell me not to."

"Because it's like cigs," I said. "Life experience requirement for teenagers?"

"Good memory." She looked uncomfortable.

"What's your dog's name?" I asked.

"Scruffy. But mostly I call him Scruff Boy." She picked him up and scratched his head like she was scrubbing a dirty dish.

"What will happen to Scruff Boy if you run away?"

"I don't know. I might take him with me. I haven't decided yet." Gertie sucked on her cigarette, then spoke as she exhaled smoke, "So what's the big message from my mom?"

"She's just..." I hesitated, unprepared for the question. "She's concerned for your safety. The whole latchkey thing. You're home alone while your dad is at work. You keep the doors locked, right?"

"Don't need to. I've got Scruff Boy. He's little, but he's ferocious. Like, if you grabbed me right now? He would be all over you. And his teeth are sharp. I've learned the hard way."

"I don't doubt it." I reached out and gave him a pet. "Do you like school?"

"That's a joke, right? School is stupid. I've done some research. Did you know that David Lean was a high school dropout?" she said.

I must have looked puzzled.

"The director?" she said. "Lawrence of Arabia? Dr. Zhivago?"

"Oh, sure," I said. "David Lean, huh?"

"And Quentin Tarantino? He was a dropout, too. Same with John Huston and Peter Jackson and Walt Disney. All great directors. None of them bothered with high school. Instead of going to school, I could be formulating my debut."

"What's that mean?"

She flicked another ash, took another drag. "Formulating means coming up with a concept for a film. And debut is your first film. I got it from Tarantino. He has a big vocabulary. I heard him interviewed about film making. I had to write down nine different words to Google. I've learned all of them. Do you know what a parody is?"

"What is it?" I said.

"It's one of the film types that Tarantino makes. An art film that makes fun of something. Only most viewers don't get it unless they're in-the-know. Like Tarantino. He's in-the-know."

"No doubt," I said.

"It's not just directors," she said. "The actors I respect the most were high school dropouts, too. It's practically a requirement to be an actor. I've memorized a bunch of actors who've won Academy Awards and were also high school dropouts. Wanna hear? Angelina Jolie, Bob Hope, Nicolas Cage, Lee Marvin, Julie Andrews, Marlon Brando, Ellen Burstyn, Michael Caine, Hilary Swank, Sidney Poitier, Charlie Chaplin, Russell Crowe, Groucho Marx, Patty Duke, Greta Garbo, Whoopi Goldberg, Maurice Chevalier, George Burns..."

I waved my hand to try to let her know that she'd made her point, but she kept going.

"Cary Grant, Cuba Gooding Jr., Catherine Zeta Jones, Heath Ledger, Sophia Loren, Clark Gable, Cher, Peter O'Toole, Al Pacino, Joe Pesci, Anthony Quinn, Frank Sinatra, Charlize Theron, Robert De Niro, Sean Connery, Humphrey Bogart, Gene Hackman." She paused to take a breath before continuing.

I put my hand palm-out like a stop sign in front of her face.

"I can keep going," she said.

"I'm sure you can. Probably, those actors became educated in other ways, don't you think? They didn't just quit school to hang out and smoke. They studied acting or something."

"God, you are such a predictable adult," Gertie said. "Anyway, that's what I'm gonna do."

"Study acting?"

Gertie made a guffaw. "Look at me. You think this mug belongs in front of a camera? I belong behind the camera. Directing."

"Mug," I said.

"Ratty hair, cleft lip scar that drives my mother nuts, body like a discarded inner-tube. I'm not exactly starlet material. Anyway, I learned the word mug from Noir movies. Do you know what noir means?"

"What?"

"It's French for dark. Or maybe it's black. But Noir movies aren't just dark in the lighting style, they're also dark in mood and subject. So noir is a metaphor. Get it? That's another word I had to learn after I heard the Tarantino interview."

"Sounds like you're learning a lot when you're not in school."

"No way. I've learned this all during school. I have a Blue Tooth earpiece for my phone. You can't even see it in my ear, especially if I turn to the right a little and pull my hair over it. I heard the Tarantino interview in Mr. Torres' class. What's it gonna be, Pulp Fiction or Pythagoras?"

"I bet Tarantino won that contest," I said. "Have you worked on – what was it – formulating your debut?"

"Yup. I'm going to run away to Hollywood and be a director." She reached into her pocket, pulled out a card, and handed it to me. It said,

Gertie O'Leary
Screenwriter, Director, Film Mogul
Below it was her phone number.

"Mogul?" I said. "You've got big plans. Here, we'll trade," I said. "You can put me on your list to notify when you have your premier." I handed her my card.

She tucked it into her pocket.

"When will all this happen?" I asked.

"Going to Hollywood? Could be any time. I'm almost there. Maybe I just need to take a road trip. Like Geena Davis and Susan Sarandon in "Thelma and Louise." That could give me my final inspiration. I could leave this afternoon. Running away would give me a new life, a life with purpose."

"Gertie, at the risk of sounding like a boring adult, running away isn't the best way to handle disaffection with your current life. You might want to think about alternatives."

As soon as I said the words, I regretted it. A little fire grew in Gertie's eyes. She squinted at me.

"There's no risk of you sounding like a boring adult. You are a boring adult. You have no vision. I bet you've never even had a dream of a new life." Her eyes moistened. "A dream that you could really do something. That you could be somebody. Am I right?" Her voice wavered.

"I'm sorry, Gertie. I didn't mean to insult you."

"Did you ever see Brando in "On The Waterfront?" Where he says he coulda been somebody? Well, I'm not going to wait while boring adults force me to go through all these boring classes all so I can get a boring job. I'm going to be what Brando wanted to be. A contender. Maybe I'm only fifteen, but that's an advantage. I'll still be a teenager when my debut has its premier. And boring adults like you will be thinking, 'Wow, I didn't believe that girl could do it.'"

She took a last drag on her cigarette, her cheeks shiny with tears, tossed the butt onto the sidewalk at my feet, turned and went inside the house. She shut the door behind her.

It was as good an exit as I had seen in any movie.

EIGHT

I drove east and found the building I was looking for just south of the freeway and 50 yards from a nice restaurant that looked out of place – and hence, hip – among several warehouses. I bypassed the front office and walked around the side of the building. There was a lot of asphalt and a wide area where trucks could pull to one side and back up to loading docks.

At every fourth dock there was a ramp where drivers could walk up. It was shortly after 3 p.m. when I trotted up to the loading dock. Several of the big overhead doors were open. Inside were aisles of heavy steel shelving units that were two stories high, accessible only by forklifts, scissor lifts, or monkeys. The shelves were loaded with big cardboard boxes.

There were no workers around that I could see. I walked down one aisle, turned, then came back another. At an intersection, I saw a group of men off to the side, clustered around some long tables. Most had cans of soda. Some had thermoses of coffee. Several smoked.

As I approached, one of the men jumped up and intercepted me before I got close.

"You can't be in here."

"I need to talk with Merrill O'Leary."

"You'll have to wait. He's on break."

"I thought his break would be a good time to talk, keep from interrupting his work. It's urgent."

"So's our break. Union rules."

"What if I said his daughter's in trouble?"

"She in the hospital or something? An emergency?"

"No."

He pointed back toward the loading dock. "You'll have to wait on the dock."

"How long's your break?"

He looked at his watch. "Another fifteen minutes."

Twenty minutes later, a big, rotund guy marched out onto the loading dock. He was red of face, hair, and suspenders, and blue of eyes, jeans, and shirt. A toothpick barely poked out the left side of his mouth. He frowned, his eyes narrowed, and his lips scrunched up. His hair was a messy, crumpled bunch of thin wire. If he was half as mean as he looked, he would have been in prison, not out driving a forklift. I could not imagine him ever being married to Nadia.

"Looking for me?" he said. Deep voice, half growl.

"If you're Merrill O'Leary."

Maybe he made a partial nod, but not that I could notice.

I reached out my hand. "Owen McKenna," I said.

He looked at my hand but didn't reach out his.

"I'm a private investigator from Lake Tahoe. Your ex, Nadia Lassitor, just lost her husband to drowning." I watched to gauge his reaction, but there was none.

"So?" he said. "Maybe now she'll finally get the money she's been wanting all her life."

"Yes, except she's being blackmailed for that money."

The toothpick twitched, then went still. "What's that got to do with me?"

"Maybe nothing. But I'm worried about your daughter."

"Not your business," he said. I noticed that it was the same phrase Amanda Horner had used when I questioned her about following Nadia.

"If the blackmailer wants leverage with Nadia," I said, "he might threaten Gertie."

"That wouldn't matter to Nadia. She don't care 'bout Gertie. And anyway, nothing's gonna happen to Gertie as long as I'm in charge."

"How do you know? Is it because you are so close to her?" I asked.

"What's that supposed to mean?" His eyebrows tipped inward, the outer tips rising up in pronounced arches.

"Gertie told me about your loving parental attention. Half the time, she eats dinner alone. And when you finally come home, you have more of a relationship with your beer than you do with her. Or was that just a story she made up for the movie she's writing?"

Merrill reddened further. He made fists at his side and his arms came out a couple of inches. "I broke the nose of the last guy who insulted me."

"I believe it."

"She never said nothing about writing a movie."

"I believe that, too," I said. "Has she talked to you about directing? Has she told you about the interview with Quentin Tarantino? Did she ask you about movie parodies?"

He frowned. "Never heard about 'parrot eats.'"

"That's all I need to know. Let me leave you with this. I came down from Tahoe to warn you and Gertie to be careful. Until we catch this blackmailer, I don't think she should be left in your house alone. Especially with the doors unlocked."

The man looked like he was about to attack me. "What happens with my daughter and my door locks is my business. It's time for you to split, bub."

"Bub? I see where your daughter gets her flair for description."

The man lunged for me, his arms out like he'd seen NFL football players do it.

I feinted, stepped the other way, grabbed one of his arms and swung him around in a circle like the end person on a crack-the-whip game. He floundered as he sped up, windmilling his other arm and flailing his feet in an effort not to lose his balance. As he was about to spin out, I shifted and jerked him the other way, back over his feet. Twisting his hand and wrist so that he yelped, I walked him backward over to a forklift. I reached out a single finger and pushed on his chest. He tried to take a little step back. But the metal arms of the forklift were about knee level. One of his calves hit the metal, and he went down, arms windmilling, his giant butt jamming between the forks. Merrill sat with his arms out like he was lounging in an easy chair. He panted so hard, I thought he might be having a heart attack.

"Cost me a day and several bucks to drive down here just to let you know about the threat," I said. "In return for my efforts, you attack me. Next time I'll send you off the end of the loading dock and see how well you fly."

Merrill was still gasping. He probably hadn't moved that fast in his life.

I turned away from him, taking care not to let my own heavy breathing show. It was a stupid move, letting him out of my sight, directly behind me. I hadn't even frisked him. But I was mad, and like an adolescent boy, I wanted him to try me one more time.

"Try it, Merrill," I said over my shoulder. "See if you can get your ass out of that chair and come after me." All I heard behind me was his breathing.

As I walked away, I reached into my wallet, pulled out a card, and dropped it onto the concrete floor.

"If you change your mind and decide to care about Gertie's welfare, there's my card."

I walked away without looking back.

It was getting dark as I went through Placerville and headed up the ridge toward Pollock Pines. I pulled over when I got to 4000 feet of elevation and before I dropped down into the American River Canyon and lost cell reception. I called Street.

"I'm coming up from Sac and was wondering if you could break away from your bees and have dinner with me at my cabin?"

"Hmmm. Their honey is sweet. What's the competition?"

"Barbecued steelhead trout, a Central Coast Pinot, and whatever else you'd like me to pick up when I get up to Tahoe."

"How about serving it on a bed of kale and garlic mashed potatoes, the little red ones with the skins still on them?"

"Always the healthy choices," I said.

"Tasty choices," she said.

So Street came up to my cabin for dinner, and we feasted. Over dinner I told her about Gertie O'Leary, the unwanted child of Nadia and Merrill.

"A kid who wants to be a director, not an actor," Street said. "That is so cool."

We stayed up late, and before she left, we stepped out onto my deck for a brace of the cold air at 7200 feet and a look at the world's greatest view across the lake to the Sierra Nevada crest.

There was just enough light to show thin clouds racing from southwest to northeast. Here and there were openings to the sky, moving black patches with hundreds of stars. Across the lake to the northwest, fifteen miles distant, were bright flickering lights crawling high across the mountains of Squaw Valley. It took me a moment to realize that they were the groomers driving the big snowcats, no doubt rocking out to their headset music while they laid down corduroy tracks for the next day's skiers.

I stood behind Street at the deck railing, my arms around her, feeling shapes which, despite her slender build, were the stuff to generate hormone surges.

"Romantic isn't it," she said as she leaned her head back against my chest, "snow-covered mountains lit by stars. And as the earth rotates, the stars trace slow curves through the sky."

"Those aren't the curves I was thinking about. But yes, it's very romantic."

NINE

I slept in the next day, and called Nadia after I'd had my second cup of coffee. She came to my office that afternoon. Her first words were to ask if I'd seen Gertie and Merrill. I nodded.

She took a deep breath and let it out slowly. The idea of me seeing Merrill made her tense and worried.

"Did it, you know, go okay?"

"Yeah, great. Merrill is a loving, caring dad, and he's rearranging his schedule to be sure that Gertie isn't at risk."

"Gertie? Not Trudy?"

"Nadia, Gertie made it very clear that she prefers to be called Gertie and that everyone in the world but you calls her by the name she prefers."

Nadia hesitated. "I... I like the name Trudy."

"Yes. I can see that. At every step, you care more about your likes than your daughter's."

Nadia colored. Her jaw muscles bulged. Her eyes moistened. She blinked multiple times. But no tears spilled over the dam.

"Did Ian have substantial assets?" I asked.

She blinked some more, then focused on the new subject.

"I didn't know that at the time I married him. But later, I learned that his company was a much bigger deal than he'd led me to believe. I also found out that his vacation home here in Tahoe is practically a castle. It's this big stone place with a matching stone boathouse. Much bigger than the house in Santa Clara. I learned that he collects expensive toys like that fancy old wood boat that he died in. He used them for employee perks and for entertaining clients. Of course, they all were lost when Symphony TechNation went out of business."

"How did that happen?"

"Another lawsuit. Or maybe it was mostly a prosecution thing. Anyway, this time Ian was on the receiving end. He had to liquidate everything. Even the Tahoe castle was sold. Although he got the new owners to lease it back to him for six months. The only thing left was the house in Santa Clara."

"Besides the insurance, what are you left with?"

"Just my car and the house, and that's about it. I could always sell the house. It's small, but it's still worth about two million, so I could move to a nice apartment and still be okay."

"You said Ian was prosecuted? For what?"

"I don't know the details. But one of the companies Ian sued some time back counter-sued a few years later. Something about discovery and whether or not Ian or his lawyers had been forthcoming during the first lawsuit. So the next thing Ian knew, the District Attorney came calling. It took a couple of years for the lawyers to do their dance. That's what Ian calls it. Lawyers dancing. In the end, they made a deal. Ian paid a fine to the government and pleaded guilty to some minor thing, and he also paid a giant settlement to this other company on some civil case. He said it cost him about twenty million, which was all he had including all his property."

"Tell me about his insurance."

"I don't really know anything about it. I just went through the file about a week ago after I got over the shock of Ian dying. There was a form that I found. I filled it out and sent it in along with a certified death certificate. Now I just wait."

"Was Ian worried about dying?" I asked.

"I doubt it. He was too cocky for that. He probably thought he was going to live forever. I think that the only reason he even had insurance was that some salesman sold him on the concept. Probably, there was something else that Ian got out of the deal."

"Like what? A bribe from the agent?"

"Maybe. I don't know. But I don't think that Ian would have bought the policy out of the goodness of his heart."

"Do you inherit his entire estate?"

"I guess so. As far as I know, he didn't have a will. But the Santa Clara house was in both our names, so now it's mine."

"Most people like Ian have some other investments, even if small. Stocks, bonds, that sort of thing."

"He never mentioned anything to me."

"This all must be quite the shock," I said, thinking that it didn't seem like much of a shock to her at all.

"I wasn't prepared," Nadia said, a serious understatement. "Ian was only forty-two. I never imagined that he would die. Probably people think about that sort of thing when they get into their sixties or seventies. The news knocked me down for the first few days. Then I got the email from the blackmailer. So I looked you up and put your number in my purse. I hoped they might think I've been out of town and haven't gotten their email."

"Nadia, the fact that the email self-deleted tells us that they know how to do fancy stuff. There are companies that specialize in vanishing emails. I'm pretty sure they can embed code in it that tells them it's been opened."

Nadia looked sick, but it had a feigned quality to it.

"How did the woman following you find you?" I asked. "Did she wait outside your house?"

"I don't know. I just noticed her SUV on the highway. Following me forever. It was relentless. So scary."

"Have you had your car looked at for a GPS device?"

"I don't need to. My car came with GPS." She paused. "You mean they could use that to track my location?"

"Sort of. But to use the built-in system, they'd have to hack into the network your car uses. That would require serious expertise. Much easier just to attach a separate GPS unit. Something they could put under your car."

"Oh, my God. That would explain how the woman found me. They could find me again. I might be in danger. What should I do?" Her forehead was a network of worry lines.

"I can solve the problem."

"How? Can you inspect my car for the GPS and remove it?"

"No. Those things can be very small. It could take a long time to find. There is an easier way."

"What's that?"

"We switch cars."

TEN

Nadia stared at me.
I waited.

"That car is my baby," she said, as if it were much more dear to her than her daughter Gertie.

I didn't comment.

"But I can see that it would make me safer," she said.

I nodded. "Where are you staying?"

"I got a room at the Marriott."

"What was your plan when you drove up here?"

"I was coming up to visit the new shops at Heavenly and Northstar when I saw that person following me."

It was dark when we walked down to the office entrance. We traded keys. In the dim light spilling over from a neighboring building, I saw her scowl as she turned my key over in her hand.

"I have to put the key in the lock to unlock it," she said.

"Right. Old vehicle. You've never unlocked a car with a key?"

"I've seen it done. But I didn't get my driver's license until I got married the second time. Ian's cars just use key fobs."

She put the key in, turned it both ways several times until it finally turned.

"It's a bit sticky," I said.

"I see." She opened up the car door. "It smells of dog."

"Yeah. It's Spot's car, too. You'll get more of his hair on you."

"That means that his hair will get in my car, too."

"The price of safety," I said. "But he will enjoy it."

Nadia hesitated but didn't protest. She got into the Jeep, and reached down and found the seat lever to move the seat. It

lurched all the way forward with a screech of old metal. I showed
her the headlight switch, how to work the parking brake, and I
made certain that she understood where to smack the dash when
the defroster fan tried to die.

"We'll talk late tomorrow morning," I said.

"I always get up early," she said.

"I don't. I'll call you after I've had my coffee."

She nodded. She started the Jeep, got the lights on, shifted,
and drove off very slowly.

It was possible that an observer could have seen her get into
my car in the dark, but I hoped that the blackmailer was relying
on GPS in her car, if, in fact, he was tracking her at all.

Spot was excited when I opened the back door of the BMW.
He stuck his head into the leather-lined space, taking deep
breaths, wagging his tail. He'd never ridden in such a fancy car,
especially one permeated by fancy woman scents.

"Get in, boy," I said.

He turned and looked at me, wondering if I was serious.

"It's our new ride. For a bit, anyway." I pointed into the car.
"Climb aboard."

Spot jumped in. Sniffed the seats. Turned around, excited.

I got in front. Leather aroma mixed with perfume and soap,
essence of pampered woman.

I started the engine. It was smooth and muted but with a hint
of growl. Music came on. Mexican. I found the headlight switch
and turned it on. There were as many lights on the Beemer's
dash as in Reno on a busy night. I took some time to familiarize
myself with the knobs and switches.

Switching from my old Jeep to a modern German luxury
sedan was like trading up from talking through cups-and-string
to talking on an iPhone. There were obvious advantages, but the
learning curve was steep. It would take a ride-along tutor weeks
to teach me how to work all the BMW systems.

I spun the radio dial looking for something more muscular
than Mariachi, but the music didn't change. Maybe the music
was on an unseen CD, or a satellite subscription, or an iPod
hidden in the glove box.

I couldn't figure out how to change the music, so I hit the power-off button.

I heard Spot nose-bumping the rear passenger window.

"Sorry, largeness. We're in stealth mode. Can't have you flopping your tongue out an open window. We want them to think that Nadia is in this ride."

I pulled out and found that you have to go easy on the gas. At the first touch, the Beemer made me think of a horse rearing before it leaped ahead with instant acceleration. I felt like the horse whisperer communicating without touching the reins. In a moment, I was going 50 in a 30 zone, and I couldn't remember how it happened. I braked to a more reasonable speed. It seemed to take only a few minutes to get to my turnoff north of Cave Rock.

Nadia's BMW powered 1000 vertical feet up the private, winding mountain road that I share with my far-flung vacation home neighbors as if the road were level. Its power and cornering were more like a big motorcycle than a four-wheeled vehicle.

When I pulled onto the parking pad of my little cabin and got out, I had a vague sense that I should get out the towel and curry comb to calm and reassure the high-strung Beemer's nerves after our trail ride. Spot pushed out as I cracked the back door. He ran a large circle around the BMW. Probably ravenous for fresh air after Nadia's pineapple-disinfectant perfume.

After a short walk with Spot out in the cold breeze, I said, "C'mon, largeness. Let's fire up the wood stove."

I popped a Sierra Nevada Pale Ale when I realized that I hadn't locked Nadia's Beemer. I never locked my Jeep, but then no one would want to steal it. A BMW was a different matter. Not many people drove up the road. But leaving a $70,000 car unlocked was not wise.

I reached to open my cabin door. Remembered the key fob. Cool. I wouldn't even have to go outside.

I moved to the big window, pushed aside the blinds, pointed the key fob and hit the lock button.

There was a blinding flash of light and a sharp, muffled snap like a breaking tree as the BMW exploded.

ELEVEN

I spun around, my back to the wall next to the window. Spot had been in the kitchen at his water bowl, so I knew he would be protected.

The explosion was loud, but it didn't blow out my front window. I waited a moment to be sure no shock wave or second explosion would follow. Then I looked back out. I could see nothing in the dark. I realized that the flash had given me night blindness.

I reached over and flipped on the outdoor light. It was hard to see with my eyes shut down, but I could tell that the Beemer was a mess, its windows shattered, roof bulged up a few inches, gray-black smoke billowing from the interior. No flames, no sparks.

I dialed Diamond's cell.

"Sí?" he answered.

"You remember Nadia Lassitor, the woman I told you and Street about over lunch?"

"The woman being tailed and blackmailed?" he said. "Yes."

"We worried about her Beemer having a GPS unit and making it easy for someone to follow her. So we switched cars."

"She took your Jeep without protest?"

"No. There was protest. Anyway, I'm at my cabin. I went to lock her wheels with the key fob, and the windows blew out," I said. "I'm guessing a stun grenade."

"Hold on."

I waited. I looked toward Spot. He watched me from over in the kitchen nook. His ears were up, focused. Tiny flickers came from the faux diamond that Street got him after a previous explosion had pierced his ear with a splinter of wood. As a veteran of explosions, he was somewhat traumatized by loud noises. As long as he could see me from the kitchen, he didn't feel the need to come forward until I gave him the okay.

Diamond came back on the phone. "I turned around. I'll be up your mountain in fifteen minutes. You okay?"

"Yeah." I hung up.

Spot and I went outside. Spot approached the BMW with tentative steps. He held his nose up high, pointing toward the BMW. He kept his distance as he sniffed. No doubt the acrid smoke was wicked to a dog's sensitive nose.

A short time later, Diamond pulled up and got out of his patrol unit. Spot was relieved to have him there. In times of stress, the familiar is reassuring. He poked his nose at Diamond's abdomen and wagged. Diamond put him in a headlock and growled in Spot's ear. Spot wagged harder.

Diamond said, "You think someone hoped to fry you? Or just scare you?"

"The flash and bang were impressive and might have killed anyone in the car. But anyone a few feet away would probably live."

"The distance most people are when they press their key fob button," Diamond said.

"Right. So it was probably a warning. They just wanted to show Nadia that they are serious and capable."

"Or show you," Diamond said.

"Maybe. They could have programmed the explosive package in advance. Set it to go off the third or fifth or tenth time she hit the key fob. That way she'd be multiple steps removed from them when it went off. They could have attached it to her car at any time. All it would take is a half a minute to run up and stick it under the floor panel."

"And when it went off," Diamond said, "she would be rattled and perhaps more eager to pay the blackmailer's demands." Diamond shined his flashlight into the blown-out windows. Smoke made the beam an undulating column of light. "Hard to see anything in here. I'll get a team up here and see what we can find."

He called the sheriff's office and explained the situation.

Most of the smoke was gone when two other sheriff's vehicles arrived. Four deputies got out and began their work, collecting evidence, taking photographs. Diamond and I went inside.

"Seems like the first of these incidents was the husband of Nadia Lassitor dying in Hurricane Bay, right?" Diamond said.

"Yeah. Ian Lassitor," I said.

"Hurricane Bay is Placer County, and Santiago's still their sergeant at the lake. He probably handled the drowning."

I nodded. "I worked with him on the Neo-Nazi case last fall. Seemed like a good guy."

"I'll give him a call in the morning," Diamond said.

I stepped outside with Diamond. It was two in the morning. Heavy clouds, back-lit by the moon, raced across the sky. The deputies had set up some lights and were bagging evidence.

"The woman has your wheels," Diamond said as he stared at the BMW wreckage. "Maybe I could loan you my pickup."

"I'll promise to baby it," I said.

Diamond nodded. "Especially important not to slam the doors too hard."

"Why?"

"Each vibration shakes off more rust. Pretty soon, there won't be any rust left."

"And with the entire body being rust, that would be bad," I said.

"Yeah, the doors would fall off. And you can only use so much duct tape to hold a windshield in place. Gotta have the rust to tape it to."

"Should I come with you now?" I asked.

"I'll bring it by in the morning. I'm showing our new deputy the ropes. Guy named Denell. He should know where you live, anyway."

"'Cause a lot happens up here," I said.

Diamond touched the fried-out Beemer. "Case in point," he said.

TWELVE

The next morning, I was up early drinking strong, black coffee. As dawn arrived, the wrecker showed up and hauled the BMW away. Diamond pulled up in his ancient pickup a few minutes later, followed by a Douglas County patrol unit.

"Your road gets steeper and steeper," Diamond said as he got out of the ancient pickup. "My pride and joy barely made it up. The little rubber band engine was whining. I had to put that three-in-the-tree shifter in the upper position."

"You mean first gear."

"That what you gringos call it?" He reached over and burnished down a loose bit of duct tape on the edge of the windshield. The movement reminded me of a man giving a gentle caress to a woman's forehead.

A young man got out of the patrol unit.

Diamond introduced us. "Owen, meet Cory Denell. Cory, Owen McKenna."

We shook. Denell was what older cops like to see in rookies. He acted engaged, appeared to care, wanted to impress his sergeant, and even stood straight. And when he looked me in the eyes, he radiated intelligence.

We made small talk for a bit. Then Diamond and Cory left in the Douglas County vehicle, Cory driving.

I went inside and dialed Nadia Lassitor's cell.

"It's Owen McKenna," I said when she answered. "Any more emails from the blackmailer?"

"No," she said.

"Anyone following you?"

"Not that I've seen."

"Good. Okay if we meet at my office?"

"When?"

"Twenty minutes?" I said.

"Okay."

I squeezed Spot into Diamond's pickup, shutting the door gently to minimize the rust raining onto my parking pad. The truck was slow starting, and it puffed white smoke when it finally caught, a sign of moisture getting into the system. We coasted down the mountain, Diamond's pickup making little backfiring noises the whole way. We turned south at the highway. Miles later, I'd gotten the truck all the way up to 45 mph by the time I had to slow for Kingsbury Grade.

Nadia was in the lot waiting for me.

"I smell like your dog and I've got dog hair all over me," she said when we got out of the truck.

"The hazards of hiring a private investigator."

"Why do you have an old pickup? Where's my BMW?"

"The people after you are trying to send a message about how serious they are."

"What's that mean?"

"Your car blew up last night."

Nadia looked stunned. "I don't understand." She sounded devastated.

"It was in my driveway. Someone rigged a bomb to go off when I pressed the key fob lock button. You could have been in it. You need to stay in hiding as much as possible."

Tears wet her cheeks. She looked like a child who's just lost a favorite doll. "That was my baby. That car was the best. It was expensive, too."

The statement struck me as absurd. "Your life is at stake, and you're fussing about your car?" I didn't mention her lack of concern for whether Spot and I were okay.

Another pause. "I'm sorry."

"Your car was insured, wasn't it?"

"I don't know. I hope so."

I ushered her inside the building and up the stairs to my office.

After I'd made coffee and poured two mugs, I said, "Tell me about how you and Ian handled your financial affairs. You said that you didn't know much about his business. Did you pay the household bills?"

She was still in shock, her face blank.

"Nadia?" I said.

She nodded, a slow, deliberate movement. "Ian set up an automatic deposit that gave me four thousand a month for the household account. The mortgage is paid off. At least, that's what I think. Ian took care of the real estate taxes. So I paid all the miscellaneous stuff. Groceries, utility bills, lawn service, clothes."

Nadia brushed her hand over her pant leg as if she'd seen more dog hairs. She didn't pull out her sticky roller. Maybe she realized it was hopeless.

"Ian died during that big storm," I said. "Do you have any idea why he would take his woodie out during a serious winter blow?"

"No," she said. "But I'm not surprised. Ian was stubborn and headstrong. If someone told him that he shouldn't do something, then he would do it."

"Has he gone boating in the winter before?"

"I don't know. He usually came up to the Tahoe house alone. I stayed in Santa Clara."

"I understand the Tahoe house is on Hurricane Bay?" I said.

She nodded. "Just south of Tahoe City."

"You said it was leased back to Ian for the next few months. Why aren't you staying there?"

"I wouldn't stay there even if it still belonged to us. It's a huge, cold stone house, not at all cozy. The first time Ian ever took me there, I told him that I wouldn't sleep there."

"Can you write down the address?"

Once again, she had to look it up in her little address book. She wrote it with such perfect handwriting, one would think she taught cursive at grammar school.

"What is the name of the company that bought the assets?" I asked. "You could write that down, too."

"I have no idea of the company's name. I just heard about it from Ian. A Mexican company was all he said. But he never gave me details."

"Where did Ian keep his papers?"

"Papers?"

"Insurance, real estate deeds, vehicle titles, tax records."

"They're at the Santa Clara house. At least, some of them, anyway."

"Does he still have an office in the Bay Area?"

She shook her head. "No, that went with all the other assets. He has his home office, of course. And maybe he keeps some stuff at the stone castle. I wouldn't know."

"Did he have any other places? A condo someplace?"

"No." Nadia paused. "At least, not that I know of."

"Who is Ian's lawyer?"

"I don't know. That's bad of me, isn't it? I should know more about my own husband."

"What happened to your husband's body?"

"It was cremated according to his wishes."

After Nadia left, my phone rang.

"Owen McKenna," I said.

"This is Gertie."

"The film mogul," I said. "How's your debut formulating?"

"Well, I just got a good idea for how to add creepy noirish emotion into my screenplay."

"Great," I said.

"Maybe not. I think a man is watching me."

That got my attention.

"Where did you see him?" I asked.

"Outside my school. I didn't pay any attention. He was just a guy standing there."

"What did he do?"

"Nothing. I left with some other kids and got a ride home."

"Have you seen him again?"

"Yeah. That's why I'm calling you. He was there again today. He started to follow me when I left the school. Maybe it was just a coincidence. But I ran and caught up to some other kids and I got ride again."

"Gertie, you know about a person's gut instinct, right?"

"You mean, like, a feeling?"

"Yeah," I said. "Something that you don't know in a logical way but you feel it anyway. I want to tell you an important law of human perception. When you have a gut instinct about safety, it's very important to give it higher priority than your logical feelings."

"You're saying that my uncomfortable sense that the man was following me is a gut instinct."

"Yeah. Always heed those kinds of feelings. They will save your life more often than any logical thoughts will."

"Okay, I will."

"Can you describe this guy?"

"Big. Strong. Not pretty. Kind of a lunk. Like someone who might have worked at my dad's warehouse."

"How old?"

"I don't know. Maybe my dad's age."

"Where are you now?"

"At home."

"Okay, here's what you do. First, lock your doors and keep them locked. Always."

"I did."

"Don't open your door unless it's someone you know."

"Okay."

"You never go anywhere alone. Call other kids, get them to walk with you or give you rides. Get your dad to give you rides. If you can't get a ride or escort to school, you stay home."

Gertie hesitated. "That's pretty extreme, don't you think?"

"No, it's not. Remember your gut instinct?"

"Right. That's why I called you."

"I'll make some calls. I can get you a taxi service. And any time you use a taxi, you tell the driver to wait until you're inside your house or your school, wherever you're going. Okay?"

"Okay."

We hung up and I called Nadia.

"Someone is following Gertie," I said.

"What? Someone bad?"

"Yeah," I said. "Someone bad."

"How do you know this?"

"She called me and told me."

"She called you, not me?" Nadia sounded whiny.

"Yeah. I need you to call Merrill and tell him to give Gertie money for a taxi. If you need to, send him money immediately. Whatever it takes. I also need him to make sure she has the phone numbers for two or three taxi services. She can no longer walk anywhere by herself. Either she gets rides, or she stays home. Do you understand that this is serious?"

"Yes, I get it."

"And you will call Merrill right now?"

"Um, yeah. I will."

We hung up.

Gertie worried me. I went over everything I'd said, wondering if I'd sufficiently impressed her with safety concerns. I paced back and forth. There were bills to pay and other desk work I needed to get done. But I couldn't concentrate.

I took Spot down to Diamond's pickup and we left.

A block down, I saw that Street's VW Beetle was at her lab. I pulled in and stopped. Street was the world's most supportive person, but I didn't want to stress her out about possible danger to Gertie, so I took a moment to calm down before I got out.

THIRTEEN

Spot and I walked up to the door of Street's lab. I made my secret rap against the door.

Street opened the door.

Spot wagged and pushed past her through the doorway.

Street saw Diamond's pickup. She raised her eyebrows.

"Where's your Jeep?" she asked.

"I traded the Jeep for Nadia Lassitor's BMW. But it blew up when I pressed her key fob lock button."

"What? Why didn't you tell me?"

"I just did. It happened late last night."

I heard the sound of a vehicle behind me. I turned to see a Douglas County patrol unit pull off Kingsbury Grade and come to a stop next to the pickup. For a short moment, the patrol unit's Christmas bar flashed blue and red LEDs and the siren began the briefest bleep before it was truncated. All went silent. The driver's door opened, and Diamond got out. He looked at his pickup as if checking to make sure it was still okay. Once again, he reached over and smoothed down the errant piece of duct tape.

"Running okay?" he asked.

"Yup."

"Gonna invite me in, or do I have to find some fine print building code infraction to gain admittance."

"Help yourself," I said. "But keep your sidearm close. There are bugs in there that take at least two nines to put down."

With his left hand, Diamond raised his flashlight alongside his temple and flipped it on. He put his right hand on the butt of his gun and walked into Street's lab.

"Watch out for the large hound," I said.

Street and I came in after him. I shut the door behind me.

Spot ran up to Diamond, sniffing and pushing and leaning

and wagging.

"Hound has a casual, carefree insouciance insufficient to his stature," Diamond said.

"What I think every morning at my point of deepest slumber when he wakes me by sticking his nose in my face," I said. "But he's rebounding from the slight of not being allowed to sniff a woman who indulged in excessive makeup while he looked on. So we may need to extend him some tolerance."

"What kind of woman would say no sniffing to Spot?" Diamond said.

"The Beemer lady, Nadia Lassitor."

Diamond walked over to a counter and looked at a terrarium, standing a safe distance away. Inside were dirt and twigs and leaves that looked like fresh spinach and lots of bugs, the make and model of which were unclear.

One of the bugs in the terrarium leaped an inch or more. Diamond jumped back, his right hand moving back to the butt of his sidearm.

"You think the woman tailing her was for real?" Diamond said.

"Amanda? You're wondering if Nadia might have made up the blackmail scheme to deflect questions about whether she arranged her husband's death in order to get the insurance payout. And then she might have hired Amanda to give her story a sense of legitimacy."

Diamond nodded. "Vanishing email threats have a high threshold of proof."

"That's what I thought. But Amanda seemed like an actual dirtball. Of course, hiring Amanda would be a great setup to make it seem real."

"Lot of work for some verisimilitude," Diamond said. "And then there was Amanda's supposed boss, the guy who said you were going to get dead. Nadia could have arranged that, too."

"I don't like this," Street said. "It's possible that this is all real. You could be in real danger."

I thought of Gertie's phone call about a man following her. But I didn't want to alarm Street further.

"Amanda said she was going to get dead, right?" Diamond said. "All because she let you relieve her of her gun and ID and phone."

"Time to change the subject," Street said.

Diamond nodded as he moved around Street's lab. He stopped at another large container not unlike an aquarium. Inside was an impressive beehive and a fair number of bees that were buzzing their wings if not flying around with energy.

"You collecting honey?" he said.

"No," Street answered. "It's winter, so this hive is dormant. I'm joining with a thousand scientists to try to find out what ails bees worldwide."

"With enough ailing, they'll go extinct and we'll no longer get stung?" Diamond said.

"You Luddite," Street said. "Bees are the most important..." She saw him grinning. "Oh, you're kidding. But this isn't something to joke about. Bees pollinate a huge portion of human food. If we lose all the bees, our species will be stricken. Imagine a world with almost no fruits or vegetables or nuts. Bees have reached a tipping point. They are dying off in record numbers."

"Sorry for joking," Diamond said. "Do we know why they're dying?"

"We know some of the reasons. At first we thought that a couple of the diseases they suffer from were the primary causes of death. But when we dissect a bee, in addition to opportunistic viruses that attack weakened bees, we find an average of six or more different pesticides and herbicides. And when we look at the landscape where they range, we find thousands of acres of a single crop that all blossom at the same time and that have been bombarded with pesticides and herbicides. By comparison, the natural landscape of bees consists of hundreds of plant species that produce flowers at different times. The single crop landscape gives bees a poisonous feast for a week or two. The natural, multi-crop landscape feeds them healthy food all around the year."

"So you think bees are dying because we've destroyed their habitat?"

"Yes," Street said.

Diamond moved around the honey bee aquarium, peering through the glass. "But we still need them."

"Yes, we do."

Diamond stepped to the far side. There was a snapping sound at his feet. He looked down.

"Sorry," he said. "I've stepped on a mousetrap." He bent down and picked up broken pieces. "Apparently, you don't want to save all of Mother Nature's creatures."

Street grinned. "I want to save mice, too. But not the ones that are making nests in my lab. That was my last trap. And the hardware store is out."

"You could use a Paiute Deadfall," Diamond said.

"What's that?" I said.

"You know of the Paiute," he said.

"Kinda," I said. "The Native Americans from the Nevada territory. Ferocious fighters. The Pyramid Lake War of Eighteen Sixty."

Diamond nodded. "And they were some of the most famous Native Americans. Sarah Winnemucca, who published the first Indian autobiography. Wavoka, the spiritual leader. The Paiute were also ingenious hunters and trappers. One of their clever inventions was a kind of trap called the Paiute Deadfall. It was designed for catching small rodents to eat, from mice up to squirrels. The simplicity and effectiveness was something to see. It's basically a universal trigger device that can be used in lots of different ways. Kind of the same principle as a mousetrap. But instead of a spring supplying the power, the Paiutes used a heavy rock and let gravity supply the power. All it requires is four little sticks of wood, a piece of cordage, a..."

"What is cordage?" I interrupted.

"A cord made from fibrous plants. Dogbane, milkweed, the inner bark from cedar or basswood, wild hemp, reed grass. I was just reading about it last night. Here, I'll show you how it works. It's really cool."

Street and I had often seen Diamond's enthusiasm in the past. He's always learning something new, and then we get a show-and-tell lesson. It had made for many interesting discussions.

We'd also learned that when Diamond gets excited about something new, there's little chance of postponing his song and dance.

"Gimme a sec," Diamond said. "You're gonna love this." He went outside. I watched out the window as he reached into a small tree and broke off a couple of dead sticks. He brought them inside, got out his pocket knife, and shaved the end of a stick to a point. He looked around Street's lab.

"What do you need?" she said.

"Something I can push a stick into the way you'd push it into the ground."

"How about this?" She handed him a flat piece of Styrofoam packing material about an inch thick.

"Perfect," he said. "This will be our ground. He pushed the back end of the pointed stick into the Styrofoam so that it stood with the pointed end up.

"This point is the fulcrum," he said.

Then Diamond cut a notch in the other stick about one quarter of the way from the end. He balanced the stick like a seesaw, so that its notch rested on the point of the vertical stick and the long end rested on the Styrofoam ground.

Diamond picked up the other sticks he'd brought inside.

"Now we need to use this small, short stick and a twig and some cordage." He looked at Street. "Do you have any cord of any kind?"

She thought about it. "Would dental floss work?"

"Sure."

She went into the bathroom and came out with a floss dispenser and handed it to him.

Diamond took a piece of floss and tied one end to the lowered, long end of the seesaw stick. He tied the other end of the floss around the third, short stick. The fourth stick was just a twig, and he wedged it between the vertical stick and the short stick at the end of the floss. The floss was now stretched tight to the long end of the seesaw.

"Next, I need something like a flat rock," he said. "Big enough to squish a critter."

"I know just the rock," Street said. She pulled her thick Random House dictionary off the corner of her desk and handed it to him.

"Perfect," he said. He set one end of the dictionary on the ground, then lifted the other end and carefully leaned it against the short, upper end of the seesaw. The dictionary's balance on the seesaw seemed very precarious, but I realized that that was the point of the design.

Diamond pointed to the twig. "This is the trigger," he said. "The slightest bump to this trigger twig will release the short stick that holds the floss. When the floss lets go, the seesaw will tip, which will drop the rock, killing the rodent."

"This is one of those skills that makes Diamond irresistible to women," I said to Street.

"You joke," he said, "but I have my ways."

We were intrigued, and we watched with focus as Diamond took an eraser off of Street's desk and tossed it onto the trigger twig. The sticks collapsed and the dictionary fell onto the eraser with a solid thump.

"A simple and effective way of getting some protein for your dinner," Diamond said.

"I'll definitely use this the next time I get a hankering for a rodent dinner," I said. "You think I should roll the mice up in tortillas and bake them? And what kind of cheese do you recommend I sprinkle on top?"

Diamond gave me a withering look.

FOURTEEN

When I drove home and turned up the road to my cabin, I saw what Diamond meant about his pickup struggling up the steeps. The engine was so weary that I had to putt-putt at fifteen miles per hour to get up to my cabin.

The next morning, I took Spot for a walk in the snowy forest. I came back to a ringing phone. It was getting so that if I wanted my phone to ring, all I had to do was to leave and come back.

"Yeah?" I said.

"Got something you might want to see," Diamond said.

"What's that?"

"The woman you told us about?" he said. "The one you relieved of gun and cell phone and wallet before she ran?"

"Amanda Horner?" I said.

"Yeah. This morning we got a call from an unhappy tourist on one of the cruise boats. Said there looked to be a woman's body on the bottom of the lake, off Nevada Beach. Two of our deputies went out in a kayak and found it. Meantime, we trailered the Douglas County Sheriff's boat to the boat launch. But after we got our diver down there, he couldn't retrieve the body because it's tied to an anchor with a steel cable."

"And a tourist spotted it," I said.

"Not the best advertising for a vacation in Tahoe," Diamond said. "Wrong kind of photos to bring home."

"You think it might be Amanda?" I said.

"Can't tell from up on the boat."

"Sounds like she didn't die of natural causes."

"Correct," Diamond said. "Suicide is a possibility, but I doubt it."

"You got an ETA on retrieving the body?"

"We're coming back to get a bolt cutter as we speak. If you can come down to Cave Rock in about fifteen minutes, you can come with us on our second trip out. The body is positioned to be noticed. I'm guessing it's a message to you and the widow lady you're working for."

"Okay, I'll be there in a bit."

Spot and I got back in Diamond's pickup and drove down to the Cave Rock boat launch. I parked where the rotary plows had cut the snow walls a bit wider than normal. Even with the unintended ventilation from the rust holes in Diamond's truck, there was enough sun to keep Spot warm on the blanket I'd spread out on the seat. I told Spot to enjoy his nap.

The Douglas County Sheriff's boat was idling next to the rocky breakwater to the side of the boat launch ramp. Diamond was standing at the captain's chair.

I put my hands on the boat's gunnel and boosted myself up.

The Douglas County Sheriff's boat was a compact, classic inboard, designed with the prop and rudder just forward of the stern so that divers could use the small swim platform without fear of contacting the prop.

I nodded at Diamond, then turned toward the stern.

A man in a one-piece ski suit with large pack boots on his feet sat on the rear seat. He was bent over a scuba tank. Under the collar of the ski suit was the edge of a blue wetsuit.

"Chilly for wetsuit diving," I said.

He nodded. "When that water first rushes inside the suit, it pretty much sucks the life out of you. I have a friend who has a drysuit, but I couldn't get hold of him to borrow it."

On the bench seat next to him were swim fins and a face mask. The water drops on them looked to be frozen.

Diamond said, "Here comes Denell with the cutter."

A county patrol unit came to a stop near the boat ramp. Denell got out carrying a bolt cutter and a coil of slim nylon rope like a water skier's tow line. He trotted through the snow to the patrol boat. I reached out and he handed me the cutters and the rope.

"You want me onboard?" he said to Diamond.

"No," Diamond said, pointing at the patrol unit. "You should go back to your office. Keep the county trails safe. I'll call when we're on our way back to the boat launch. I'm guessing a good hour or more."

Diamond shifted into Reverse and backed away from the breakwater. When we were 30 yards out, he turned, shifted into Forward, and sped up until the boat climbed up on plane, motoring south at maybe 20 knots. After three or four miles, Diamond slowed enough that the boat dropped out of plane and plowed water, bow high, stern low. The boat threw off a large wake. Soon, he slowed further, staring at the water off the starboard bow.

There was a medium chop, which obscured the view down into the water. Diamond slowed further.

"I'm guessing two hundred yards," the diver said.

Diamond nodded.

After a minute, Diamond dropped the shifter to neutral. He pointed. "There's the buoy marker," he said. We coasted at no-wake speed, turning a bit to port as the boat slowed to the point that the rudder ceased being effective. The diver was frowning, staring at the water.

Diamond shifted into Forward, brought our speed back up to that of a person walking so that he regained steering control, then pulled it back into neutral.

Something caught his eye, and he shifted into Reverse for a second, just long enough to bring the boat to a stop. "Hard to work a crime scene when it's forty feet under water," he said.

The diver unzipped his ski suit and pulled it off.

I still couldn't see anything under the water. The waves reflected sunlight like thousands of camera flashes going off at random. It was difficult to focus my eyes on the shifting dark areas of the water's surface. There seemed to be nothing but light-colored sandy bottom.

Then the corpse appeared like an apparition, far below us, but easy to see, fully clothed, tied ankle-to-anchor, and floating vertically, the arms lifted up by a float.

FIFTEEN

The body looked closer than it probably was because of the water's clarity. One of the ankles was tied to a tire that stood upright on the bottom. The tire probably had some kind of weight in it. The body position was vertical, held up by a life ring that was tied to the body's wrists. The life ring was buoyant enough to keep her vertical but not enough to overcome whatever weight was in the tire. The body's free leg floated up and out at an angle. With her arms up, hands together, she looked like a dancer or a yoga practitioner in a workout position.

It was easy to drown someone by tying a weight to them and dumping them in the lake. It was easy to drop them in the middle of the lake where the bottom was in permanent darkness 1600 feet below and where no one would ever find the body. But someone had decided they wanted this body found, and he had gone to extra trouble to use a float to arrange the body for maximum visual impact.

For a brief moment, the water's surface became calmer and the image of the body stopped jumping around. I got a glimpse of the face. Although it was a long way down, the water was very clear. It looked like the woman who was pursuing Nadia, the woman whose ID said her name was Amanda Horner.

If the news media reported the death, that would suit the killer well because it would increase the chances that Nadia would see or hear about it, likely hastening her delivery of the insurance money when she got it.

The diver pulled on his swim fins, picked up the scuba tank, and slid the harness straps over his shoulder. He pulled a neoprene hood over his head, then picked up his face mask. He spit on the inside of the glass and rubbed it around with his finger, a common way of keeping a mask from fogging up when diving. He pulled his gloves and the mask on, put the regulator into his mouth, took a breath from the tank, then looked toward the bolt cutters, which was with the coil of rope on the seat near Diamond.

I handed the diver the bolt cutter and the rope.

The diver raised one knee, carefully lifted his swim fin through the small transom door and stepped onto the little swim platform. He shifted his weight, lifted the other leg, and then did a kind of sideways fall into the water. He put one hand to his face mask and twisted as he went so that he was back first when he hit, avoiding any impact that would knock off his mask.

We watched as he descended, his fractured image jumping around as it appeared through the waves. The bubbles from his exhalations rose in groups as he descended.

When the diver got to the body, he first tied the coiled rope to the tire. When done, he put his arm through the rope coil. We saw him reach out with the bolt cutter. The body came free.

The life ring pulled the body toward the surface, hands first. As the body rose, the water pushed the free leg down. It looked like a swimmer had pushed off the bottom, hands outstretched above her head, and feet together. Like a slow torpedo, the body made a long, graceful, coasting trajectory toward the surface.

After long seconds, the life ring popped out. Inertia brought the body's hands out of the water. As the hair broke the surface, the body stopped rising, then slipped back beneath the surface. Freed of its anchor, the body now hung from the life ring.

There was a gentle splash to the side as the diver surfaced. He kicked with his fins and came over to the side of the boat. He lifted up his hand and held the end of the line. I bent down, took it from him, and began pulling up the heavy tire, reeling the line in, left hand, right hand, over and over.

The diver swam over to the life ring and towed it to the boat, moving slowly because of the drag of the body. Diamond came over and took it from him. The diver removed his fins, tossed them in the boat, then climbed in.

I stopped reeling in the tire and tied the line off on a tie-down cleat. Diamond bent down and lifted gently on the life ring until he could get hold of the woman's arms. He pulled the body part of the way out of the water. Then the three of us hoisted the body into the boat and laid it on the floor of the boat. The life ring was still tied to the body's hands. It looked old and faded as if it had hung in the sun for thirty years. Water ran from it, sparkling in the sun and trickling across the boat floor to join the much larger stream coming from the body and its clothes.

"This the woman you told me about?" Diamond said.

I nodded.

The wet clothes looked to be the same black jeans and shirt Amanda had worn when she followed Nadia. Her skin was now blue-white, and she looked oddly beautiful, like the good ghost in a movie. Whatever terror had stricken her in the moments before she died was gone now. Her face was placid, as if being interred in Tahoe's ice water was relaxing.

"Doesn't seem like this senorita would be good at putting the squeeze on anyone. Very slight of build." Diamond paused. "I never thought much about my image of bad guys. But I see her and I realize that I've been indulging in stereotypes."

"No way to know if this woman was an effective predator," I said. "But Nadia was certainly shaken. Simply having someone follow her made her feel pressured and scared."

"You said she was carrying?" Diamond said.

"She had a pocket Glock, but no permit. According to her driver's license, her name was Amanda Horner. Age thirty-two. The license looked like a forgery."

Diamond turned to the diver. "See anything down there?"

"Just wavy sand in all directions. The life ring and the cable to her ankle are here." He turned and pointed to the cut cable attached to the body's ankle. "The rest of the cable is attached to the tire." He looked over the side where the tire cord stretched from the cleat down into the water.

I un-cleated the cord and continued to reel in the tire. When I got the tire to the surface, it was too heavy to pull out by the line alone without the line cutting my hands. I bent down and grabbed the tire to lift it aboard.

One side of the tire was filled with concrete. It probably

weighed 50 pounds, and it made an effective anchor even if it didn't have anchor plates to dig into the bottom. Certainly, no one could swim with such a weight tied to their ankle.

"An old Goodyear," I said to Diamond. "Standard size. Probably only ten thousand like it in the basin."

Diamond looked over. "Right. Maybe concrete has a chemical finger print. If we could identify it, maybe we could learn where the concrete was bought."

"Concrete DNA?" I said.

"Yeah. Better yet, look for a fingerprint in that concrete."

"No prints that I can see," I said, angling the tire, trying to get it into the light. "But here's a creepy crawly that might give up some secrets."

"What?" Diamond asked.

"A really long bug," I said. "Stuck in the concrete. Dried. Well, totally soaked, now. But it looks like it died and dried out when the concrete was poured."

"And now it's reconstituted?"

"Practically," I said.

"What kind of bug?"

"I don't know. It's got legs, wings, creepy little antennas. Looks like a giant black wasp."

Diamond came over and looked. I pointed.

"Think Street would know?" Diamond said. "She could do that forensic entomology thing, figure out that the concrete was poured into the tire in some distant place, the only place on the planet where the bug grows."

"Maybe," I said. "I'm going to lean this tire against the rear seat. If we're careful, maybe we can get this to Street before it self-destructs."

"Probably should keep it moist," Diamond said. "I don't know that bugs can be repeatedly dried, moistened, and dried again. Could be, if this guy dries out, he'll turn to dust and blow away."

"Good point," I said.

"But you slosh water into the tire, I bet it washes him away," Diamond said.

"Tricky business, bug stuff," I said. I wondered how long we could keep ignoring the corpse lying on the floor of the boat.

Diamond leaned over the woman's body and felt the pockets of her jeans. "Too tight and wet to feel inside the pockets," he said. "But I don't feel anything from the outside. 'Course, it sounds like you already took what she carried."

"And gave it to Mallory," I said.

"The coroner might learn something," Diamond said.

The diver sat with Diamond up front, and I sat on the rear seat as Diamond drove back to the boat launch. The day was spectacular, the chop making the waves a deep indigo with the snow-capped peaks as a 360-degree backdrop. It was hard to appreciate the scenery out of the boat with a dead woman lying in front of me, staring open-eyed toward the sky. She'd been in the water long enough for her corneas to fog a bit. Except for a series of scratches on her left jawline like those a gnawing fish would leave, it looked like scavenging water creatures had left her alone. With no specialized knowledge, I guessed that she'd been under just overnight. In warmer water, the body would have been in much worse shape. In the icy cold of Lake Tahoe, bodies tended to stay relatively preserved.

It was disconcerting how thoroughly lifeless a dead human body was. Bodies don't look like people without animation. They look like strange objects, a new kind of cold plastic. I'd often seen sculptures of people, most of which had more life than a dead body, even those sculptures made of bronze or marble. I didn't know how it worked, a sculptor imbuing a hard lifeless material with some essence of life when an actual body had no essence of life. It was the inscrutable magic of art.

Diamond was driving the boat at medium speed, just enough to be up on plane. He took a sudden turn to port. Probably avoiding some floating debris. Just as quickly, he took another turn back to starboard. The boat leaned one way, then the other. The turns made Amanda's head roll back and forth as if she were shaking her head. 'No, no, no, don't do it,' she seemed to be saying.

Diamond cut the power as we approached the Cave Rock

boat ramp. Denell was ready with the boat trailer. We hooked the tow cable onto the prow of the boat, then winched the boat up onto the trailer.

I leaned over the edge to look inside the cockpit and see if the body should be secured in some way before we drove off. Her head lolled again. I put my foot on the trailer tire and boosted myself up higher. I reached over and in and took the life ring that was tied to her wrist and propped it to hold her head in place. The line made her arm move, and I noticed some discoloration just visible below her sleeve. I pulled the cold wet fabric up.

There was writing on the inside of her arm. The letters looked to have been written with an indelible marker. The handwriting was scrawled, but the words were clear.

"The American Dream"

"Diamond," I said.

He looked at me. I gestured toward the boat's cockpit.

Diamond pulled a little step stool out of the back of the patrol unit, set it on the pavement next to the boat trailer, and stepped up to look inside.

He saw what I was pointing at.

"I'm guessing she didn't write it," I said.

"No." He pointed. "The letters are on her left arm. If she'd reached over with her right hand and written them herself, they would be facing the other direction. Unless she's good at writing upside down, somebody else must have written them."

"A murderer's calling card?" I said.

"Could be."

"Do you have anything we can use to cover the body?" I asked.

Diamond thought about it, then shook his head.

Perhaps a few curious people would notice the sheriff's vehicle towing a dripping boat in the middle of winter, but unless we pulled next to a tall truck, none of them would know that lying on the floor of the boat was the body of a young woman, staring at the clouds, about as far from experiencing the American Dream as possible.

SIXTEEN

Spot was excited to see me as I approached the pickup. He wagged hard enough for me to hear his tail smacking the back of the front seat, then the dashboard, then the seat again. The rhythm was syncopated like the padump of a heartbeat. I'd never noticed that before, his right wag a bit faster than his left wag.

When I opened the door, he wagged harder as he sniffed me. His tail slowed, then stopped. He kept sniffing, but his enthusiasm was gone.

It seems that the default emotion of most dogs is happiness. But they are very sensitive to the smell of human death. It runs a hard counter to their enthusiasm for all things connected to people.

"Sorry, largeness. It didn't turn out well. You can probably smell death even when it's been refrigerated in ice cold water."

He sat down, leaning against the passenger door, and looked away.

I started the pickup and turned on the fan to begin to dry the window condensation from Spot's breath.

I stretched the end of my sleeve over my hand and used it to wipe the inside of the windshield. Then I pulled out and followed Diamond and Denell as they headed south. They turned up Kingsbury Grade and pulled in at Street's lab.

I parked next to them, got out, and lifted the tire with its concrete fill out of the back of the boat.

Diamond was frowning hard. "Looks like you should consider the threat to you to be serious."

"Yeah," I said. I thought about the body's eyes, staring lifeless, and I tried to convince myself that I wasn't to blame for her death. I bore no responsibility because I didn't kill her. All I did was challenge her boss when he called on the cell phone.

Yeah, right.

Diamond and Denell pulled out fast, probably to eliminate any possibility of Street coming out and seeing the body of Amanda Horner lying in the back of the boat.

I carried the tire into Street's bug lab. Spot followed me, his movements lackluster. I told Street about what we'd found. Her face went dark, but then she rallied.

"Bring it over here so we can see it in my exam light," she said.

I did as she said and lifted the tire up onto her counter.

Street pulled the light over and angled it to illuminate the inside of the tire. The concrete in the tire was still a bit wet from the lake. At the edge of the concrete plug, where the concrete met rubber, the big, long bug was still visible. It looked mangled and soggy and scary as a bug gets.

"Oh, my God, it's a Tarantula Hawk," Street said.

"So it's a regular bug," I said. "Not some mutant, one-of-a-kind freak?"

"Yes, of course, it's a regular bug. They are common wherever tarantulas are found."

"I'm sorry to hear that," I said. "I don't like to think that anything so large and nasty-looking could be common. Please tell me that Tarantula Hawks look worse than their bite."

"Yes, absolutely. They rarely bite humans."

"Good."

"But they sting," Street said.

"Now I'm unhappy. Is it a gentle, benign sting?"

Street smiled. "Maybe we shouldn't go further down this line of inquiry."

"Not gentle? Not benign?" I said.

"On the Schmidt Sting Pain Index, the Tarantula Hawk is number two."

"Number two least painful, or number two most painful?"

"Most. The Tarantula Hawk is a type of spider wasp. It has the second most painful sting in the world after the bullet ant, which feels like getting shot by a bullet. Justin Schmidt, the guy who created the Schmidt Sting Pain Index, was actually stung by a Tarantula Hawk. I recall that he called the pain 'blinding, fierce, and shockingly electric, as though a running hairdryer had been dropped into your bubble bath.'"

"That's all?"

"Right. But you probably don't want to know the details of what this wasp does."

I inhaled a deep, calming breath. Breathed out. Repeated. "Okay, I'm ready."

"This specimen in the tire is a female Tarantula Hawk. She can smell a tarantula from a long distance. She attacks the tarantula and gets into a death battle. She usually wins by stinging the spider. The sting paralyzes the tarantula but doesn't kill it. Then she drags the tarantula to her nest."

"Wait." I pointed at the wasp carcass. "This girl is big, but tarantulas are huge. They must weigh many times what the wasp weighs."

"True. But she's incredibly strong. She can drag a paralyzed tarantula up hills, over obstacles. It's amazing to watch. When she gets the tarantula where she wants it, she lays an egg on its abdomen. When the larva hatches, it drills a hole into the still-living, still-paralyzed tarantula and burrows into the spider's body. There the larva eats the tarantula from the inside, voraciously consuming everything but the most vital organs, which keeps the tarantula alive for several weeks while the wasp larva grows."

"That's disgusting," I said. "It sounds like something out of a horror movie."

"Mother nature at her most inventive," Street said. "Never underestimate insects."

I glanced at the big, dead wasp. "I may move to Antarctica, where it's too cold for insects."

"Sorry, there are insects there, too. But none like this one." She pointed at the Tarantula Hawk. "May I have this specimen? I'd like to check it for parasites. Parasitoids are often victims of parasites themselves."

"Divine retribution from an insect deity?" I said, feeling smart.

"Maybe." Street put on magnifier glasses and used a tweezers to pull the waterlogged insect body out of the tire. "It looks like it got one of its wings trapped in the concrete. I'm surprised it didn't tear itself free. Oh, but here's some damage to the thorax. That's probably what did it in."

"You have an exciting profession," I said.

"Sarcasm hides insecurity," Street said.

"Ouch. But you're probably right. I should get going. Will you be okay alone with your dangerous creatures?"

"They're dead, so unless they have ghosts, I'll be okay."

"But the mice are still alive. At least for now." She pointed to the Paiute Deadfall with the Random House dictionary weight. She'd rigged up Diamond's sticks and re-balanced the dictionary on the stick seesaw.

"I put some peanut butter on the trigger twig," she said. "We'll see if it works."

"It certainly looks like a medieval rodent-crushing device," I said.

"Diamond said the Pauites invented it long before the Middle Ages," she said.

I'd stepped close to Street to give her a hug goodbye. I put my hands on her waist and slid them around her back. After being around death, I felt a desire for closeness and touch, an affirmation of life, of energy, of spirit, of everything that was the opposite of death.

"What's this sudden affection?" she said.

"I don't know. You seem very alive, and you have inordinate smarts, and your shape is a dream, and you possess a kind of woman's insight that seems an utter mystery to me. I find the combination endlessly alluring." I bent down and kissed her temple.

"You think a woman's insight is more insightful than a man's?"

"Of course. What does your insight tell you now?"

"It's not telling me anything," Street said. "It's asking."

"What?" I said.

"If I ever unloaded all those boxes that I stacked on my

overnight cot in the back room."

"I can unload them. Exercise is good."

"But you weren't thinking about that kind of exercise." Street's voice was a whisper.

"Well let's check your back room and see what our options are."

Street turned, held my hand behind her back, and, tugging me past Spot, who was spread out in a serious snooze on her rug, she pulled me into her lair.

That evening, I called Nadia.

"You okay with the Jeep?"

"Aside from the dog smell and hair, I guess so. But I'd like to get a rental car. Would that be okay? I could call up one of the agencies that delivers cars."

"I think that would be fine. Just keep a low profile. Have them bring the car into the hotel parking lot. I don't want you out on the street. Then call me later tomorrow?"

She agreed. "Do you think Trud... Gertie will be okay?" she asked.

"If she keeps out of sight and doesn't go out alone, yes."

"I hope so," she said. "I've thought about it, and I do love her. I just don't know how to do it right."

"Skill comes with practice," I said.

We hung up.

SEVENTEEN

In the morning, I called Special Agent Ramos at the local FBI office.

"I heard from Sergeant Martinez that you helped him bring in a body from the lake yesterday," he said.

"Yeah. She went by Amanda Horner. I gave her wallet, ID, gun, and cell phone to Mallory a couple of days before that. I'm calling about something that was written on her arm. Did Diamond tell you about that?"

"'The American Dream,'" Ramos said. "It reminds me of something from way back, but I can't remember. We're running it down. If we find something, I'll let you know."

"Thanks," I said, and we hung up.

I called Street at her lab.

"Hey," I said when she answered.

"Oh, my Lothario," she said, "you are quite – how shall I say it – effective with your, um, physical attentions. But I really must work today. All day."

"Attentions," I repeated.

"I'm a scientist. I'm not sure you'd want me to compare you to the scent of a rose or a lovely summer's day."

"You're right. I just have a question, darling, nothing more."

"Ready."

"I want to see if I can find out where that tire was filled with concrete. So I'm thinking of doing a search on used tires, and another search on tarantulas and/or Tarantula Hawk wasps. I could find the common areas and cross-reference them with areas proximate to Tahoe. Brilliant, eh?"

"Yeah, except that tarantulas are like tires, they are found nearly everywhere in California except cold, high-altitude areas like Tahoe."

"Bummer."

"But," Street said, "when I was trying to remove the bit of wasp wing from the concrete, I wondered if you had noticed that little symbol."

"No. What do you mean?"

"There's a kind of logo stamped into the concrete. It could be accidental, like something got dropped and hit the concrete while it was still curing. Maybe it's a fluke, but I think it was formed by pressing a shape into the concrete."

"What's it look like?"

"Sort of like a small circle inside of a larger, irregular ellipse. The ellipse is lopsided and dented on one side. The inner circle is round. And there are two straight lines."

"I better come by and look," I said.

"What happened to, 'a question, darling, nothing more'?"

"Extenuating logo circumstances," I said. "I'll be there in fifteen."

I hung up the phone. Spot jumped up.

"Largeness," I said. "Why the sudden leap to your feet?"

He looked at me, his tail on medium. He made me think about Nadia's description of her childhood dog, Señor Inteligente. "I've not used the word for perambulation," I said to Spot. "Nor any of the words for tasty, canine ingestibles. I haven't reached for the metallic instruments with which to start Diamond's mobile rust experiment. I'm still wearing my indoor shoes and haven't even glanced toward the Sorels. The front entrance to this manse is still out of my field of vision. Yet you wag. Please reveal the secret."

He wagged more.

I gave up, walked over, and pulled on my snow boots. His wag ratcheted up to high speed.

We went out and drove Diamond's pickup down the mountain through three more inches of snow.

Fifteen minutes later, we pulled up at Street's bug lab.

Spot greeted her with excitement, doing the little bounce on his front paws as if he hadn't seen her for months instead of only being separated overnight.

Street pet him first, kissed me second, then walked over to the counter where the tire still lay and turned on her light.

I leaned in for a look, and Street pointed with a pencil.

"It's over here at the corner of the concrete."

The wasp was gone, but the mark was easy to see once you looked for it. It was three-eighths of an inch long. It looked like it was made by taking an embossing tool of the type one might use on leather or wood and lightly pressing it into curing concrete. No one would ever notice it unless you looked very close with a bright light, as Street did.

"Does it mean anything to you?" Street said.

"No. But the shape looks like an artist's paint palette next to a railroad track."

"That's it!" Street said. "I thought the palette part seemed familiar, but I couldn't remember why. The hatch marks could be anything, but I guess a railroad track is as good a guess as any."

"And I agree that it looks like an intentional mark. I don't see how something so fine and clear could be an accidental impression."

I gave her a kiss, picked up the tire, and turned to go.

"Wow," Street said. "A brief visit. Affection voluntarily truncated after a mere kiss. A man who keeps his word."

I carried the tire outside and put it into the back of the pickup.

My cell rang. It was Nadia.

"I got a rental car delivered to my hotel."

"Great," I said. "How 'bout you meet me at the Sheriff's office. It's near my office. I'll drop off Diamond's pickup, and you can drive me to my Jeep."

She agreed, and I told her where to go.

I drove over to the Sheriff's lot and parked the pickup in the far corner to be out of the way. While I waited for Nadia, I called Diamond and told him where to find his wheels.

"If that doesn't work for you," I said, "then I can deliver it back down to Carson Valley just before the next time you come back up the mountain, and I'll catch a ride with you."

"No problem. Our guys are always going back and forth. I can make arrangements."

"Gracias very much," I said.

Nadia pulled up in a bright red Mustang.

I took the tire anchor from Diamond's pickup and put it in the Mustang's trunk.

It took some coaxing to squeeze Spot into the micro space they call a back seat. Nadia drove off fast. I had to hang onto the door handle.

"Hard to stay incognito in this red color," I said.

"Isn't it pretty?" She sounded delighted.

I wondered how someone could be so clueless. I reminded myself that some people get a burst of neurotransmitter feel-good chemicals when they see bright colors. The desire overwhelms any common sense about the benefits of drab.

Nadia took me to the underground hotel lot where she'd left the Jeep.

"Please watch where you park," I said. "If someone wants to accost you, the most likely time is as you are leaving your car or coming back to it."

She'd turned on the radio and was nodding her head to the beat. She gave me a smile, still nodding, but I don't think she paid any attention to what I said.

I grabbed the tire from her trunk, and Spot and I transferred back to my Jeep and drove home.

A romantic idea had been bouncing around in my head. I found Shakespeare's sonnets online. I scanned several of them for the most notable two lines, found a good example, and memorized the words. I was about to call Street and whisper them into her ear when my cell rang.

I hoped it was Street calling, but the number was blocked.

"Hello?" I said.

"Mr. McKenna?" A big deep voice I'd heard before but couldn't immediately recognize. Then I realized it was Merrill O'Leary. "Gertie's gone," he said.

EIGHTEEN

Spot and I got back in the Jeep and headed west over Echo summit. There was light snow, but the road was open. It was late enough that there was little traffic. The sky went dim with twilight, and the American River Canyon was lonely and dark. By the time we'd dropped down to Kyburz at 4000 feet, the snow had turned to drizzling rain. By Placerville, the rain had stopped.

We were in Sacramento two hours later.

The broken sidewalk up to the O'Leary house was dark, and there was no light outside the door. Blue light danced on the window drapes. TV voices came through the wall. A sportscaster. People cheering.

I knocked to an immediate response of high-pitched barking.

Merrill opened the door. With no light outside the door, I could only see the sides of his face, back-lit from behind. It was enough light to see beads of sweat on the skin of his cheeks and temples.

Scruff Boy was at his feet, his tail wagging.

"Come in," Merrill said. He turned and walked into the house.

I stepped into the entry, past the posters of Dietrich, Dean, and Grant. We went into the living room.

There was another man sitting on an old couch.

The big TV was turned up loud. The Heat were playing the Warriors.

"This is my bro Ellison," Merrill shouted over the TV. He gestured at the other man on the couch. Ellison was taller and narrower than Merrill, with obvious shoulder muscles. He had the kind of good looks that girls like Gertie might notice.

"I'm Owen McKenna," I said, reaching out.

Ellison leaned forward in his chair and gave me a quick handshake.

While I stood, Merrill sat next to Ellison on the couch, picked up a remote off a low table in front of the couch, and turned off the TV. Merrill put down the remote and lifted a lit cigarette off the top of a beer bottle where it balanced on the narrow opening. He took a drag and set it back down on the bottle. The bottle sat on a stained white plate, which caught the ashes. At the base of the bottle were multiple butts. There were other bottles on the table. Merrill picked one up and held it in front of his face as if to see if it contained beer. It was empty. He set it down and tried another. That one was half full. He took a long drink. Then he leaned back on the couch and set the beer bottle between his legs.

He gestured to the only other chair in the small room, a big easy chair that was partway reclined. I lifted my leg up and over the raised footrest and sat down. Scruff Boy jumped up on the footrest and stood looking at me. I grabbed the arms and tried to raise the chair to the upright position, but it didn't want to go.

"Chair's broke," Merrill said, smoke still drifting out of his mouth. After a moment, Merrill said, "Gertie's still gone. I was hoping that she'd come home after I called you. Like maybe I was just jumping to conclusions. But I haven't heard anything." His voice was tense and worried in a way that made me not sure that he was actually tense and worried. Maybe it was an act. Or maybe he was just so awkward that nothing about him seemed sincere.

Ellison stared vaguely ahead toward the darkened TV screen as if he wasn't listening to his brother.

"The last time you spoke to Gertie," I said, "did she say anything out of the ordinary?"

Merrill shook his head. Then he looked up at the ceiling, which was spray-textured. The white paint was mottled by a thin, fuzzy coating of spider webs and cigarette smoke. "I don't remember exactly when the last time was I spoke to her."

"This morning before you went to work?"

He shook his head. "I leave for work at seven. She's still in her room."

"What time does she go to school?"

Another shake. "I don't know. Eight, maybe."

"So the last time you saw her was last night?"

He thought about it. "I didn't see her. I came home kinda late. Her door was already closed." He pulled the beer from between his legs, drank the rest of it, and leaned forward to set it on the low table. The balancing cigarette wobbled. Merrill picked it up and sucked it down to the butt, the end glowing bright. He stubbed it out on the plate.

"The night before, then. Was that the last time you saw Gertie?"

Merrill shrugged. "Maybe. I really don't remember."

"Nadia got hold of you, right?"

He thought about it. "She left a message on the machine saying that Gertie was to take taxis if she couldn't bum a ride and that she'd pay for the taxis. Like she'd ever voluntarily pay for anything other than her designer clothes."

Scruff Boy lay down on the footrest, his chin between his paws. He watched me carefully.

"What about you, Ellison?" I said. "When was the last time you talked to Gertie?"

He reacted slowly as if thinking carefully about how he should respond.

"I, uh, don't really remember. Gertie and I are close, you know, like good buds." He gave me a grin. "But I don't keep track. I'm around here and there. I stop by to say hi, maybe give her a lift to the mall. She likes my wheels, so that's always fun. Get her in the ol' Stingray, she lights right up. You know what I'm saying?"

"No, I don't."

Ellison flashed a quick frown and then went back to a grin. "Girls are impressed by cars. And I've got an impressive car."

"Give me a guess, then?" I said.

"About what?"

"About when was the last time you spoke to Gertie?"

"Oh, that. Let me think. About three days ago. Yeah, that would be about right. I stopped by to pick up some DVDs that Merrill borrowed from me. We played catch in the driveway. You maybe don't know this, but Gertie's an awesome softball pitcher."

"You go to her games?"

"Heck yes. Five, six times I've been. Gertie loves me for it, an uncle that pays attention to her life."

"What about you, Merrill? Do you go to her games?"

Merrill gave me the same mean look he used at the warehouse. "I can't. Some people have to work."

I looked at Ellison. "What do you do for work, Ellison?"

"What's this, like an interview with the police?" He pronounced it like 'poe-lease.'

"Yeah. That's exactly what it is."

"And you are?"

"Detective McKenna. Former Homicide Inspector SFPD."

"Ah," he said, his tone heavy with condescension. "And now you're a private cop. Which technically means you've got no authority."

"Is there something about you that would make it matter whether I have authority or not?"

Ellison shrugged.

"When I talk to the Sacramento police, they will act on my recommendations." It was a statement that may not turn out to be true, but Ellison didn't know that. "Back to my question. What kind of work do you do?"

"I'm a businessman." Again, he looked at the blackened TV screen."

"What kind of businessman?"

"General purpose. I look for opportunities. I have investments. Just three months ago I met a guy who was onto a great new supplement vitamin that helps old people's memories. All he needed was some capital to set up a sales network into old folks homes, and he was willing to give me a huge return in exchange for investing."

To Ellison's side, Merrill was gritting his teeth.

"There are opportunities all over if you know where to look," Ellison said.

It was the kind of line that scammers and schemers and con-artists use, white-collar dirtballs one step up from corner drug dealers.

He pulled out a card and handed it to me.

I read the card. "O'Leary Enterprises. A phone and website but no address. Sounds like a catch-all name," I said.

Ellison acted affronted. "It's the real deal. I even have a website and a blog."

"Good for you," I said. "You live around here?"

"Yeah." Non-committal. Wary.

"Where?"

"Got a great deal on a nice two-story a couple of neighborhoods away. But I'm... if you want to reach me, I'm rarely at home. Best to call my cell. It's on the card."

I looked at Merrill. He was looking at the wall. His jaw muscles clenched.

"Merrill, when you got home tonight, was there any note from her?"

"No."

"What makes tonight different from last night?"

"What do you mean?" He frowned.

"You came home last night, you thought she was in her room. You came home tonight, you thought she was gone."

"Last night her door was shut. So I knew she was in her room. Tonight, Scruff Boy was at the door when I walked in. And Gertie's door was open, and she wasn't there."

"Was the front door unlocked when you came home?" I asked.

"Yeah. It's always unlocked."

"Don't you tell Gertie to lock it when she's home alone?"

"No. We live in a safe neighborhood. There's no gangs here. Just families."

I gave him a hard look and tried to squelch my desire to go over to him and rip his nose off his face.

"Is everything here the same as always? Nothing out of place?

No indication of struggle?"

"Everything's pretty much like before. I didn't really look around. I just saw that she was gone, so I found your card and called you."

"Could you look around now?"

"What would I look for?"

"Anything out of place. Anything different."

He sighed, leaned forward to put his hands on the edge of the couch, pushed down and heaved himself to a standing position. He breathed hard from the effort. Scruff Boy jumped to his feet and watched.

Merrill walked down a short hall. I got up and followed. He walked into one of two bedrooms and flicked on the light.

He leaned into the doorway and looked around. Then he did the same with the other bedroom.

"Nothing's different," he said.

"May I look in Gertie's room?"

"Sure." He pointed. "It's that one." Merrill was big enough that he filled the hallway. He had to back up so that I could step into Gertie's room.

It was a small space, maybe eight by ten feet. There was a single, narrow mattress on a box spring along the wall. At one end of the room was a small closet and next to it a four-drawer dresser. At the other end of the room, a small desk with a metal fold-up chair. The desk was neat and orderly with a stapler and some pens and a pad of paper on the left side. On the right side was an old desk lamp. There was an impressive stack of books about movies, all used and tattered. A guide to classic movies, two books on how to write screenplays, books on directing by David Mamet and Sidney Lumet, a collection of interviews with Francis Ford Coppola, and several books on Tarantino including his screenplays for "Pulp Fiction," "Reservoir Dogs," and "Natural Born Killers."

Merrill saw me looking at them. "I give her an allowance, and she pretty much spends it all at this used bookstore she likes. Everything they have about movies. I guess they order books, too. Gertie also finds the books on her phone. Used books. I don't have a credit card. So the store orders the used books from Amazon."

"Does she have a computer?"

"They have computers at school. And her phone is actually a computer, right? She can use it for everything. Homework, even."

"Texting her friends?" I said.

Merrill looked down. "She doesn't really have any friends."

"None?"

"Pretty much. I've seen her text people. But I think that's more school related."

"Does she ever go over to anyone else's house? Or does anyone come and see her here?"

He shook his head.

"Has she ever mentioned a boyfriend?"

"No. I even asked her once. She said boys only care about two things."

"Sex and video games?" I said.

Merrill looked surprised. "Yeah. That's exactly what she said."

"So she doesn't do anything social with boys? No dates?"

"No."

"What does she do for fun?"

He hesitated. "Well, I'm always at work, so I'm not real, you know, tuned into what Gertie does. But as far as I can tell she just reads her books and watches movies." He pointed at the stack of books on the desk. "It's pretty weird, if you ask me."

"What do you do when she watches movies?"

"Well, she pretty much does that when I'm not at home."

"You mean, when you're at work," I said.

"Probably more like after work. Before I get home."

I waited.

"Sometimes I stop at the Corner Tap for a pick-me-up after work," he said.

"A few brews to relax after a hard day," I said.

"Exactly. I work hard."

"Who cooks? You or Gertie?"

"I'm no good at cooking. And besides, after a hard day, I can't usually make it home early enough for Gertie's dinner. So she'll usually make something for herself and then leave the rest for me."

"What do you do when you get home?"

"I usually watch a movie while I eat."

"One of Gertie's movies or one of yours?"

"Mine. I pay the cable bill."

"What does Gertie do when you watch your movie?"

"Usually she, you know, does the dishes. And then she does her homework and stuff."

"In her bedroom."

He pointed at her desk. "That's where her desk is."

We walked back out to the living room. Ellison had turned the TV back on. Merrill sat down on the couch. He picked up the remote and turned down the sound, but left the game on.

"Do you care about your daughter?" I asked.

"Sure I care about my daughter. What kind of question is that?"

"She told me she wanted to run away," I said.

"What? I don't believe that. She never told me that." He turned to Ellison. "Did she ever tell you that?"

"Sure. But I thought it was just a joke. Don't all kids say that at some time?"

"What does she talk to you about?" I directed the question at both of them.

Merrill said, "I don't know. School stuff. And movies. She always tells me about movies." He pointed at the movie posters. "I bought her those. We went to the mall before school started last fall 'cause she needed some new clothes, and she found them. They were expensive, but I bought them for her. I'm real supportive of her."

"Do you watch movies together?"

He looked at me. "Just once. She really wanted me to watch this movie with her. It was real old. Black and white. Nothing happened. I like action movies."

"But you watched it with her," I said.

"Most of it. It had Katherine Hepburn. I might've fallen asleep. I don't really remember."

"What about you, Ellison? What else do you do with Gertie?"

"I told you. I hang with her. We're pals. And I give her rides. She likes the other kids at school to see that. They all think my car is cool, too."

"You think I'm a bad dad," Merrill said, his voice subdued.

"It sounds like you could pay your daughter more attention."

"I have to go to work. Every day I go to work. Unless the company is slow. But most days they need me. Usually all day. Once in a while, half days. I know some guys, if they don't feel like working, they stay home. And some dads split and are never there for their kids." He flashed a look at Ellison. "But I'm always there, working. There's rent to pay. And the cable TV. And I gave Gertie a phone. Do you know how much that costs every month? She doesn't even use it to make calls. It's just a camera to her."

"It's hard being a dad," I said.

"Yeah. Real hard. Not like her mom was ever there, either. At least I have a job. Always did, too. I'm, like, the rock in Gertie's life. The one thing she can count on."

Right, I thought. His perspective on being a dad reminded me of men I'd met who believed that they were rock-solid husbands because they never beat their wives. Merrill had a job and gave his daughter a phone, so that made him a stellar parent.

Ellison looked at his watch, one of those fancy types with the thick gold case and multiple gauges on the face. "I gotta go," he said. He slapped his hand onto Merrill's knee, then stood up.

Ellison walked past me without glancing toward me. More wariness.

"Can you help find Gertie?" Merrill said to me after Ellison had left.

"I'll try."

NINETEEN

I walked out of Merrill's house and went out to the street.
A block down, I saw the taillights of his brother Ellison's Corvette going around a corner.

I sprinted to my Jeep and jumped in. Spot leaned over the back of the seat and sniffed out the smells of beer and cigarettes and infrequently-washed men as I raced after the Corvette. My speed was high as I came to the corner. The Jeep skidded through the turn, but I made it without colliding with the cars parked to the side.

The 'vette's taillights were up ahead, making another turn, moving fast. I pushed my speed, made the next turn, gradually got closer, then eased off to minimize the chance he'd see me.

Ellison turned onto 16th, took that north past the capital, then went east on J Street. After a few blocks, he pulled over and parked, leaving his flashers blinking. I couldn't find an open parking spot, so I stopped in the right lane with my blinker going as if waiting for a parked car that was leaving.

Ellison jogged into one of the restaurants. He came back about five minutes later, too fast to have even had a drink. He ran diagonally across the intersection and stepped into a bar with blue light coming out the door and some high windows. Once again, he came out in a few minutes.

He jumped in the Corvette, drove down to 21st, turned left, drove to I Street, and turned left again. Once again at 16th, he went right and parked near the old Historic Governor's Mansion, a grand Victorian from a grander era before California governors were forced to fend for themselves and stay in hotels.

I found a parking spot, got out, and followed Ellison for a couple of blocks. He turned up the steps of one of the old Victorians on 18th Street. Someone was opening the door and letting him in as I got close. I stayed back until they were inside. Then I walked up and noted the house number.

I waited in my car down the block. After an hour went by, the lights in the house began to turn off. I decided that Ellison was staying in for the night.

It didn't fit with what he'd said at Merrill's. He lived nearby, he'd said. But he'd been let into this house, so it wasn't his. Why was he staying at another person's house and not his own?

When all but one light went off, I went back to the first restaurant he'd stopped at on J Street. I too parked in a no-parking zone and left my flashers going.

The inside of the restaurant was busy with all the tables full and the bar crowded. The maitre d' approached me.

"A drink or dinner at the bar? I'm sorry that we don't have single tables."

"Actually, I was supposed to meet a gentleman named Ellison O'Leary. We got our times crossed. Turns out he was in here an hour ago and then left. He was supposed to come back around now. Have you seen him?"

The maitre d' frowned. "I don't know Ellison O'Leary."

"About six-one, wearing a blue polo shirt and jeans."

The maitre d' shook his head. "Sorry."

"Could you ask the waitresses or the bartenders? It's very important."

He gave me an icy look. "I've been here all evening, no breaks, and I haven't seen him."

"Thanks."

I left and ran over to the bar across the intersection, opened the door, and walked into essence of blue.

At one end of the long, granite slab was a man wearing a white shirt that looked blue in the strong blue light, his sleeves rolled up, his black bow tie loose.

I made the similar request.

"O'Leary? I know O'Leary. Why do you ask?" As the bartender spoke, I smelled tequila on his breath.

I realized that most answers I might give him would sound false to someone who knew O'Leary. I decided to be flip. I spoke in a low voice. "I don't want to suggest anything negative, but I lent him some money and..."

The man smiled. "This is where I'd normally say, 'get in line,' right? Ha, ha!" Then the man frowned. "I thought I knew everyone in O'Leary's world."

"I don't really know O'Leary, and I don't make book. I just met O'Leary a few days ago when I was moving up to K and Twenty-fourth. He came walking along right when we got the couch stuck between the van and a car that parked too close. So he helped us free it, then he helped us haul our stuff up two flights. Great guy. So when I found out he was tight until his next paycheck, I offered to help. He said he'd meet me outside this bar. But I haven't seen him."

"Sorry for you," the bartender said, "because he was just in here an hour ago. He paid me my loan plus vig. The guy was high and happy, so he must have made a good score."

"Damn, I guess that's good news, huh? All I gotta do is find him. I don't even know where he lives."

"Now that's funny!" the bartender said. He reached under the counter, lifted out a lowball glass, took a sip, and put it back. "Like O'Leary has a regular crash pad? You must not know him well. He's never had enough financial control to pay rent. So he just crashes wherever he can. He told me he's even slept in his 'vette. Imagine that."

"I guess I'll just wait then," I said. "I'm sure he's planning to come back and pay me."

The bartender guffawed. "You don't read personality types very well, do you? He's not coming back unless you've got some kind of hold on him. And the paycheck story he gave you? He's never had a regular job in his life, so there's never been a paycheck and never will be. O'Leary just lives from one scam to the next."

I nodded, thanked him, and left.

I got a room at a hotel just a few blocks from the Governor's Mansion. After I checked in and found my room, I took the back stairway down, then came back with Spot.

"Hustle, largeness," I said when we got into the stairwell.

"Top floor."

Spot trotted up the stairs twice as fast as I could take them. At every other landing, he stopped and looked back to see if I was coming. We went through the door into the hallway. Half way down, the elevator opened, and a couple came out.

I took Spot's collar. When the couple saw him, they gasped.

"Animal control officer," I said. "Found this dog loose in the hotel. Is he yours?"

They shook their heads, alarm in their eyes, and flattened against the wall as we went by.

Spot and I turned into the elevator and waited. When I heard their room door shut, we reversed and hurried to our room.

I dialed room service and ordered up a Porterhouse steak dinner for two.

The man taking my order spoke with a strong accent that I didn't recognize, "I should to let you know that we have the steak very special, no? The Porterhouse is the twenty-four ounces. So the couples, they should to most times split the one dinner."

I remembered that the front desk thought I was alone, so I said, "It's just for me, but I'm hungry, and I always eat two."

"And the beers is the sixteen ounces," he said.

"I always drink two beers."

"Very pleased, sir. We will to bring your dinners fast."

I had Spot hide in the bathroom when the man wheeled the dinner cart into our room. In the center was a single red rose in a narrow vase.

"Smells good," I said as I tipped him.

The man glanced at the closed bathroom door and winked at me. "Your, eh, wife will enjoy, I'm sure."

"No doubt," I said.

After the man left, I cut the bone out of Spot's steak so that he wouldn't gnaw it on the hotel carpet and make a mess.

Spot was drooling when I let him out of the bathroom. I sat at the little table, and he stood. He finished his steak and potatoes in twelve seconds, and I finished mine in seven minutes. I poured his beer into the ice bucket, and he drank it in thirty seconds. I stretched mine out for an easy ten minutes just to prove that I still have self-discipline.

After dinner, Spot immediately jumped up on the king-sized bed and went to sleep while I sat in the dark and called Street and told her about Gertie, the street-smart kid who didn't like school and might have run away but maybe was kidnapped instead.

We talked a long time, both of us saddened and unsettled by her disappearance.

The breakfast buffet started early, and I was first in line. I ate a muffin fast and took two more out to Spot in the Jeep.

We were outside O'Leary's latest crash pad house by 7 a.m. He came out at 7:15. Instead of heading to his car, he walked the opposite way.

I let Spot out, and we followed Ellison over to 15th, then down to Capital Avenue, where he headed into the big park that surrounded the capital dome. There were some homeless people behind the bushes, but the beautiful park was mostly empty. I kept back, watching for an opportunity.

Up ahead was one of the huge redwood trees, its giant trunk maybe eight feet wide. Nearby were some heavy plantings of small trees and bushes. There were no intersecting paths and no one else near on our path.

I sped up and caught O'Leary from behind as he came to the place where the path curved around the redwood. I reached my right hand around and grabbed his throat, pinching his trachea and carotid arteries hard. He choked and gagged. Almost immediately, he began to lose body tone from lack of blood to the brain. I marched him into the thick growth and up against another tree. Unless someone came walking down the path, no one could see us. I figured I had thirty seconds.

I turned him sideways to me, my right fingers still clamping down on his neck. By easing up my thumb and fingers on his carotid arteries, I was able to keep him conscious, if weak. He looked at me, eyes wide and worried as he realized who I was.

I spoke in a vicious whisper. "You make a move, I'm going to rip your throat out. I know you're a fraud. You have no house like you claimed, nothing but your 'vette and your lies. You owe money all over town. But suddenly you are able to pay off debts." I eased up on his throat.

"I... I can't breathe!" His voice was a choked whisper.

"I'm giving you one chance to tell me where you got the money. If I believe you, I let you go. If I don't believe you, my dog will eat your balls, and they will find your body but probably not soon enough to keep the birds from pecking out your eyeballs."

I turned to Spot. "Show him we mean business," I said.

Spot wagged a slow one, two.

"Show him, Spot!" I said in a hard whisper.

Spot growled. It wasn't the deepest, loudest, longest version, but it was scary enough, and Ellison's eyes strained and rolled. Spot moved forward, lifted his exposed teeth up toward Ellison's neck, and upped his growl toward a deep roar. Ellison started shivering.

"Okay, Spot."

He stopped growling.

I tightened my squeeze on Ellison's throat. Tears came out of his eyes.

"Where did you get the money?"

I loosened my grip on his neck a bit.

"A man wrote me an email. He got my email address off my website. Said he knew Gertie was my niece because I put a picture of her on my business' social media pages." Ellison gasped for breath, his throat wheezing. "He said I could make two thousand dollars cash for telling him where Gertie goes to school and where she lives. He said if I didn't tell him, he would come and cut me up. There was a picture in his email. It was like one of those snuff pictures with a real body all bloody and dead and a knife sticking out of its throat. At least, it looked real."

"So you emailed him the info about where Gertie lives and goes to school."

Ellison attempted a nod. "After I hit send, his email disappeared. It was gone from my inbox. And my reply to him was gone from my sent box." Ellison's tears were flowing harder. "I didn't take Gertie," he whined. "He's the one who took Gertie.

All I did was give information. And he forced me to do it."

"When was this?"

"A few days ago. Four. Maybe five."

"How did you get paid?"

"He sent me directions to a garbage can in this park. I went there, and the money was under the garbage. All there in cash."

"Gertie told me that you were her favorite uncle."

He cried.

"And you sold her out for two thousand dollars, and then you happily went to collect your pay."

His eyes were shut, tears streaming.

"You are scum of the lowest order. If that man hurts Gertie, I'm going to come back and find you. Do you understand?"

He tried one more nod. The small movement flicked tears off his chin.

I gave him a shove into the bushes. He collapsed hard.

"Guard him, Spot," I said, pointing at Ellison.

I stood over him as I dialed 911.

"Sacramento Emergency," a man's voice answered.

"This is Owen McKenna, Private Investigator from Tahoe calling." I gave them my license number. "I'd like to report a probable kidnapping."

The man had lots of questions for me, which I answered with the limited information I had. I carefully explained for the recorded call that they could get background from Special Agent Ramos at the FBI's Tahoe office as well as Sergeants Martinez and Santiago from the Douglas and Placer County Sheriff's offices.

"I also have a suspect in custody at the State Capital Park. I believe he has engaged in child trafficking. I'll wait here while you send a unit over."

I gave him my location and hung up.

Ellison made a move as if to sit up.

I touched Spot on the throat. Already primed, he growled.

Ellison dropped back down to the dirt.

Sirens grew from the north side of the capital. Two patrol units pulled into one of the wider access paths. They stopped at a gate. Two cops jumped the gate and came trotting up. I said my name, and showed them my license.

One of the cops said, "I'm Sergeant Cutler." He stared at Spot.

I pointed to Ellison.

"His name is Ellison O'Leary, uncle of the missing child Gertie O'Leary." I held up my phone. "I have a recording of him admitting that he sold information on her whereabouts for two thousand dollars. The likely purchaser is an unknown suspect who is blackmailing the girl's mother out of life insurance proceeds on the death of her husband, the girl's stepfather. Special Agent Ramos in Tahoe can give you more details."

I played the recording for the men. Ellison squirmed as he lay on the ground.

"You pat him down?" Cutler asked when he heard the recording.

"No. He's too slimy to even carry a nail file."

"Check him," Cutler said.

I pulled Spot back so the other cop could step past. The man hoisted O'Leary to his feet.

"Arms out, hands on that tree, spread your legs."

He patted O'Leary down, pulled O'Leary's hands behind his back, cuffed him, and read him his rights.

"We'll need that recording." Cutler pointed at my phone.

"I've got critical calls that may come in. I'll email you the recording while you watch. A voice expert can substantiate O'Leary's identity at a future time. The email time stamp will match your report."

Cutler thought about it. "Okay," he said.

He gave me an email address and watched as I sent it.

"When do you want to come in to make a statement?" he asked.

"Now isn't good. Can I call later and set up a time?"

"Yeah."

They took my card and left with Ellison.

Ellison turned back to me and said, "You said if you believed me, you'd let me go."

"I lied."

TWENTY

When Spot and I got back to my Jeep, I was breathing the hard breaths of anger. The human species had a subgroup of scum parasites that scientists had not yet named. On the scale of revolting, they were just one notch behind murderers and rapists and other violent offenders.

And Gertie was gone.

I got Nadia on the phone.

"Are you driving?"

"Yes, but I'm on hands-free," she said.

"Can you pull over? I'd like to talk."

"Okay, hold on." Thirty seconds later, she said, "Okay, I'm in a little parking lot."

"I don't know for certain and I could be wrong," I said to her. "But it looks like Gertie may have been kidnapped yesterday afternoon."

"What?!" she shrieked.

"I spoke to Gertie yesterday, and then talked to Merrill last night. Again, we don't know for sure. Gertie told me that she was thinking of running away. She even said she might go that afternoon. But I think it was just a story. I have reason to believe someone took her. You will probably get an email notice from the blackmailer. And you should know that Merrill's lovely brother Ellison sold her out. He took two thousand dollars in exchange for telling the kidnapper where to find her."

"I can't... I can't believe..." Nadia was crying.

"I've got some leads to pursue," I said, stretching the truth. "I'll call you as soon as I learn more. You should take some deep breaths. Then drive to your hotel and get some rest."

She didn't respond.

"Okay?" I said.

"Okay," she finally said.

As soon as I hung up, my cell rang.

"Owen McKenna," I said.

"This is Special Agent Ramos calling." Always more formal than he needed to be.

"Glad you called," I said. I told him the news about Gertie O'Leary and explained that the Sacramento cops would probably be in contact for information.

"Got it," Ramos said, betraying no emotion. "We'll talk more about the girl later. I'm calling about the body that was tied to the anchor. You told me about The American Dream writing on her arm. I've learned something that you should know. Sergeant Diamond Martinez is going to meet me at my office at two this afternoon. Any chance you can come by at that time?"

"I'll be there."

"See you then." Ramos hung up.

I dialed the Placer County Sheriff's Office and asked to be put through to Sergeant Santiago.

After a minute came a deep voice, crisp with enunciation. "Santiago."

"Owen McKenna calling," I said. "You and I met last fall."

"How could I forget," he said. "You pulled that fingerprint evidence trick in the Tahoe City restaurant. We used it to arrest the guy who wore the cowboy boots and tight-crotch jeans. The Neo-Nazi militia case."

"Good memory. I'm calling about the drowning death in Hurricane Bay about two weeks ago, Ian Lassitor."

"That was a crazy one. Gotta wonder what kind of guy takes a little boat out in a gale. I heard about another strange death on the lake. Douglas County found a woman's body under water."

"I was there," I said. I told Santiago about Amanda Horner. Then I explained that Lassitor's wife Nadia had contacted me. I also explained about Gertie. "Her disappearance may be connected to Ian Lassitor's death."

"You're saying that the step-kid of Ian Lassitor was kidnapped yesterday in Sacramento."

"I believe so, yeah."

"And this is an effort to pressure the kid's mom – Lassitor's widow – into paying the blackmail, which will now be ransom."

"Yeah."

"I don't like it."

"Me either," I said.

"Thanks for letting me know," he said.

We hung up.

When I got back to Tahoe, I had a few minutes before my meeting with Diamond and Agent Ramos. I stopped by Street's lab.

"Any news?" Street's face was heavy with sadness and worry. "Do you know for sure if Gertie has run away or if it's something worse?"

Spot stood next to Street, looking at me with a wrinkled brow, mirroring her worry.

"I learned this morning that it's likely she's been kidnapped."

Street puffed air and moved back as if she'd been hit in the diaphragm. Her back hit the counter, and she reached sideways with her arms and grabbed the counter's edge as if to keep from sliding down to the floor.

I stepped next to her and put my arm around her shoulder.

I told her what Gertie's uncle Ellison had admitted to me.

Street was outraged. "That is so sick!"

"And Gertie looked up to him," I said.

Street shook her head. She reached for a tissue, wiped her eyes, blew her nose.

Street's concern for all victims of predators was profound, and it came from both her natural empathy as well as her miserable childhood and a father who beat her brother to death. With all other crimes, she talks about rehabilitation over punishment, education over retribution. But if she were in control of the fates of predators, she would probably let them fry.

We talked until I had to go meet Agent Ramos and

Diamond.

When I left, Spot was in a deep sleep, crammed up against Street's laboratory wall so that his shoulder caught a corner of the square sunlight beam coming in the window. I left him with Street and walked to Ramos's place.

They'd moved the South Shore's FBI office. It was now just a short distance from both my office and Street's lab, on the south side of the highway. No wonder Ramos and I were so chummy. We were practically next-door neighbors.

I saw no Douglas County vehicles nor Diamond's Green Flame Karmann Ghia nor the ongoing rust-experiment pickup that I'd returned to him, a vehicle he sometimes drove when he wanted to recall the life of the migrant lettuce picker he once was. So I waited.

A minute before 2 p.m., a county patrol unit pulled into the lot. It parked and Diamond got out. We gave each other the imperceptible nod like two taciturn cowboys coming from different directions and different cultures to meet the head rancher and join forces to help root out a band of rustlers.

We walked up under the cameras, and Diamond hit the button.

A speaker crackled. "Yes?"

"Hola, amigo," Diamond said. "Your humble Douglas County sergeant and rogue private gringo cop reporting, sir."

A buzzer buzzed, a lock released, and Diamond opened the opaque metal door.

"Rogue private gringo cop?" I said as we walked into the glass-walled inspection chamber where we were probably photographed and recorded and irradiated with X-ray and MRI waves. On the other side of the glass, I saw Ramos push back his desk chair and stand up.

"Sorry," Diamond said. "Was it rogue or gringo or private that sounded pejorative? If rogue, I meant it in the solitary and unpredictable sense, like a large wave to watch out for. If gringo, the Spanish and Portuguese etymology makes it clear that it bears no ill will and just refers to an English-speaking wanderer. If private, you know how enamored I am of your job, the tough-guy gunslinger for hire. Except, of course, you have a thing about not slinging a gun."

"So you meant it as a fawning description of awe," I said.

Diamond made a serious nod. "Always the awe when I think of you."

Ramos pulled open the door. "Come in, please." He waved his hand toward a circular group of four chairs and made just the tiniest of bows. Not a bow of respect, but a bow of invitation. Ramos had always erred toward ceremony. His manner was as careful and scrupulous as the cut of his hair and mustache. He wore a white shirt with a narrow navy tie that matched his navy dress slacks. His cuffs were folded back twice and smoothed just so. His nails were trimmed with care.

We three sat. I spoke first.

"Before we discuss the body of the dead woman and the writing on its arm, I need to tell you about a girl I met named Gertie O'Leary. She is Nadia Lassitor's daughter by a previous husband. I believe she was kidnapped yesterday in Sacramento."

I gave Ramos and Diamond all I had.

When I was done, they looked troubled. Kidnapping of children was one of the most nightmarish crimes that people in law enforcement ever face.

They asked a few questions. Ramos said he'd be in contact with the Sacramento police.

After a minute, he said, "What I'm about to tell you may connect to this child. I learned something about the writing on the left arm of the body you pulled out of the water."

"The American Dream," Diamond said.

"Right," Ramos said. "It turns out that there are some ugly antecedents to this. If the connection we've found holds, we may be dealing with a significant adversary."

"There have been other killings with the same words written on the victims?" Diamond said.

"Six of them ten years ago, one seven years ago, and two of them three years ago. Nine murders. The first eight were on the East Coast. The last was in the South."

"So we're dealing with a serial killer who's moved to the West

Coast for his tenth victim," Diamond said.

"Probably," Ramos said. "It could be a copycat, but I looked at pictures of the various victims' arms from years ago, and it looks like a match. The media got pictures of one of the victim's arm, but it was fuzzy. A copycat might have been able to get close, but the writing on the woman's arm is closer to the earlier examples than one would expect from a copycat who had only seen the one photo in the media."

"What do we know about this killer?" I said.

"We think we know nearly everything about his past. This is all information we got from past interviews, especially two neighbors who have since died. But we know nothing about what name this killer is currently using, where he lives, or who his contacts are. We were never able to link him to the crimes other than motive on the first six victims. We had nothing with which to charge him. And over the last few years, we've learned nothing else." Agent Ramos leaned back in his chair.

"Here's what we think happened based on some interviews the FBI conducted years ago," Ramos said. "Twenty years ago a young family emigrated from Russia. They were Cossacks. A professor of mathematics, his wife, and their three children, two boys, Petro, sixteen years old, and Mikhailo, twelve years old, and Kateryna, a girl six years old. They moved to Brooklyn where the professor got a job teaching at Brooklyn College. In less than a year, the man caught a sudden lung infection and died. After such a short period of employment, there was no death benefit for his family, and he had not purchased any insurance. His wife ended up cleaning houses to support her family.

"From the moment they arrived in America, the oldest boy did well. He was big and strong and amiable, and he got along well in his high school. But the younger twelve-year-old Mikhailo was skinny and shy and awkward, and he suffered taunts for his skinniness, his accent, his lack of sociability, and his artistic bent. Mikhailo was always drawing little sketches, and he was bullied for it relentlessly.

"In particular, there was a group of school children who were a kind of ruling clique. Most of these kids came from upper middle class families. For some reason, this clique of kids took a special dislike for Mikhailo, and they hounded him. Among other insults, the bullies would taunt Mikhailo by saying that he'd come to our country for the American Dream and, as they would strike him, they'd say, 'Here's your American Dream, Rusky boy.'"

"Ain't children sweet," Diamond said.

"They learn from their parents," Ramos said. "One winter Saturday, Mikhailo was watching his little sister Kateryna while their mother cleaned a house that belonged to the family of one of the bullies. Mikhailo and Kateryna were walking along a small creek that flows through the nice neighborhood. The group of bullies happened upon them. They started throwing rocks. Mikhailo and Kateryna tried to run away. But the bullies jumped them, pushing Kateryna down a steep bank toward the creek and then beating Mikhailo severely, hitting him with rocks.

"Kateryna tumbled down, struck her head on the frozen ground, and fell into the creek where she drowned.

"Mikhailo was hospitalized. After he recovered, he was able to give a full and complete report of what happened, and he provided the names of the bullies. The police launched an investigation, and two of the boys, including the one who lived in the house that Mikhailo's mother cleaned, were charged with voluntary manslaughter. However, both of those boys had well-to-do families who hired good lawyers."

Diamond took an audible breath and sighed. No doubt this story was resonating with some previous experience he'd either had or heard about.

"In the end, the charges against the bullies were dropped, and no one paid any price except for the mother who was fired from the cleaning job. Worse, the bully's family knew most of the mother's other cleaning clients, and they convinced all of those families to fire her as well."

"The making of a killer," I said.

Ramos nodded.

"Mikhailo withdrew into his own internal world. He played violent video games. He broke off what few friendships he had.

Just a few years later, he started taking steroids and working out. He went to a gym with a reputation for catering to young men with problems. There he met a guy who ran an MMA school."

"Mixed martial arts," Diamond said.

"Right. That man coached Mikhailo in fighting techniques. Mikhailo got better and more fanatic. He lived in a world of violence, bodybuilding for strength not show, and fighting in non-sponsored MMA events."

"By that you mean, shadow matches?" Diamond said. "Not sanctioned by the regular fight promoters?"

"Right. Like dog fights or cock fights. Mikhailo was christened Mikhailo the Monster. He won every fight he entered, all in the heavyweight class. And in two of them, he reportedly killed his opponent with kicks to the head, but the shadow matches are so secretive that nothing came of it. He was twenty-eight when he became a kind of unofficial national heavyweight champion, and the rumor was that the sanctioned champion on the regular circuit was afraid to fight him in any kind of match."

Ramos, as if suddenly cold, unrolled his sleeves and buttoned the cuffs at the wrists.

"That was the year the first murder victims were found," he said.

"The kids who had bullied him," I said.

"Right," Ramos said.

Diamond said, "And on each body's arm was written, 'The American Dream.'"

Ramos nodded. "Two of the bullies had grown up to become soldiers, but that didn't deter their killer. In fact, we think it might have inflamed him."

I asked, "How were the victims killed?"

"The first ones were all drowned. Their bodies were each found within a dozen miles of where they lived or worked, two in Brooklyn, one each in Newark, Atlanta, Hartford, and Buffalo. As with Amanda Horner's body, the victims' bodies were displayed in obvious ways so that passersby would see them, although none of the previous victims was completely submerged under water. Two were found on ocean beaches, one near a creek, two near lakes, one near a slough."

"No witnesses?" I said.

"No."

"And the three bodies that have been found more recently?" I said.

"Victims seven and eight were burned. Number nine was drowned. The burn victims had a type of insulating metallic tape over the writing on their arms."

Diamond made a slow head shake. "So that when they found the charred bodies, they could peel off the tape and still find the writing."

"Right."

"The more recent victims weren't bullies from Mikhailo's past, were they?" I asked.

"Not that we can tell. We think that Mikhailo's transformation from injured, persecuted kid to vigilante killer sated him for a few years. But it is likely that, as he endured other insults or slights over the years – as we all do – he cracked further. He was already a murderer, used to playing God with peoples' lives. So it is possible that he couldn't resist the pull of resurrecting his brand of justice."

Ramos paused as if to take a breath.

"The two burn victims were being blackmailed. Apparently, they had collected cash as instructed and gone to a meeting where they were to make payment."

"Where they were relieved of their cash and then burned?" Diamond asked.

"Yes. One was an unlicensed doctor who'd been banned from practicing medicine, yet who sold quack cancer cures to desperate, unsuspecting cancer patients. The doctor was found in an old cabin in the Great Smoky Mountains in North Carolina. The cabin had been torched. The other burn death took place in a mansion in Palm Beach, Florida. That man made his money as a Miami pimp. A couple of his sex workers had been killed by johns over the years, leading people in the trade to accuse the man of not providing even the most basic protection for his workers."

"So both of those killings could have a vigilante component?" I said.

Ramos nodded. "And the blackmail also suggests that money was a secondary motivating factor. We don't know how much the doctor brought to the blackmailer before he was killed. But the pimp's associates said he was being blackmailed for a hundred thousand dollars."

"You mentioned the six people who bullied Mikhailo when he was a boy, a pimp, and a predatory doctor," I said. "That's eight murders. What was the last murder?"

"A lawyer in New Orleans who sued small businesses for disability-access infractions, businesses that he'd never even patronized. He was non-disabled himself, and he drove around looking for potential victims to prey on through the court system, businesses without wheelchair-access restrooms and such. A journalist ran a series on one of the businesses that was forced to close after one of the lawsuits and reported that the owner committed suicide. The lawyer who sued the business owner was found drowned in a bayou. We have no specific evidence of blackmail. However, the lawyer withdrew fifty thousand dollars in cash from his account the day before his death."

"All this fits with Lassitor's drowning because he engaged in predatory patent infringement lawsuits," I said. "And whether or not he paid money to his killer – if he was killed, that is – his widow Nadia is being blackmailed after the fact."

Diamond was shaking his head. "But how would Amanda Horner's drowning fit into this? The death method fits, but there is no vigilante aspect and no other apparent motive."

"No," Ramos said. "And that is disturbing. To have Mikhailo step outside of his MO and find other targets for his twisted violence gives us less chance of anticipating his moves."

"It seems like he might be a suspect in Gertie O'Leary's kidnapping," I said, "if only because her step-child connection to Ian Lassitor seems like too much of a coincidence. But do you have any indication that Mikhailo has kidnapped in the past?"

"Not in a ransom sense, no," Ramos said. "But it appears that he abducted several of his other victims simply for the purpose of dragging them to their death sites. The main thing we know about him is that he has no moral boundaries. In the beginning, he saw his life as a war against people in power. It may now be that he sees his life as a war against anyone in his way. If he thought that taking Gertie O'Leary was part of striking back against what he hates, the evidence suggests he's capable of that."

"Does he always work alone?" Diamond asked.

"We have no indication either way. But if he did bring in comrades, one would expect him to use men from that same shadow world where he grew up, disaffected men who live in a world of violence, psychopaths who've been burned by society and have developed into predators who can kill without remorse."

Ramos turned to me. "Tell me about these predatory lawsuits you said Ian Lassitor was involved in."

"According to Nadia's account," I said, "Ian earned some or maybe even most of his money by suing companies for infringement of patents that he'd bought cheap from a company going through bankruptcy. He chose targets that were rich enough to pay a handsome settlement but poor enough not to be able to afford to fight a prolonged case. Nadia said he'd been called a patent troll."

Diamond said, "A predator who Mikhailo might murder."

Ramos nodded. He looked at me. "Have you found anything to suggest that Ian Lassitor's drowning was murder?"

"Santiago said that there were marks on the boat wreckage that could have come from a boat collision, but there was no evidence beyond that. But it would have been easy for someone to run over his little woodie with a bigger boat."

"And Amanda Horner?" Diamond said.

"If we assume that she was working for Mikhailo, maybe she learned about Lassitor's death and was trying to squeeze Nadia Lassitor herself," Ramos said. "If Mikhailo found out that she was running a blackmail scheme on the side, he would want to punish her and get her out of the way."

I said, "Or she could have been exactly what she told me, a worker who botched the job of following Nadia. Her boss had warned her that the punishment for that was death."

Ramos nodded. "The bottom line is that Mikhailo could be our murderer. If so, I can't overestimate how dangerous he is. Coming from a professorial family, he is probably very bright. And of course, his fighting skills are significant."

"Do you have any pictures of him?" I asked.

"No. For obvious reasons, photos are banned in the shadow MMA fighting circuit. He's never gotten a license or any other ID under his given name. We also think that he's changed his looks. One account said he was shaved bald. Another gave him a goatee and a ponytail. He's never held a regular job under his given name. So he's effectively stayed out of all the databases that we take for granted. The only photo that we could find was from his class picture in seventh grade."

Ramos pulled two photos out of his manila folder and handed them to us. "Here are two copies of that photo. Extrapolating from a twelve-year-old boy to a man in his thirties is, of course, difficult, but it's all we've got."

"You said he had an older brother," I said.

"Yes. Petro. A cardiac surgeon at Brooklyn Hospital. Several years ago, he fell off the Staten Island Ferry and drowned."

"Did anyone see this accident?"

"No. It was late. He didn't show up at home. The body was found the next day."

Diamond asked, "Do we know if Petro and Mikhailo got along as children?"

"No. There's no one to ask. The mother went missing some years ago. They didn't have friends as I've already outlined. All of their relatives are back in Russia or Ukraine." Ramos looked at the wall clock. "I'm sorry, but I'm out of time. Please keep me informed if you learn anything."

TWENTY-ONE

B ack at my cabin, I spent the next hour online trying to
find information on the paint palette logo that Street
found imprinted in the concrete of the tire anchor. I took a break
to eat some lunch, and then went back to the computer. After
another hour, I'd gotten nowhere.

I paced my little cabin, trying to see the logo in a new way.
Spot watched me for awhile, no doubt wondering why I kept
going to the deck door, then turning around without going
outside. After several circuits, he gave up watching, put his head
down and sighed.

Perhaps I was using the wrong words. So I looked for
substitutions. The words tire, concrete, and anchor seemed
required. But palette wasn't. I wrote down substitutions. Painter,
Paint, Mixing, Artist.

That was obvious. Only took me two hours to think of it.

A short time later I found a listing for a website called The
Dock Design Artist.

I clicked through to the website. It took a bit for the banner
at the top to load. It was a picture of a dock projecting out into
a lake. Next to the picture was the palette and the line-drawing
logo that was pressed into the concrete in the tire.

There were several pages showing designs, most of which
featured dock posts with tire anchors for bases rather than posts
that had to be sunk into the lake bottom. Once the posts were
set out into the water, the posts were attached to each other with
X braces.

I scrolled down and found the address of The Dock Artist.
It was located in Carson City not far from where the new 580
freeway crossed Highway 50. The posted hours said The Dock
Artist was open until 5 p.m. There was still enough time to make

the 40-minute trip.

"Okay Spot, time for another ride."

He scratched the floor with his nails as he jumped up and ran the two steps toward the door.

We went up and over Spooner Summit, then dropped down 3000 feet to the desert floor and Carson City. As I drove, I tried to puzzle out the reasons why someone might have a dock business in the desert.

The cross street on Highway 50 was easy to find. A block down was a small sign attached to a chain link fence that surrounded The Dock Artist's outdoor show space.

I pulled over, parked, stepped around a white cargo van that was parked in front, and walked in through the open gate.

It was like walking through a junkyard, stepping on crusted snow, winding through piles of materials. Metal posts, white pre-assembled dock sections, what looked like treated wooden posts, an open shed sheltering stacks of concrete bags, tires. In the rear, right corner was a building sided with corrugated metal sheathing. The front wall had a walk-in door and a garage door. Three drooping power wires ran from a utility pole to the corner of the garage. Music thumped loud enough to be heard outside.

Outside the door stood a metal sculpture as tall as me. It was made of metal pipes and automobile components welded together. It was both crude and effective and clearly showed a man standing on one foot, his other leg kicking out and up as if in a karate move. The man's hands were fists in front of his face.

I stepped past the sculpture, opened the door, and went inside. Heavy metal rock boomed in my ears. It sounded like Black Sabbath.

The garage was dark with only two four-foot fluorescent light fixtures. Above them were four panels of skylights. They probably provided great lighting most of the time, but they were currently covered with enough snow to block out most daylight. The dim surroundings were punctuated with staccato flashes of strobe light. A large man was in the corner using an arc welder. He wore a heavy leather shop coat and a big helmet with a darkened face plate. The electrical arcing hissed and snapped and popped. The flashes reflected in his face mask.

I didn't want to startle him, so I waited. In the corner of the garage was an open area covered with a padded floor mat. Hanging over the middle of the mat was a large punching bag of the type that I'd seen used for kickboxing practice.

After a minute the man turned off the welder and lifted his face mask to look at his work.

"Afternoon," I called out.

"Oh. Didn't see you," he said with a very slight accent. He lifted off his helmet and gave me an unusual look. I couldn't immediately tell what it was. Recognition combined with wariness, maybe. After a moment, his face shifted to something more pleasant, like one that a businessman would use with a potential customer.

"I'm Dan the Dock Artist. What can I do for you?"

He shrugged off the big shop coat and hung it on another sculpture. Without the coat, he was still large, and his hard muscles were thick under a tight sweatshirt.

"I'm Owen McKenna, a private investigator from up at the lake. Sorry I'm not here for a dock," I said. "We're trying to track an anchor we found that may have been purchased from you. May I bring it in for you to look at?"

He looked at me for a bit longer than is normal when you first meet someone. "I'll come out," he said.

I turned and walked out to the Jeep, wondering if the man following me was Mikhailo the fighter and killer. I wanted to open up the Jeep's back door and let Spot out. But that would be awkward, and if in fact Dan the Dock Artist was really Mikhailo, letting my dog out would telegraph that I may have figured out Mikhailo's identity.

The man followed me out to the Jeep. I opened the rear hatch, reached in past Spot's probing nose, and lifted the tire out. The man looked at it.

"Yep. That's my tire."

"I don't suppose it's easy to tell who got it from you," I said.

"I go through a lot of tires," he said. "People think, what's a Dock Artist doing out in the desert? But we have lakes and reservoirs and man-made waterski parks. This one is a buoy anchor. I have two kinds. The ones that are fully prepped and filled are for small boats. But they're too heavy for some people who need to pull an anchor up and down frequently. For my light anchors like the one you have, I only fill those with concrete on one side. Of course, with less weight, they won't secure anything that takes heavy stress from waves or wind. I always tell clients that even a small dinghy can get blown away with a light anchor."

"Why would someone need a light anchor?"

"Lots of reasons. For example, swimming instructors like to put up a perimeter of colored, floating markers to keep students inside a certain shallow area. Party hosts like to put up a line of markers to mark the boundaries for water volleyball and other games. A light anchor is perfect for that."

"Have you sold any of these lately?" I asked.

He shook his head, then looked down, as if thinking. "But two were missing when I got here... Was it two, no, three days ago. The marks in the snow were as obvious as can be. Here, look. They're still here." He walked over to the corner of the fence and pointed. "See? Someone climbed the fence, walked across here, and took them right off the top of the pile." He pointed to some vague footprints that had been degraded by sunshine. "Maybe the anchor you've got in your Jeep is one of the stolen ones."

"Yeah, you might be right. I'll give it back to you as soon as I finish my investigation. You don't have an alarm here?"

Dan pointed over at the garage. "Sure. On the garage. But out here in the yard? Everything is too heavy to be worth hauling up and over the fence. At least, that's what I thought before that theft. The fence is ten feet tall. Even that light anchor you've got, it would take a real big guy to hoist that over the fence."

"And you'd need a ladder to get over a fence that tall," I said.

Dan nodded, then pointed at the cargo van. "Or a van like mine to climb on top of."

"I assume you don't have a surveillance camera," I said.

"No, but look at the convenience store across the street." He pointed. "They've got cameras everywhere. Inside, out at the pumps, at the corner looking back at the store. You could check with them."

I thanked him. "Oh, one more thing," I said. "Do you ever see tarantulas around here?"

He frowned. "Not much. This is a city. But I've seen them twice. Two different summer evenings. It makes an impression on you when you see a spider that big. So I told people about it. And this one guy I told said that the boy spiders go cruising for girls on summer evenings. Isn't that a hoot? Just like us. Why do you ask?"

I pointed at the Jeep. "When we found this tire anchor, there was a dead wasp stuck in the concrete. We showed it to an entomologist. Turns out those wasps prey on tarantulas. They're found where tarantulas hang out."

The man nodded.

"Of course, tarantulas aren't crawling around in the snow," I said.

"That tire anchor you've got?" Dan said. "I poured that concrete last summer. It sat in that stack until it was stolen."

"Thanks again."

I went across to the convenience store, flashed my license to the manager, explained that the Dock Artist had been robbed, and asked if they had a surveillance camera that pointed toward the Dock Artist. The woman came out of the store, walked around the side and looked across the street. Then she went over to the dumpster and looked up at a camera.

"Could be our dumpster monitor catches the street at the edge. Let's go look."

We went back inside and into her office. She sat down at a desk and worked a computer, clicking through different screens. "Here we are. This is the dumpster. This uppermost corner kind of shows the Dock Artist across the street. Down here in the corner of the screen is the time scroll. What time are you wondering about?"

"I have no idea. Could be any time during the night after he closed three days ago."

The woman glanced at a clock on the wall. "Look, I have to run my register tape every hour on the hour. You sit here. You click here for fast forward, here for fast reverse, here for regular forward and here for regular reverse. Got it?"

"Got it," I said. "Thanks."

She left me in the office. I went back and forth, slow and fast. Nothing happened at the dumpster or in the uppermost corner.

Five minutes later, the manager came back. "Find what you're looking for?"

"No. Sorry. But I haven't gone through the whole time frame, yet."

"Here, let me sit there again."

We switched places.

She started clicking on menus. "The owner thinks this neighborhood is real bad, so he got all these cameras and this software upgrade that allows you to automate a search, skipping by any section without movement and stopping whenever something happens. But I've never used it because the neighborhood is a lot safer than he thinks. We've never been held up, rarely been shoplifted, either. If only I can remember how to use it." She kept exploring.

"Here we are," she finally said. She found a menu, used the mouse to draw a rectangle around the area in the uppermost corner, then hit enter. "There. Anything moves in that corner, it should stop at that point."

The little hourglass symbol showed passing time. Then it stopped. In the uppermost corner was a white cargo van that hadn't been there before. She cruised forward and backward until we'd seen the entire sequence. The van pulled up at the corner of the fence, its left side facing the camera. The top of the van was cropped off by the camera. If someone had climbed on top of it to get over the fence, it wouldn't have shown in the video. Nothing happened for several minutes, then the van pulled away.

"How long total was it there?" I said.

The woman clicked on the time symbol, subtracted in her head. "Looks like three minutes. A little more than three minutes."

I noticed that the van's visit was shortly after 4 a.m.

"Thanks very much," I said.

TWENTY-TWO

I called Sergeant Santiago.

"Do you have lunch plans for tomorrow?" I asked. "Maybe we could meet and grab a bite."

"Sure. Where do you want to meet?"

"Tahoe House Bakery?" I said. "Noon tomorrow?"

"See you there," he said.

I next called Agent Ramos.

"Do you know about a guy called Dan the Dock Artist in Carson City?" I asked.

"No."

"He designs docks. He's a big strong guy with a slight accent I can't place, and he's got a kickboxing setup in his workshop."

"Interesting. Does he look like Mikahailo?"

"Hard to compare a steroidally-bulked grown man to a photo of a skinny young kid, but it could be him. Same eyebrows. He has a dock-design and installation business in Carson City. You will remember that when Amanda Horner was dropped into the lake, she was tied to an anchor made from an old tire filled with concrete? Diamond and I found a dead wasp stuck to the concrete. I showed it to Street. She said it was a tarantula wasp, and we thought that might help us find the origin of the tire anchor. But she also found a logo stamped in the concrete. That logo belongs to The Dock Artist. I showed him the tire anchor that helped drown Amanda Horner, and he says that he made it. He also says that two of the anchors were stolen from his place of business three days ago. He showed me footprints in the snow.

"So I walked across the street to a convenience store and looked at the security footage from their cameras during the night that the anchors were stolen. A white cargo van pulled up to the Dock Artist's yard and stayed there for several minutes, long enough for someone to climb the fence and steal the tire anchors. Of course, every tenth vehicle on the road seems to be a white cargo van. Even Dan the Dock Artist has a white cargo van."

Ramos asked for the Dock Artist's address, and he said he'd check it out.

The next morning, the roads were icy, slowing traffic. I took it slow going north around the lake, through Incline Village and Kings Beach. In Tahoe City, I turned left at 89 and took Fanny Bridge over the Truckee River where it flows out of the big lake. About a mile south, I turned into the Tahoe House restaurant. Santiago was waiting in his patrol unit. I found a parking spot in the lot, told Spot to be good.

"Sergeant," I said. He nodded as we shook hands.

Santiago and I chatted as we walked inside, scanned the menu board, then ordered gourmet sandwiches on fresh-baked bread.

We found a table.

"Creepy, the way that woman was tied under water," Santiago said.

"Yeah."

"Are you thinking that somehow she is connected to Ian Lassitor's drowning?"

"It appears that way," I said. "Turns out that Nadia Lassitor is being blackmailed," I said. "Apparently, Ian had a life insurance policy worth two million, and Nadia is the beneficiary. Someone knows that and is blackmailing her for the two mil."

"What's the blackmailer's leverage?"

"First, he said that Nadia would die if she didn't pay him. Now, it looks like he kidnapped her daughter in Sacramento."

"You haven't been able to track the ransom demand?"

"His only communication was a vanishing email."

"Great," Santiago said. "Score another win for technology. They say there isn't any privacy anymore, but when we want to find someone, good luck."

"I could pursue a court order, try to pry open the email service that Nadia uses and work backward from there, but that could take months. Agent Ramos thinks our perpetrator might be a guy named Mikhailo who's possibly been killing people for years."

Santiago said, "Unfortunately, we found no evidence in the Lassitor drowning that would point one way or another. No one appears to have witnessed anything. The nearby houses are all vacation homes, vacant in the winter. We interviewed the only two neighbors who are ever around. One, a part-time resident who lives in Minden, Nevada most of the time, saw nothing. The other is a crazy lady who lives in a cabin across the highway. She gave us nothing."

"A crazy lady?"

"That's what we've called her ever since we first tried to talk to her years ago when we had a string of burglaries. She won't answer her door. Once, she was outside when we pulled up, but she wouldn't talk other than mumbling something about aliens."

Santiago sipped coffee. "Maybe you should check from the insurance angle. Who did Nadia tell about the policy? Did Ian tell someone about it? Stuff like that."

I nodded.

The waiter brought us our sandwiches.

I bit into turkey, lettuce and tomato on whole grain Ciabatta.

"Have you learned anything about Lassitor's drowning?" I asked.

"Not much," Santiago said with a full mouth. "The boat was broken in two. Lassitor's body was in the bow section, which was still floating. The stern had sunk. There were scrape marks on the bow that made it look like some other boat had run over the woodie."

"You think there's any chance of recovering the stern?"

Santiago shook his head. "The body and bow were found about a half mile offshore. My map says the lake is seven hundred fifty feet deep there. Too deep to find any wreckage unless we had a submersible and the budget to drive it around. And even if we found it, bringing up the wreckage is another problem."

"What was the body's condition?" I asked.

"Bad. One elbow was broken in multiple pieces, and it looked like Lassitor tried to smash the cockpit dash with his face. But there wasn't much swelling or bruising. Probably the cold water iced him so thoroughly that the body shut down before it could react to the facial blow. Also, his hand was impaled with a shard of wood that also penetrated the dash of the boat. We had to saw the wood to disconnect Lassitor from the boat. Other than that, his body was fine."

Santiago nodded as he chewed and swallowed. He showed no discomfort at talking about dead bodies while he ate, the mark of a seasoned law officer.

"Who ID'd the body?"

"The neighbor first, then later, the widow."

"The neighbor is the one who lives in Carson Valley?"

"Yeah. Craig Gower. Carson Valley and Tahoe. Has a dainty little beach house of maybe seven thousand square feet. Compared to Lassitor's castle, Gower could feel a bit inferior if he was given to such thoughts. But he's an old guy and wheelchair-bound, so maybe house size isn't at the top of his worries. We know him from a few years ago. A real sad story. He was driving with his wife and daughter and got in a head-on collision. His wife and daughter were killed, and he was paralyzed. He's about as broken as you can get. But he still has his business in Minden. A factory that makes thermostats. But even with money and a nice house or two, I don't know how he keeps on going."

"The circumstances of Lassitor's death suggests a lot of questions," I said.

"No kidding. Like how could Lassitor be so stupid to go boating in a storm?" Santiago shook his head.

"If there was a collision, it could have been intentional."

Santiago grinned. "Two million would be a nice bank account for a woman who wanted to start over, wouldn't it?"

I nodded.

"But how would you do it?" he said. "Run Lassitor out into the lake, hope that there were no witnesses, and then arrange the collision? Why not just tie a concrete block to him, and toss him overboard?"

"Unless the killer wanted the body found."

"Like the woman who was drowned on the South Shore," Santiago said. "A kind of a message."

"I should go chat with Gower," I said.

"Actually, I have a couple of questions to ask him that I forgot the last time around. You can join me, if you want."

"Don't want to interfere with official sheriff's office business."

Santiago was shaking his head before I finished my sentence. "You handed us the big collar last fall. I owe you."

Santiago got out his cell, dialed, and arranged a visit.

When he hung up, he said, "I've spoken to old man Gower a few times and he sounds more fragile each time."

"In addition to being paralyzed, he's probably got survivor's guilt too," I said.

"What makes it worse is that he was driving and it was his fault. Apparently, he drifted over the center line."

Santiago drove his patrol unit, and I followed. We continued south on 89, passed the Sunnyside restaurant, and after another mile Santiago turned left into a long, narrow drive that had vertical snow walls like those near Nevada Beach but that were much higher because the West Shore gets three times as much snow as the East Shore.

I turned in after him. After winding through the trees for sixty or seventy yards, Santiago pulled up at a rambling home that probably dated from the 1950s. Sided with cedar shingles, it looked like someone had slid wooden boxes up against each other in a scatter-shot combination, which created unusual roof lines intersecting like geometry puzzles.

I left Spot in the Jeep and joined Santiago at the front door.

TWENTY-THREE

The door opened sooner than I expected. Perhaps a sensor had picked us up as we turned into the drive. A man in a wheelchair looked out. He looked to be in his mid-70s, with a gentle if sad face and soft gray hair. A lap blanket covered his legs.

"Sergeant Santiago," the old man said. "Back to ask more questions about Ian Lassitor, I presume."

"Just a few things I'd like to go over, if you've got a minute," Santiago said.

The man seemed to think about it. A gust of air swirled in through the open door, fluttering the corner of the lap blanket.

"Come in. We can talk near the fire. Get you boys warmed up."

He reached down and pulled on one of his chair's push rings and pushed on the other, rotating the chair. I noticed that Gower's chair was outfitted with a motor and a small control stick on the right arm, but he propelled himself across dark oak floors. I shut the door behind us, and we followed him through the entry.

There was a staircase that was fitted with a platform lift that Gower could roll onto and then it would travel up the stairs.

We went by a large, open kitchen area with long, polished, black-granite counters and a black-granite dining table. In the center of the table was a big glass bowl of oranges. The orange color reflected off the black granite.

Gower rolled past the dining room, then turned left into another room.

In striking contrast to the modern kitchen, the living room felt like the lobby of an old lodge, with a row of small-paned windows facing the lake and, on the opposite wall, a crackling fire behind a heavy screen in a stone fireplace. There was a low wooden table, rustic in design. On it was another glass bowl of oranges.

The man turned his chair to me and reached out his arm. "Craig Gower," he said.

"Owen McKenna." We shook. Gower's grip seemed fragile.

He saw me notice the oranges.

"I own part interest in an orange grove in Southern California. Valencia oranges. The best for peeling and eating. Of course, I'm biased. The grove doesn't supply a significant income, but it allows me the indulgence of oranges for much of the fall and winter."

"They are beautiful," I said.

"I see you have no uniform," he said.

"I'm a private investigator. I'm helping with the Lassitor case."

Gower nodded. "You boys want a beer?"

"Thanks, but I'm working," Santiago said.

Gower turned to me. "I always thought that the point of self-employment is that you can have a beer during the day, right? I've got Paddleboard Pale Ale from the Tahoe Mountain Brewing Company."

"Sounds great," I said. Many times in the past, I'd noticed that the camaraderie of a shared beer resulted in people saying things they wouldn't have said had they been in a formal interview without libation.

Gower turned the chair again and slowly rolled himself out of the living room. I wasn't sure, but I guessed that it might have been inappropriate to offer my help. He was obviously independent in his wheelchair.

I looked out the windows. There was a path that led out to Gower's dock where a good-sized cruiser was moored under a rigid canopy. It was like half a boathouse, providing protection from snow and rain. In the distance to the side was a stone boathouse that must have been Lassitor's. I couldn't see Lassitor's house, or castle as they referred to it.

Gower returned in a minute with two tall glasses of beer, each set in holders on the sides of the chair. "They don't bottle their beers in regular bottles yet," Gower said. "But I get them to bring me the large-size growlers. With that and my fire, I've pretty much got what I need."

Gower handed a glass to me, raised his, and said, "To your health," and drank. I joined him.

"Good stuff," I said.

He nodded, licked some foam off his upper lip.

"You have a motor on your chair," I said, "but you roll yourself."

"Only exercise I get. Motorized rigs are great for quads and others who need them," he said. "And it's handy for me when I'm going up ramps or trying to hold a couple of grocery bags in my lap as I'm going from my van into the house.

"But lots of people in chairs have use of their upper bodies. Like everybody, we can use all the exercise we can get. Unfortunately, some of us just end up using the motor for convenience. Then our upper body strength goes away."

"Just like able-bodied people taking the elevator when they could walk the stairs," I said. "I'm guilty of it, too. Like going to the club for exercise and driving around the parking lot trying to find the closest space."

Gower smiled. He looked warm and pleasant with a smile, but I guessed that he didn't find much cause for it.

"I'm determined to get exercise even if nothing works in the lower half of my body. I crushed my lumbar vertebrae in a car accident a couple of years ago."

He paused.

After a moment, Santiago said, "Mr. Gower, unlike before when we spoke of the details of what you saw when Lassitor went out in his boat, today I'd like to ask you about your opinions rather than facts."

"Opinions about what?"

"What did you think about Lassitor's death?"

"How do you mean?"

Santiago seemed to hesitate. "In trying to figure out how Lassitor drowned during a winter storm, the facts don't seem to help us at all. Whereas your thoughts about Lassitor could give us an indication of what to look for."

Gower frowned. "I'm not sure what you want from me."

"I'd like your personal opinion of the man. For example, do you think he was the kind of man who could get mixed up in something that would lead to his murder?"

"Oh, whoa. I didn't see that question coming. You think it could have been murder? Let me think." Gower's frown deepened. "Well, the simplest way to describe Lassitor is that he had bad judgment. Long ago I had the thought that he would probably die as a result of a stupid decision. He liked to live hard and fast and dangerous. I saw him drive drunk and also drive like a wild man. I saw him go hiking just to climb mountain peaks in cold weather with no extra clothes or food or water or even sunglasses. He called it speed climbing, and he said that having extra water or clothes took the excitement out of it. And he was a base-jumper, that crazy sport where you leap off buildings or bridges or cliffs with a parachute. Another thing he told me – and this will make you think he was truly nuts – was that he occasionally played a game called Ten Little Pills where he would pour a bunch of different prescription pills into a bowl and mix them up. He'd also pour himself a tall glass of Scotch, straight up. Then he'd put on gloves and close his eyes and pick ten pills out of the bowl. Because of the gloves, he couldn't tell by feel which pills he was getting. Then he'd down the ten pills with Scotch."

"That's insane," Santiago said.

Gower nodded. "But then look at me. Here I am being judgmental about Lassitor, and I'm paralyzed because I veered over the center line in a car. So forget everything I just said."

Santiago stared at Gower as if shocked at what he heard.

I noticed that Gower didn't mention losing his wife and daughter in the accident. Probably that was too painful for him to even think about.

After a silence, Santiago said, "Did Lassitor ever say he was going to take his little boat out in a winter storm?"

"Not specifically. But like I said the last time you came here, it's the only thing that made sense. He'd try any idea that came to him, regardless of whether it was crazy. He had no impulse control. He probably was going too fast, hit a wave and swamped his little woodie, breaking it in two."

"Which would explain his injuries," Santiago said.

Gower nodded. "Or someone didn't see him and plowed into him in another boat. Although, leaving him there to drown is beyond comprehension. But if he was murdered, then I have no idea how someone would know when and where he would be out in his boat."

"Did he have a friend he liked to visit across the lake?"

"He never said anything about knowing someone across the lake. Frankly, I'd be surprised if he had any friends." Gower drank some beer and stared into the fire.

I spoke up, "You have seen Lassitor go out in his woodie in the past, right?"

"Sure. Several times. And I'm gone half the time or more attending to my business. So I have to assume that he went out quite often."

"Did he always wear a flotation vest?"

Gower looked up at the ceiling. "I never thought about it, but as I think back, no, I don't think I ever saw him put one on. I can see him standing up at the wheel, sometimes even standing up on the seat, whooping and hollering as he raced across the waves. But I can't remember any life jacket."

"Yet, he had one on," Santiago said. "Going out on a nice summer day isn't like heading into a winter storm."

"What kind of business are you in?" I asked Gower.

"I have a small thermostat manufacturing company. Down in Minden. That's why I live down in Carson Valley for a good part of the year, although I love to be up here in the winter when there is solitude. I have twenty-nine employees. I started it forty-three years ago after I bought a thermostat that didn't work properly. I've done quite well with it, although there is new competition from all over the world. My company has some modern, programmable thermostats, but any tech device more than six months old is in danger of obsolescence. We're not good at keeping up. I would like to sell the business, but to tell the truth, I would never recommend that anyone buy it. So I'll probably just give it to my employees and let them try to find a way to make it relevant to the new world."

Santiago turned to me. "Just to be thorough, we should take a look inside Lassitor's house. Lassitor's wife is probably technically in charge of his lease rights on the castle. Do you think that she would allow us to look at his house?"

"Yes. Implicit in our relationship is that I look into all aspects of Lassitor's life and death. However, she did not give me a key or alarm code."

"I can show you the house, if you like," Gower said.

"You have a key?"

"Sure. Ian has mine as well. We don't share opinions about politics or religion or business or maybe anything else, but we both try to be good neighbors. If something happens like you get a frozen pipe and your house floods or something when you're not around, you want your neighbor to be able to go in to turn off the water. I'll go get it."

Gower wheeled himself away.

"I don't imagine there is anything to find," Santiago said. "But it can't hurt to look."

TWENTY-FOUR

"Would you like to drive over there?" I said when Gower came back.

"No, no, not at all. You may have seen the path between our properties. It's a broad sidewalk in the summer. The paths and our driveways allow me a little circuit I can roll for the exercise and fresh air. I have the snow service keep it clear in the winter."

We waited as Gower put on his jacket and gloves. He telegraphed a strong sense of independence. I thought it best not to go out of my way to hold the door for him. When Gower rolled to the front door, I followed him outside.

Gower rolled down the ramp. He showed a bit of caution as he used his hands on the push rings to brake. He was focused and cautious on the icy surfaces, never noticing Spot in the Jeep as he went across the driveway and over to the walkway that headed toward Lassitor's house. I followed.

The winding path was like a narrow canal with snow walls five feet tall. I could see over, but Gower couldn't. As we approached the Lassitor house, I could see why everyone referred to it as a castle. It didn't seem like someplace that people would call home. While it was impressive, nothing about it was inviting.

The pathway went close to the castle, then curved around to the drive, which had also been cleared of the recent snowfall. Like most castles, the place had few windows, mostly small. One large section of stone wall had no windows at all. Near the top of the roof was a line of clerestory windows, the kind that were designed only to let light in. Looking out from the inside, one would probably only see sky and trees. On the lake side, the sloped roof gave way to a horizontal section fronted with crenelations just like something out of King Arthur's time.

Gower continued past the garage with its four individual

doors designed to look like castle gates, and he headed up the walk to the front door. The door was recessed beneath a large overhang. There were light cans in the ceiling and heavy iron-framed sconces on the walls, but with them off, the area was very dark even in the middle of the day.

Gower slipped the key in the deadbolt and opened the door. A soft beeping signaled an alarm warning as he bump-rolled over the threshold inside. He stopped at a numeric panel, pushed five buttons, and the alarm stopped.

"Very trusting for neighbors to give each other their alarm codes," I said.

Gower looked at me, frowning. "How else could a neighbor help with a problem? We both set our alarms to the same code for that reason." He said it with the tone of a rebuke.

"Good idea," I said.

"So this is it," Gower said, gesturing at the cavernous space before us. "An unusual building that, like most unusual buildings, sacrifices the normal comforts for a big statement."

The huge main room had walls made of stone. One wall had an out-sized fireplace with windows on either side looking out at a large deck and the spectacular lake view in the distance. Opposite the window wall was a built-in entertainment area with TV and shelving for speakers and multiple glass bowls filled with different kinds of pine cones, Jeffrey, Lodgepole, Ponderosa, California Red Fir, and, in two of them, huge Sugar Pine cones. To one side of the entertainment center was a big upright piano. On the other side was a built-in cabinet.

The kitchen was a galley design with a long counter and appliances along the outer wall. There was a parallel island, just as long, with a large gas stove top and a grill.

Gower waited by the lakeside windows while we looked around.

There was a stairway near the kitchen and a large arched opening in the wall next to it. I walked through the arch into an entertainment room. In the ceiling above were the clerestory windows I'd seen from the outside. On the outer wall were substantial built-in bookshelves maybe twelve feet high and thirty feet long. There was a top rail which supported a rolling ladder for access to the upper shelves. The shelves held a wide range of books, hardcover and softcover, along with vases with silk flowers and small, bronze figure sculptures that were tall and skinny like those of Giacometti, but without the rough surfaces. The bookshelves and their contents showed more of the owner's personality than anything I'd seen in the living room, but nevertheless, nothing was notable. There was no TV as in the living room, but there were stereo components stacked in the shelving.

Back in the main room, I trotted up the stairs, a wide, grand design that rose a flight to a landing, turned ninety degrees, and then rose another flight. All but the last portion of the stairs looked out over the living room.

The castle's second level was all bedroom suites, each with a sitting area and a bath. All the beds were made and unruffled. All of the bathroom sinks were polished and had no water stains. The towels appeared untouched.

At the far end of the hallway was a spiral staircase. I went up and saw that it opened onto a rooftop deck. The deck perimeter was the crenelated castle wall I'd seen as we approached. Stepping out onto the deck and looking past the crenelations to the stone boathouse and the lake beyond, it almost felt like I was back in the Middle Ages, in the smallish castle of a minor feudal lord.

I went back inside.

"Nice place," I said as I came back down the stairway.

Gower nodded. His chair faced the dark front door instead of the view windows. He seemed depressed.

"You okay?" I said.

"Yeah. Lassitor wasn't what I'd call a friend, but it's hard to come back into this place and realize he's gone."

I took another look around. "The garage is this way?" I pointed to a door by the entrance.

"Yeah. Have a look."

I walked in. The four-car space had extra depth, extra width and extra height. It contained a Mercedes sports sedan and a Porsche Cayenne, and the remaining space was almost twice the size of my cabin.

Nowhere in the house was anything that spoke of Ian Lassitor or his life. It was like a sterile vacation home, set up with all of the expected comforts but no personal effects.

"What about the boathouse?" I said to Gower when I came back into the living room.

"I'll show you when we head back. The lock uses the same key as this front door."

Santiago walked back in from the entertainment room. "Seen enough?" he said.

I nodded. "Want to stop in the boathouse?"

"Sure."

"Come with me," Gower said. Then he paused. "I should probably set the alarm, right?"

"Yeah," Santiago said. "This place belongs to some company. Until they come around and take over, they'd probably appreciate it if you kept it closed up tight."

Gower punched the buttons, then rolled out the front door. After we passed through, he turned and locked the door. Then he rolled down the walkway that we had followed to the castle. Halfway to his own driveway, there was an intersecting path that was cleared of snow. He turned down it and rolled another winding path to the boathouse. He unlocked the door and let us in.

The boathouse was built with its rear half on land and its front half projecting out over the water. At the water end was a roll-up door that allowed someone to come and go in a boat just like driving a car into a garage. At the rear of the boathouse were racks that held three kayaks, red, green, and yellow. There was also a built-in case not unlike the bookshelves in the entertainment room. Instead of bookshelves, it had a closet in which hung wetsuits, rain jackets, and flotation vests. There was a vertical rack with four water skis and five kayak paddles.

Like the main house, there was nothing notable.

TWENTY-FIVE

W e followed Gower as he rolled back to his house. Santiago thanked him for his time and help.

When we drove down to the end of Gower's drive, I beeped the horn. Santiago stopped. I got out and walked up to his patrol unit.

"The other neighbor you mentioned?"

"The crazy lady?" he said.

"Where does she live? I thought I'd go talk to her."

He reached his arm out the window and pointed. "Go down the highway a block, then turn up the next street. Her cabin is closest to the highway. You can almost see it from here."

"Thanks."

"Let me know if she actually talks to you and has any information?"

"Will do." I made a little tap on Santiago's roof and walked back to my Jeep.

Santiago turned north on 89 back toward Tahoe City. I drove south a bit, then turned in on the next street, which led to a small neighborhood of old cabins with a few nice vacation homes mixed in. I pulled over next to the snow wall and parked.

"Be good," I said to Spot as I once again left him in the Jeep.

I walked down the slippery road to the cabin that was closest to the highway. From the way it was positioned above the street, it had a good view of the trees around the Lassitor castle. It's possible one could even see the castle from the cabin's front windows. As I approached, I sensed movement near the house. I stopped.

The backyard had a six-foot fence around its perimeter. There was a porch on the back of the cabin with a gabled roof. A substantial snow drift curled down from the roof and hung in a cornice off the eave of the gable. My view from the street was very limited. But I could see over the top of the fence and under the edge of the hanging snow cornice. A woman was moving around on the porch. I could only see her head and shoulders. From her movements, it looked like she was sweeping. Probably, snow blew off the roof and swirled around under the gable overhang.

She was humming a little tune, the notes disorganized as if she made it up as she went along. There was a refrain where she sang words. The first time she sang it, the words were too garbled to make any sense of them. The second time, it still sounded like gibberish, but I could imagine what words they might be. It sounded like she was saying, "He thinks he's king, hums and crows, true the crown."

I walked up her short driveway, which looked like it hadn't been plowed since the last two snowfalls. There was no car in her drive, no garage, and no footprints either. How did she get her groceries and other supplies? Did someone shop for her? Did someone plow intermittently just so she could walk out?

I trudged through foot-deep snow up to her door and knocked.

There was no answer.

After a minute, I knocked louder. Still no answer.

After another minute, I called out, "Hello? Anybody home? My name is Owen McKenna. I'd like to talk to you, please." Then I knocked again.

There was no loud music or TV on inside, so I knew she could hear me from anywhere in the cabin or even from out on her back porch.

But she wouldn't come to the door. I listened carefully for the sound of running water in case she had decided to wash the dishes. But all was silent.

I walked back out to the street. The woman was no longer on the back porch. For whatever reason, she didn't want to talk to me.

When I got back home, I had a message from Agent Ramos.

I called him back.

"I'm thinking you haven't checked the widow to see if she had a record," he said.

"Correct. I probably should have."

"I saved you the trouble," Ramos said. "Her sheet shows an arrest for shoplifting when she was eighteen. She pled guilty, and her mama paid a large fine. Less than a year later, she had gotten a job working in accounts payable at a perfume distributor and after only a half-year on the job she was fired and convicted on a misdemeanor embezzling charge. She served four months and paid a thousand-dollar fine."

"I obviously have a top-drawer client."

"Good luck," Ramos said and hung up.

Then I called Nadia's cell number.

"Are you okay?" I asked when she answered.

"I think so. I just got another email from the blackmailer."

"What did it say?"

"It had a bank account number. It said something like, 'You have twenty seconds to read this email and write down this number. If you tell anyone the number, we'll kill your daughter. When you get your insurance payment, you will have twenty-four hours to make a bank transfer to this account.'"

The news hit me hard. We now knew for certain that Gertie had been kidnapped.

I heard Nadia take a deep breath. "So I wrote down the number," she said, "and then the email vanished."

"There was no other information about the bank account?"

"No. How does that even work?" she asked. "Don't I need to know what bank the account is in?"

"Does the account number have both letters and numbers?"

"Yeah."

"It's probably an offshore account in a country with strong bank secrecy laws. The country and bank codes are embedded in the account number. Your bank will know how and where to make the transfer."

"If I pay them," Nadia said, "then they will probably kill

Trud... Gertie. Maybe me, too. Don't you agree?"

"I don't know. But yes, it's possible. Have you heard from your insurance company?"

"No. I sent them an email. I hope they write back soon."

"Nadia, why didn't you tell me about your past run-ins with the law?"

There was a long pause. "I was very young. I was a kid. Sometimes kids do stupid things. I paid my debt to society."

"Don't you realize that with this large insurance settlement coming to you, people are going to wonder if you somehow helped your husband to his end?"

"That's ridiculous! He died in a boating accident. What could I possibly have had to do with that?"

"That's exactly the question that people are asking. If you want to allay those concerns, it's best to offer up your skeletons before someone else finds them. That makes a big difference in how you are perceived. Especially when the information omitted is about a carefully-plotted, manipulative theft as opposed to a simple smash-and-grab burglary."

It sounded like she was crying. "I can't believe I can never get past that little mistake."

"It wasn't little, Nadia. Next time you are in a similar situation regarding a potential crime with financial implications, don't forget to bring it up."

"I get your picture loud and clear." She was obviously angry with me. I was the bad guy. Her daughter was kidnapped, but she was the poor, sad person being unjustly persecuted.

"Are you staying out of view?" I said, trying to change the subject.

"Well... Pretty much."

"Nadia, I want you to stay out of sight."

"I can't just sit in my hotel room. Trudy... Gertie is gone and probably is terrified beyond description. If I just sit, I'll go crazy. I should go to Sacramento and see if Merrill knows anything. I should do something!"

"I don't want you to leave. I'm concerned for your safety. Please stay where you are."

Nadia didn't reply.

"What's wrong with me doing a little shopping? There are some great shops around here. I'm not in the car. I'm just walking around a little bit. And I'm being very careful."

Her tone was so self-focused that it exasperated me.

I said I'd be in touch and hung up. If Gertie hadn't been involved, I would have walked away from the case. I'd known many narcissistic, self-absorbed people over the years, but Nadia appeared to be the shallowest person I had ever met.

TWENTY-SIX

I contacted both sergeants Diamond Martinez and Santiago as well as Agent Ramos and reported the email that Nadia had gotten, confirming Gertie's kidnapping.

Then I paced my cabin, stressing about the young softball pitcher who was full of life and had wisdom beyond her age, a girl who'd become a victim in a deadly scenario that I didn't even understand. Even if Nadia paid the blackmailer, he might kill Gertie. I felt helpless. I could feel my blood pulse in my temples.

If Ian Lassitor was murdered, the killer knew what his boat looked like and might have come to Lassitor's house at some point.

The eccentric neighbor lady was a potential witness to any activity in and out of the driveway. But she wouldn't answer her door.

I needed help, a new perspective. I thought of Ellie Ibsen, search-and-rescue dog trainer extraordinaire and sage older woman who lived in the foothills. I got her on the phone.

"Owen!" she said when I told her who was calling. "How nice to hear your voice. A woman my age doesn't often get a call from a young man."

"I'm in my forties," I said. "Not what most women call young."

"Then you're talking to the wrong women. And how is Street? And his largeness?"

"Street is still the greatest," I said. "And Spot's so special that my pastry budget is up like the NASDAQ during the dotcom bubble. I'm wondering if I can come down and ask you a question."

"Well, you can probably ask me on the phone. But I'd love to have you visit. The gate is always open at the Three Bar Ranch."

"I could bring tea or whatever a lady of your stature likes for social engagements."

"Jack Daniels works well. But this old lady has recently been rocking single malt Scotch."

"You take your medicine neat? Or should I bring ice?"

"Mr. McKenna, I'm shocked. You would pour great Scotch over ice?"

"Sorry. Can't trust the Philistines," I said. "Would tomorrow morning be okay?"

She agreed.

The next day, I put Spot back into the Jeep, drove down to Dart Liquors to pick up a bottle of The Balvenie, and headed out toward Echo Summit. I went up and over the pass. By the time we got down to Placerville and turned north on 49, we'd driven from winter to spring, the grass green from the rain they'd gotten when we were getting the big snow dumps. I drove toward Coloma, the fateful little valley where the discovery of gold at Sutter's Mill in 1849 changed the world.

As always, Ellie's Three Bar Ranch looked like a postcard. The big log arch over the entry to the fresh-sealed blacktop drive was like something built for a movie set. The drive was wet from rain, and it looked like a black ribbon as it wound back toward the dream ranch house. Foothills rose on all sides, framing the picture.

The large lawn was like a golf course, lush from the natural moisture that flowed from the hills on all sides. Less than one hundred yards away was the South Fork of the American River, draining the big mountains just west of Tahoe. Around the edge of the lawn were two rows of fruit trees. In another month or so, they would be heavy with blooms.

In the center was the ranch house, which looked like it had just been repainted white with red window trim and a dark green door. The wrap-around porch had a red railing with white balusters.

Ellie came out of the house, moving at a good pace. She showed a bit of stiffness, but nothing like most people in their

late 80s. Her age had slowed her down about the same amount
that age slows down a typical 50-year-old.

Ellie comes up to a little above my waist, so she had to reach
up high – and I had to bend down low – for us to hug. Although I
was careful not to give her old bones a hard squeeze, she surprised
me with the vigor of her grip on my shoulders.

"Aren't you going to let that big beautiful canine out of your
car?" she said as she kissed the side of my neck.

"You're more eager to see his largeness than me," I said.

"Did you expect it to be otherwise?"

"No." I walked over and let Spot out of the back seat.

He was excited to see Ellie. He ran an enthusiastic circle
around us, then another, this one with a greater diameter and at
higher speed. Then he tightened his arc and zeroed in on Ellie
like a planet falling out of orbit and crashing into its mother star.
He came to a halt just as his head reached Ellie's outstretched
hands.

"Anyway, you're probably about to ask after Natasha and
Honey G," Ellie said as she rubbed her hands down the sides of
Spot's head and neck. "I'm not the only one who can't resist a
dog."

"How are Natasha and Honey G?" I said.

"See? I knew it. Come with me." She turned, put her arm
over Spot's head, his neck coming up under her armpit, and the
two of them walked off toward the kennels, which were painted
white with red trim to match the house. Spot never even glanced
back to see if I was coming. If I drove away and left for a day or
seven, he wouldn't think of me. And when I returned, he'd barely
have the I-think-I-remember-you reaction.

Ellie opened the door to the kennel building. I couldn't see in
the building. But Spot could. His tail was on high speed.

They went inside. In a moment, a German shepherd charged
out, followed by Spot. Natasha couldn't run as fast as in the
old days before her bone-breaking fall in the forest fire. But she
remembered that Spot had saved her life, and she would run
through pain to play with him.

Another dog shot out of the kennel, Honey G, the Golden

Retriever who seemed to suffer no gender confusion despite his name. He was younger and uninjured. He could run faster than Natasha and dodge faster than Spot. If each dog had trailed a cord, the three of them would have woven an elaborate braided rope.

Both of Ellie's dogs were certified search-and-rescue dogs, with Honey G having his Avalanche certification as well.

As the dogs raced around, I fetched the Scotch from the back of the Jeep, and we went inside, leaving the dogs outside to run. Ellie had a brick fireplace, painted white on the sides and top. The hearth was smooth granite. A small fire burned behind the screen. It snapped and cracked and periodically sent tiny sparks in all directions.

Ellie held up The Balvenie. "Join me?"

"Please."

She walked over to a sidebar and pulled out two large shot glasses, filled each half way, carried them over, and handed one to me.

"To dogs," she said, holding up her glass.

"To dogs."

We sipped.

"Like heaven on fire," Ellie said, breathing, her eyes shut.

"It is."

We sat near the fire, Ellie in a tiny chair that was upholstered in leather, and me in a big chair. The tiny chair sat low so that Ellie's feet could touch the floor.

"You said you had a question," she said.

"Yes. I'm investigating a death that appears to be a boating accident. But the victim had an insurance policy payable to his wife. Soon after he died, someone began attempting to extort the insurance money from the wife."

"Suggesting," Ellie said, "that the extortionist may have arranged the death?"

"Right. Worse, the wife has a daughter by a previous marriage. That girl was just kidnapped in a further effort to motivate payment from the wife."

"Oh!" Ellie brought her hands up to her mouth. Her eyes

misted. "I can't imagine how terrible. How old is the girl?"

"Fifteen. Her name is Gertie. She's strong, but a kidnapping can break you pretty fast."

"Please tell me you don't think the kidnapper will harm her, you know, physically."

"Impossible to say. But it would seem that the whole point of the kidnapping is blackmail, so I'm hoping there isn't twisted behavior in the mix."

Ellie's forehead was a complex pattern of worry wrinkles.

"Oh, my lord, I can't think about that little girl," she said. "I'll go crazy. Focus me on something else. How can I help?"

"There is a woman on the periphery. She lives in a little run-down cabin across the street from the big house that belonged to the husband who died."

"This woman in the little cabin is old?" Ellie said.

"How did you know?" I asked.

"You called me saying you had a question. I'm an old woman. I'm looking for common ground."

"Ah. I'd guess she's in her seventies."

"And she lives alone and is a little bit unusual," Ellie continued.

"But you don't live alone and there's nothing strange about you," I said.

"I have help, but I live alone in the main. I don't have any family. Not even nieces and nephews. That also makes me a bit unusual. Some old ladies love to knit caps for their grandchildren. Whereas my idea of a good time is to walk my dogs."

"And drink Scotch with younger men?"

"That, too." Ellie leaned her head back and laughed with as much gusto as a 90-pound woman can get out of her throat.

"Okay, but you are not strange," I said, "whereas this woman appears reclusive to an extreme."

"What does she do?"

"I don't know. She appears to stay indoors or inside her fenced backyard. She appears to be a shut-in. She doesn't have a car. I have no idea how she gets food and supplies. Someone must bring them to her or take her to the store, but we haven't seen them."

"What did you want from me?"

"Because the woman lives within sight of the dead man's driveway, I'd like to talk to her about what she's seen. She may have witnessed someone coming and going. But she won't talk to me or anyone else. She was there when I stopped by. I saw her on her back porch. But she won't even answer the door. I thought you might have an idea of how to approach a shut-in, an older woman who may have good reason to distrust strangers."

"It could be that she isn't afraid," Ellie said. "Maybe she just wants to be left alone. She may know nothing useful."

"True. But it would be good if I could pick her brain about any activity around there. Normally, I would knock louder and call out through the door. You can often irritate a person into responding. But my instincts tell me that this woman wouldn't respond."

"And if you wait for her to come out the front door, it may not happen for months," Ellie said. "Does she have any neighbors who might know her?"

"It doesn't seem like it. The closest houses are behind her cabin. They are vacation homes. Because of her location, surrounded by forest or vacation homes, she's quite isolated."

Ellie sipped Scotch.

"When I was there," I said, "I heard her moving stuff on her back porch. Her backyard is fenced. I quietly walked over and listened from outside the fence. She was humming a little tune, then singing some words, then humming some more. When she spoke, it sounded like gibberish."

"What kind of gibberish?"

"I couldn't make it out for certain, but the clearest part sounded like, 'He thinks he's king, hums and crows, true the crown.'"

Ellie nodded. "Maybe it's a Medieval English phrase about the king. 'True the crown.'"

"Yeah. I thought 'true the crown' could imply correcting or adjusting the Kingdom or the king's reign, like truing your course at sea, or truing your instruments. Calibrating them. But I can't make any sense of it."

Ellie nodded again. "Okay, here's what I think," she said. Ellie paused as if thinking how best to explain. "When women get old, they often get dismissed in a way that men don't. You've heard the phrase, 'She's just a little, old, white-haired lady. What does she know?' A woman could be a nuclear physicist, but that doesn't change the dismissal based on appearance. That is why many old women refuse to let their hair go white. White-haired men can still get respect. But it's much harder for women."

"I love your white hair," I said.

"I don't doubt it. But I also know that the first time you came to visit me, you already knew of, and respected, my work with search-and-rescue dogs. If you'd first encountered me driving in front of you, slowing to search for my turn-off, you may have thought of me as just a little old lady."

"You're probably right."

"And if I didn't get to live on this ranch and have people come to me for dog training, I might have to be out on the road more, spending more time in the larger community. If so, I might not let my hair go white, either."

"Am I so transparent that you know how I think?"

"No. You're just a man in the prime of life, not yet fully aware that when people get old, they are still the same people inside, still like you in many ways. We old folks are slower and weaker and have whiter hair. But we still have a fire burning, just like you."

"And you have more wisdom. I drove past a lot of young people to come to you for advice."

Ellie smiled. "I'm honored," she said. "But I fear my advice won't suffice."

"I'll find out. So how does this woman's age connect to how I approach her?"

"Show her respect. She may well be unbalanced, but even unbalanced people respond to respect."

"You have a suggestion how I go about it?"

"Sure." Ellie held her Scotch up in the air as if looking at the color, studying the refraction of light. "Go knock gently on her door. Wait a bit, then knock again. You want to get her attention. Then you sit down on her doorstep and talk to her through the door."

"What should I say?"

"You'll think of the words. Just tell her that you're a cop and you have questions about an important case, and you think she can probably help. Through it all, if you show your respect for her, she'll pick up on that. After a bit, you can tell her about the kidnapped girl, but don't use it like a hammer. Be gentle. The girl's plight will bring out this woman's concern, but not if she feels manipulated.

"Eventually, she'll talk to you. You might have to keep talking for a long time, but I'm guessing that after she gets a sense of your personality, she'll open the door to you."

"If she does, do you think I can trust what she says? Or will she spin it to suit her perspective?"

"Of course. We all spin everything. And she'll probably say some unusual things, maybe even some crazy things. But don't dismiss her."

I nodded. "I'll be careful not to hurt her feelings."

"That's not what I meant. I don't want you to miss what she's trying to communicate."

"Even if she's saying crazy things," I said.

"Right. She will speak the truth as she knows it. It may be couched in craziness, but it's still there for you to translate. Remember that all people, even old unusual people usually make sense from their own perspective. Get into her brain that way, and you'll understand what she's trying to say."

I nodded. We sat there in silence in front of her fire.

Ellie and I had never spent a great deal of hours together, but we'd been together on multiple searches that yielded dead victims. People who share such stress develop a kind of bond.

After a couple of minutes, one of Ellie's dogs made a soft bark outside the door.

Ellie jumped up with the energy of a young woman and opened the door. "Oh, my, three very wet and dirty hounds on the porch, smelling like, well, wet hounds. Time to get them back to the kennel and clean them up before I let them back in the house. You may stay or go as you wish."

"I'll head back up the mountain. Thanks so much for your help."

I went out with Ellie, collected Spot, and said goodbye.

"Respect," Ellie said. "That's the key to gaining anyone's trust. Especially little, old, white-haired, eccentric ladies."

"Got it," I said. I bent over, kissed her cheek, and left.

TWENTY-SEVEN

B ecause Emerald Bay was closed due to avalanche hazard, it wouldn't be easy to get to Hurricane Bay from the South Shore. So I drove the Gold Country highway north from Ellie's to Interstate 80, and took that up and over Donner Summit. When I dropped back down to Truckee, I took 89 south to Tahoe City and continued on to Lassitor's neighborhood.

I turned up the eccentric lady's road and parked in the street in full view of her cabin.

I paused a moment, remembering the things that Ellie Ibsen had told me about showing respect, then got out. I let Spot out of the back, and we walked up to the cabin.

We trudged through the snow and walked up the three front steps and knocked on her door. I was careful to make my knock loud enough to be obvious but not so loud as to be insistent. I even tried to space my raps with the same goal. Not too demanding, not too meek.

There was no response, which was no surprise. After my previous attempt to talk to her the day before, I hadn't expected her to answer.

After a minute or more, I knocked again. Again, she didn't answer.

I had no idea if she was home. There was no sound. But she'd been home the previous time I'd knocked and gotten no response. Time to do what Ellie suggested. Start talking. That would draw her curiosity. Or maybe her ire.

I moved back from the door, brushed the snow off the first step, took off my gloves and sat on them so that the snow and ice wouldn't melt into the seat of my pants. I faced sideways, my upper body turned so that my head faced the door at an angle and I could be heard through the door.

My first words were nothing significant. I figured that she might not be close enough to hear them clearly. She might not even realize that the low tones coming from outside her door were from me speaking. So I made my first words about the weather and the time of day and how long it takes to drive around the lake from my place, which was almost exactly on the opposite side of the water.

I wanted my first words to simply establish that I was talking and give her time to quietly come near the door to figure out what I was doing. I figured that she'd be curious about what was happening on her doorstep. And if she looked out her window and saw Spot sniffing in her drive, that would help.

I spoke softly with the goal of reassuring her, convincing her that I meant no stress.

Periodically, cars went by on the highway, their sound competing with my voice. At those moments, I spoke a little louder.

Eventually, as Ellie had suggested, I worked my little speech around to my line of work.

"Anyway, I'm a cop. Well, not technically a cop anymore. I was with the San Francisco Police Department for twenty years, and worked my way up to Homicide Inspector. I liked the work, felt like I was doing an important thing in society. Of course, much of the time cops feel like they're spinning their wheels. You get a case that you can crack, and you mostly end up filling out reams of paperwork, satisfying all the rules, organizing evidence, and trying to get the warrants and such. I always tried to work by the letter of the law. Meantime, the bad guy sometimes disappears. It can be beyond frustrating.

"Worse, sometimes you manage to put the collar on the bad guy and bring him in. Everybody including his mother knows he's the bad guy, and there's no doubt that the only place he belongs has concrete walls three feet thick. But a clever lawyer finds an inconsistency, the judge makes a ruling that your key evidence is inadmissible, and the guy walks. A variation is when the scumbag has money and he gets a team of good lawyers who overwhelm the prosecutor. Maybe the prosecutor is just as good on technique, but she doesn't have the resources, can't hire the help. Our system is about as good as legal systems get, but that doesn't mean we get justice. In fact, often justice in this country is a crap shoot. Sometimes it works and sometimes it doesn't."

A truck went by on the highway, its engine roaring as if it weren't used to high altitude and it had to gasp twice as loud as normal in order to function. I had to stop talking until it was far down the road.

"Sometimes, of course, we do get justice," I said, "and the bad guy goes inside. Later, when we ask ourselves why the system worked this time, it usually gets down to a single little thing. The testimony of a witness, a person who was willing to come forward, point at the defendant, and say, 'Yes, I saw that man pull the murder weapon out of his pocket.' Or, 'The defendant told me about the party after he got home, so I know he was there.' Or, 'The defendant said that he hated the murder victim and would do anything to sink her to the bottom of the lake.'"

I paused, thinking that I was making it seem like valuable witnesses always have something big to say. So I amended it a bit.

"Sometimes there is a witness who knows something that turns out to be important, but the witness doesn't realize that. Usually, nothing about the information is dramatic. It could be as simple as having seen someone drive through the neighborhood. It couldn't possibly matter, right? Because the person didn't do anything wrong. They weren't even speeding. They didn't toss litter out the window. They were behaving like all other upstanding citizens.

"But what the witness doesn't know is that the defendant has previously claimed to have been in Hawaii on the day the witness saw him in the neighborhood. Simple testimony like that can blow apart a defense. Often the most basic observation can help put a bad guy in jail where he belongs. But without that testimony, the bad guy stays on the street and commits more crimes."

I paused and took a breath. I had still heard no sound from within the cabin. I was feeling ridiculous, rattling on to no effect, wasting my time and, probably, the lady's time as well.

Five cars in a row went by. They all had ski racks on their roofs. One was an Audi, two were BMWs, and two were Mercedes, like a German car commercial shot in Tahoe instead of the Bavarian Alps.

There was still no response from within the cabin. I didn't know what to do to increase my chances that the woman would talk to me. Assuming that she was even in the cabin. I wanted to go back home, but I'd invested a lot of time driving down to get advice from Ellie. So it made sense to keep trying for a bit longer.

"This is the dilemma that we in law enforcement face on a continuing basis. We do the leg work of pursuing a killer, but without a single good citizen coming forward, we can't assemble a solid case to put before a jury.

"This case is like that. We have the death of your neighbor Ian Lassitor. Maybe you've met him, maybe not. He lived across the highway. There's a big stone house on the lake. You can't see it from here because of all the trees.

"One morning a couple of weeks ago, your neighbor Ian Lassitor apparently went out on his boat. It was, no doubt, a bad decision. It was very cold, and the wind was deadly. We're not sure what happened, but it appears that he collided with another boat. His boat broke apart and most of it sank. He had a flotation jacket on, but the ice cold water killed him by hypothermia.

"Shortly after Lassitor died, his wife Nadia got a note extorting the life insurance payout. It could be from a low-life who simply saw an opportunity to profit from Lassitor's accidental death. But it could also indicate that the blackmailer helped arrange Lassitor's death.

"Then something much worse happened. Nadia Lassitor has a daughter from a previous marriage, a girl named Gertie. I was worried about her. So I went and visited Gertie and her father to warn them about the threat. I ended up talking to Gertie for some time.

"Gertie is fifteen years old. She's got more personality than any three kids put together. She's smart and sassy and wry and grown-up beyond her years. I didn't specifically lay out the potential threat to Gertie, because I didn't want to scare her. But I told Gertie to be careful, to lock the doors and windows.

"Turns out that shortly after I left, Gertie was kidnapped."

I paused. Just talking about Gertie made my breath short.

"I ache whenever I think about Gertie. It's a sharp ache behind my ribs. Maybe my rib muscles are knotting up. Or maybe it's an actual heartache.

"Either way, it's likely that someone knows something about this. It could be that someone came to Lassitor's house. Maybe to sabotage his boat so that it would stop out on the lake and make him an easy target. I don't know.

"So I'm looking for any information connected to Ian Lassitor. It could be information that doesn't even seem like it would be helpful. It could be some person who visited Lassitor in the last few weeks.

"Such a person might not have even talked to Lassitor or his neighbors. Maybe he just went down to Lassitor's dock and looked in the boathouse. Maybe he stayed back here in the street and looked through binoculars. However this person made an appearance, it probably seemed innocuous."

I paused as a line of loud cars went by.

"I don't know you," I said. "But I saw you here when I came around before. So it made me think of asking you for help. You might not want to help me. I get that. Like most people, you've probably had some experience with crime, either as a victim or as someone who knows a crime victim. I understand if you think that you should just mind your own business. Whatever your reasons for choosing to talk to me or not, I understand. I don't want to pressure you. But of course, I'm still sitting here talking to you, so obviously I want to encourage you. I should probably give you a bit more time to consider. But I'm really worried about Gertie..."

The lock clicked and the door opened a few inches. An unkempt woman in her seventies looked out. Her long gray hair looked as if she'd been swimming under water and got her hair wound up for maximum entanglement before she got out of the water. Then she let it dry without ever trying to brush it.

In spite of her wild hair, she was handsome, with graceful eyebrows, pronounced cheekbones, and gentle lips.

Her eyes were wide open and reminded me of those of a frightened horse. She looked past me, left and right, afraid of something.

Spot came trotting up. I reached out and grabbed his collar.

I didn't want to alarm the woman by standing up tall, so I stayed sitting.

"Thank you for talking to me," I said, even though she hadn't said a word. "Anything you can help me with would be much appreciated."

She didn't speak. Just stared. Squinted her eyes, then opened them wide once again.

"Anything at all," I said. "Gertie could die. Kidnappers often kill their victims as soon as they get a payoff. Gertie could be next."

"I've seen a light," the woman finally said.

"Where?"

"Through the trees," she said. Her eyes glanced behind me.

"Which trees?"

She looked past me toward the highway.

I turned and looked. There was nothing to see across the highway but trees.

"Do you think it came from Ian Lassitor's house? The stone castle?"

"I've never seen the castle. I don't go out. But I heard it's like the Thunderbird."

I assumed she was referring to the famous stone castle that George Whittel built across the lake during the 1930s.

"Maybe Lassitor left the light on before he died," I said, even though I didn't remember any light from when neighbor Craig Gower showed us Lassitor's house.

The woman shook her head. "Sometimes the light is off."

"And it turns back on," I said.

She nodded. "It flashes." She stepped over the threshold, raised her arm and thrust a long, graceful finger out. Her finger shook.

I tried to see where exactly she was pointing.

"It looks like you're pointing just to the right of those firs. A bit toward that really tall Sugar Pine tree. Is that where the light is?"

She squinted toward the tree, then nodded.

"I think that would be closer to Gower's house than Lassitor's house," I said. "Does that seem right to you?"

"Maybe. But in the Middle Ages, people were tortured in castles. They had oil lamps. Oil lamps make an evil glow. This light is evil. So the light could be from the castle."

"But oil lamps don't flash."

"These do," she said.

I tried to think about what I'd seen inside Gower's house and Lassitor's house. "Could it be a light on one of those timers that are designed to make it look like someone is home?" I said.

She shook her head. "It doesn't come on when it first gets dark. The times vary. Sometimes it turns on at four in the morning. Sometimes not at all. But it always flashes."

I wondered how often she was up at four in the morning. I also wondered how any light from Gower's house or Lassitor's castle could be seen from her cabin. The castle had almost no windows facing this way, and there were enough trees to block any light. Gower's house was behind an even thicker bank of trees.

I pointed across the highway toward the lake. "At night, you can see lights across the lake at Glenbrook and Cave Rock. Some of them seem pretty bright even though they're twelve miles away. Could it be you are seeing a light from across the lake? Shining through the trees?"

She shook her head. "No. If it came from Glenbrook, it would be a tiny light. And it wouldn't flash. This is closer."

"What is it about the light that makes it seem evil?"

"The light is golden. Like a fallen angel. It is Lucifer. Satan."

"Satan?" I repeated, not knowing what else to say.

She said, "'No wonder, for even Satan disguises himself as an angel of light.' Second Corinthians."

I paused. "Have you seen any strange person in the area?"

"You. And Mr. Gower. He might be the Pale Rider."

"Do you mean that in the biblical sense?"

She made a solemn nod. "Death."

"Why do you think that?"

"Riding that wheelchair. I think he's faking it."

The statement seemed harsh, and her comments taken together seemed to make no sense.

"You think he can walk without his chair?" I said.

She nodded, squinted her eyes. "Maybe."

"Have you seen anything else unusual?"

She thought about it. "Only the light."

"How often does it come on? Every night?"

"Sometimes two or three nights in a row. Sometimes not at all. Sometimes four nights in a row."

"How do you know this? Are you up in the night?"

She nodded.

"Did you ever see this light before Lassitor died?"

"I don't know when he died. I've been seeing it for two weeks. Or more."

"Do any other lights come on when it comes on?"

"No. Only one evil glow."

"Yesterday, I was talking to Craig Gower, Lassitor's neighbor. Afterward, I came over here to talk to you. When I got out of my car, I heard you on your back porch. You were talking and singing. I apologize for overhearing you, but it sounded like you sang, 'He thinks he's king, hums and crows, true the crown.' You sounded like you were angry. Or frustrated at minimum. So I'm just curious. What does that mean, 'He thinks he's king, hums and crows, true the crown?'"

The woman shook her head. "I never said that."

"Are you sure? I'm pretty sure it was you behind your fence."

"I would never say that."

"After that, I knocked on your door, but I guess you didn't hear my knock. Or maybe it was someone else here at your house."

"No one is ever at my house but me."

"Okay." I turned to leave, walked down her steps, then looked at her again. "Thanks very much for talking to me. I'm grateful for your help."

"Don't go in those trees by those houses. There is evil."

TWENTY-EIGHT

S pot and I got back in the Jeep. We drove back to Craig
Gower's house.

I knocked.

Gower came to the door after a couple of minutes. He looked
more tired than when Santiago and I visited the day before. But
he seemed in good spirits, which, considering his recent history,
was admirable.

"Owen McKenna," he said. "Come on in." I followed as
Gower rolled his chair into the living room and up near the
fireplace. The fire was low. He reached into a log bin, pulled out
a split, and tossed it onto the coals.

As he moved, I watched his legs. A person faking paralysis
might tense their legs as they moved around. But his had a sense
of limpness about them. If he was faking it, he was good.

"What can I do for you?" he asked.

"When Sargeant Santiago and I were here yesterday, I had a
question I forgot to ask. I know there are a lot of trees between
your house and Lassitor's, but I wondered if you can see his place
from any of your windows. Specifically, if anyone were to visit
the castle, would you be able to tell?"

"It depends. If someone came and went when I'm on this
first floor, then I couldn't see them from inside my house. If I'm
out on the deck, then I can see through the trees to his driveway."
Gower waved his hand toward the living room windows. "But
as you can see, I don't have the deck shoveled, so that would
only apply in the summer. If I'm upstairs, then I can see a bit of
Lassitor's drive and house from a couple of the windows."

"Have you ever noticed anyone over there?"

Gower shook his head. "But I should add that I don't look
out those windows very often."

"What about lights? Can you see light from any of Lassitor's windows?"

"No. The few windows he has are small, and my filtered view is mostly of the drive."

"Would you see the lights of a car pulling in or out of the drive?"

"Yes. Sometimes when I'd be near those upstairs windows, I'd notice Lassitor or one of his visitors coming or going."

"You haven't noticed any vehicle since he died?"

Gower shook his head.

"Do you think that Lassitor might have a light on a timer? Something that turns on at night to make it look like someone is home?"

"I never noticed any when I've been over there. But I never looked for one, either. Do you have reason to think that someone has been to his house?"

"No," I said. "But I'm trying to be thorough. I've learned that he made some enemies in business."

"That doesn't surprise me," Gower said.

"Do you leave lights on at your house when you go to bed?"

Gower frowned and shook his head. "I have no outside lights on at night. I don't want to add to light pollution. One of the nice things about Tahoe is that it is relatively dark. You can see the stars. Why do you ask?"

"It occurred to me that if some of the other people in the neighborhood ever saw a light from this direction, it might help to know that it didn't come from your house."

Gower nodded. "If you're concerned that someone is going into Lassitor's house, you could go over and check it again. Then you could look for timers at the same time. Would you like the key? I can't imagine that anyone would care."

"Yes, I'd appreciate that. It would answer the question."

Gower fetched the key and handed it to me along with a piece of paper with numbers written on it. "Here's the alarm code. I can't imagine that I'm violating anything by giving it to you. I just don't feel up to going out into the winter weather today."

"I'll only be a few minutes."

He nodded, and I left.

The stone castle was exactly as we'd left it the day before. Dark and cold and heavy, the opposite of a cozy Lake Tahoe getaway. I made a quick circuit of all the rooms, looking at all the lamps to see if any of them were on timers. I also paid attention to all of the windows. There were only three that faced toward the old woman's cabin, and from them I could only see trees.

I also opened desk drawers, kitchen cabinets, and closets. I found nothing interesting.

Back at Gower's, I handed him the key.

"Thanks," I said. "No light timers that I could see."

"I'm curious why you and Santiago are even interested in the house? Not that it's any of my business, of course."

"Lassitor had an insurance policy," I said. "That always motivates questions in an unusual death."

Gower made a big nod. "Ah, now I get it. Perhaps it's possible that the death wasn't as accidental as it looked." Gower made just a touch of a grin. "Your job may be more interesting than I first thought."

I thanked Gower and left.

TWENTY-NINE

I drove clockwise around the lake, not stopping at my cabin but continuing on to my office on the South Shore. Eager to be out of the Jeep, Spot trotted up the office stairs.

I hadn't checked my email in a while, so I brought it up on my laptop. It looked like mostly junk mail. I scanned the subject lines and checked all of the spam. I was about to click on purge when I paused.

One of the subject lines was A Photo You Should Know About.

It seemed like a classic junk mail teaser. I didn't recognize the sender. But something made me uncheck it before I deleted the others.

I went back and opened the email.

It had no photo, just a link followed by a short message.

I didn't recognize the link, so that reinforced my spam sense. Almost as a reflex, I again went to delete it. Then paused again.

No harm in reading the message.

'I found your email online. I saw a photo Gertie posted. It said your name. It said you were a private detective. Maybe this isn't the right Owen McKenna. But you might want to know that Gertie didn't run away like people at school think. If you want to text me, here's my number. You could even call.'

I clicked on the link. It took me to a website where people post photos. The page loaded with my photo in the center. I was walking across the street, facing the camera. I recognized the area. It was Gertie's neighborhood. She must have taken it with her phone as I approached her house. On the sides of the photo were soft, white lines. The window drapes. She'd seen me coming.

Under the photo it said, 'A man came to visit. He said his name was Owen McKenna and he was a private detective looking to protect me from the big, bad wolf. Like Scruff Boy couldn't do the job? He was sent by my weird mom. First time she ever cared about me!'

I went back to the email with the phone number.

I dialed. It rang five times, then went to voicemail.

A girl's voice said, "Hey, Emily here. I'm all busy with Justin Timberlake right now. Probably will be all night. Text me. Maybe I'll text you back."

It beeped.

"Emily, this is Owen McKenna calling. I got your email about Gertie. Please give me a call right away. This is very important."

I left my number twice and hung up.

Five minutes later, my phone rang.

"Owen McKenna," I said.

"This is Emily." The voice was so soft, it took me a moment to figure out what she said.

"You're a friend of Gertie's," I said.

"Yeah. Something's wrong. Gertie hasn't texted or tweeted. She always tweets what she's doing. I'm, like, her only follower, so I pay attention. I feel like it's my responsibility to be a friend to her. I haven't heard from her since she tweeted that a detective had come by and to check out the guy's photo. So I went to the website and saw your picture and what she wrote."

The girl must have been nervous. Or scared. I could hear her fast breathing.

"I thought about it for the last three days," Emily said. "When she still hadn't texted or tweeted, I knew something must have happened. So I Googled your name and found your contact email."

"Thanks for getting in touch with me. I'm sorry to tell you this, Emily, but Gertie's been kidnapped."

She gasped. "You haven't found her?"

"No. We have no clues about where she is. Do you have any idea of how it happened?"

Emily was quiet for a bit before she spoke. "Well, it's a pretty out-there idea, but maybe she went with the other man."

"What's that mean, the other man?"

"The other guy she posted. The other photo."

"Is there a way for me to see that photo?" I said.

"'Course. It was the last one she posted. Right above yours. Just scroll up."

I went back to the photo website and scrolled up on my computer. Another photo came into view above mine. It was of a big guy, buzz-cut dark hair, heavy brow that obscured his eye color. He wore a brown bomber jacket that rose at an angle from his shoulders to his neck, lifted by thick webs of muscles. He had on faded jeans and running shoes. The man was smiling, but it looked to my jaded eyes like the fake grin of a predator. Like that of the Dock Artist. I looked at the photo, trying to see the Dock Artist in the face. It was a possibility. But not a certainty.

To the sides of the photo were the same white curtains as in the photo of me.

Under the photo it said, 'This could be the wolf the detective told me about, ha, ha. But he's a hunk, that's for sure.'

"It looks like she took this photo from the same place as mine," I said. "Looking out her living room windows."

"'Course," Emily said. "I recognize the neighbors' cars."

"All of them?"

"All the cars, yeah. But not the van. That must be the man's."

Behind the man, at the left side of the photo was part of a white cargo van facing out of the picture. It looked like a standard, generic cargo van. Just like the one that belonged to the Dock Artist. Just like the one that was in the convenience store security tape. Just like tens of thousands of other white cargo vans.

"Have you ever seen that van before?" I asked.

"Na, uh."

"Do you think Gertie may have willingly gone with the man in the photo?"

"Well, it would be unlikely. Gertie likes to make others think she's kind of reckless. But she's pretty much a quiet kid who lives low."

"What's that mean, lives low?"

"She stays out of the light. Away from attention. Partly, she's kind of embarrassed about her cleft lip scar. Maybe you noticed. Other kids sometimes make fun of it. They call her 'Lip.' She acts like it doesn't bother her. But inside, she's real sensitive about what people think. Anyway, that man would need a real good story to convince her to go someplace with him."

"Is it possible she knew him?"

"I don't think so. She would have mentioned it. She would have already posted his picture before. She tweets about all of her postings. I've seen every picture. So I don't think she knows him. Do you think he's the one who kidnapped her?" Emily's voice was shaky-worried.

"I'm not thinking anything, yet," I said. "I'm just wondering the same things you are. Did you tell the police about this photo?"

"I thought you were a detective. I just told you."

"I mean the Sacramento police."

"No. I... I wouldn't know how. What would I do? Would I dial nine-one-one? Would they investigate me? I didn't do anything wrong."

"I'll call them. And no, they wouldn't investigate you. But they will ask you questions just like I did."

"That sounds kinda scary."

"It isn't. If they contact you, just tell them what you told me. You know Gertie pretty well?"

"I'm her best friend. But it's not like we're real close. I should probably say I'm her only friend. We stay pretty – I don't know what word to use – casual. It's not like she confides her secrets."

"Who would she tell them to?"

"Nobody. That's the thing about Gertie. She's self-contained. Even if she has something burning her up inside, she's the only one who's ever going to know."

"Is there anyone else I could call who knows Gertie well?"

"Nobody knows Gertie well. All she cares about is movies. It's her escape from the real world. That's why she's going to be a director. So she can live in that made-up world."

"Right," I said. "Can I call you back if I have any more questions?"

"Yeah. But it's better if you text. I don't always take calls."

"Thanks for contacting me," I said. "I hope we talk again."

"Okay. Bye."

I was about to hang up when she said, "Oh, Mr. McKenna?"

"Yeah?"

"Something else you should know? Gertie's not a slut."

The statement made me pause. "Why do you say that?"

"You saw how Gertie wrote that the other man was hunky, and I just wanted you to know that she wouldn't hook up with him or anything like that. Gertie's got good dreams."

"What's that mean?" I said.

"It's what Gertie and I say when someone isn't, like, after bad stuff. I don't know how old people would say it. What Gertie wants is all about good stuff. Some kids want to drink and do drugs and get in trouble and back-stab their friends with gossip. Gertie just wants to make movies. She says a movie is telling a story with a camera. She has this video app on her phone, and she showed me a little movie she made. It was good. She's got good dreams."

"Thanks, Emily. I appreciate that."

I hung up.

I called Agent Ramos and told him about Gertie's friend Emily and the photo she'd seen.

"I'll forward the link to you," I said. "The photo that Gertie posted on the website shows a man who vaguely looks like the kid pic you showed us of Mikhailo, although that's a reach."

"Does it look like the Dock Artist man you told me about?"

"Yeah. Kinda."

"Is that a precise legal term?" Ramos said.

"Kinda. Also, the background of the photo shows a white cargo van on the street behind the man who may or may not be Mikhailo or Dan the Dock Artist."

"I'll check it out," Ramos said.

"Because this case is Tahoe-centric, whoever grabbed Gertie may have brought her to Tahoe. I'd also like to disseminate this information to local businesses with a request for no public posting or Amber Alert. I'm worried that the perpetrator would see such a posting and flee. But if we keep it private, he has no reason to think we know about his van behind his picture on the website. Because Tahoe is small, I think the advantages to not posting an alert out-weigh the disadvantages. I'd like your permission on that."

"I don't believe you need my permission."

"Agreement, then," I said.

I heard Ramos breathing. I don't think it was frustration, just thinking. "It is true that Amber Alerts can send a kidnapper into hiding and impede an investigation. It's a hard call. I think your idea of a partial notice, just to Tahoe businesses with a request for privacy, is a good compromise in this situation."

"Thanks. I'll get this over to you as soon as possible."

We hung up.

I got Sergeants Diamond and Santiago and Commander Mallory on the phone in a conference call and gave the same information to them.

Then I emailed Emily's link to all three of them.

THIRTY

The time was 4 p.m., still some time left before businesses closed.

I'm the opposite of tech-fluent, but I brought up the image program on my computer and struggled for a long time. Eventually, I created a graphics file and managed to paste the picture of the man and the white van. Underneath I typed my flyer message.

KIDNAPPING ALERT
PLEASE DO NOT POST THIS
ONLINE OR ON ANY PUBLIC FORUM
LAW ENFORCEMENT – PLEASE NO AMBER ALERT

15-year-old Sacramento resident Gertie O'Leary has been abducted. Indications are that she may be held in the Tahoe area. Suspect pictured above is believed to be driving a white cargo van. Suspect may be watching the news and Amber Alert notifications. If he sees this information, he will flee. If you see a suspicious, white cargo van, please call or email Detective Owen McKenna, Douglas County Sergeant Martinez, Placer County Sergeant Santiago, SLT Commander Mallory, or FBI Special Agent Ramos ASAP. Thank you very much for your help.

I put contact info at the bottom of the flyer.

I dialed the Stateline Chamber of Commerce.

"This is Detective Owen McKenna," I said when a young man answered. "FBI Special Agent Ramos and I are sending you a notice about a kidnapped child. As the notice explains, it is important that this doesn't result in an Amber Alert because we believe the kidnapper will see it and go into hiding. I would like to email this to you and have you send it to your membership immediately. Can you do that?"

"I'll have to check it with our director, but I imagine we can do that."

"What email address should I send this to?"

He gave it to me. I thanked him and hung up.

I repeated the call to the South Lake Tahoe Chamber, the North Lake Tahoe Chamber, and the Truckee Chamber of Commerce.

They all cooperated, and I had the flyer emailed to them before 5 p.m. With luck, most of the businesses in the Tahoe-Truckee area would be on the lookout for white cargo vans within the next day.

On my way home, I stopped by Street's lab once again and told her of the developments.

While the news that we now had a photo of the suspect gave her hope, the seriousness of the situation seemed to make her even more upset.

"Would you like to come up to my cabin for dinner? Make the evening a little better? It's already getting dark. Time to call it a day?"

"I'd love to," she said. "But I'm sorry. The lobbyist the beekeeping trade group hired needs my results tomorrow. I've still got a lot to do on my toxicology report."

So I kissed her goodnight, left her with her honeybees, and headed home with Spot.

After I parked in front of my cabin, I got out, shut my door, and turned to open the back door and let Spot out. He barked and growled. It took me a long half-second to realize it was a warning, a half-second too long. I never got the door open.

A guy with the size and speed and strength of an NFL tackle came out of the dark at a run and hit me, his shoulder to my middle, one arm wrapped around my waist. He drove me back toward my log cabin as if I weighed ten pounds. A dump truck would've had more trouble moving me.

My ribs hit the outside corner of the cabin a fraction of a second before my right temple bounced off the end of one of the protruding logs. I went down, my mental world immediately darker than the Tahoe night.

THIRTY-ONE

I became vaguely aware of someone holding my wrists inside-to-inside in front of me and then taping them. The tearing tape sounded like duct tape. It could be torn edge-to-edge, but it couldn't be broken by pulling. With multiple loops, the tensile strength was probably thousands of pounds. My lower arms were next. My shirt sleeves were pulled up, my elbows squeezed together, and tape was pulled around my lower arms in a spiral from wrists to elbows. Even though my fingers were free, my forearms and palms were held so tightly together that I was unable to do anything.

Next came my ankles. Then a piece of tape over my mouth. Despite the darkness, he put a cloth bag over my head and tied it tight at the back of my head. The fabric was so heavy that I wouldn't be able to grip the edge of the tape through it, even though my fingers were free. There was movement at my wrists, the hot burn of a rope being yanked over wrist bones and then knotted.

With fabric over my head and tape over my mouth, there was no way I could bite at the rope knotted around my wrists.

Someone lifted me up off the ground and over his shoulder the way a strong dad might with a child. I got a strong whiff of cologne. He took several steps, and pitched me off with substantial forward motion.

My foot banged against something solid as I fell to a hard, cold, metal surface. Big hands gripped my upper arm, spun me around on a corrugated floor.

The bed of a cargo van.

There were noises at the side of the van. The rope at my wrists jerked. I was tied to something inside the van.

Hands went through my pockets, pulled out the contents.

A door opened and shut. Engine roared. Another door shut. Two men.

The van lurched off and went down my mountain road fast enough that I slid around in the back as we raced around corners. The rope tied to my wrists came up short. My arms were jerked one way, then another, and my body spun around.

For a moment, I'd had the brief thought that despite being hobbled with taped wrists and ankles, I could maybe roll up onto my knees, feel my way to the inside door latch, open it and push myself out to fall at high speed onto the road. But now that I was tied to the inside of the van, jumping out would leave me dragging and bouncing behind the truck. A quicker end, perhaps, than what they planned for me, but death by road rash was right up near the top of the list of bad ways to die. I stayed curled in a fetal position on the hard metal and tried to think away the fog in my brain.

If I could get one of the knots in the rope untied...

I pulled on the rope, dragging my sore body across the floor of the van, trying to move slowly so they wouldn't notice if they looked back. My fingers followed the rope to a knot that went around a horizontal support board that was bolted to each of the van's ribs. I could feel the heavy knot, but I couldn't understand how to untie it. It was tight, the rope hard with tension. If the men planned to untie it, there would be a slip tie of some kind. But without vision, I couldn't tell what it was.

I sagged back down, my head pounding.

I could tell when he slowed for the stop sign at the bottom of the mountain. Then came a pull of acceleration as he turned south onto the highway and floored the gas pedal. I noticed the change in sound when he went through the Cave Rock tunnel. A few miles later, I became aware of the van slowing and stopping.

I heard the side door of the van open. Someone untied the rope that had attached me to the inside of the van. Once again, a man tossed me over his shoulder as if I were a bag of dog food. My gut was squeezed hard as I bounced on his hard deltoid muscle. I could have tried using my elbows or knees against his chest or back, but my brain was still swimming.

The man carried me a long way. His cologne permeated my brain. I never heard him huff and puff. He dumped me onto soft ground. Snow. But not normal snow. There was sand under the snow. Somewhere nearby was the rumble of a big engine at idle.

There was a chunking sound as if something had been dropped on the ground by my feet. I felt rope-tying motions at my ankles.

For a moment there was silence. Then I felt movement on the skin of my left arm, a scratching. Someone was writing on my skin, between the spiraling strips of duct tape.

"Ready?" said a rough voice. His, I thought. One word wasn't enough to perceive any accent.

"Yeah," came a more distant voice.

I heard the swish of air, then the smack of something hitting a solid surface. The rope on my wrists went taut. Running footsteps. A big engine revving. Muffled. Gargling with water. A boat with a big inboard engine.

The rope jerked hard enough to break my arms if I hadn't been tensing my muscles. I was dragged across the ground. Something heavy pulled on my ankles. The snow turned to thin, hard ice. Then I hit ice water.

I gagged and choked as water was forced into the cloth bag around my head. But as the boat pulled me out into the lake, it sped up. My body rose, surfing just enough on the water for my head to be in the air even as a heavy weight pulled on my ankles with enough drag that I thought of the torturous dismemberment used as punishment in the Middle Ages. The boat was going fast enough that the water's surface was firm. The rope dragging on my ankles was a severe strain. It felt like I was being torn in two.

Some of the water drained from the bag around my head. I concentrated on breathing through my nose. Too fast and I sucked water into my nose. Too slow and my lungs started to pound with desperation.

Then the boat slowed. I tried to kick with my taped ankles, tried to rise to the surface. But the ankle weight was too heavy, and I was powerless to stop myself from sinking. The ice water was sucking the heat out of my body. Hypothermia was slowing my muscles, robbing me of control. My kicks with taped ankles and my arm strokes with taped wrists weren't enough to overcome the weight on my ankles. The bag over my head filled with water. I held my breath, but it wasn't enough air to last thirty seconds. And my futile efforts to swim against the weight pulling me down exhausted my air supply that much faster.

Just as my consciousness was fading, the rope at my wrists tightened. I felt myself pulled up through the water. My head broke the surface. I was lifted so that I was out of the water from my armpits up. I shook my head, trying to get the water to drain from the bag. As air came in, I sucked through my nose over and over, trying to replenish my air.

"Is it tied?" a voice said.

"Yeah."

"Listen up McKenna!"

I kept focusing on breathing.

"Time for you to die, McKenna." The man's voice was intense and creepy. A slight accent, maybe. Maybe not.

The rope holding me up by my wrists went slack. I tried to suck one last breath through my nose as I dropped back into the water. Water rushed back into the bag over my head as I tried to kick with my taped feet, fighting the weight that pulled me down into the depths.

THIRTY-TWO

I'm not the type to panic. Every time that I've faced extreme danger, I've done it with a certain calm. I've always been able to accept that I'll die someday. Not knowing when or how has never stressed me.

But this was a kind of panic-inducing terror unlike anything I'd ever experienced.

I tried to kick hard. Again and again. But my muscles were weak with hypothermia. As I thrashed my arms, I felt a gentle upward tug on them. They'd attached a small float to my arms to keep me vertical in death, displayed like Amanda Horner for the tourists to see, to send a message to Nadia to pay.

But the float was not buoyant enough to give me any chance of swimming against the weight tied to my ankles. I was unable to fight the weight, and I was losing control to hypothermia.

As I sank, I bent at the waist, reached down and felt for the knot that tied my ankles to the anchor weight. The knot was an obvious, hard ball. No way would I get it untied without time and a tool of some kind.

I stopped struggling. Not because I was giving up, but because I realized that a futile fight goes nowhere. If I burned through my last few seconds of breath doing something that didn't help, that was foolish no matter what my chance of survival.

I felt my descent quicken, the ice water flowing past my head as I sank down into the depths. As I dropped, I reached my hands to the side of my head to feel behind my neck for the knot that tied the fabric bag in place. Because my wrists and forearms were lashed together so tightly, it was awkward to even touch my fingertips to the knot. It was there at the back of my neck, a hard little tangle of cord. I pulled at it. Scraped, pinched, gripped. A portion of the cord seemed to move. I tried to get it between my fingernails. Pull again. The cord moved some more. A little loop of looseness. Hook the nails into the loop. Yank on it. Shift up on the cord. Pull again. Faster. Over and over. The loop grew.

Some part of the cord came free.

I got my fingers under the edge of the cloth bag, pulled out, stretched it to the maximum circumference, jerked the bag off my head.

The bag was off, but the world was still black. Without the bag, the ice water swirling past my head was more pronounced as the weight on my ankles pulled me farther into the deep.

With the fabric gone, I got a fingernail grip on the corner of the tape over my mouth. Tore it off. I felt a tiny bit less constrained. But to breathe was to suck in water and die.

I don't know how long I was pulled down toward the bottom. But about the time that I realized this was my end, the weight on my ankles stopped pulling on me. My anchor had hit bottom.

Reaching down against the gentle upward tug of the float, I felt the line from my ankles. Grabbed it. Pulled myself down to the anchor.

It was a tire. The twin of the one that pulled Amanda Horner to her death.

My feet hit the sandy bottom as I lifted up on the tire. It was heavy with concrete.

But, like Amanda's tire, the concrete was just in the part of the tire that rested on the bottom. Was it possible that, standing upright on the bottom of the lake, the top of the tire had trapped any air?

I lifted the tire up higher, put it over my face, tipped my head back, and thrust my nose up into the tire. There was a pocket of air. I inhaled, slowly in case I sucked water. Exhaled. Inhaled again. Exhaled. Repeated.

The air pocket was small. But it was enough to gather a bit of oxygen and blow off some carbon dioxide. I could prevent carbon dioxide build-up in the air pocket by exhaling into the water, but then the air pocket would shrink and I wouldn't be able to get my nose up into it. Better to exhale into the tire and maintain the air pocket. But if I continued to breathe it for more than another breath or two, I would exhaust the oxygen, pass out, and drown.

I took a last breath, then rotated the tire. With my hands and arms still lashed together, I could only rotate it a bit at a time. Eventually, the portion with concrete came around to my hands.

I reached into the tire space, feeling for the edge of the concrete. It seemed joined to the rubber. I tried to flex the tire rubber, spreading the tire wider, moving the rubber. I got my fingertips under the edge of the concrete. Tried to curl my fingers. The concrete seemed immovable. A fingernail broke off. The ice water was numbing. My muscles were weak. Focus. Bend the fingers. Flex the rubber. Get another fingertip under the concrete. Pull. Jerk.

My lungs burned. Consciousness was fading. I was standing on the sandy bottom of a dark, freezing, mountain lake, arms taped, ankles taped. The surface was an unknowable distance above me, and the end of my life was assured by a tenacious tire anchor.

The concrete loosened.

I got my right fingers under the edge of the concrete. My knuckles abraded against the inner, ribbed rubber of the tire. I put my knee against the inner rim of the tire. Pulled. Jerked harder.

The concrete came out of the tire and fell away.

Without the weight of the concrete, the tire became a mild anchor. Still heavier than water, still a bulky weight and difficult to drag through water, but no longer a guarantee of death.

I pulled down with my arms, kicked with my feet. With wrists and ankles taped, and with my boots on, it was the crudest of swimming motions, a shackled dog paddle. The float tied to my wrists, a plastic bottle filled with air, was not enough to overcome the weight of the tire, but it didn't hurt.

Then I thought about the plastic bottle.

It would have a tiny bit of air, but it might make a difference.

I pulled it down to me as I continued to kick. By turning

it upside down, I was able to unscrew the top without its air escaping. I exhaled a tiny bit of the air in my lungs, then put the end of the bottle in my mouth. Squeezing the bottle very gently as I inhaled, I got most of the air into my lungs, good, I hoped, for another few seconds under water.

My kicks and strokes were feeble. On each kick, my legs pulled up on the tire, ensuring that I would rise almost not at all in the water. My ascent was torturously slow. My consciousness was almost gone. My lungs felt as if they were going to explode. Or collapse.

Through my fading thoughts, I had the vague awareness that I was moving up through the water. Toward the surface. Toward air. The thought motivated me a tiny bit more and pushed off my resignation and acceptance of death for another few seconds.

If I could make a few more strokes and kicks...

If I could hold my breath a bit longer...

There was no more point. I was at my end.

I gave a last, final, death kick.

My head broke the surface.

I gasped. Over and over. Sucked air as if it were the essence of existence.

While consciousness returned, I had to keep making the ineffective kicks and arm strokes. I had to keep breathing.

After many seconds of rushed breathing while I tread water, I realized that my arms and legs were losing their function to hypothermia. I thought to look around.

There. To my left. Lights. The shore.

I tried to swim. Kick. Arm stroke. Kick. My movements were weak from hypothermia. The tape on my wrist and ankles made my movements ineffectual. It was an enormous effort to get my head far enough out of the water to breathe. I was hobbled by the tire dragging my feet down and the empty plastic float interfering with my arm movement.

The shore seemed to stay distant. The cold became more numbing. My fatigue was overwhelming. I tried counting my kicks and arm strokes to help me focus, to help me keep going. One, two, three...

At the bottom of each arm stroke, my head lifted up enough to get a small breath.

Ninety-nine, one hundred, one hundred one...

The black water went on forever. The lights never got closer.

Four hundred twenty-two, four hundred twenty-three, four...

The cold took the last of my strength. Once again, it was over. I was sinking for the last time.

My feet hit bottom. My head was still above water. I hopped forward, sluggish, awkward leaps, dragging the tire with tied ankles. I tried to leap like a tied dog would. It moved me a foot forward. Again. And again.

An area of white appeared, dimly lit by distant lights. It was a stark contrast to the blackness of water.

The snow-covered beach.

I kicked and thrashed. My hands hit ice. I pushed down, pulled forward. My hands broke through the ice. Dug into sand. I pushed. Writhed. Thrashed.

Eventually, I was half out of the water.

I tried to shout, "Help!" It was a tiny, meek chirp. I tried again. No sound at all.

The cold continued to suck my strength until I could no longer move, until I no longer cared.

THIRTY-THREE

I never heard any voices or felt anybody move me. My first awareness was of shivering violently while being burned with fire. Gradually, I realized I wasn't breathing fire, but was inhaling very hot, humid air. That same air seared the exposed skin on my face and neck. I was in a tiny room, lying curled up on a wood bench. There was a dim light in a corner by the ceiling.

I heard a noise. A door opened. Ice fog swirled in. A man materialized in the fog. He wore a jacket and under it a beige shirt and slacks. He had a gun and radio on his belt.

"You alive?"

I tried to say, "Maybe." It came out as a staccato grunt. My shivering was so violent that my teeth banged hard enough to chip each other.

"I'm Cory Denell, Douglas County Sheriff's Office. We met."

"I 'member."

"We got a call, and the caller said a person was lying on Nevada Beach, maybe freezing to death. Hey, it's some kind of hot in here. Gimme a sec to cool off." He stepped outside and shut the door. Came back a minute later. The jacket was gone.

"We were carrying you from the water's edge up to the street when this homeowner came out and said he had his sauna all fired up. It was snowing pretty good, and it looked like it would take a long time to get you to the ER. So we called the hospital, and a doctor said to go ahead and put you in the sauna but to turn down the heat so it was gentle. Then he said to turn off the heat when you stop shivering, not to let you cook yourself even if you wanted to."

"Yes, I want to," I mumbled.

"I'm curious about how you ended up in the lake, arms and ankles tied. They tried to drown you like Amanda Horner."

"Yeah."

"But you got away."

"Yeah."

"We got all the duct tape off."

"Thanks. Maybe you should call Diamond. He'll want to know."

"Okay. I'll do it outside, if you don't mind. I can't take this heat."

He stepped out and shut the door.

When my shivering eased a bit, I sat up on the bench. There was a heater in the corner. I was too weak to pull my clothes off, so I stood by the heater. When I felt my pants burning my legs, I turned a quarter turn. In a few minutes, another quarter turn.

Deputy Denell came back in. "Sarge is on his way. You still okay?"

"Yeah." I turned another quarter turn.

"Like a rotisserie," he said, pointing at the heater. "I'm gonna wait outside while you get those threads dry." He went out and shut the door.

Three full rotations later, I started to sweat. But my clothes still weren't dry, and I still wanted to bake. I found the switch and turned off the heater. Cracked the door. The sauna would cool, and my clothes could continue to dry.

The door swung wide and Diamond walked in.

"You okay?" he asked, looking me up and down.

I nodded.

"There's a group up in Minnesota," he said. "Town called Duluth. One of the stranger gringo activities. They call themselves the Polar Bears, and their idea of a good time is to use chain saws to cut through the ice in Lake Superior and then jump into the hole to take a swim."

"I can now say with some expertise that it is not a good time," I said.

"Maybe why Mexico City is located where it is," he said. "A sane climate helps keep people acting sane." He paused. "Same guys who dropped Amanda in the drink?"

"Yeah."

Diamond reached out and touched my wrists. "They hang you by your wrists before they dropped you in the drink?"

"From a boat. Drove the boat a little with me dragging behind. The tire weight tied to my ankles made it more exciting."

The sauna door was open a few inches, letting cold air in. Diamond was standing next to it. He reached over and shut the door.

I pointed to a thermometer on the wall. "It's still ninety degrees in here."

"Perfect," Diamond said. "In Mexico City, my mother turns on the heat when it gets down to ninety. You think those guys know that their plan for you didn't work out?"

"If they did, they would have caved my head in and then dropped me in the lake again."

"Your Jeep here near the beach?"

"No. Those men were gracious enough to give me a ride all the way from my cabin. Spot is probably still shut inside the Jeep at my cabin."

"I'll give you a ride. Maybe I should bring you to the hospital for a quick check?"

I shook my head. "Spot is waiting."

THIRTY-FOUR

My Jeep was still in my drive and Spot was still in the Jeep. Cold and no doubt miserable, but very happy to have me let him out. He jumped all over me.

Because the men had taken all my pocket contents, I had no keys. But I found my hidden house key.

Diamond came inside with us.

"You gonna be okay?"

"Yeah, as long as I don't walk outside and leave Spot inside, or close him inside the Jeep. He and I are going to be real tight for the foreseeable future." I remembered my arm. "Oh, one more thing," I said. "Denell or one of the others pulled off the duct tape that was holding my arms together."

I lifted up my left sleeve and showed Diamond my arm.

"The American Dream," he said. "You tell Ramos, yet?'"

"Maybe you could do the honors," I said.

He nodded. "Those men will find out that you are alive. They could have been in the area as we pulled up. They might already be planning a more permanent repeat performance."

"I'll be fine. You can go."

Diamond hesitated.

"Thank Denell and your other guys for saving my ass."

"Will do," Diamond said. He left.

I noticed my answering machine was blinking. It was Street saying she hoped I was okay and that she'd try again in the morning.

I built a hot fire in the wood stove, drank of couple of Sierra Nevada Pale Ales, and went to bed.

I dreamed that I was cast to the bottom of the icy lake and had to hold my breath for eternity.

Dawn came three hours later, and I was up an hour after that, happy to leave my nightmares behind.

I called Street and gave her the basics of the assault without sharing the worst details.

She was worried and upset and stressed, and she said all the right things to be soothing and comforting. She made me promise to be more careful.

I made a hot breakfast and ate it sitting in the rocker, pulled up close to the wood stove. Then I poured another cup of coffee, nuked it until it was boiling, and drank it while again sitting close to the fire. I took Spot out for a walk, a short one because the cold air bothered me.

Back inside, I put more wood in the stove, stared at the flames through the glass, and appreciated the burning sensation as my jeans seared my legs.

Through it all I imagined where Gertie was and what she was doing. My imagination can go very dark, and every thought about Gertie was black with foreboding. I'd experienced what Mikhailo – if it really was Mikhailo – could do. I sensed his sadistic pleasure at my torture. The idea that he may be holding Gertie was both nauseating and terrifying.

After an hour of cooking myself with wood stove heat and miserable thoughts, I found my spare key ring. Spot and I got back into the Jeep and headed north around the lake to the old lady's cabin.

This time, as I pulled up, her cabin looked haunted. Maybe it was her previous comments on Satan and evil. Maybe I just hadn't noticed before.

As before, when I knocked on the woman's door, she didn't answer. There was no indication that she was home. No visible lights on inside, no sounds of TV or radio.

The last time, she opened the door after I spoke for many minutes.

"Hello, it's Owen McKenna again," I said toward the door, loud enough that she would likely hear it inside. If she was inside.

"You were so helpful to me the last time," I continued, "that I wanted to stop back and thank you. I checked Ian Lassitor's house for the light you mentioned, but I couldn't find any timer. I also asked Gower if he had any lights that go on at night, and he said no. I really appreciated your help. I don't know how this case will shake out, but I think your input will make a difference. I wanted to check back and see if you've noticed anything else. We still haven't found Gertie, but we think the person who kidnapped her may be driving a white cargo van. I wondered..."

I heard the deadbolt turn, then the doorknob. The door opened a few inches. The woman peered out. Her hair was even wilder than before. It would require dipping in motor oil to brush out the snarls.

She didn't speak. So I spoke as if she'd said hello and asked how she could help me.

"When I talked to you before, I asked if there was anything you'd noticed that was strange. You said that, mostly, what was strange was a light that comes on at odd hours."

She nodded. "Satan's disguise," she said.

"I wondered if you've seen other strange things besides the light."

She shook her head. "No."

"Nothing else is unusual about the Lassitor house?" I said.

"Lots of things are unusual."

Her circuitous way of speaking frustrated me. "But you just said that you've seen nothing else unusual."

"That's true. But I've heard things."

Immediately, I realized that despite her strangeness, it was me who was frustrating her. If I'd been listening carefully, I wouldn't have been confused. "I'm sorry. You're right. The light is the only strange thing you've seen. What have you heard?"

She looked behind me to one side, then to the other, as if checking to see that no one had sneaked up to listen.

In a quiet voice, almost a whisper, she said, "The ghost boat."

"What's a ghost boat?" I asked, using a low voice myself.

"The ghost of a dead boat," she said.

"You mean... a boat that has sunk?"

She nodded. "A boat spirit."

"Is it like the golden light that you said was a fallen angel?"

She shook her head. Very serious. "That was Lucifer. This is different. The Bible says that dead people can't come back as spirits. But the ghosts of dead boats come back to haunt those who sank them. It is a crime against the oceans to build a boat, give her a name, then cast her to the bottom forever."

"And you've heard these ghost boats?" I asked.

Her eyes grew intense. "Every night. A low moaning."

"Where does the sound come from?"

She raised her arm and pointed to the south. Then she swung her arm in a slow, dramatic sweep toward the north, her long index finger just missing my chest.

"The sound goes from south to north," I said.

"Then back," she said. "Over and over."

"Can other people hear it?" I asked, aware that she might be insulted by the question.

"I don't know."

"Is there any light on these boats?"

She shook her head. "Ghost boats don't have lights."

"Is there more than one ghost boat?"

"I don't know. I can't see it. I hear it. If it stopped and then started, would it be the same boat? Or two boats?"

"Right," I said. "Do you have an idea where it comes from or where it goes?"

"It's on patrol. That's what ghosts do."

"They patrol."

She nodded.

"The sound you hear, is it like a typical boat motor?"

She seemed to think about it. "Softer."

"Could it be a boat going slow?"

"Maybe."

"Have you heard the difference between an outboard and an inboard? Could you guess which one it is?"

She shook her head. "Ghost boats have their own kind of motor."

"Oh." I wanted to change the subject. "I also visited Craig

Gower again," I said. "I think his paralysis seems pretty real."

She nodded.

"But you thought he was faking it," I said.

She shook her head. "Maybe not," she said.

"You seemed pretty sure before. You acted like he was evil."

"I don't think that now."

"Why? Did something happen to change your mind?"

"When I was a little girl, my uncle had a wheelchair. He was evil."

"And that affected how you thought of your neighbor?"

She shrugged.

THIRTY-FIVE

I thanked the woman and headed home. That evening as twilight descended and I was stressing about Gertie, my phone rang.

"Owen McKenna," I said.

"Oh, hi." A high-pitched man's voice. Tentative. He spoke softly, almost a whisper. "I'm calling because we got an email from the Chamber of Commerce about a missing girl in a white cargo van? Well, I'm in Homewood. We run one of the cafés here? Anyway, a white cargo van pulled off the road into our lot. It's got a flat tire. Three men got out. From where I'm standing, I can see that they're working on getting the jack set up. But what's funny is there's a utility light near our door. Yet they didn't park near it. Instead, they parked in the corner of the lot, away from everyone else. So they're working in the dark. That got me to thinking. What if they had that girl that's on the email flyer? And what if she's, you know, tied up in the van or something? They wouldn't want anyone to hear her, right? So they might park like that. Don't get me wrong, I'm not saying the girl is there, or anything. I'm just saying it's possible, right? So I thought I'd call and let you know."

"What's your address?"

He gave me the number and then said, "Oh, I better go. One of the men is coming across the parking lot toward the café. Maybe he wants takeout coffee or something."

"I'll be over. Try to delay them any way you can, as long as possible. I'm an hour away. Can you keep them that long?"

"I'll do my best."

"Thanks much," I said, and hung up.

"C'mon, Spot. We're not having any dinner just yet."

I drove around the lake to Homewood. Homewood sits just south of Hurricane Bay. It, too, is in Placer County, so I put in a call to Santiago to ask if he could send a patrol unit over to check out the van. I got his voicemail. I left a message, then dialed the sheriff's office. As I expected, I got a recording stating the office hours and saying that if I had an emergency, I should call 911.

With no other options, I called 911 and told the dispatcher who I was and why I was calling.

"It's not necessarily an emergency and I've got nothing but a white cargo van and a report of unusual parking while they change a flat tire, but if you could send a patrol unit to check it out, that would be good."

"I'll put in the request, but I may as well let you know that a big rig jack-knifed on eighty-nine west of Tahoe City. Two cars hit it and we've got reported injuries. So all of our units are on the scene. It could be a while."

I thanked him and hung up.

Despite the snow, the traffic was light, and I got to Homewood just 50 minutes later.

I saw the café and the cargo van. Its lights were on, engine running. One man was using a windshield brush to clear snow off the glass. I slowed as I drove by. I saw what looked like an All-Wheel-Drive insignia on it, but it looked just like any other cargo van. I continued a couple of blocks, pulled over, and turned out my lights.

Watching in my review mirror, I could see the van pull out of the lot and turn south toward me. I realized they would be able to see me and Spot through the windows.

I shifted into Drive, moving the lever fast so it would minimize the flash of my back-up lights as it went past Reverse. Without touching the brakes, I drove forward and turned into a parking lot. The Jeep rolled past some parked cars and two large trees.

The van went by on the highway. I kept rolling in a circle, came back out to the highway, and turned out behind them. My lights were still off. I let the van increase its distance in front of me.

The moonlight was low and intermittent as the cloud cover

flowed by overhead. The road was dark with tree shadows, but it was enough to drive by. I aimed for the middle of the road. Any approaching vehicles would almost certainly have their lights on. I could turn mine on when I saw them. Because it was the middle of the night, there would likely be no one out walking.

The lake was on my left, a black plate of steel bordered by distant white mountains. Then the road veered away from the water, and we cruised through Tahoma.

Oncoming headlights appeared ahead. I turned on my lights and slowed. I went by a sedan, sped up, and shut off my lights once again.

The van sped up as we drove through Sugar Pine Point State Park and the speed limit changed to 55 mph. I stayed far enough back that their taillights disappeared whenever they went around a curve. They reappeared in the straighter sections. Then they disappeared at the end of a long straight stretch.

The tree shadows over the road became thick, so I had to turn on my headlights. That allowed me to speed up. If I eventually saw red taillights, I could turn off my headlights. Maybe any driver ahead would think the vehicle in his rear view mirror had simply turned off the highway.

The red taillights didn't reappear.

Either the van driver was a maniac, or they'd turned off, and I missed them. I could start driving down turnoffs. It would take days to explore all the roads. Or I could drive ahead, hoping they were still in front of me.

I braked for a tight curve. With only the moon for illumination, I carried too much speed for the icy road. The Jeep slid. I corrected, but the Jeep continued sideways until it hit the snow wall. I hit broadside. Spot hit the door, but it was a soft blow, and the Jeep bounced back, the tires regaining footing. I'd probably have a shallow dent on the right side doors, but I'd lucked out. Driving slower, I came out of the curve and saw red taillights flash ahead where the road crested a hill and made a curve.

There was no way to tell if the vehicle ahead was the van, but it gave me hope. I powered back up to an unreasonable speed and raced up the slope. At the top, the red lights came back into view. I sensed a large vehicle, but it was in the shade of trees. Not wanting to get too close, I eased off on my speed.

The vehicle came out of the tree shadows and popped into full moonlight. A white van. There was a sharp curve ahead of the van. Its brake lights came on. The van went into the turn. Before it went out of sight around the snowbank, I got a glimpse of its side.

No windows. A cargo van.

I kept my distance.

We went through Meeks Bay, climbed up the grade, and came around the sharp curve that leads to a long straight stretch of road high above the dark lake. In the distance was the necklace of lights that line the southern half of Tahoe's East Shore.

The van's taillights went bright once again as it went around the next set of curves. I sped up to try to keep it in view. When I next saw the van, it was slowing. It turned west on Scenic Drive and climbed up into the neighborhood that stretched up the mountain above Rubicon Bay.

I went easy on the accelerator to minimize engine noise. The van was visible above me, turning to the north and heading along a group of vacation homes. I turned up the same road. It was so steep that my wheels still slipped even in four-wheel-drive. It was an area that demanded one have four-wheel-drive with chains or at least studded snow tires or, better yet, stay out of the neighborhood until summer.

The van kept climbing. It must have had studded tires.

As I watched the van above me, it turned onto another street. I followed. After another block, it turned again, climbing higher. I slowed to let it get some distance up the mountain.

We came to the highest part of the neighborhood, a road that ran along the ridge line. The van turned along it.

As I approached the turnoff, I had to swerve a bit to avoid a stop sign that had been broken off by someone who'd come down a sloped section of the road and was unable to stop. Just past the sign, I turned where the van had gone, my headlights still off.

The van pulled broadside to a snow wall and stopped in front of a dramatic vacation home that perched on the edge of a steep slope. I used my parking brake to stop well back so that my brake lights wouldn't turn on.

I pulled out my binoculars and studied the van.

As I looked, I felt Spot beside me, thrusting his head forward from the back seat. He was tense, staring through the darkness at the men down the street.

The van's right side was facing me. The van's left front corner seemed to touch the snow wall. The only window on the right side was at the front passenger seat. Behind the passenger seat, the cargo van had two windowless side doors.

Through the passenger window, I saw movement. The driver's door had opened. Then the passenger door opened. Two men got out. They met at the front of the van and appeared to talk. One of them pointed at the slope below the house. The other nodded, pulled out a large handgun, and racked the slide. The first man turned and pointed toward the snow wall at the far side of the van. They moved around the far side of the van, out of sight. They must have stopped between the van and the snow wall.

I couldn't get a sense of their intentions. Was the display of the gun just some macho play? Was the man with the gun going to burglarize the house? Or did they in fact have Gertie in the van? If so, were they planning to execute her in a place where they could toss the body far enough down the steep mountain slope that it wouldn't be found until spring, if ever?

THIRTY-SIX

I went from chilled to hot. The men who had just tried to drown me appeared to be planning to kill Gertie. My desire to incapacitate them first was intense. But I had no weapon except Spot. If he could attack unseen, he could possibly disarm a single man. But we didn't have time to approach unseen. And there were three men. The only other thing I could do would be to ram them.

The thought seemed audacious, but maybe it was my best option. The third man was still in the van. Most cargo vans did not have a bench seat in front. Which meant that the third man was in back.

With the other two men outside, why would a third man stay in the back of a windowless van?

Was he watching Gertie? Untying Gertie? Molesting Gertie?

My imagination made my throat constrict.

If Gertie was in the back of the van when he got in, that would put her on the left and him on the right. The right side cargo doors were facing me.

If I timed it just right...

I put the Jeep into drive, released the parking brake, and started toward them. I accelerated gradually so that my engine wouldn't roar. I mentally rehearsed the skid I'd made earlier when I slid out on a turn and bounced the right side of the Jeep onto the snow wall.

I heard what I thought was a shout over the sound of the Jeep. The van's cargo door opened just as I spun the wheel.

The Jeep began to turn left, then broke into a skid and slammed broadside into the side of the van, striking it on the open cargo door.

The collision wasn't severe, but it was significant. The van probably outweighed the Jeep by one or two thousand pounds, but I thought that my Jeep had bumped the van to the side, hopefully pinning the two men between the van and the snow wall. Because it was a sideways collision, my old Jeep hadn't deployed airbags. It was still drivable.

I pulled left and forward, my right doors scraping as they separated from the van. I stopped and jumped out. The icy road was treacherous as I tried to run around the Jeep to the van. I jerked open the crushed cargo door.

A man sat on the floor. He looked dazed. There was blood on his forehead. He held his arm. I grabbed him, lifted him up, and patted him down. I found no weapons. But he had a phone. I put it in my pocket and threw him out onto the road.

From the other side of the van came angry voices, swearing. I heard thumping against the wall of the van.

I leaned in and looked through the partition toward the front seats to see if the key was in the ignition. It would be worth the time to grab it.

But it wasn't there.

Gertie huddled at the left side of the cargo compartment, sitting on a blanket. In the dim light, she looked shocked but didn't look like she'd been injured from the Jeep ramming.

"Gertie, it's me, Owen McKenna. We talked in Sacramento. Let's get you out of there. Hurry."

She didn't speak and acted comatose as I pulled her out of the van. I kept my arm around her as we moved across the ice-covered road.

I didn't know if the passenger doors on my Jeep were operable, so I pulled Gertie to the driver's door and pushed her inside. She made no sound, but she did make a weak effort to crawl across the center console and sit in the passenger seat.

I followed her into the Jeep, then shifted into drive. I hit the gas, spinning the tires, sliding the Jeep's rear end once again until we were facing back the way I'd come.

The wheels spun as I accelerated. I let off the gas, and we straightened out. The ridgeline road was slippery with snow. The road made a curve. I braked, put the Jeep into a fast turn. We skidded as we went around. Before I completed the turn, I was aware of headlights in my rear view mirror.

The van was coming up behind me at a fast rate. I powered down a short dip in the road, then flew back up the other side, took another turn, and hit the accelerator as the road went up a gradual slope.

The van came behind.

The road made another gentle turn, then a hard 90-degree cut in the opposite direction. I tapped on the brakes. Even though I was gentle, the road was polished ice from previous braking vehicles. The anti-lock system kicked in, and it pulsed continuously as we came to the corner.

The Jeep's delayed seatbelt alarm went off because neither of us had taken the time to put them on. No time now.

I turned the wheel. Once again, we slid sideways. We came to the intersection where someone had broken off the stop sign. Beyond the intersection, the mountain dropped down a steep slope toward the lake. There was nothing to see but the darkness of black water far below and the distant lights of the far shore.

I tried to ride the brakes, tried to keep us from skidding past the broken stop sign and into the snow wall. But the Jeep would have needed chains on all four tires to stop in time.

We slid across the intersection, fishtailing. The tires seemed to grab pavement for a moment, then lost traction. We skidded clockwise. The left side of the Jeep plowed into the snow wall at the far side of the road.

I turned the wheel, gave the Jeep gas, tried to pull away from the snow. But the left front of the Jeep was jammed into the snow, and the tires spun. I shifted into Reverse and tried again. Same result. We were on ice, with no traction.

Headlight beams washed over us as the van came from behind.

"C'mon, Gertie, time to run."

She made no response.

I pulled my door handle and pushed. The door opened an inch before it jammed against the snow wall.

"We have to go out your side," I said. I reached over and tried her door. It, too, was jammed. The right side of the Jeep wasn't against snow. The sheet metal must have gotten crimped when I rammed the van.

I pushed up and back in my seat. Got my right knee out from behind the steering wheel. I turned, lifted my foot, and swung my leg over Gertie's lap.

"Pull on the door handle to free the latch, while I kick," I said.

Gertie didn't respond.

I reached over and grabbed her hand, which was rigid with tension. I put her fingers on the door latch and pulled.

"Pull this door handle out while I kick the door."

She did as told.

I kicked. The door didn't budge. I shifted in my seat to get a better angle. I leaned my back against the driver's door and kicked again.

Gertie's door popped open with a metallic screech.

"Out," I said. "Quick!"

She climbed out in slow motion. I scrambled out after her.

I had to make an instant decision about Spot. Would he hinder us more than he could help us? With three men with guns and no place to run except over six-foot snow walls into deep powder, it seemed it would be best to leave him in the Jeep. "Be good, boy," I said as I shut the door with him inside. We turned down the street. The road was like a tunnel. The men would catch us easily. Or just shoot us from a distance.

"We have to climb the snow wall," I said. "Hurry."

The van came fast. It didn't appear that they even tried to slow down as they approached the intersection. They slid, rotating, studded tires grinding on the icy pavement. The van came to a stop about 20 yards behind the Jeep.

I kicked a step into the snow wall, then another above it, then a third.

"Put your shoe into this step, Gertie. I'll give you a boost. Quick!" I turned her toward the wall, put my hands on her waist. She slowly put her foot into the notch in the snow. I lifted her. She put her bare hands on top of the wall and made a weak effort to pull herself up. I wrapped one arm around her waist so I could use my other hand to guide her feet into the other steps.

Noises came from behind. Van doors opening. The heavy breathing of angry men.

One of them shouted. "Don't try to catch him, just drop the bastard!" The voice sounded like the man who tied the anchor to my feet and dropped me over the side of the boat into the lake. I heard a weapon being cocked.

Gertie got her knee over the top edge of the snow wall and rolled onto it. If I could make it up before they shot me, we could maybe roll down the mountain. As soon as I had the thought, I realized that the snow was too deep. Without snowshoes, we'd just sink in and be mired. The men would get to us in a few moments.

A shot cracked through the night. Then another. They sounded like cannon fire against the quiet of the forest. With the speed of fire and depth of the boom, it was probably a large caliber semi-auto with serious stopping power should a round hit us. In addition to multiple weapons, they probably had large-capacity magazines. It would be easy to keep drilling us until we were both dead.

My refusal to carry a gun seemed the stupidest decision I'd ever made. Gertie's life and mine were now as short as the time it took the men to take a calming breath, aim, and pull the trigger.

Maybe I could run the other way, get them to follow me, and give Gertie a chance to get away. But it was a foolish thought. Without snowshoes, she couldn't go anywhere except along the hard surface of the highway. I hadn't saved her. I'd only prolonged her agony.

Then I had an idea. It seemed ridiculous, but I had no other options.

I ran away from Gertie, back across the road.

One of the men shouted. I glanced behind me. One man ran toward me, cutting across the street at an angle. The other man lifted his weapon and pointed it at me. I kept running. A shot fired, its deep crack thudding in my ears.

I got to the other side of the road, skidding in my boots. The broken stop sign lay on the road. I picked up the sign.

The sign was much larger than I imagined. With its 4 X 4 wooden post, it was heavy as a log. I sprinted with the sign, back across the street to the snow wall.

The man who'd chased toward me changed his course and angled back toward where I'd helped Gertie up the snow wall.

With my hands on the top of the stop sign, I planted the base of the 4 X 4 into the snow at the wall. It wasn't like a pole vault, but the sign gave me support as I scrambled up and over the top of the snow wall.

Another shot cracked, loud and percussive, and blasted through the stop sign.

I pulled up on the sign as the other man got to the wall. He grabbed the 4 X 4 post to yank the sign out of my hands. Instead of trying to pull it away from him, I shoved it toward him. Hard. The end of the broken post hit him on the shoulder and turned him around. He lost his grip. I pulled the sign up, rotated, then dropped down to the snow next to Gertie, who hadn't moved.

"Quick," I said as I positioned the sign in the snow, shiny red side down, the post angling back toward the street. "Lie down on the sign. Like a toboggan."

Gertie made feeble moves. I knew that the man would scramble over the snow wall in a moment. I grabbed Gertie, pulled her into position on the back of the sign, putting her legs on either side of the post that was bolted to the back of the sign. I realized that she had no gloves, no winter clothes, no hat. I could put my jacket on her, but if I took more time, we'd be dead. But if I tried to send Gertie on a toboggan ride with no gloves, she'd never make it.

"Reach up your hands!" I said. She looked dazed. I grabbed her arms, took a grip on her sweatshirt and yanked down on the fabric. I pulled the sweatshirt sleeves down over her hands, then positioned her hands on the front of the sign. The sweatshirt had a hood. I pulled it up over her head.

"Hold on tight. Don't let go!"

I jumped on the lower edge of the sign and its protruding

post. My arms were over Gertie's legs, pinning them in place.

A grunt came from behind me. I kicked at the snow, trying to get the sign to slide. We were stuck in place. I jerked my body. Over and over. We didn't move.

The man leaped onto my legs. One of his hands gripped at my jeans. I kicked at him. He grunted but held firm. I reached down to try to dislodge his grip. His fingers wormed into one of my pockets. I couldn't break his grip. I kicked again. I rolled onto the side where his hand gripped my jeans. The move forced him down and under me. I tried to press down, tried to crush his hand. But he held firm.

I got my other leg up and kicked at the man's crotch as the second man came over the top of the snow wall.

The man beneath me exhaled an angry groan. I kicked again and again.

The force of my kicks loosened the sign from the snow. We started to slide down the mountain, Gertie and me and the man holding onto my pocket.

Then the fabric of my jeans tore, and the man lost his grip. Another kick and the man came loose from us. I looked back and saw the other man up on the snow wall. He raised his gun with both hands. Took careful aim.

I swung my legs to the left of the post, dragging my boots in the snow. The sign-toboggan swerved left as another shot rang out. The bullet blew another hole in the stop sign, just to the right of Gertie's chest. Another shot splintered wood near my face.

The slope pitched down at a steeper angle, and we shot down into the dark forest. A third shot pierced the night, but didn't hit us. We slid, mostly out of control, into the dark forest and away from the men.

THIRTY-SEVEN

As we tobogganed down the mountain, I trailed my legs off the back edge of the sign. By swinging them left or right, they acted as a rudder, steering us between the trees. It also kept my weight back, forcing the front of the sign to stay up so that Gertie's hands on the leading edge stayed in the air and didn't dig into the snow. I controlled our speed by how much I pushed down with my boots.

It was dark in the forest as we left the open area near the ridgeline road. I didn't know where we were going other than to escape the men and head down toward the lake. This part of Tahoe had a few vacation homes down on the lake, accessed by a narrow road that wound down from a neighborhood to the north. Maybe we could get to one of them.

As I steered between the trees, arcing left and right, powder snow flew up into our faces. At one point I heard Gertie gasp.

"Tuck your head down!" I shouted. "Concentrate on hanging on. We'll be down the mountain in a couple of minutes."

Gertie lowered her head, her face to her right shoulder.

As we went farther, I saw Gertie's right hand loosen its grip. I grabbed the right edge of the sign, my fingers pummeled by the snow as we rushed along. By squeezing my grip and pressing down on Gertie's legs, I was able to pin her to the sign.

At times, snow flew into my face, making it impossible to see. Down below us came lights.

A vehicle on the highway.

I dragged my boots to slow our descent, and we came to a stop at the snow wall.

"Okay, Gertie. Time to get off."

I helped her down the snow wall onto the highway.

The vehicle that had gone by before was not in sight. There

were no other headlights. But we could walk to somebody's house.

Headlights appeared in the neighborhood above us, where we'd come from.

The cargo van was coming down to the highway.

"Sorry, Gertie, we're going to have to take another ride. Let's put my jacket and gloves on you."

We got my clothes on her, and then got ourselves and the sign up the snow wall on the lake side of the highway.

"Ready?" I said as preparation for our next descent.

The cargo van turned onto the highway and its headlights washed over us as we pushed off again.

As the mountain slope steepened, our speed grew. We were far enough down the mountain that I dared to brake harder with my boots and slow our speed. But I saw up ahead an open area that was much more shallow. If we didn't carry enough speed, we would slow to a stop and be stuck in the deep snow, unable to move far enough to get to a steep slope and continue our escape. On this part of the mountain slope, in this part of Tahoe, slowing to a stop would be guaranteed death. Without tree branches to cut into makeshift snowshoes, we'd be trapped by the deep snow, and we'd freeze to death.

I bent my knees and lifted up my legs to minimize drag. Our speed increased immediately. But before we got going very fast, we came to the transition and hit the shallow slope.

We slowed. Slowed more. We were probably on a meadow area, covered by six feet of soft snow. By the time we were halfway across, our speed was cut in half. It was like a boat going fast enough to plane on the water's surface. You can slow a little and still plane. But once you slow too much, you sink down and come to a fast stop.

I scanned the snowy surface in the darkness, looking for any area where the slope angle increased, where our momentum could carry us to a steeper slope. There was a bit of a dip to the right, but the landscape continued at the same angle for a long distance. I didn't think we could get across.

Straight ahead was a steady slope but probably too shallow to make it across.

To the left, the slope was even shallower than where we were now. But it was shorter to the steeps.

It was a gut decision. I went left.

I didn't want to steer with my boots because that would slow us more. So I leaned to the left by pulling up on my right hand.

We made a slow arc toward the shallower, shorter area.

Our speed was now down to a gentle ride. No more powder lofted up toward our faces. On a sunny day, and without three killers chasing us, it would have been pleasant. As we slowed toward the planing threshold, the prospect of Gertie freezing to death in the wilderness gripped me. I hoped that she wasn't aware of the consequences.

The tipping point where the mountain pitched down was just ten yards ahead. We came about a yard short before our makeshift toboggan stopped.

"You did great, Gertie," I said. "Now I just have to budge us a little farther to get back sliding down the slope. Then we'll have one more short ride. So don't move. Just keep hanging on. This will take me a few minutes. You should flex your hands. Make fists inside of my gloves, then straighten your fingers. Over and over. When we are ready to move again, you'll be able to grip the front edge of the sign like before."

There was no indication that she heard me. The deep cold combined with fear had made her withdraw to a place that I probably couldn't access until I got her warmed up.

I let go of the edge of the sign and slid off Gertie's legs, allowing my legs to drop down into the snow. Suspended from the sign at my waist, my feet didn't touch ground. I shifted farther back off the sign and pushed off. I dropped up to my neck before my feet touched something solid.

As I tried to push off, the firmer layer under my boots crumbled, and I went in deeper. I wasn't on ground. I was on snow crust that had formed before the last series of storms.

With my head at the level of the sign, I pushed up and forward on the sign and its 4 X 4 post. The sign, with Gertie on it, moved a few inches, and I sunk down a few more inches.

I spent some time doing chopping motions, cutting snow with the edge of my hands, pushing it down, and then marching and packing it beneath me. It took a few minutes to widen the hole I was standing in. With more snow beneath my boots, I was able to again move Gertie and the sign forward another few inches.

Moving a yard was going to take a long time.

I chop-cut more snow, marched my feet to move it beneath me. Stomped my feet to compress it. Pushed up and moved Gertie and the sign another few inches.

As I continued, another concern was that if I pushed her too far, she could take off down the mountain without me. So I kept one hand on the 4 X 4 post.

I repeated the process, huffing like a sprinter, until I believed that the sign was on the verge of tipping over the crest between meadow slope and steeper mountain slope. By continuously stepping more and more snow beneath my feet, I raised myself up. I pushed the sign with Gertie until it wanted to slide, but my grip prevented it from escaping and kept me from dropping back into my hole.

I pumped my feet and knees against loose snow until I had clambered out of my hole. As the sign began to move, I climbed on.

We accelerated fast, and soon I was once again dragging my feet to slow us down. The trees got very thick, and I had trouble choosing a line between them in the dark. Once, we were in a thick grove and went off what might have been a giant, submerged boulder. For a moment, we were airborne. Gertie made a gasp, which pleased me because it indicated that she was still aware. Then we landed with a soft thwump into deep powder.

Ten seconds later, we cruised into an open glade with the trees well-spaced. There was a sudden drop into a gully, and our speed increased as if in a downhill race. Then we shot up the other side, burning off speed. Our sign toboggan came over the sharp rise and nearly went into the air again as the slope pitched down.

Then in a moment the landscape got very dark. But it wasn't

a heavy forest cover. It was the lake, and we were about to shoot into the black water.

"Let go, Gertie," I shouted as I grabbed her shoulders.

I took Gertie with me as I rolled off the shooting sign. We tumbled into snow at the shoreline. The sign hit the water and skimmed over the waves for five yards before it came to a stop and then sank.

THIRTY-EIGHT

The snow at Lake Tahoe's shoreline was crusted, uneven, and slippery, the result of waves crashing and throwing freezing spray into the air. Because of its depth, Tahoe never freezes across. But the shore edges freeze into breaking sheets of ice, and the rocks become coated with layers of ice.

I pulled Gertie to her feet. "We're okay, Gertie," I said knowing that we were far from okay. "We made it. Those men will never find us. Now all we have to do is walk to one of the vacation homes near here. Then we can go in and warm up.

"We'll walk next to the shore where the snow isn't deep. It's uneven and slippery, so we'll have to be careful."

I turned her north toward where I thought the closest vacation homes were, and I walked closest to the lake so that any splashing water would hit me more than her.

The walking was treacherous on the uneven ice. Gertie was uncoordinated, no doubt from hypothermia. Her Sacramento shoes and pants were much too thin for winter night in the mountains. I believed she'd be okay as long as I kept her moving, but I worried about frostbite on her fingers and toes.

I put my arm around Gertie's shoulder, keeping a strong grip and holding her up when she slipped. The shore went in and out. Fallen trees forced us to bushwhack away from the shore and into deep snow. We stepped over many glistening ice-covered boulders and detoured around the larger ones.

As soon as we found a house, we'd be fine. I could call Santiago and Diamond and have them send out a rescue party. I reached for my phone in its cargo pocket, and then remembered that the men had taken my phone when they carried me off to drown me. But there was something hard in my pocket. The phone I took from the man in the van.

I turned it on. The screen asked for the passcode. The phone would do us no good. I put it back in my pocket.

We kept trudging through the crusted shore snow.

There were no vacation homes. No boat houses. No boarded-up cabins. We were alone on a frozen, desolate stretch of Lake Tahoe, getting colder and weaker with every step.

I tried to talk to Gertie, but she didn't respond. Her steps became more wobbly. Mine did as well. At times, the snow at the water's edge was deep, and I had to help Gertie as she struggled to raise her legs high enough to march through.

Her shivering was violent, a good sign when one is concerned about hypothermia, because shivering keeps the body's heat up. But after we'd gone maybe a half mile, her shivering lessened and then stopped. That was a major step on the descent into hypothermia. I tried to speed up her walk to generate more heat, but she could barely walk.

If it got much worse, I'd need to find a place to dig a snow cave and crawl with her underground until morning. But I wasn't convinced that would save her. I had no idea how much she'd eaten in the previous 24 hours. She may have had little if any food stores in her system. And I was cold enough that I doubted that I'd be able to dig a snow cave. I had no shovel, no extra gloves or jacket, and my own body heat was fading. It would be difficult or impossible to warm up Gertie by crawling next to her in a snow cave.

I decided to keep going, even if I had to carry Gertie.

After what seemed like an hours-long death march, the wind had come up and was blowing snow into our faces. The fatigue was greater than any I'd ever known. Like Gertie, my shivering grew and then faded as I began my own descent into hypothermia.

As my brain grew foggy, I decided it would be best for us to sit and rest. Just a short rest. Maybe we could take a little nap. It would be so pleasant. Gertie would be glad to stop, too. Up ahead was a nice mound of cushy snow. It would be comfy to curl up in it. Winter explorers in the dark forest.

I stopped. Gertie collapsed to the snow and flopped over

sideways. Her movement startled me.

Hypothermia had taken my common sense just as it had taken my body warmth.

We were both on the verge of no return.

I gritted my teeth, visualized Street urging me on. 'Just a little farther,' she would say. 'You can't let Gertie down,' she would say. 'That girl is depending on you,' she would say.

I bent over, grabbed one of Gertie's arms, and hauled upward.

"C'mon, Geree," I said, my lips frozen, brain numb, words slurred. "We ga'a kee wahing. Wah, Geree, wah."

I held her, and we stumbled ahead.

Twenty yards, I thought. If we could just make it twenty more yards. Then another twenty. Just another twenty yards. But the forest got too thick, too dark. There was a huge tree near the lake, and we walked right into it. My cheek bounced off rough bark. I turned to go around, but I couldn't even get past it.

A vague thought danced just out of reach. I tried to focus on it. It was like being drunk to the point of unconsciousness. Then I captured the thought. I was brilliant. My brain was a magnificent calculator of complex equations, stunning insights, ruthless conclusions.

It wasn't a tree.

It was a cabin. A very old cabin with tree-bark siding.

THIRTY-NINE

I don't remember how I found the window. I don't remember breaking the glass.

I do remember boosting Gertie up, poking her through the window head first. She fell through to the floor on the inside.

Like an Olympic gymnast, I climbed in head first and fell next to her.

We lay in the dark for a time. The cabin had no heat, but we were out of the wind.

In time, I rolled to my hands and knees, pushed up and stood, wobbling. I walked like a zombie with my hands out in front of me, feeling my way through the cave-dark cabin.

Operating by feel alone, I thought there were three rooms. The one we were in had a bed. Another was very small and had a door and a rack of hooks on the wall nearby. The third was bigger and had a counter with a sink in the middle. I felt along the counter. Something metallic clattered to the floor. Nothing else. I raised my hands. Found a shelf. It had cups and some plates that were curved. Shallow bowls. Some cans.

Above was another shelf. I came to a small box. Cardboard. Lightweight.

Wooden matches.

It took nine tries to light one.

The match flared bright, blinding me for a moment. I turned and looked around the room. Eventually, the match went dim. An acrid odor burned my nose. I looked at the match. It was burning the flesh of my fingers. I hadn't felt it because my fingers were so numb.

I dropped the match to the floor. It went out.

I struck another. Up on the shelf where I found the match were little candle jars. I lit one. It took a moment to get bright. I tried to blow out the match but I couldn't form the right shape with my lips. I dropped it to the floor, and it went out.

After a few more tries, I had eight candles lit. They illuminated the main part of the cabin, a rustic space with a plank wood floor, an old wood stove in the corner, a kitchen area with a counter, table, and two wooden chairs. Near the wood stove was an upholstered chair and a small couch. I pulled the upholstered chair over in front of the wood stove, then took a candle into the room where Gertie still lay on the floor and set the candle on a small table next to the bed. I picked Gertie up. She was not responsive.

I carried her into the bigger room and sat her down on the upholstered chair.

"Stay 'ere, Geree," I slurred, unable to make my lips move. "I'll geh to 'erk on a 'ire."

Gertie was clearly in trouble.

Near the wood stove was a box of kindling and a metal rack holding split logs. I found some paper, added kindling, and lit a fire.

The stove drafted well, and in a few minutes I had a good fire going. I held my hands in front of the fire, flexing my fingers to get them to thaw out.

After a couple minutes, I began to feel the intense prickling as sensation returned.

I fetched a blanket off the bed in the bedroom. I didn't want it over Gertie's front, as that would insulate her from the fire's warmth. So I got it behind her back and draped it over her head and around her shoulders.

As the fire began to warm the room, a freezing draft from the broken window in the bedroom became more obvious.

I looked around for some cardboard and found nothing. But the kindling was sitting vertically in a cardboard box. I took the kindling out and stacked it on the floor.

I took a candle and the box into the bedroom. The broken window was bigger than the box. I set the box on the floor and used my feet to break one of the box seams and then crush the box this way and that. When it was the right shape, I held it up to the broken window opening. It wasn't great, but with something to prop it in place, it might work.

Back at the kitchen counter I found a small tool box. Inside was a tack hammer. I dug through the detritus at the bottom of the box and found five finishing nails.

Hammering with frozen muscles was like when you give a two-year-old a hammer and nail. I missed nine times out of ten. And half of the times that I hit a nail, my blow was off-center enough that the nail flew across the room.

Fifteen minutes later, I finally had the cardboard nailed in place. My efforts had warmed me up enough that the skin pricks in my fingers were gone and the finger I'd burned with the match felt like it was stuck on red-hot metal.

On one of the kitchen shelves were some pans. I took two of them out the cabin's door and scooped them full of snow. I expected the kitchen area to feature a propane camp stove of some kind, but there was nothing. The wood stove would do.

I set the pans of snow on top of the stove. They sizzled and crackled as snow melted and water ran down the outside of the pans. While they warmed, I took the third and final pan outside to collect more snow and added it to the two cooking pans as the snow melted into very little water.

I searched the kitchen for something to add to the water and found two boxes of tea. I put tea bags into mugs. Five minutes later, I poured boiling water into the mugs.

After they cooled a bit, I sat on the arm of Gertie's chair and held a mug to her mouth so she could sip it. She dribbled and drooled and demonstrated just how close she'd come to dying from cold.

After she'd consumed most of a cup, she began to shiver, a sign that she was emerging from hypothermia. Her spasms were so violent that I could no longer feed her tea without risk of her choking.

Fifteen minutes of wracking spasms later, Gertie's shivering slowed. She still hadn't said a word. Her eyes began to dart toward the door and the windows, fear returning as she warmed.

On one end of the shelf above the counter were a dozen cans

of soup, all minestrone. I found a can opener and emptied two cans into one of the pans. It heated fast on the wood stove, which was now very hot. We ate it without speaking. I asked Gertie if she wanted more tea. She shook her head.

I got Gertie to stand up. Then I switched the chair out for the couch, but positioned the couch a bit back from the stove.

"You sleep on the couch in front of the fire," I said.

The kid who almost wouldn't stop talking in Sacramento made a vague nod but said nothing. I found a pillow and another blanket. Gertie sat down on the couch. I got her to lie down, spread the blanket, and tucked her in.

I pulled the mattress out of the bedroom and laid it on the floor, not far from the couch and the wood stove. Then I blew out all the candles but one and, out of excessive desire for safety, set it in the kitchen sink. It would make a night light with no danger of burning the cabin down.

When I turned back toward the wood stove, Gertie was already asleep. I quietly added two more logs to the fire, shut the stove door and dialed down the air intake to the lowest setting so the fire would burn slow and long. I lay down on the mattress.

I didn't know the time. My best guess was somewhere around four or five in the morning. Two or three hours to daylight.

My last thought before I fell asleep was how glad I was to have gotten Gertie to a safe, snow-bound location where the men couldn't drive in to find us.

Sometime later, another thought jerked me awake. I realized that it would be easy for the men in the van to find a toboggan and, come dawn, follow our tracks down the mountain. In addition to our tracks, the smoke from the wood stove was like waving a flag to get attention. I turned away from the wood stove to look at the cabin window. It was beginning to get light outside. If the men had found a toboggan in the last hours of the night, they would probably be at our cabin in less than an hour.

FORTY

Gertie was taking long, deep breaths. It was a relief to see that she was, for the moment, not freezing or terrified. The fire was still burning with a low, wavering, yellow flame. The logs had turned to mounds of coals. I stood up and, tip-toeing, added two more splits to the fire.

With light in the cabin, I took another look around.

It was a classic, small summer cabin, probably built 70 or 80 years ago and never updated. No electricity. And no phone line. The small, removable water tank over the sink and the collection bucket under the sink were the only plumbing. In a small closet by the door was a porta potty of the type that people take in their RVs for camping.

I stepped outside and saw that a weather system was building. Light, tiny snowflakes peppered my face. I hoped a good storm would bury our stop-sign toboggan tracks, even though I knew that the men in the cargo van would either be coming down the mountain on a toboggan at that moment, or they'd be studying Google maps and satellite photos, figuring out where the closest plowed road would be in relation to our probable location. They could drive to that spot, wherever it was, and with snowshoes, winter clothing, and weapons, come through the forest to find us.

Either method of finding us could happen fast.

It was likely that Spot would still be in the Jeep. He'd be cold, but I thought he would be able to last a day or more. Hopefully, someone would come along and find him. I was worried, but there was nothing I could do.

I studied the landscape outside the cabin door, where the forest was thicker and thinner, where it rose and fell, how the slope came down to the lake, how the land would direct the route of anyone making their way toward the cabin. Somewhere near the cabin was the road or lane that I knew had to be there to bring people to the cabin in the summer. It might be the easiest path on which to go from the cabin. But it was hidden under the thick blanket of snow and the tangle of numerous trees and brush. The snow was so deep that no one could walk through it. Without snowshoes, skis, or a plowed path, we were trapped.

The best emergency snowshoes were made from thick boughs of fir trees. There was a smallish one ten yards from the cabin. Away from the lake. In the deep snow. So close, but I had no idea how to get there through six feet of soft snow. Maybe it was just as well, because the road would also direct the men into the woods. I went back inside.

As before, I took the two pans outside and filled them with snow, packing it in to make for more water. I carried them in and set them on the stove top, careful not to wake Gertie up.

While I waited for the water to heat up, I looked around the cabin more closely than I had earlier.

There was nothing in particular I hoped to find. But I scanned the entire room, checking the shelves, looking in the few drawers, opening a few containers that I found. A jar at the corner of the kitchen counter had miscellaneous nuts and bolts. A wooden box with a lid had three decks of cards, a small pad of paper, and two yellow, #2 pencils. Hanging on the wall on either side of the largest window were two framed watercolors of Lake Tahoe, each looking like the fabulous view out the window.

In the corner closest to the door leaned two kayak paddles. Next to them hung two flotation vests. I picked up a paddle. It was a modern, lightweight design, a blue fiberglass handle with plastic blades at the ends, one blade turned 90 degrees from the blade at the other end of the paddle. On a nail hung a small key. I lifted it off. It was tarnished brass, and it looked just like the key for the padlock on my bike lock cable. I slipped it into my pocket.

There was no way to know, but I guessed that somewhere outside, buried in the snow, was a kayak. If I could find it...

I opened the door, stepped out, and closed it behind me. If

this were my cabin where would I stash my kayak?

The snow was not so deep right next to the cabin walls. The overhang reduced the accumulation, and the way the wind whirled around objects often created a kind of a low-snow zone like the tree wells that trap unwary skiers. I walked along the outer cabin wall, stepping through two-foot-deep snow that quickly rose to six feet just out from the cabin. I didn't expect to see a kayak, but I'd seen people hang them on racks mounted to the outside of sheds.

I went around the outer corner and marched along the next wall. No kayaks. At the far corner, the wind micro-climate had behaved differently, and the snow was drifted against the cabin wall eight feet deep, flowing up and over the eave and onto the roof in a seamless mountain. There were no kayaks. I turned around and retreated.

From the door, I went the other way and once again got around two sides of the cabin before I came to another impenetrable snow mountain. No kayaks anywhere to be seen.

Back inside, I found Gertie still sleeping. I stood at the main window that faced the lake and looked out. If this were my place, I'd probably keep my kayak near the water, secured under a small lean-to, or lying on the ground, locked to a tree.

All I could see was snow. No dock, no boat shed, no gazebo, no kayaks.

But there were several large, rounded humps of snow. Under them were likely fallen tree stumps or boulders or groups of Manzanita. Or kayaks.

Back outside, I marched toward the lake. As when we'd arrived a few hours before, the lakeside snow was frozen and crusted from wind-driven spray. It wasn't easy to walk on, but it could be done. At each big, long hump of snow, I kicked and probed. On one hump, I hit nothing. Two humps turned out to be logs. The fourth covered a bright green kayak lying upside down. It was difficult to uncover because the big white hump of snow was mostly white ice. I kicked and stomped. I scooped up ice-chunk conglomerations in my arms and tossed them aside. Once, my kick slipped and hit the kayak hard. I worried that the plastic material would be brittle in the cold and crack under the blow. After that, I hand-chopped the ice that was next to the kayak.

It took a quarter hour or more of kicking and chopping to free the kayak enough to break it loose from its frozen mooring.

It was a tandem kayak, with two small seats, one in front of the other. There were storage compartments at the bow and stern. I thought I was done with my project, but I discovered that it was still stuck beneath snow and ice at both bow and stern.

After another serious chopping session, I finally exposed the bow, which revealed a bike lock just as I'd imagined. I pulled out the key, but was unable to insert it into the padlock. The opening was filled with ice.

I got down on my knees and breathed on the lock, gradually warming it. When I thought it was no longer cold enough to freeze to my lips, I put the end of the padlock in my mouth, sealed my lips around it and blew hard. Not much air moved, but my breath was hot enough that I could sense the internal ice gradually thawing. I put the tip of my tongue on the key opening, transferring more heat.

Again, I tried the key. It slid into the lock, turned easily, and the lock popped open. I unhooked the cable from the bow ring, and the kayak was now free.

By taking some of ice chunks I'd removed and wedging them in next to the kayak, I hoped to prevent a gust of wind from blowing it into the lake. I left it there and went back inside.

Gertie was sitting up on the couch, the blanket wrapped over her shoulders. From her angle, she probably had seen me out the window, trying to free the kayak. I saw her eyes glance in my direction, but she didn't turn her head.

I moved slowly so I wouldn't startle her and sat down next to her.

"Are you okay?" I said.

She made a slow nod.

I didn't know if her hypothermia would have any lasting effects. I didn't want to push her in any way. I wasn't sure what to say.

"You're a tough kid. I want you to know that."

She didn't nod. Still didn't speak. I saw her eyes look from the left side of the window to the right as if wondering if someone might be lurking just out of view.

"Tell you what. I'm going to make us some breakfast. Our food choice is the same as when we got here in the night. We have many cans of minestrone soup to choose from. You sit tight, and I'll go pick which can looks best."

I consolidated the melted snow from both pans into one pan. I used the empty pan to heat another can of soup.

I put new tea bags into mugs, poured in hot water, and brought Gertie a mug.

When the soup was hot, we ate. When we were done, I again sat next to her in front of the fire.

"They were going to kill me," Gertie said in a tiny voice.

I didn't know what to say. I wanted to ask her if she had an idea why, but I thought it best to wait. She'd just been through one of the most traumatic experiences a person can have. I patted her leg.

"They're still looking for me, aren't they?" Her voice was soft, her tone wooden, the voice of a girl in shock.

"Probably. But I found a kayak. We can get out of here in a way that won't leave any tracks."

She was silent. She sipped her tea.

"Where will we go?" she finally said.

"We paddle down the shore, find another house, and see if it has a phone."

"This one doesn't."

"No," I said. "I assume the men took your phone."

Gertie nodded.

"Most of the houses on the lake aren't this rustic," I said. "Many of them will have landline phones. We can call the police and get them to come get us with the sheriff's boat."

"You don't have a cell phone." It was a statement.

"I had one, but it got lost." No point in telling her about how they tried to drown me. I reached into my pocket and pulled out the phone I got after I crashed the Jeep into the van.

"I took this from the man who was in the back of the van

with you. It's got a passcode lock. Any chance you can hack it?"

She shook her head. "When will we go?" she said.

"Sooner the better," I said.

"Because the men are coming," Gertie said.

"It's possible."

Gertie made another slow nod. "Scruff Boy is stuck alone with my dad. That's torture for him."

I nodded.

"I saw your dog in the back of your Jeep, but I was too scared to think. I would have pet him if... if things had been different."

I nodded again.

"Where is he now?" she asked.

"I don't know. Maybe still in the back of the Jeep."

"Oh, my God! He will be frozen! He could die!"

"Someone will find him and let him out, maybe take him into a warm car or house. He'll be okay."

After a minute, Gertie said, "What's his name?"

"Spot."

She was silent.

"I'm sorry about all of this," I said. "It must be very hard to be ripped out of your family life and very difficult for your parents, too."

"You forget," Gertie said. "I was the unwanted child, remember? I'm sure they don't want me to suffer, but it's not like they want me around, either."

"Okay, but you'll call them when you get the chance? Tell them you're okay? I know they are both worried."

"Maybe you could call them. They'd probably rather talk to you, anyway."

"What about your friends?"

"I don't have any friends except Scruff Boy." Gertie's voice was flat.

"Emily was very concerned when you went missing."

"She's probably more worried for Scruff Boy than me. She tolerates me. The only reason we connect at all is because she doesn't have any friends, either. So I should be grateful. But you're a better friend to me than Emily." Gertie took a deep breath. Let it out. "Okay. I saw you dig out the kayak. Let's go," she said.

I walked over and picked up one of the pencils I'd found earlier, found a scrap of paper and scribbled a note to the cabin's owners. I apologized and said that I would pay for the broken window and other damages. I set a glass on the note and my business card so they wouldn't blow away if the wind blew down the cardboard I'd put in the window. I knew that Mikhailo and company might find it, but they already knew who I was, and if they came to this cabin, that meant they already knew we'd been here.

"We'll get you into the front of the kayak," I said. "You can hold your arms close for warmth, then I'll wrap that blanket around you." I didn't add that I would wrap the blankets loosely so she could swim in case we capsized. And I didn't ask if she could swim. This was our best chance of escape, and we'd take it whether she could swim or not.

"No," Gertie said. Her voice was soft, but her tone was firm. "I want to paddle. I know how. I've gone on a kayak on the American River two different times."

"Okay." I was pleased to see her assert herself. It was the best sign that she would recover from what had happened.

I shut down the air intake on the wood stove, and put the furniture and pans back where I'd found them.

As before, I had Gertie wear my jacket over her hoodie. She got the jacket zipper stuck on the big plastic fob that was attached to the hoodie's waist drawstring. I helped her to free it. With my big gloves over her hands, she could hold the kayak paddle. It wouldn't be warm, but it would help.

I ignored the flotation vests I'd found earlier. They are life savers when the water is warmer. But in the winter in Lake Tahoe, a vest merely allows rescuers to find your body after you succumb from hypothermia. And before you die, the vest gets in the way and restricts your movement.

We grabbed the paddles and headed out into the cold.

FORTY-ONE

As we marched through the snow, Gertie in front of me, she looked around through the forest, her nervousness obvious.

I pulled the kayak out from the depression where it had been buried and positioned it in the ice and snow at the shoreline.

"You climb into the front seat," I told Gertie. "Then I'll slide the kayak into the water and get into the back seat."

Gertie didn't speak. She stuck her paddle into the snow, leaned on it like a crutch, stepped into the kayak, and sat down.

I slid the kayak out. When the stern dropped down from the snow into the water, I turned the kayak broadside to the shoreline and stepped into the rear seat.

The seat was small, the space for my legs smaller still, and the kayak was very tippy as I got in. I leaned the end of my paddle against the icy shore to stabilize the boat as I lowered myself down to the seat. Gertie inhaled as we rocked.

Gertie's paddle strokes were mild but impressive considering what she'd been through. Because there were few houses to the south heading toward Emerald Bay, we went up the shore to the north. In just five minutes of paddling, we came upon a good-sized, modern house. I used my paddle to turn us into shore.

"You can go farther, faster on the lake than walking through the snow," Gertie said in a substantial understatement.

"Yeah," I said, pleased that she was focused on something positive.

I angled the kayak sideways to the shore and, using my paddle as a crutch, stepped out onto the snow. I bent down and steadied the kayak as Gertie stepped out. I pulled the kayak onto the shore, turned it topside down, and pushed it down into the snow so it wouldn't blow away.

Even though I found a wind-blown area with less-than-normal snow accumulation, it took a great deal of energy to fight our way through the deep snow up to the deck of the house.

There was a sliding glass door with drapes on the inside. At the edge of the drapes was a gap through which I could see an alarm panel with a blinking red light. I didn't want a loud alarm bell to announce our presence, but I hoped there was a silent alarm that would alert the police.

I'd spoken to Tahoe vacation home owners who told me that they open their Tahoe houses to friends. The problem is that it is hard to communicate how to work the alarm without setting it off, and it is also difficult to get a key to the person. Much easier to leave the alarm visible, blinking, but not set. Easier, also, to hide a key on the property.

The best hiding place for a key is inventive and well-hidden. Nevertheless, the standard locations are still popular. There are three places that produce a key about 50% of the time.

I started with the door mat. I kicked snow off the mat, then lifted it up. No key. Next to the door was mounted a cute little red bucket. Inside sat a ceramic flower pot from which dried flowers still rustled in the breeze. I pulled out the pot and looked into the bucket. No key. I took off my glove and ran my fingers along the top edge of the door molding. There was a little finishing nail that stuck up a quarter inch at one corner. Hooked onto the nail, lying out of sight, was a key.

I used the key in the slider lock, then replaced the key. I opened the door. The little red light continued to blink. No bell clanged. Maybe it was dialing the monitoring company.

I shut the slider behind us, locked it, and closed the drapes.

To the side of the slider was a light switch. It turned on three canned lights. The house had power, a good sign.

As we walked into the luxury home, I thought how ironic it was that I had to break into the old cabin. The house with a hundred thousand dollars in furnishings was basically open to the public.

The house's climate control was set quite cool, but at least the heat was on. Another bit of luck.

There was a great room next to the kitchen area. The room had a sitting area in front of a gas stove. I couldn't find the switch or valve. Then I saw three remotes sitting by one of the overstuffed chairs. The room had a giant TV and a fancy sound system, needing, perhaps, two remotes. One of the remotes had just a few buttons. I pressed some of them. The gas fire lit.

Gertie stood in front of the fire as it slowly warmed up.

I walked around the house looking for a landline phone or a misplaced cell phone that could be charged. I found neither.

When I came back to the great room, Gertie had moved to a big leather chair that faced the fire. Gertie still had my jacket on, the sleeves pushed up so she could use her hands. She looked at the gas fire. The yellow and blue flickering light shone on her red cheeks.

I sat across from her in a matching chair.

"How did you find me?" she asked.

"Your friend Emily called me. She'd seen your post of my picture and my name. She also saw your post of the other man who came to your house after I'd left. When there were no more posts and you didn't tweet what you were doing, she assumed that something bad had happened. So she looked up my name and sent me an email with her phone number. I called her, and she told me what she thought had happened."

"Wow, she answered the phone when you called? She never answers her phone. She's a texter only."

"She was worried about you."

Gertie was silent.

I continued. "In the background of the photo you posted online was a white cargo van. I also found a piece of evidence that led me to a company in Carson City. There was another indication of a white cargo van. So I put out some notices about a white cargo van and got a call from a man who'd seen a suspicious van on the West Shore of the lake. I drove there and followed the van. That was how I found you."

Gertie stared at the fire. She hugged herself as if she were still cold. "You told me not to open the door to anyone I didn't know. I should have taken that more seriously. But how many people can just listen to someone knocking and not open the door a crack? That was my mistake. When the man knocked on my door and I opened it, he batted Scruff Boy out of my arms, and took my hand. He squeezed so hard that I wanted to scream. He said that if I made a noise, he would crumble my hand bones like they were soda crackers. I knew he meant it. So I couldn't do anything but walk with him out to his van. One of the other men was inside it. They kept me in back, so I couldn't see where they drove me. I thought they took me to Lake Tahoe because my ears popped multiple times. I knew I was going up in elevation."

"Where have they kept you?"

"I don't know. When the man first dragged me into his van, his partner made me put on this hooded sweatshirt and pull the hood up over my head and face. That way if someone looked into the van, like at a stoplight or something, it would be hard to see me. It was night when they took me out of the van. Before they opened the door, they put a cloth bag over my head. I couldn't see anything. They also taped my mouth so I couldn't scream, and they taped my hands. They led me a long way."

"Through the snow?"

"Not much. At least, I didn't notice it. I could tell that we went through a door inside someplace. But it was like a warehouse or something. The air wasn't really cold, but it wasn't warm, either. We walked a long way and went up stairs. When they took the bag off my head, I was in a little room. It was a storeroom or a walk-in closet off a bathroom. There was cleaning stuff on some shelves and a mop bucket in the corner. There was a small mattress on the floor. They attached a chain to my ankle. The chain was bolted to the floor. It was just long enough that I could get to the bathroom. There were two TV cameras. One in the storeroom and one in the bathroom. I thought it was disgusting that they would watch me in the bathroom, so I turned off the light when I went in there. They said I'd be locked in, so there was no point in trying to escape. They said that it was sound-proofed, so there was no point in screaming. The other door in the bathroom was kept locked."

I was worried about bringing up a difficult subject, but I

needed to know. I said, "Did they ever hurt you?"

Gertie glanced at me, then looked away. "If you mean, did they rape me, then no. But they scared me to death. The one guy, I thought of him as Max. Max Cady from De Niro's character in "Cape Fear." He kept touching me. Every time he came near me, he'd grab at my boobs or my butt."

"Is that all he did?"

She paused. "Pretty much all. The two guys always came together. The other guy didn't seem as mean. But Max, he said things that made me think that if he ever came alone, I'd be in real trouble."

I felt my blood pressure rising as she said it. "Did he make a specific threat?" I asked.

"Not specific. But they were still threats. Like, 'I bet you've got a soft little body under all those clothes.' And, 'Some day I'm going to come and show you what a man can do with you.' Stuff like that. It made me sick. And they were both rough with me, pushing me whenever they wanted me to move."

"What does Max look like?"

"Dark hair, cut real short. Tall. Not as tall as you, but real big. Lots of muscles. He always smelled of cologne. He's one of those guys who puts on way too much, but they don't have a clue how gross that is."

From her description, I thought that the man who'd picked me up and carried me on his shoulder was Max. He was probably the man that Agent Ramos said was born Mikhailo and emigrated from Russia as a child.

"What did the other guy look like?"

"Shorter and softer. Messy blond hair. He wasn't so scary, like, physically. But he's scary in a twisted way. Like I bet he still lives with his mother. She probably calls him her baby. I don't think he'd rape. Or fight. But he's a kind of sicko, for sure. Probably tortures people."

"He didn't touch you?"

"No."

"Did you get his name?"

"No. Remember the Anthony Perkins character in "Psycho?"

Well, that's what this guy reminds me of. So I thought of him as Norman Bates. Neither Norman or Max ever used a name. I guess they were careful even though they were rough and weird."

"When I drove my Jeep into their van, Max and Norman were outside of the van. There was a third guy inside the van with you."

"Yeah. He's the guard. He doesn't speak, just plays with his gun. He takes the bullets out, looks into the barrel and stuff. Max always told him to guard me, to stay in the bedroom on the other side of the bathroom door."

I thought about what she'd said.

"They kept you locked up for five days. Then they came and took you off in the van."

"They were going to kill me," Gertie said.

"Do you know why?"

"I think so. The day they took me out to kill me, they were gone for a few hours. I thought I was alone. But the other door into the bathroom opened. It didn't open much, just six inches or so. I wasn't in the bathroom. I was sitting on the mattress in the storeroom, so I wasn't very close. But I heard a man inhale and then swear like he was surprised to see me. I turned to look, but it was dark in the bedroom, and I couldn't see anything through the door. Then the door shut. I think whoever it was thinks that I saw him. If whoever is in charge didn't like that I supposedly saw that guy, then they might have ordered me killed. It's the only thing that makes sense."

Gertie was gripping the arms of the big upholstered chair, her fingertips making impressions in the leather.

"That night, the silent guard came and got me. He put the bag over my head. But when Max and Norman arrived, and they all took me out to the van, they told the silent guy that he didn't need to use the bag. That told me that they didn't care what I saw because they were going to kill me."

"Did you see anything of where you were?"

"No. Once the silent guy put the bag on my head, the others just left it on until they were going to kill me."

We sat in silence for awhile.

"Did they ever say anything that would indicate why they kidnapped you?"

She shook her head.

"What about anything that would suggest their business?"

Another head shake.

"What did the man in the dark want?" I asked.

"I don't know."

I stood up. "Okay with you if I find some food for us?"

"At home, I'm always hungry," Gertie said, "but I'm not hungry now."

"You need fuel. Trauma can make you lose your appetite."

She made a small nod.

I stood up and walked over to the kitchen. I opened some cupboards, found the ones with food. The fridge was cold but empty of all fresh food, and the freezer was mostly empty. It looked like the homeowners did not plan to be back before spring.

"I could make spaghetti with tomato sauce."

Gertie nodded.

Twenty minutes later, I served up two large bowls on the island counter. We sat on tall stools and ate without talking. When we were done, I rinsed the dishes.

"Are we going to sleep here?" Gertie asked.

"Yeah. It's almost dark. We should go to bed early and get up early so we can paddle before dawn. That way we can't be seen."

"Do you think it would be okay if I took a shower here?" Gertie asked. "I haven't showered in days."

"I think it would be fine. We broke into this house because this is an emergency. That makes the rules different. We'll pay whatever they charge."

"You mean you will," Gertie said. "That doesn't seem right."

"Your mother hired me. She'll pay."

Gertie made a slow nod. "What if I looked for some clean clothes? Mine are filthy."

"I think you should do that."

"Then I'll go look." Gertie got up and turned toward the bedrooms when we heard a noise outside.

FORTY-TWO

I jumped up and ran to the slider wall to turn off the lights. Back in the kitchen, I turned off those lights. I picked up the remote and killed the gas fire.

"What's wrong?" Gertie said.

"Sssh," I whispered.

I walked over to the window that was near the slider but faced south, the direction I thought the sound came from. I gave a tiny twist to the control rod for the blinds, and peeked out, looking through the forest, down the shore.

It was twilight, and the shadowed, snowy woods were deep blue. Combined with the black lake, there was barely enough light to see anything. A fine mist of falling snowflakes put a gray haze over the view. It looked as cold as it was. I saw no lights, no movement.

I moved to a kitchen window that faced west, toward the rising mountain. Because of the thick forest and the slope blocking the twilight from the west, the view was darker. I stared longer. Again, no light, no movement. Half of the possible view was obscured by the house's garage, which projected out from the house. The garage wall was near the kitchen window, and it went out maybe twenty-six feet. If I found a window to that side of the house, I could see more. I trotted into a study. Its window was farther from the garage wall. I could see more of the mountain that rose up. But still, I saw nothing.

To look in the third direction, to the north, I went into a hallway that led to the bedrooms. It was too dark inside to see. I held one hand in front of me, ran the other lightly along the wall. I went past several doors and turned into the one that faced most directly north. There was just enough light to see the master bed and the door over to the bath. This room had a type of blind that pulled up. I didn't dare raise it, as the movement would be obvious to anyone who might be outside. I got my fingers around the edge and bent the material just enough to see out.

The snow in the forest was deep blue and so thick and deep, it blocked the view of nearly everything.

But just 20 or 25 yards out, I saw the top of the white cargo van. It was obviously sitting on a plowed road, a nearly invisible white canal in a white landscape. The road had been plowed to within a short distance of the house we were in, and we'd never seen it as we approached the house by kayak from the other direction.

Wearing snowshoes, and trudging through the deep toward the house was a big man. Behind him was the third man, the silent guard I'd bloodied in the collision. Even though I was looking through the fine mist of falling snow, I saw the rage on his face and the big gun in his hand. He held the gun up, ready and eager to fire at the first opportunity.

I let go of the window blind and sprinted back to Gertie.

"We have to go!" I said in a whispered shout.

She looked stunned and didn't move.

"Now!"

I grabbed my gloves, handed them to her, and pushed her as she trotted, stumbling, toward the slider. The slider slid open without a sound. We stepped out, and I gave the door a thoughtless push behind me. The door slid closed fast and hit the stop with a loud thud. Unless the men were making some significant noise at the same moment, they would have heard it. I'd betrayed our presence.

The only reasonable way back through the snow to the kayak was to retrace the way we'd come. Unfortunately, as soon as we stepped down off the deck at the corner of the house, we'd be visible. But we had no other option. Trying to take a roundabout path from the far side of the house would take a week of burrowing through six feet of powder. Our only hope was to move fast and hope that the men had lousy accuracy at this light level and this distance.

"Stay bent low," I whispered to Gertie. "I'll go first."

I took her gloved hand and stepped into the track we'd made coming in. I marched fast, moving sideways so that I could pull Gertie by the hand. We'd gone less than ten feet when I heard a shout.

"There they are!" a big, thundering voice shouted. It sounded like the voice of the man who dropped me overboard to my intended death. "Send in our coordinates!" he shouted.

A loud shot cracked the air. Then another. Gertie made a soft scream.

"Concentrate on running!" I whispered.

Another gunshot.

Gertie whimpered. Her drag on my hand increased.

"Pay no attention!" I pulled harder.

Our path made a curve as we approached the shore. I slipped and fell in the gathering darkness, jumped back up, jerked on Gertie's arm. She cried out.

We got to the kayak. I pulled it out of the snow. Slid it into the water. We were bent down, possibly out of view from the men.

"Get in! Hurry!"

Gertie jumped in. The kayak tipped. I grabbed the paddle in one hand and held it as I put both hands on either side of the rear seat. In a jerky, running motion, I stepped into the water with my right foot as I pushed the kayak out with my hands. The kayak swerved in a big arc to the left. I swung my left foot into the rear leg compartment. Then it swung back to the right as I lifted my water-logged right foot out of the water and snaked it into the kayak.

We were still coasting as I took my first stroke with my right hand. I pulled too hard. The kayak's stern went down into the water, and the bow arced to the left. Gertie gasped as we began to flip over.

I stopped pulling just in time, jammed the left paddle into the water, and pulled with my left hand.

The kayak arced back the other way. Levelled out.

A shot thundered. Then another. I began paddling in smooth, regular strokes, strong pulls, but no longer the desperate tugs that threatened to capsize us.

There was more shouting from behind. The voices were hard to understand. I heard the words 'green kayak' and 'find a boat.'

I paddled harder. We were moving at high speed. Faster than a person could walk. When I glanced back I couldn't see anything specific on the shore, just a general sense of forest. The sky was a dull gray twilight of clouds and falling snow. I couldn't see the men, which hopefully meant they couldn't see us. I pulled harder on my paddle, wanting to get as far away as possible. Gertie paddled too, her strokes weak but regular. Then I had a frightening thought.

If we got too far out, we'd be lost on the vast expanse of lake, unable to see anything. If I lost our bearings and began paddling toward the center of the lake, we'd die on the water.

I thought I could get a sense of the wave direction and use that as a kind of compass. But it was too dark. The kayak seemed to have a regular agitation from the waves, but it didn't give me a sense of direction in the near dark.

We had to go back closer to land. If we could at least sense the shore, we wouldn't get lost. I worried about Mikhailo and his comrades. But they wouldn't be able to see us in the dark unless they had infrared sights. As I had the thought, I accidentally bumped my paddle on the kayak. It made a loud, resonant thump as if I'd struck a bass drum. If I did that more, they'd be able to track us by sound alone.

I turned toward where I thought the land was and stroked hard. I thought the dark sense of shore would appear in a few moments, but it didn't. I kept making strong strokes through the water, even as I tried to slip my paddle blades in and out of the water so they didn't make a splashing noise. Instead of worrying about them hearing me, maybe we could hear them.

"Hold up," I whispered. We stopped paddling and coasted.

I heard nothing except a soft, distant hum, like the hum of old-fashioned electronic equipment.

"What's wrong?" Gertie said in a low voice.

"Sssh," I whispered. "I'm listening for shore noises."

"What do you mean?" she whispered.

"Men talking. Waves hitting rocks. Night animals."

"Are we lost? Oh my God. We could be lost at sea."

"No. We're fine. I can always slap my paddle and listen for the echo, but I'd rather not."

I heard nothing. I slipped my right paddle blade into the water and took a soft stroke. Paused and listened. Pulled my paddle out and made a stroke with my left blade. I tried to make the strokes equal in effort. Like most kayaks, this one had no rudder. The only way to keep it going straight was to alternate left side and right side strokes and give them the same power. But I'd been in kayaks enough to realize that, without vision, it would be nearly impossible to make a rudder-less kayak go straight for any length of time.

I stopped again to listen. There was no sound that indicated the shore. Was there a breeze? Yes, a light breeze that brought the tiny snowflakes onto my left cheek more than my right. Which way did they come down on the land? I couldn't remember. How stupid could I be? At a time when I should have been hyper-vigilant, I didn't pay attention to my surroundings.

Again, I heard no sound except the low hum. It sounded like it was everywhere. Maybe it was just ringing in my ears. "Do you hear that low hum?" I whispered.

"Yeah," Gertie said.

"Where do you think the sound is coming from?"

"I don't know. Maybe behind us?"

"Do you think the sound is moving?" I asked.

"No. Yes. It's just kind of wavering. It's doing a soft wa, wa, wa."

What Gertie said made me uneasy.

"I think the hum is getting louder," she said.

I remembered that the lady in the cabin across the highway from Craig Gower's and Ian Lassitor's houses talked about the ghost boat moaning. Could it be that the ghost boat was out on the lake? I didn't know what to think of the idea. But if any boat was on the lake, I could use the direction and movement of its sound to get a general sense of where land might be by the simple awareness that a boat can't go on land. So if a boat noise came

from the south and went north – as the eccentric lady described
the ghost boat – then I could turn the kayak until the track of
the sound was behind us. If I paddled forward, I'd likely hit land.
It wasn't foolproof, and I'd already proven that I was a fool for
getting lost at sea.

But what if the boat was swooping in and out near the
shoreline? Then I was out of luck.

Now it was obvious that the hum was getting louder. Although
I was no marine expert, it sounded to me like an outboard motor.
The sound of the boat hitting the waves had a metallic quality to
it, like the sound I'd often heard with small aluminum fishing
boats.

The wa, wa rise and fall that Gertie mentioned grew in my
mind to the regular bounce of a boat going across regular waves.
At first, I was skeptical of my guesses. But as the boat grew a
bit louder, I started to think that maybe I wasn't too far from
reality.

In a little bit, the sound made a small jump in volume. I tried
to guess why. The pitch of the motor hadn't changed, so there was
no rise-and-fall Doppler shift like when a train goes by on the
track. Maybe the boat was near shore and it came around a point
so that now its sound was in direct line with us. If so, we should
be able to see its lights.

I looked in the direction of the sound. There was nothing to
see. The sound was now loud enough that there was no doubt
about its source. Our kayak sat low in the water. Perhaps the
boat's lights were out of sight behind waves. Or maybe the sound
coming over the water was playing tricks, and the boat was
actually still miles away. In that case, the curve of the earth could
block the lights. Either way, it wouldn't be long if it kept coming
closer.

After another minute, it was obvious that the boat was getting
close, but no lights showed. The driver was committing a serious
error in piloting his boat without running lights. The eccentric
lady said the ghost boat had no lights. I dismissed it. But maybe
she was right. When another minute had passed, I made an
obvious, but startling, realization. The sound had gotten louder,

but the direction of its source hadn't changed. Simple geometry meant the boat was coming toward us.

We had no lights, either. Two boats striking each other out in the lake was a very unlikely event. But if the other boat did, in fact, have no running lights, and if it were on a collision course with us, I had only its sound to avoid it.

Gertie turned around and looked behind us. It was dark, but there was enough cloud light that I could see the fear in her face.

I started paddling, trying to go left at a 90-degree angle to the course of the incoming boat. I thought about how you can't outrun a tornado, so you go at right angles to it. We couldn't outrun any motor boat. But by turning more to the left and paddling fast, we could easily get out of its way.

I stroked hard. The sound of the boat got louder. What was its driver thinking?

I adjusted my course even more to the left. The approaching boat got louder still.

It still sounded like an outboard on a runabout, and the pitch of the engine sound hadn't changed. But the engine seemed to be running at a much higher throttle setting than I'd earlier thought. The closer the boat got, the more its engine seemed to race. I paddled harder. Left side, right side, left side.

I glanced around behind us. There were still no running lights on the approaching boat. I saw nothing in the darkness. As I turned more to the left, the boat always seemed to be coming from behind us. But we had no running lights, either. And as a human-powered boat, we made no sound.

I started to wonder about the worst scenario. What if Mikhailo or one of his men were out on the lake, trying to kill us?

But there was no way for someone driving a boat in the night to know where we were. It made no sense. We were invisible. Yet we were being chased. Maybe the woman was right. Maybe there was a ghost boat. Maybe it was chasing us.

The boat seemed to roar behind us.

Gertie turned around in her seat again. Her face showed the strain of horror.

I paddled furiously as the boat behind us came closer, its whine like the growl of a night predator chasing down its prey. I turned again. Paddled harder. But no matter what I did, the dark, unseen, ghost boat followed us. By some magic, its captain could see us in the dark.

In a moment, Gertie's face transformed from concern into a fright mask. She screamed.

The sound behind us multiplied. I jerked my head around to see.

In the dark gray of the last twilight, I saw the shine of an aluminum hull's bow hit a wave behind us and loft into the air. The boat was a touch to the right of our stern, but it was going to slam down onto our kayak.

I stabbed the right blade of my paddle down into the water and jerked it back through the water with as much power as I had.

Our kayak's bow lifted and turned left. My effort pushed the stern down into the black water as the kayak arced to the left.

The ghost boat slammed down onto the waves. The left part of its hull hit the right side of our kayak. Gertie gasped. The kayak bounced left. Water rushed into the kayak. The ghost boat's momentum carried it forward. I strained as I made another paddle stroke with maximum power and speed. We pulled farther to the left. The ghost boat continued forward at high throttle. I turned to watch it go, to see the crazy, idiot skipper. But the boat went into the darkness, and I couldn't see anything.

Our kayak sloshed with the water we'd taken onboard, but it was still floating. Gertie was crying, and I couldn't get enough air. I continued paddling into the darkness. I didn't know which way was land and which way was sea. I just wanted to put distance between us and the boat that nearly destroyed us.

But by my third paddle stroke, a chill permeated my body.

The sound of the ghost boat was changing. It twisted in the night, unseen, but heard. And then it began to get louder.

The boat was coming back to run us down again.

But we were invisible! We were a silent kayak in the darkness!

I was frantic. I couldn't breathe. The racing motor grew in the night. How could the driver know where we were?! He had no searchlight. Even with an infrared scope, the waves would make it nearly impossible to see us.

Then I had an idea. Maybe it was crazy, but everything about this was crazy.

"Gertie," I shouted. "Take off your hoodie!"

She turned, horrified at my own craziness.

"Take it off!" I shouted.

"But it's under your jacket!"

"Take off the jacket. Then take off the hoodie. Throw the hoodie overboard! Hurry!"

She struggled with my jacket. The zipper wouldn't work.

The ghost boat was coming closer.

The sleeve caught as Gertie tried to pull her arm out. She pulled the jacket over her head, but her hand was still stuck inside the sleeve.

"Pull it off!" I shouted as the ghost boat bore down on us from the side.

Gertie leaned her arm and jacket back behind her seat as if I could help. I grabbed the fabric. Set my paddle down across my lap. Reached for her arm with my other hand. Pulled. Jerked. Gertie cried out. I gritted my teeth and ripped the jacket off her arm.

The ghost boat roared toward us.

I dropped the jacket across my knees and grabbed Gertie's hoodie at the top of her head. "Lift your arms up!"

She did as told. I pulled the hoodie up and off her. I felt her hair get caught in the fabric.

The ghost boat was almost on us, its engine at full throttle.

I pulled on the hoodie, felt Gertie's hair tear. She made a small whimper but didn't scream.

The hoodie came off. I balled it up and threw it over my head behind us. Then I grabbed the paddle and took multiple fast strokes, straining arm and back muscles to make the kayak shoot forward in the water. Left side, right side, left side, right side.

The ghost boat went from loud sound to sudden apparition

in the night, bouncing on the waves, slamming shiny aluminum hull against black water as it bore down on us. It was twenty feet away, about to cut us in two, when it veered slightly away, behind us, and missed our stern by inches.

I paddled again, turning away from the ghost boat, trying to get some distance between us. Another boat appeared in the dark. It was motionless, moored to a buoy. Then came another buoy without a boat. We were near a marina of some kind. Or a residential area with boat moorings. I kept paddling. More buoys appeared, all floating quietly in the harsh winter waters waiting for spring when a plethora of boats would be brought out of storage to spend the summer on the lake.

The sound of the ghost boat changed once again, signaling another change in its course as it came around in another high-speed arc. I paddled faster, trying to get away. But this time the boat's sound didn't get much louder. Maybe it was still chasing us. Maybe not. I turned to watch and saw a vague movement in the dark as if the ghost boat were circling back toward the hoodie. But its path was interrupted when it hit the moored boat broadside. There was a tremendous screech of ripping metal. Crunching, splintering noises. A miniature meteor streak of sparks flew like fireworks. Then came a small flame, followed by a muffled explosion. A fireball the size of a compact car blinded me as it rose into the sky. Yellow light glowed bright on the side of Gertie's face. Heat radiation was hot on our skin.

Flaming debris arced through the night, curved streams of fire trailing gray smoke plumes. The fireball puffed out in a second. There was a ring of fire on the water's surface as gas and oil burned. Burning debris hissed as the shattered boat hulls sank into the water. Soon, there was only a choppy scatter of flaming detritus. What we could see of the wreckage disappeared beneath the water. Two minutes later, the last of the fires went out.

I never heard the skipper call out. I never saw any other movement. But the collision was forceful enough that whatever ghostly skipper was onboard, he would have either been badly hurt or flung forward into the night.

But maybe there was no skipper at all.

FORTY-THREE

I had no desire to paddle back and no light with which to inspect whatever debris remained. If there was a skipper trying to swim in the freezing water, it didn't bother me to leave him. He was an attempted murderer. Trying to save him would just give him an opportunity to grab onto our kayak, tip it over, and drown us.

"Here's my jacket," I said to Gertie. "You'll want to put it back on." She took it and, without unzipping it, pulled it over her head like a huge sweater. It engulfed her, and it took a moment for her to find the neck opening and get her head through it.

"Why did you have me take off my hoodie?" she cried, her voice shaky with fear and trauma.

"I don't know if I'm right, but the boat that nearly killed us found us in the dark. We should have been invisible, but we weren't. Your captors made you wear that hoodie. It seemed like it was about keeping your face out of view when they brought you up from Sacramento. But I'm guessing it was also a way to track you in case you got away. It may have had some kind of electronic chip sewn into it."

Gertie didn't respond for a few seconds. Then she said, "The hoodie had a drawstring at the hem. The logo tag on the end of the drawstring was thick. Like the key fob for my dad's car. Could that be it?"

"That's what I'm thinking, yes."

"And they could, like, home in on me wherever I was?"

"Yeah. GPS or something. Maybe the boat chasing us was automated."

She went silent.

I paddled slowly and quietly in case someone on the shore had seen the collision and fire and was looking out toward us. We came upon another empty buoy. From it, I ventured this way and that, my eyes gradually regaining their night vision. The snow increased, making a constant mist of melting flakes on our faces. After a few minutes, I saw a looming presence of darkness more complete than the darkness on the water.

The shore.

I stayed close enough to land to keep sensing the darkness while I paddled north, parallel to the shoreline, staying close to not get lost. Maybe a mile later, I found another group of buoys, all without boats, save one. There was one lonely, dark sailboat, maybe thirty feet long. If we could get inside its cabin and keep it dark, it would be a good, safe place to spend the night.

We faced the stern of the boat as we approached. I could just make out the boat's name in the dark. Nāmaka. I didn't know the name, but it was probably something to do with sailing or water.

I pulled up next to the boat's side. It was a deep-keel design with a high lifeline rail. From down on the water in the kayak, the sailboat's hull was imposing. I reached up and grabbed one of the stanchions near the stern.

"Gertie, there's a cable along the top edge of the boat," I said in a whisper. "Like a really thin railing. Can you grab it?"

"I can't see it." Her voice was loud.

"Please talk quietly. Sound carries great distances over water."

She lifted her arm but didn't quite have the reach. "I'll have to stand. Is that okay?" This time she whispered.

"Yeah. I'll steady the kayak."

I put one of the paddle blades into the water, ready to react if Gertie made the kayak rock too much. She stood up slowly, leaning one of her hands against the sailboat hull. The kayak was very tippy and it shook, transmitting her shakiness. She reached up and out, her hand sweeping the air. She waved her hand up and down, and her fingers touched the cable. She grabbed onto it.

"Great," I said. "Hold on while I grab it, too."

I stood up and reached over to the sailboat.

"Before we both get into the sailboat, I need to find a line to tie the kayak. Stay put while I climb aboard."

I set my paddle inside the cockpit of the sailboat, swung my leg up and over the gunnel, and climbed aboard. The only light was the faint glow coming out of the clouds. I felt around in the dark, touching surfaces, running my hands back and forth, looking for a coiled line. I found cleats and grab rails and the backstay, one of the cables that attaches to the top of the mast and helps hold it in place the same way utility power poles are held by guy wires. There was a storage locker drawer. I opened it. It had gloves and tools and a flashlight. I shielded the light with my hand, turned it on, and shined the beam around the cockpit. There were two large cockpit lockers. I opened them and looked inside. They were full with stuffed sail bags. I lifted up on them to see underneath. Nothing. I tried the companionway door. It was unlocked. Tahoe sailors were as trusting as vacation home owners.

"I'm going down belowdecks to look for a line. Don't move, okay?"

"You'll be right back?" Gertie's voice vibrated with fear.

"It won't take more than a minute to see if I can find a line."

I stepped down through the companionway and used the flashlight to look around. The boat was neat and clean. The cabin was spacious but only six feet tall at the highest point, so I had to duck as I moved around.

The main cabin was both a galley and saloon with a settee area that had a dining table and a bench seat. Forward of the galley was the head, and past that, the V-berth visible in the forward stateroom.

There were many storage lockers and galley drawers. Near the head was a clothes closet. Probably, none of them would hold lines or other sailing tools.

At the base of the companionway was the chart table and on it a marine radio. If the boat's battery was charged, I could call for help. But I'd underestimated Mikhailo and his men regarding the ghost boat. They could have a scanner and be listening. I didn't want to take the chance. Not this night, anyway. Gertie needed a break from trauma, and we both needed sleep.

I'd wait to use the radio until I had a plan for our next move.

Next to the chart table was a narrow closet. I opened the door. On the floor were rubber boots. Hanging on hooks were two sets of foul weather clothes, hooded jackets and waterproof pants. In cubbyholes were several flashlights and gloves. On another hook were nylon lines, neatly coiled. I took one of the coils and went back up to the cockpit.

Gertie was still standing in the tippy kayak, hanging onto the lifeline cable with both hands. I could hear her teeth chattering. The snowflakes were now visible in the night. They'd grown to medium size, and they floated to the lake like those in a snow globe.

"I have a line," I whispered as I tied one end of it to a cleat on the sailboat.

Working together, Gertie and I got her and the kayak safely aboard. I was able to lash the kayak in place along the cabin roof. I used slip knots so that I could free the kayak in a hurry if I needed to.

Gertie's shivering had increased.

"Let's get you inside and warmed up," I whispered.

I shined the flashlight so that she could see the steps of the companionway. We went down. She sat on the settee. I closed the companionway door behind us. I shined the flashlight into the galley cupboards and drawers and looked for candles. I knew there were cabin lights, but I didn't want to turn them on for fear they would be too bright and alert anyone on shore. A candle would be dimmer, but I couldn't find any.

I turned back toward Gertie and saw a hurricane candle lantern hanging on a hook above the settee table. On the cabin wall nearby was a shelf. The shelf had holes cut into it. Inserted into the holes were jars for organizing small items. One of the jars had matches. I lit the hurricane lantern. The single flame was too bright for comfort. In one of the galley drawers, I'd seen a dish towel. I draped it around the outside of the lantern, careful not to let it go over the top edge where the heat from the candle would be hottest. Now the candle light was dim.

While Gertie sat and shivered, I moved around the cabin and into the forward stateroom to make sure that all of the drapes were shut tight over the little windows and portholes.

In the main closet, I found some sweaters. One was woman-sized. I helped Gertie get my wet jacket off and pull the sweater on.

There was a built-in propane heater near the settee. It had an electronic ignition. I followed the procedure for turning on the gas, then pressed the ignition button. The little pop of spark fired several times, and then the pilot lit. I turned up the thermostat, and the burner turned on. In moments we had a blast of warm air coming into the cabin.

There was little to eat in the galley. I found some bottled water and a bag of dried cranberries. We munched them in the near dark of the draped lantern as the heater made the space warm.

"We'll spend the night on this boat," I said. "There's a large bed in the forward stateroom. You can sleep there. I'll sleep here on the fold-out settee."

"I've never slept on a boat," Gertie said. "Is it... safe?"

"Yeah. Cozy, too. I saw several sleeping bags. You'll be warm. And the gentle rocking of the waves is the best sleep aid there is."

"How will we ever get back to the shore without those men finding us?"

"We'll go to a different shore. If the weather is okay in the morning, we'll sail across the lake. The men won't know where we spent the night or where we're going. They may even think we died in the boat collision."

Gertie was quiet for a bit. "So you think we're finally safe?"

To hear the question from a traumatized girl was heartbreaking. Kids should all have shelter and food and clothes and, perhaps even more important, love. But safety was the number one thing a kid should be able to expect.

"Yeah, Gertie. I could be wrong, but I think we're finally safe."

FORTY-FOUR

"When you say we'll sail this boat, how does that work? I've never been on a sailboat."

"It's just like you imagine from pictures you've seen."

"Do you know how to drive it?"

"Yeah. I've never rigged a boat exactly like this one, but they all operate on the same principle. It shouldn't be difficult."

Gertie thought about it. "What if the wind is blowing the wrong way?"

Her question was a good sign. She was thinking about something other than the terror she'd been through.

"That's what's cool about sailboats," I said. "You can sail any direction regardless of which way the wind is blowing."

"That doesn't make sense," she said. "What if the wind blows hard from, like, the north and you want to go north?"

"Well, you can't actually sail directly into the wind. But you can sail somewhat into the wind. So you go northeast, then you turn and go northwest. It's called sailing close to the wind or beating upwind. When you turn back and forth, that's called tacking or coming about. You'll see how it works tomorrow. It's fun. You'll love it."

"I doubt it. I was on a Jet Ski once. That's fun because you have all this power, and you can race around any direction you want. But having no power and having to do tacking or whatever to go, it seems lame compared to a power boat."

"Power boats are great," I said. "They go fast, and they are very fun, especially small power boats. But power boats make noise and they create smelly exhaust like trucks and cars. It's impossible to hear the birds and the waves and the natural wind when you're on a power boat. It's impossible to smell the pine trees and flower scents blowing from the nearest shore."

Gertie looked skeptical.

"Most of the time, sailing is about quiet and calm, about contemplation," I said. "On a sailboat, you're using your wits and smarts to extract your power from the wind. It's one of the oldest kind of transports that man ever invented. Sailing can take you anywhere in the world. So when you go out on a sailboat, there's a historical connection that takes you back to the great seamen who first explored the planet. The Vikings, Columbus, Magellan, Captain Cook. The Polynesians who populated all the islands in the Pacific. You feel that history when you're on a sailboat."

"You talk about it like sailing is art or something."

"It is. There's a kind of poetry to sailing. You think about the rhythms of nature. You watch the birds to sense the coming breezes, even the weather. You study the waves to see squalls. You see the fish jump. You can talk without shouting. Sailing connects you to the beauty of movement, the beauty of nature. It even gives you an appreciation for math and physics because that is what makes a sailboat go."

Gertie looked at the candle flame.

The subject was a good mood change from the fear of being pursued by killers, so I continued my little talk.

"I think of sailing as a cousin to kayaking and canoeing, bicycling and hiking. It's transport that doesn't burn gasoline. And a sailboat, its sails filled with wind, is one of the most beautiful things there is to see. It's romantic. You'll think I'm nuts for saying it, but sailing is like using a candle compared to using an electric light. It still gets the job done but has much more warmth and beauty than those things that require technology."

"You're like a sailing pep club or something."

"Yeah, maybe."

There was a jar of toothpicks in one of the shelf holes. Gertie pulled out a pick and stuck it through one of the openings in the hurricane lantern, touching the pick to the flame. When it lit, she pulled it out and watched it burn.

"So if you think sailing is about beauty, does that mean you think beauty is important in everything?" Gertie blew out the toothpick. It issued a smoke plume. She drew ellipses with it in the air.

"I think it's good to find beauty where you can. It makes you appreciate life more."

"What about people? Is it important for people to be beautiful?"

I saw where she was going with her question. I paused before answering. "There are lots of kinds of beauty. I assume you're referring to physical beauty. That is the only kind of beauty that doesn't matter. Beauty based on things outside of your control is meaningless and ephemeral. Beauty based on qualities you can create is meaningful and long-lasting."

"So even though the whole world is fixated on beautiful celebrities, you don't care if someone is physically beautiful?" she asked. There was a hardness and a wariness in her voice.

"Some people are born beautiful. To me they're like flowers. They're nice to look at, but their beauty doesn't impress me."

"Why wouldn't you be impressed?"

"Because physical beauty comes from the luck of birth, from DNA, from genetics. Some people win the lottery. Lucky for them. But it's not impressive. Except for good grooming, you can't do a great deal about the way you look."

"If you're not impressed by physical beauty, what are you impressed by?"

"I'm impressed by a person who gets results from their effort, not from their natural gifts. If a person succeeds in spite of disadvantages, that's someone to celebrate. But if a person succeeds through the luck of birth, there's nothing impressive about it."

"You're telling me you don't look at pretty flowers?"

"No, I'm not saying that. I do notice pretty flowers. But I think they're lucky. I don't think they're any better for it."

"Men don't have a clue what it's like to suffer prejudice. The rudeness of people who fixate on beauty."

"That's mostly true. But it does affect men, too."

"How?" Gertie asked.

"I read a study about the CEOs of the Fortune Five Hundred companies – those are the chiefs of the biggest corporations in the world. They include several women, but generally, they're mostly men, and other than the heads of the countries with the biggest economies, they are the most powerful men in the world. It turns out that on average, the company CEOs and presidents are taller than average by a substantial amount, they have more hair than the average guy, they are thinner than average, and they are better looking than the average guy, although that last concept is obviously subjective."

"What does subjective mean?"

"It's sort of like personal opinion that can't be verified by any facts. There are, of course, notable exceptions to the rule of CEO looks, but the principle is solid. It even carries over to our country's presidents. If you go back through all of the presidents, in a majority of the elections, the winners were taller and had more hair."

"Really?"

"Again, there have been notable exceptions, but yeah, people take those preferences into the voting booth. So what about the guys who are short or bald or fat or all of the above? Do they matter less? Should we pay them less, value them less, promote them less? Of course not. But when a company's board of directors chooses its next president and CEO, they are invariably affected by the looks of the candidates. More often than not, they choose the tall, handsome male. While it's true that these issues affect women much more than men, men still have to deal with it."

"Beautiful people have so many advantages," Gertie said. "They get favors and jobs and attention and opportunities. It's not fair."

"You're right, it's not. But those who realize that life is unfair can turn that knowledge to their advantage."

"How?"

"By not trying to compete on the level of physical beauty."

Gertie looked up at me.

"If you're a short, bald guy," I said, "instead of investing time into putting lifts in your shoes and getting a lofty hairpiece, you can put your energy into your skills and climb your way up in spite of not having physical advantages. I remember that you are interested in movies. You want to be a director, right? Well, a woman interested in movies can study them and practice writing them. You can make videos and learn from the reactions while you – what did you call it? – formulate your debut."

Gertie made a little smile.

"This is all stuff that you can work on while other girls are fussing about their looks."

Some wax had pooled at the bottom of the lantern. It broke through an opening and ran out onto the table in a thick pool.

I used my fingernail to shape it into something like a fir tree. Then I picked up Gertie's burnt toothpick and drew some branches on it.

"Some kids make fun of the way I look," she said, finally getting to the reason she brought up the subject.

"Then those kids are either immature or stupid or both. The appropriate response is to ignore them and remind yourself that you are far beyond them in terms of ambition, drive, self-education, and so forth. Look at all you've learned about Noir movies while they learned about makeup or pickup trucks."

"But I'll never have the opportunities that the beautiful kids have."

"No, you won't. But I think you're ultimately better off as a result."

"That's ridiculous. What could possibly be better about being homely and having a cleft lip?"

"Several things."

Gertie scoffed.

"Hear me out. First, beautiful people get so much handed to them that they never learn as many valuable skills as other people learn, skills that help you make it through life. Then, in the middle of life, when their youthful beauty begins to fade, the attention and the advantages fade, too. Without attention, they often flounder and sometimes collapse. Without skills, they sometimes find they have no way to earn a good living anymore. Of course, many former beauties cope. People are adaptable. But other former beauties feel like dried up flowers, left alone and passed over for the next crop of beauties. Many Hollywood celebrity actors stop getting job offers when they turn forty. Models stop getting job offers at thirty or thirty-five. Just when people start to really know something, their beauty advantage goes away, and they suffer. Meanwhile, directors are just getting warmed up. And, as you must know from looking at directors, no one cares what they look like.

"The second advantage to not being beautiful is that you get to operate under the radar. You get the gift of privacy. If you were beautiful and tried to make a movie, you'd be scrutinized intensely just when you really wanted to be left alone and out of the spotlight while you developed your chops. If the first movie of a beautiful director was bad or even embarrassing, everyone would gossip about it and write bad reviews of it. The scrutiny would be excruciating. Whereas, the non-beautiful director doesn't get much attention for her failures. She will be comfortably overlooked until she creates a hit.

"But maybe the best part of not being beautiful is that you get credit for your accomplishments. When a beauty succeeds at something, the world says that she got her acclaim for her beauty as much as anything she accomplished. People remark that anyone can be successful when they're beautiful, and the hard-won accomplishment is dismissed. And if the beauty fails, the condemnation is more severe because people will say, 'How could a person fail when they have so many advantages?' By comparison, the accolades bestowed on the accomplishments of people with ordinary looks are sincere.

"Gertie, when the day comes that you direct a good film, you will get genuine praise and admiration. No one will take away your accomplishment and say that you really don't have ability and that you only succeeded because of your beauty."

Gertie was still bent over the table. She made a slow nod without looking up.

She said, "You said that there are lots of kinds of beauty and that physical beauty is the one kind that doesn't matter. What are the kinds that do matter?"

"Well, I haven't thought about it much, but there are many. Passion, desire, interest, hunger for ideas, charity, attention, focus, kindness, and skills that you acquire through practice and hard work. Like your softball pitching. No one is born knowing how to do that. You learned that through constant practice. Your pitching is the kind of beauty I'm impressed with. These are all the things you have control over. These are the kinds of things that can make you beautiful in ways that are a thousand times more important than how you look."

We sat in silence for a bit.

"I want to tell you one more thing," I said, "but I worry that it will weaken my earlier point, so please keep those things in mind."

Another slow nod. "What is it?"

"My hobby is studying art. I'm no expert, but I like art. I'm kind of like a little kid with a picture book. I like to look at the pictures that people make. I have a bunch of books on art, and in some of them, the artists talk about what makes something art. Of course, I'm pretty naive about this stuff, so don't take me as an expert. But anyway, one of the categories of picture art is portraits. I've looked at a lot of them over the years. And I've learned something interesting. When it comes to portraits, those of beautiful people are almost never as interesting as those of people who aren't beautiful. Physical beauty in people, for all of its pleasantness, doesn't make you think or wonder as much as when you look at interesting-looking people.

"So here's where I'm going with all of this. You don't think you're beautiful. But I think you have a very interesting face, and I'm hoping you agree with that. And talking to someone with an interesting face is more interesting than talking to someone who has a perfect, pretty face."

"But do artists do much of that?" Gertie said. "Paint people who aren't beautiful?"

"Absolutely. In fact, some of the most famous portrait artists today are Lucian Freud and Chuck Close and my favorite, David Hockney. The portraits they make are captivating. Fascinating. And to my knowledge, none of them ever did a portrait of a beautiful person. They only paint people who have intriguing faces. For them, beauty is nothing compared to intrigue."

"You're just saying that to make me feel better."

"No. It's what I care about. Maybe someday you'll meet my girlfriend. Her name is Street Casey. I think she's wonderful, and to me, she's beautiful. She has a fascinating face. But it's not what other people would think of as beautiful. She's all angles and has acne scars."

"But you think she's beautiful."

"Yeah. It's all those other kinds of beauty that I mentioned. I like looking at her face because it intrigues me. It has character. Someday, if not already, people will think that about you, too."

Gertie looked down at my wax tree. She seemed pensive to a greater degree.

"What is that?" she said.

"My name is Irish, Scottish, and Welsh, which all have Celtic origins. This is a fir tree, an important symbol for the Celtic people." I turned the wax tree over and used the toothpick to scratch an F, H, R, and S into the wax. "The Celts said that the fir represents Friendship, Honesty, Resilience, and Strength. These are real characteristics of beauty, and I think you have them."

I picked up the wax tree and handed it to Gertie. "This is for you."

She took it and stared at it.

"My name's O'Leary," she said, "so I have a Celtic background, too."

I smiled, and we sat in silence for a bit.

I'd said enough, so I went into the forward stateroom and spread out a couple of the sleeping bags for her. I came back and handed her the flashlight.

Gertie carefully closed her hand around the wax fir tree and went to the front of the boat. I folded and lowered the dining table to be level with the settee base. Then I pulled out the settee cushions and blew out the hurricane lantern.

It was a very comfortable bed, which, even though I slept diagonally, was still six inches too short.

My feet hung out, and Gertie was troubled, and there were still men out there who wanted to kill both of us.

But we were safe for now.

FORTY-FIVE

I couldn't sleep. All night long I heard thumps and bumps and possible voices. Waves that seemed too big splashed up against the sailboat's hull. Once, I thought I heard the hum of another ghost boat. Each time I got concerned, I opened the companionway door and went up topside, stood in the dark, snowflakes still falling, and listened. The noises that I'd heard below were not there. Back down in the cabin, I remembered that sound travels underwater like it travels through steel. It might well be possible to hear the hum of a far-off engine through the sailboat's hull and have it be impossible to hear through the air.

By the time morning came, I was more exhausted than I'd been before. But Gertie was still asleep and safe. I didn't know if the onboard water was potable, so I dipped water out of the lake to make coffee, finding some old instant coffee powder in a jar. There was a teakettle to heat water on the propane stove top.

I took my coffee topside and drank it while I brushed three inches of fresh snow off the boat and its rigging.

I was on my second cup when Gertie came out of the head and said, "What's for breakfast?" She had a smile on her face. It was obviously good to have put some hours between her and her would-be killers.

"We have more cranberries. Or you can eat anything you want once we get this crate down to the South Shore of the lake and stop at the Red Hut Café."

"What is it, a drive-in restaurant for boats?"

"No. But it's just across from the Ski Run Marina where we'll dock and call for help."

"How long will it take?"

"It's a long way, maybe ten miles. The wind has shifted out of the north, and it's a pretty good breeze. It stopped snowing, and the cloud ceiling has moved up to over ten thousand feet. So all the mountains are visible and navigation will be easy. It'll be a straight shot on a broad reach. If we average six or seven knots, we'll be there in an hour and a half, give or take."

"You're saying we have to sail ten miles before we can even eat breakfast." She put her hands on her hips in mock critique.

"Yup. I also have to get the boat rigged and sails hoisted. But it's worth it to avoid those men who are after us. And if you help, that'll speed things up."

"How can I help?"

I opened the narrow closet where I'd found the foul weather gear. I pulled out the smaller waterproof jacket, flotation vest, and waterproof gloves and handed them to Gertie. There was a green scarf and a red kerchief hanging in the closet. I stretched the kerchief out, long and flat. While I was still bent into the closet and out of Gertie's view, I tied it around my head so it covered one of my eyes.

I turned around, squinted at Gertie with my other eye, and said, "Aye, me hearty lass, get ye topside, and I'll show ye how to be hoistin' me colors."

Gertie laughed, saluted me, and said, "Aye, matey."

"Well shiver me timbers, we got us a pirate," I said.

I put on the other, larger, waterproof jacket and flotation vest, and with Gertie's help, I pulled the sail bags out of the storage lockers in the cockpit. We sorted the mainsail from the jib, threaded it onto the boom and started sliding it into the base of the mast track. With the halyard line hooked on, it was ready to hoist.

The jib sail was next. Gertie did most of the work rigging the jib as I explained the process.

I was checking the rudder wheel, the compass, and other gear when I noticed that the boom wouldn't clear the kayak. So I untied the kayak, shifted it farther forward, and secured it again.

When we were ready, I said, "Avast me hearty, prepare the cannons fer a blast o'er the blue, and we be off."

I pointed to the cockpit and Gertie, giggling, sat down on

the cockpit bench.

I remembered the green scarf in the closet below decks and went down to fetch it.

I climbed out to the bow, lay down, and leaned out to reach the mooring buoy. I tied the green scarf to the buoy to mark which one belonged to the sailboat, then unhooked the bow line. We began to drift away. I hoisted the jib. The wind caught it and turned the boat downwind. We began moving at slow speed toward the South Shore. I moved back to the cockpit and set the rudder wheel where I wanted it.

Gertie watched with great attention when I showed her how the boom swung back and forth, and I mimed how it could hit me on the head. She nodded understanding. As I hoisted the halyard, the mainsail rose and filled with wind. The boom swung out to starboard and strained at the sheet line, and the boat sped up by a factor of four or five.

Gertie laughed and bounced on her seat. The wind made the sails crackle as they stretched out long-pressed wrinkles and folds. I had her stand behind the wheel, and I showed her how to steer.

"Me enemy scallywag buccaneers took me doubloons to hide at the Ski Run Marina," I said. "Yer steering target be that mountain thar." I pointed at ten thousand-foot Heavenly, 15 miles distant.

Gertie kept a steady course southeast. We came out of the lee of the Meeks Bay Point to the north and moved into an area where our tailwind increased to a strong steady breeze of maybe fifteen miles per hour. The wind shifted to northwest. We went from a broad reach to running downwind.

Time to check the spinnaker.

Gertie was a focused skipper as I got out the spinnaker sail in its sock. The spinnaker is something you can only use when you're sailing on a downwind course. A striking contrast to the triangular mainsail and jib, the spinnaker is as huge and bulbous as a hot-air balloon. And like a balloon, it is usually made of brilliant colors. Looking into the sock, I saw that this one was yellow, orange, and red panels. Spinnakers can explode in too much wind, but this one appeared to be heavy enough to handle the current breeze, and it looked in good shape.

On many sailboats, when you use the spinnaker, you don't use the jib, so I dropped the jib and rigged the spinnaker lines.

When the sock, with the spinnaker inside it, was in place and ready, I shouted, "Arr, me hearty, raise yer grog fer toastin' and be tight on yer lines. This gale ain't fer the lily-livered!"

I raised the sock. The spinnaker came out. The wind rushed into the spinnaker, and the sail blew open and formed a huge, hot-colored balloon out in front of the boat. It snapped into place with a thunderous clap. The sailboat immediately accelerated to high speed.

Still wearing the red kerchief over one eye, I put my shoulder against the headstay, the front-most cable that runs to the top of the mast. Braced against it, I leaned forward over the bow, and raised my arms out wide like a conquering pirate flying into the wind. Back in the cockpit, Gertie whooped and shrieked with excitement.

FORTY-SIX

The Nāmaka ran well with the wind, pitching little despite a rolling swell that got bigger as we went south. With increasing distance of windswept water behind us, the waves would be pushing four feet by the time we got to the South Shore. There was little to do but steer for the next 40 minutes. Because we were running with the wind, it didn't blow strongly in relation to us. But the windchill was still significant. Gertie was wrapped up in my jacket with the foul weather gear on top of that. With her back to the wind, she looked warm enough.

"I assume you knew your stepdad?" I said. I sat on the rear bench of the cockpit. Gertie stood behind the wheel, making careful adjustments as the boat shifted with the wind and waves.

Gertie snorted. "I met him once. And it wasn't at their wedding. I wasn't invited. Mom called later and invited me to San Francisco. Dad gave me permission to go. Mom said we could do whatever and go wherever I wanted. So I said I wanted to visit all the locations where Hitchcock's "Vertigo" was filmed. Mission Delores and the Golden Gate and Lombard Street and the Palace of the Legion of Honor and Coit Tower. So mom picked me up and drove me to the Bay Area."

"Was it fun?"

"No. We didn't go to any of the places I wanted. She brought me to her house in the South Bay and said that things had come up, so if I wanted to meet her new husband, it would have to be at Starbucks. Mom knows I don't like coffee, but she and Ian do. So they took me to Starbucks in Santa Clara, and I had a cookie and water while they fussed over fancy coffees and discussed what time it would be best to go to the De Young art museum where Ian had to attend some kind of meeting."

"Tell me you went to the museum?" I asked.

"I said maybe we could all go there together, but mom said I wouldn't like it, that it was for adults."

"More fallout from unwanted child status?"

"That," Gertie said, "and mom's continuing embarrassment to be seen with me. She always has the perfect hair, perfect makeup, and perfect outfit like she's a model or something. Wouldn't want to be seen with the imperfect daughter, would we?"

"Did they go to the museum without you?"

"Yeah. They had a babysitter come over. So I spent most of my visit talking to a Mexican girl not much older than me. She was nice. But that was the closest I ever got to Hitchcock."

"And you went nowhere else?"

"No. I told mom maybe she could at least take me to San Carlos so I could see where Kathryn Bigelow was from."

"Who's that?"

"The only woman who's ever won a Best Director Oscar. It was for "The Hurt Locker." I thought it would give me inspiration to see where she was born."

"And San Carlos is just up the peninsula from Santa Clara," I said.

Gertie shook her head. "Mom said San Carlos was too far and that Santa Clara was nicer, anyway."

"I don't know what to say, Gertie. I suppose your parents could have been worse, but, short of beating on you, it's not clear how."

Gertie looked off the side of the boat at the water rushing by.

"So Ian wasn't like a stepdad to you?"

Gertie laughed. "Other than that one time at Starbucks, I only spoke to him once more. On the phone."

"How did that happen? Was he trying to reach Merrill and got stuck talking to you instead?"

"No, he called me."

"Really?"

"Yeah," Gertie said. "I was shocked. The phone rang one night. My dad answered and then gave the phone to me."

"What did Ian want?"

"He said he'd heard from mom about how I was into films and how I'd made some short videos with my phone. He said he wanted to make a film, and he wanted my advice."

"Do you think he really wanted advice, or was he trying to flatter you?"

"It turns out he actually wanted advice. Of course, I was flattered that he would ask me. But later I realized he would rather have asked someone else if he knew someone to call who didn't know his associates. Instead, I was the only person he knew he could ask who wouldn't be able to spread the word to anyone in his circle that he was asking about filmmaking."

"Any idea what kind of film he wanted to make?" I asked.

"Not really. He said it was going to be a cross between fiction and documentary. I asked if he meant docufiction or docudrama, and he didn't know the difference."

"I don't either," I said.

"Docufiction is like a documentary with a real person playing his real life, but it adds some made-up stuff to help make its point. Docudrama is kind of the opposite. It's pretty much all made up and it has actors playing the parts. But it's inspired by real events. Docufiction is more real than docudrama."

"After you explained that, did he say which direction he was going?"

"No. I think he didn't want me to know. But I also think that he didn't have a clue what he wanted."

"What did he want from you?"

"It was more like equipment questions. Do you need a fancy camera, and was everything digital now, or did they still use film, and what was the best kind of editing software, and did I know if there was a short class anywhere that taught all the basics."

"Did you give him answers?"

"Yeah," Gertie said. "I told him about the basic filmmaking summer program at USC. But I warned him that it was real expensive and intensive, too. You can't do it online. You have to be there every day for six weeks. He said that price wasn't an object and time wasn't an object, either."

Gertie went silent, then looked away. After a minute, she

said, "He could plan an entire summer going to USC and buy a zillion-dollar digital setup and probably live in an expensive hotel and hang out by the pool while he played with his new camera, but he and mom couldn't take me to the Golden Gate because it took too much time."

"More fallout," I muttered, more aware than ever that a simple childhood like mine – with two parents who cared about you, whatever their flaws – is something that huge numbers of kids never experience.

She nodded. Wiped the back of her hand across her eyes.

"Have you ever been to the Golden Gate?" I asked, almost not wanting to hear the answer.

"No," she said. "It's been a great ride, this being a kid thing."

We sailed for awhile without talking.

"When did you find out that Ian had been killed in the boating accident?"

"I got an email from my mom a few days after it happened."

She said it with no drama, just a simple statement that made me wince.

The wind shifted a little just as we crested a large wave and started surfing down the front side. The boat yawed a bit to port. I reached out and pointed to the right. "Just a bit," I said.

Gertie eased the wheel a touch to starboard.

"Where did you learn about filmmaking?" I asked, thinking it would be better to go back to the previous subject. "Did you go to the USC summer program?"

"Are you kidding? I'm fifteen. My real dad has no money. Whatever money my mom has goes for shoes and makeup. Just the summer program at USC is something like twelve thousand for six weeks, and that's just tuition."

"Your mom's clothes are more important than your education," I said.

"Of course," Gertie said. "Everything I know about filmmaking comes from reading blogs on it. Not like I know that much. But no money means I have to be a DIY person."

Maybe I frowned.

"Do It Yourself," she said.

"Ah."

"I've also learned a lot by watching great films. DIY can be a pretty good way to go. Did you know that Steven Spielberg applied twice to USC Film School, and he was rejected both times? Talk about an 'Oops' moment. Somewhere there's a USC decision maker who's the butt of jokes."

"I didn't know that about Spielberg. Was he a high school dropout, too? Like all those other directors and actors you mentioned?"

"No. And he did get into Cal State Long Beach. So he actually went to college for awhile. But then he dropped out of that." Gertie said it with satisfaction.

"Pity the potential film hero who'd lose your respect because he or she finished college," I said.

"Right," Gertie said, sounding serious. "Did you know that when Spielberg directed "Jaws," he got one of his greatest ideas from watching Hitchcock films?" Gertie said.

"No. What was that?"

"It's a motif." She looked at me to see if I comprehended. "A motif is..."

"Something you learned from the Tarantino interview?" I interrupted.

Gertie grinned. "Right. It's kind of like a design element in a film. Something that repeats and builds power through the repetition. Well, anyway, in "Jaws" there is a motif of the shark's fin cruising through the water. Why show the whole shark, when just the fin is more ominous? Hitchcock often did that where less is more. Instead of showing someone getting killed up close, just show the shadow of the murderer killing the victim. Showing less can be more powerful because the viewer fills in the rest."

"I remember," I said. "The shark fin in the water was really creepy."

"Yeah, and "Jaws" became the highest grossing film of all time. Then Spielberg directed "E.T.," and it became the new highest grossing film of all time. Then he did "Jurassic Park," and it did even better than "E.T." And all along, Spielberg got critical raves and won Academy Awards like Best Director for "Schindler's List." So naturally, a few decades later, USC came crawling on hands and knees, asking if they could please give him an honorary degree. Probably just hoping he'd drop a billion on them in his will."

"You're kind of a cynic, huh?" I said.

"Live and learn," Gertie said.

"I have a hypothetical question," I said.

"Hypothetical?" Gertie grinned. "Did you learn that from an interview?"

"Probably," I said. "If you ever got a chance to go to a good college, you wouldn't turn it down just to remain pure and unsullied by the world of academia, would you?"

She thought about it. "Depends on if they had a good film school."

"Like USC or UCLA?" I said.

"Or AFI," she said.

"What's that?"

"American Film Institute. Only maybe the best there is. But it won't happen. You have to be rich. And anyway, AFI is like a graduate school. Or what do they call it? A conservatory. Pretty snooty." Gertie put her thumbs together and then her forefingers together to make a circle and held her hands above her head like a halo. "They're all so special. And anyway, it's all old people who go there."

"How old?"

"Real old. I read that the average age is twenty-seven. And they only give out Masters of Fine Arts, so if I wanted to get a Bachelor's degree in Filmmaking, I'd have to go to USC or UCLA or one of those fancy East Coast schools. But I can still study Hitchcock on my own."

"Good idea," I said. "Did Hitchcock drop out of high school?"

"I don't know. I'll have to Google it. But if he didn't, maybe he dropped out of college like Spielberg."

I grinned at her.

"Do you know what most people think is the most exclusive

club in the world?" she asked.

"No, what?"

"People who get a college degree from Harvard. But that's not true. The actual most exclusive club in the world is people who drop out of Harvard. Microsoft's Bill Gates. Facebook's Mark Zuckerberg. William Randolph Hearst, the guy who ran the San Francisco Examiner and built the Hearst Castle. Bonnie Raitt the rock star. Robert Frost the poet. And, oh yeah, the movie star Matt Damon. Those are the richest, most successful people of all."

"Wait," I said. "You're telling me that Matt Damon didn't drop out of high school? And you still respect him? I'm shocked."

"Right. He had to wait until he got into Harvard."

"So do you still want to drop out of high school?" I said.

"I do. But it would be even cooler to drop out of Harvard. That would guarantee that people would pay attention to whatever I film."

"Isn't making really good films the best way to get people to pay attention?"

"How is anyone gonna know they're good if no one notices them in the first place?"

"You're a hard kid to argue with."

We were getting close to the South Shore, so I turned my attention to sailing. As we swept in toward the Ski Run Marina, I worried that my sailing skills wouldn't be sufficient to bring a large sailboat up to the dock without damage. Like landing a plane, landing a sailboat is much trickier than taking off, especially landing downwind.

I aimed for a point a hundred yards northeast of the pier where the Tahoe Queen was docked. When we were still well out from shore, I took down the spinnaker and stowed it.

We were running downwind on a port tack. I touched Gertie's shoulder and pointed at the mainsail and boom, which were projecting off the right side of the boat.

"We're going to jibe to starboard, otherwise known as turning to the right. When we do that, the sail and boom are going to blow across the boat from right to left." I pointed. "It will come fast, so you'll want to keep your head below this level." I held my hand up.

She nodded. "Got it."

I turned the wheel and began the turn. I pulled in on the sheet line, bringing the sail toward the center line. When the wind crossed to starboard, the sail swung to the left. We continued to turn until we were on a beam reach, sailing across the wind toward the big Tahoe Queen sternwheeler. I steered toward the base of the pier, behind the Queen, letting out the sail to minimize the wind power. When I got close to the pier, I turned upwind and let the sail luff in the breeze, which was lighter in the wind shadow of the Queen. We coasted toward the dock. When we were ten feet away, I realized that we were coming in too fast. I ran to the bow, waited a moment, then jumped off onto the pier. I turned around, reached my hands out to the sailboat's bow and pushed with all of my strength, slowing the boat, shifting its direction. The boat came to a stop inches from the pier. I grabbed the bow line and tied it to a post, then dropped the dock fenders to hang down outside the boat and protect its hull from damage as it jostled against the pier.

I fastened a stern line, then a spring line to keep the boat from shifting. When the boat was secure, I climbed back on board. I dropped the mainsail so that there would be no significant wind force bumping the boat against the pier. I didn't remove the sail, but found some bungies to wrap around it. With the mainsail still rigged, it would be easy to hoist when it came time to sail away.

"C'mon, Gertie, let's go get that breakfast."

She jumped off the boat, and we walked down the pier.

A man came running and shouted at us.

"Hey, you can't leave your boat there!"

"Sorry, it's not my boat."

"But I saw you come in and tie it up."

"That was an emergency landing. You'll be hearing from the police in about twenty minutes."

"You still can't leave it there. It's blocking our operations."

"I'm just the guy who managed to land the plane when the pilot couldn't be found. Pure luck. I wouldn't even know how to sail it away."

I led Gertie out the access road, past the marina, and across Lake Tahoe Boulevard. While Gertie talked, I looked at all the nearby vehicles.

Nothing stood out until we walked into the parking lot of the Red Hut Café. Gertie gasped.

"What?"

She pointed. There was a white cargo van near the restaurant door.

FORTY-SEVEN

I pulled Gertie to the side of the café, out of sight from the van. We stepped behind some bushes.

"Stay here," I said.

I crept around the side of the building.

The cargo van was just pulling away. It was a painting contractor with a large logo painted on the side panel.

"All clear," I said when I came back to Gertie.

We went inside the restaurant.

"Hi, Mr. McKenna," a young woman I recognized said. "Table for two?"

"Yes, please. Also, I lost my cell. May I borrow your phone for two short calls?"

"Sure." She pointed to one. "I'll get you your table as soon as you're done."

"Thanks."

Gertie stayed near me while I dialed Sergeant Santiago. He answered.

"Owen McKenna calling," I said.

"The same McKenna who apparently abandoned his dog in his Jeep halfway up the mountain above Rubicon Bay?"

"You found Spot," I said.

"Cold and hungry, but okay. Of course, he's no longer cold and hungry."

"Where is he?"

"First, he was in the back of my patrol unit. I thought about calling animal control but decided he'd rather hang out at the sheriff's office in Tahoe City. So we fed him and last I looked he was... Hold on while I check again. Yep, he's still sound asleep in front of the heat vent."

"What did you feed him?"

"One of our deputies was making a run to McDonald's in Truckee, so he brought back some extra Big Macs." Santiago paused. "That's okay, right? He sure seemed to like them."

"He was probably just being polite. How many did you give him?"

"Three, I think. Except Lance didn't eat all of his second one, so your hound maybe had that, too. Oh, and there were some extra orders of fries that were for a sales rep who was showing us new radios. But he had to go, so I'm pretty sure your dog ate those, too."

"He probably really misses me, huh?"

"Um, well, if eating and sleeping is the way he shows how much he misses you, then yeah, he really misses you."

"What about my Jeep?"

"Your keys were in the ignition, so two of the guys pushed it out of the snowbank, and we drove it here to the office."

"Is it okay if I pick up my dog and my Jeep later? Maybe this afternoon?"

"Sure. Any word on the kidnapped girl?"

"I found her. That's why I had to leave the Jeep and Spot. We were in a bit of a hurry to get off that mountain." I gave him the basics of where we'd been and how we stole the boat to escape. "We left it at the Ski Run Marina. I'm not sure the best way to return it."

"I'll work on it," Santiago said.

"I also have one of the bad guy's cell phones. I'll give it to you when I pick up my hound."

"Great. Hey, McKenna, I should probably tell you that someone shot up your wheels. We saw two bullet holes, and we weren't even looking for them."

"At least it didn't get blown up." I thanked him and hung up.

I called Street.

"Hey, sweetheart, I just came in with Gertie, and we're okay."

"You rescued Gertie! Thank God! I was so worried. And Diamond told me what happened to you, those men who dragged you out on the lake and dropped you in. I would've died if I'd seen them haul you off. I'm so glad you survived, I can't say..." Street broke off. I heard sniffling, her breath catch. She blew her nose, then was back.

"Is Gertie, you know, okay?" she asked.

"Yeah. She's strong. I'm impressed with her."

"I kept telling myself that you must be in an area with no cell coverage. But I've been so worried. It's been two days."

I glanced at Gertie before I spoke.

"I couldn't call because they took my cell when they gave me the little boat ride."

"What about his largeness?"

"Sergeant Santiago has been taking care of him at the Placer County office in Tahoe City. Can you give me a ride up there to fetch him and my Jeep?"

"Of course."

"Then we'll be over after we eat and I make some calls. You can meet Gertie, and we'll tell you all about our adventure."

"Okay. I'm so glad you're okay. Love you."

"Love you," I said, and hung up.

"Our adventure?" Gertie said.

"Just spinning it a little with a euphemistic phrase."

"What's euphemistic?" she asked.

"A description that makes something seem not so bad as it really is."

She thought about it. "Like when someone gets their head bashed in and their brains squish out, and the doctors say the person died from blunt force trauma?"

"Yes, exactly."

"I heard that in the Tarantino interview."

"I bet you did."

"So you use euphemistic phrasing when you talk to your girlfriend."

"Sometimes," I said.

"She can't face the truth?"

"No, she can face anything," I said. "I just try to soften the blows a little."

Gertie seemed to think about it.

The waitress brought Gertie and me to a table.

Gertie asked what was good, and I said the Owen's Omelet.

"Wow, what a coincidence that they serve an omelet with your name," she said.

"Yeah." I didn't tell her it was because I eat it all the time.

We didn't speak until we were done.

"Where will we go now?" Gertie asked.

I thought about where the men would look for us. "I'll call a cop friend and see if he can give us some cover."

Because the men took my wallet, the restaurant said I could pay the bill on my next visit. I borrowed the house phone one more time, and called Diamond. I got his voicemail, left a message, and was turning to go when the phone rang.

I answered it, "Red Hut."

"Got you on call back," Diamond said.

"Thanks." I gave him a brief explanation of where Gertie and I had been. "I'm wondering if you or one of your deputies is nearby. We could probably use a sheriff's escort for the next day or so until I get a plan."

Diamond said he'd pick us up in fifteen minutes.

Gertie and I waited near the restaurant door.

"I was thinking that I should probably call your mother and father first," I said.

"Why?"

"To tell them you are free and safe. They'll be worried. And they'll want to see you."

"But I don't want to see them. I'd rather be with you. I'm safe with you. Besides, you're nicer. They're selfish, and they've never cared about me. Let them worry. The only thing I miss is Scruff Boy. I just hope Emily took him to her house."

"Maybe I can put off arranging a visit with your parents," I said. "But I still have to call them."

"Is that, like, a law or something?"

"Probably. You're a minor. You're with a man who isn't a relative. That's fine in the short term. Very short term. If I go too long before turning you over to your legal guardian, then I become a kidnapper."

"That's totally lame. I'm here because I want to be."

"Sorry, Gertie. The world doesn't put much stock in a kid's desires."

"That's a law that adults made," she said.

"Right. Adults think they know what's best for kids."

"It's adults that kidnapped me." It looked like there were flames in Gertie's eyes.

"Yeah, we adults are a stellar group."

"Can you put off calling my parents for a bit? Please. Just give me some time to think?"

I thought about it. "I did lose my cell. And the bad guy's phone in my pocket is locked. Maybe it will take me a day to find another phone."

Gertie grinned.

"Those men..." she said.

"Yeah?" I said.

"Could they have followed us across the lake?"

"Only if they knew we were on that boat and had perfect timing and a lot of luck. They'd have to be watching the shoreline just as we rigged the boat and sailed away. Then they'd have to have access to a motorboat to follow us from a long distance, watching us through binoculars. A sailboat wouldn't do because I would have seen its sail. I watched as we sailed. I never saw any boats behind us or near us."

"What about following us by driving?" she asked. "They could see where we were going, then drive here."

"Again, it would be possible, but it would take luck. Once they saw us heading across the lake, they would have to make a guess that we were going to the South Shore and not about to turn east or even northeast. The road to the South Shore has many places where you can't see the lake. And even if they could see us getting closer to where we docked, they'd have to make a guess about whether we were going to dock at the Timber Cove pier, the Ski Run Marina pier, or any of several private docks. When they made that guess, they'd have to drive toward the lake on the closest neighborhood roads, park, and run out toward the water to try and see where we'd gone. There would also be time pressure. We got to the South Shore in less than an hour. The highway around Emerald Bay is closed. It takes almost two hours to drive from where we were on the West Shore clockwise around the lake to the South Shore, and that's if the weather is good, and you're driving fast. The bottom line is that it's hard to chase boats from shore."

Gertie seemed to relax a bit.

A horn beeped. I looked out and saw Diamond in his Douglas County vehicle. We walked out. Gertie seemed nervous, so I took the front seat, and she got in back. I introduced Diamond to Gertie, and she made a little wave from the back seat.

"You've had some excitement," Diamond said.

"Yeah." I told him all about the last couple of days, the old woman's story about the ghost boat, and how we escaped the men who chased us.

"The beefcake leader of the gang," he said. "He Mikhailo? The man Agent Ramos told us about?"

"I think so. We had the pleasure of meeting his two pals. I also think someone else is involved. When they were chasing us, one of them shouted to one of the others, something about sending in the coordinates."

"A person who might be behind the ghost boat." Diamond sound intrigued.

"Maybe," I said. "What do you know about stuff like that?"

"Ghost boats? What's there to know?"

"That's just it," I said. "I have no idea. But a worldly guy like you, I thought maybe you'd know something. How do you suppose it would work?"

"Lots of possibilities. Sending a robot boat after a moving target would be easiest if the target gave out a signal, like what you thought was the case with Gertie's sweatshirt. Could be any kind of signal as long as a receiver could pick it up."

"But how would the pursuing boat follow the signal?"

Diamond paused. "I don't think it would be hard. The receiving device would essentially operate as a negative feedback loop."

"What's that?"

"A device that monitors a directional input and adjusts in the opposite direction."

"So whatever the monitor is designed to watch, it adjusts in the opposite direction to keep the condition more or less the same," I said.

"Sí. Negative feedback leads to stasis. Positive feedback leads to a runaway condition, ever-increasing the condition you are monitoring. Look around and you'll see negative feedback loops everywhere. Cruise control on your car. Hormone levels in your body. Missile guidance systems. In this case, the receiver would be installed in the ghost boat and it would read the signal direction. The receiver would also have a control unit that can tell a boat to turn left or right. Any decent mechanic could figure out how to set up the steering mechanics. The receiver would be programmed to keep that signal at twelve o'clock so that the boat will drive toward the signal. Now let's say the receiver notices that the boat is going too far to the right in relation to the signal. It will steer to the left to bring the boat back in line with the signal it's chasing."

"So maybe Ian Lassitor was the only human skipper in his boat collision, and the other boat was a ghost boat, huh?"

"Yeah, just like you two," Diamond said as he glanced in the rearview mirror at Gertie.

Diamond dropped us at my office. "How long do you think?" he asked.

"An hour?"

"Okay. I'll stay here for now. If I have to leave, I'll make sure that I get a replacement."

"Thanks very much."

Gertie and I got out and walked up to my office. Once inside, Gertie walked around looking at my spare effects, running her finger along my desk, lifting the pot from the coffeemaker, and looking into the fridge.

I sat at my desk, dialed the SLTPD and waited to get Mallory on the line.

"McKenna," he said in my ear.

"Commander," I said. "You may have heard of a young woman named Gertie O'Leary who was kidnapped. I found her on the West Shore."

"That's great," Mallory said. "Congrats. But it's all out of my territory."

"Right. But now I'm on the South Shore, and we got here by stealing a sailboat, which we moored at the Ski Run Marina dock. Just thought you'd want to know when substantial stolen property is dumped in your jurisdiction."

"Are you planning to remove the boat soon?"

"Not real soon. Sergeant Santiago may take care of it."

Mallory thanked me for the information, and we hung up.

FORTY-EIGHT

I made another courtesy call, this one to Sergeant Bains of El Dorado County.

When I was through telling him what happened, I added, "Santiago is looking into returning the sailboat we stole. But it might be that we took it from south of the county line, in your territory."

"I'll talk to him," Bains said. "Maybe you should give all this to Glenda Gorman at the Herald. She could publish descriptions of the suspects. Never know who might recognize these jerks."

"Maybe. I'll have to ponder the downside potential, first. You still sweet on her?"

"We're on again, off again. As you know, she's real attractive, both mental and physical and all that. But she's kind of a powerhouse personality. I have to have high energy just to talk to her. All those questions and opinions. Do you and Street ever just sit in front of the fire and listen to music?"

"Yeah. Music and other stuff."

"Other stuff that doesn't require a big discussion. Like... Never mind. Don't answer that. It'll just make me feel bad."

I thanked him for his time and said goodbye.

I next called FBI Special Agent Ramos, told him what happened, and said that the man in charge seemed like Mikhailo the Monster. "Except, I think he's just an employee," I said. "At one point, the man I think is Mikhailo shouted about sending in the coordinates. Maybe that was just a catch phrase. But it might indicate a fourth person."

"That fits with what I just heard," Ramos said.

I waited.

"Remember when you first told me about Gertie O'Leary going missing and being possibly kidnapped?"

"Yeah?" I said.

"You said the girl's uncle Ellison O'Leary had admitted selling information about the girl's whereabouts right before she was kidnapped?"

"Right," I said, aware that Gertie was listening to my side of the converstation. I pressed the phone against my ear to minimize the chance that Gertie would hear Ramos revealing the true side of her uncle.

"So you handed him over to the Sacramento police," Ramos said. "Yesterday, one of our Sacramento informants told us about a guy he knew who was pulling down a big scam and said that the guy had originally wanted to recruit him for help."

I said, "And the guy running the scam was..."

"Ellison O'Leary," Ramos said. "We don't have any evidence as yet. And this informant has not demonstrated the greatest reliability in the past. But if Ellison isn't involved, that's quite a coincidence that this informant mentions Ellison's name in connection with a big scam, and then Ellison's niece is kidnapped, and the niece's mother is due to collect a large insurance payout."

"Have you talked to him about it, yet?"

"No. He posted bail and has disappeared."

The news put heat in my face and heart. The only reason I didn't immediately drive down to Sacramento and shake Merrill for information about his brother was that I had Gertie safe.

"One more thing," Ramos said.

"What's that?"

"The kickboxing Dock Artist who you thought might be Mikhailo?"

"Yeah?"

"He's disappeared. His shop is locked, his fence gate is locked, his white cargo van is gone, and the workers at the convenience store haven't seen him."

I thanked Ramos and hung up.

The phone rang. It was Santiago.

"So you don't know where the girl was being held," he said.

"No. They blindfolded her each time they moved her." Gertie

turned and looked at me.

"The sailboat you took. Do you know where the mooring buoy was?"

"No. It was dark when we paddled up from the house where the men found us. We paddled a fair distance north of that. So I'm guessing the sailboat was moored near Meeks Bay. Come to think of it, when we sailed away this morning, I noticed the increase in wind as we got out beyond a point of land. That was probably the point just south of Meeks Bay. If you send someone out there, tell them to look for a green scarf. I tied it to the buoy."

"Okay, I'll ask around," Santiago said. "There can't be too many boats that get left in the lake over the winter. Someone will know about it. Maybe it's already been reported stolen. And I'll see if I can track down the owners of the cabin and the house. I'll explain what happened. It was a law enforcement operation just like when an officer borrows a civilian's car to pursue a criminal or to prevent a crime from happening. Do you have a plan to handle repair costs to the cabin and rental or whatever on the house and the boat?"

"I'll get my client to pay for it," I said.

"The girl's mother?"

"Yeah. She'll be rolling in cake in a day or three."

"And now you have the girl with you," he said.

"Yeah."

"Try to hang onto her, huh?"

"No kidding," I said.

After I hung up, Gertie said, "What does that mean when you said, 'My client will be rolling in cake?'"

I wondered what the repercussions would be if I told Gertie. But I'd always thought that kids have the right to know about those things that affect them.

"Your stepdad, Ian Lassitor, had a life insurance policy that names Nadia as the beneficiary."

"Mom is getting money from his death?"

"Yeah," I said.

Gertie's eyes went wide, then narrow. She frowned and radiated suspicion like fire radiates heat.

"How much money?" she said.

"A fair amount," I said, thinking that the actual amount might not be within Gertie's right to know. And it would ratchet up her frustration.

I called Street and told her that we were on our way over to her lab.

Gertie and I walked down and out of my office building. Diamond was still there, sitting in his county vehicle.

We climbed in.

"Almost done," he said. He was slowly pecking his phone screen with his forefinger.

"Wow, your thumbs are a blur, just like texting kids."

"You forgot to mention my ESL status."

"And you're accomplishing this speed record in your second language," I said, noting that Gertie was frowning in the back seat.

"I could go places," Diamond said. "Meantime, I'm a chauffeur. Where to?"

"Street's lab."

"Long trip."

He pulled out of the lot, drove down Kingsbury Grade a block, turned into Street's lot, and parked.

"I'm hoping you or a colleague can continue to stay with us?"

Diamond nodded. "Me or a colleague."

I thanked him and we got out.

"What is this lab your girlfriend has?" Gertie asked as we walked up to Street's door.

"Street is an entomologist."

"What's that?"

"She studies bugs."

Gertie frowned. "She studies bugs for her job? That sounds really gross."

FORTY-NINE

"Sometimes I think bugs are gross. But Street finds it fascinating. And she's done some groundbreaking research that shows how pheromones work."

"What're those?"

"They're chemicals that bugs use to communicate. And it turns out that other animals and even plants use them as well."

"What, they squirt out chemicals? Like a skunk?"

"Not really. I'm not sure how it works. You could ask her."

We got to Street's door. I knocked.

The door opened. Street grinned. She lifted up on pointed toes to kiss me.

"Gertie, I want you to meet my girlfriend Street Casey. Street, this is Gertie O'Leary, an aspiring movie director."

"You want to direct movies!" Street said as they shook hands. "That's so cool. I'm a total movie nut. Come on in." Street ushered Gertie inside and shut the door behind her.

I moved over to look at Street's honey bee tank, giving Gertie and Street some space.

"I'd love to hear about your favorite movies," Street said. "I've never met anyone from the other side of the camera. I'm just a fan and a not-very-discriminating fan at that. But as a director, you must look for stuff in movies that I would never think of."

"Not really," Gertie said. "But I'm learning about how it works. Storytelling. And camera stuff. So far, I've just done a couple of videos with my phone. Pretty amateur. I uploaded them to YouTube if you want to take a look. But maybe you shouldn't. I'd probably be embarrassed."

"Okay, you think about it. If you decide you don't mind, then I'd love to see them."

Street and Gertie talked nonstop while I responded to emails on Street's computer. I've seen Street do it before, the social magic trick performed by the introvert woman who spends nearly all of her time alone with her bugs. And like all sleight of hand, I'm always focusing on the wrong thing if I want to see how it's done.

In less than an hour, Street knew Gertie better than I ever would.

I moved from email to the Paiute Deadfall trap that Diamond had set up with a few sticks. Street's large dictionary was still poised at an angle, ready to fall on any little critter that touched the trigger twig.

Soon, Street had taken a page of notes about movies. Later, she was showing Gertie bugs in jars and on display boards. She opened up some books and pointed at images. Through it all, Gertie laughed and smiled and got excited as if Street was an old friend.

Twice I'd gotten up to look out the window blinds and see if Diamond was still there. He was. Or at least, a sheriff's vehicle was.

After another 10 or 15 minutes, I said, "I'm thinking we should continue this discussion in the car while you drive me up to fetch Spot and my Jeep. Then we could plan an early dinner."

We went out. Diamond was talking on his phone. He looked at me through the window, then held up his finger. In a minute he hung up and rolled down his window.

"I have to head down to Minden. If you want to wait a bit, I can get a deputy to drive you someplace."

"Actually, we need to go up to Santiago's office in Tahoe City. We'll be in Street's car. Mikhailo and his boys probably don't know where we are or what her car looks like. What do you think?"

Diamond paused. "You could hide forever, or you can be alert and take your chances. Street has her phone, right? You can drive her car, and she can dial nine-one-one if need be."

"Yeah. What about tonight? They know where my cabin is, so maybe we should all crash at Street's. But a chaperone would be good."

"Call when you're back there for the night."

Diamond waited while we all piled into Street's bug. I had Gertie get in back where it would be harder to see her. After I pulled out, Diamond left.

Street and Gertie had another animated conversation while I drove.

There was one deputy at the Placer County sheriff's office. He'd been told I was coming.

Spot seemed excited to see me, although as we were leaving, he strained to smell the waste basket where the empty McDonald's containers were stuffed.

I drove my Jeep with Spot, while Gertie rode with Street. I had Gertie hold Street's phone in case a sudden emergency call was necessary.

Our trip was uneventful.

When we parked at Street's condo and got out, Gertie froze as Spot walked up to her.

"I saw him come out with you and get in your Jeep. I could see he was big, but I didn't know he was that big!"

Spot reached up his nose and sniffed her chin. Gertie was rigid.

"He's just like Scruff Boy. If you give him a pet, he'll be your best friend," I said.

Gertie pet him between his ears. He broke into a pant. Gertie ran her hands down his neck. Then she hugged him.

We walked through Street's front door, Spot pushing ahead of us, showing us the way. Street's phone started ringing. She answered it, then turned to us. "Sorry, but I have to take this. It'll take me a few minutes."

"No problem," I said.

She carried the phone into her bedroom and shut the door.

Gertie and I moved into Street's kitchen. Spot came with us, then went back and stood at the closed door to the bedroom. He stood facing the door, his ears turned forward. After a bit, he turned back to look at us, then listened to Street's door some more.

"Like something to drink?" I said. "Although Street is pretty health-focused, so the choices are limited. She has tea and coffee. There might be other options in the fridge." I opened it up. "Nope. What'll it be?"

"I'm not a coffee drinker, so tea it is."

I put on water to heat up.

Gertie said, "Before we went to Street's lab, did you say anything to her about my cleft lip?"

"No, why?"

"Because she didn't react at all. She didn't stare at me. Everybody stares at me. But she just acted normal. Like she was looking at me the person, not me the person with a cleft lip."

"That's just the way Street is. And it's not like you're so bad to look at."

FIFTY

"A cleft lip is a pretty big deal," Gertie said. She seemed to be a confident kid, but these talks about body image revealed the insecurity beneath her self-assured demeanor.

"It's just a little scar," I said. "It's not like it was when you were born. It was fixed up."

"It's a big scar with a little notch in my lip. I should know. Everybody stares at it."

"Do your teachers stare?"

"No. But the kids do."

"Does your friend Emily stare?"

"No, but that's Emily. She's got her own weirdnesses."

"I think when you grow up, you'll find that not so many people stare. You'll meet more people like Street and your teachers."

"I don't know," she said.

"Do you stare when you see someone in a wheelchair? Or when you're in the supermarket and you see someone in one of those riding carts?"

"Of course not. But wheelchairs are everywhere."

"Can you remember when you were very young? Did you stare then?"

Gertie made a slow nod. "Yeah, I did. My mom would hiss at me, 'Don't stare!'"

"So you adjusted. When you get older and the people around you are older, you'll find they've adjusted."

I put tea bags into three cups and poured water. I carried one to the bedroom where Street was still on the phone. I tapped on the door, opened it a bit, and held up the cup. She nodded. I stepped in and handed it to her. She smiled and kept talking.

Back in the kitchen, Gertie said, "I suppose I could do like mom says. Get more surgery."

"You could," I said. "Probably, a lot of people would. Or you could decide that it's your personal mark."

"Like Harry Potter and his forehead mark," Gertie said.

"Right. You have lots of options."

"Maybe I'll ask Street what she thinks." Spot had come halfway back to the kitchen where he stood watching us. At the sound of Gertie saying Street's name, Spot turned again and looked at the bedroom door.

"I can tell Street's really smart," Gertie continued.

"Smarter than me," I said.

Gertie paused, then made a little shiver.

"You okay?" I said.

"After they put me in the van, the guy I call Max bent down and talked to me. I could tell it was him because I recognized his voice and his awful cologne. He said that if I made any noise, he would cut out my tongue. I could tell he meant it, so I didn't move. I'd already figured out that they were probably going to kill me, but I didn't doubt that he would cut out my tongue first."

"Had he made other threats like that?"

She nodded and took a deep breath. "It was Max who mostly talked. He had a thing about tools. He said he would do things with his tools that would make me scream for mercy. He said whenever he used his tools, people begged to die. It terrified me because not knowing what he meant about tools was worse than knowing. That first night after they kidnapped me, I never slept because I kept imagining what kind of tools he had and what he would do with them." Gertie was upset.

I reached over and squeezed her forearm. "I'm sorry to bring up the memories, Gertie."

"No, that's okay. I know you have to ask." She sniffled. "I've just seen too many movies."

"What kind of food did they give you?"

"Some kind of tuna salad that came rolled up in a tortilla."

"A tuna wrap?" I said.

"That's what you call it? Yeah, a tuna wrap. They gave me that, like, three different times."

The only ready-made tuna wraps I knew of came from Trader

Joe's. There wasn't one in Tahoe, but they were everywhere else.

"They also gave me a couple of apples. And donuts."

"What kind of donuts?" When I said the word donuts, it seemed that Spot looked at me with more intensity.

"I don't know," Gertie said. "Just regular glazed donuts. Kind of a brown glaze. Maple syrup flavor. Like you get in any supermarket."

Street came out of her bedroom.

"Sorry," she said. "A potentially big client. They're interested in having me visit their vineyards and develop a natural way to control insect pests. So it was hard to tell them that I can't talk."

"No problem," Gertie said.

"I'm thinking you two might like some dinner," Street said.

"That would be great," I said. "How can we help?"

Street orchestrated a group production like she was Michael Tilson Thomas conducting the San Francisco Symphony. She put Gertie and me to work on various projects, and when we were done, we had a gourmet dinner of wild rice, broccoli, chicken with a secret sauce, a salad of kale, spinach, tomatoes, and carrots, and a chocolate parfait-type dessert that she claimed was healthy but tasted as good as any chocolate sundae.

When we were done, I brought up sleeping accommodations. Gertie hesitated, then asked if she might be able to stay with Street. "You and Spot are great," she said to me in front of Street. "But Street is... Well, I could probably get some good film ideas from her."

"Of course," I said. "Let me see what I can do about some reinforcements." I picked up Street's phone and dialed Diamond as I carried the phone into Street's bedroom as Street had done earlier.

I shut the bedroom door. Diamond answered.

"We're at Street's," I said.

"And you still have the girl," Diamond said.

"Yeah. They are going to sleep here. I haven't had more than a nap the last two nights, so I thought I'd head up to my cabin. Or do you think that's a bad idea?"

He paused. "I'll see about getting two of my guys over there and tell them to keep their hands on their sidearms. Let me put you on hold."

"Thanks." I waited.

Diamond was back on the line a few minutes later.

"Cory Denell and Joe Galant will be there in twenty minutes."

"Great," I said.

"I told Denell that you'd be back by two a.m. You can check on things, get them coffee. Okay?"

"Okay. Gracias."

We hung up, and I went back out to Street's kitchen.

Gertie was telling Street about Scorsese and how he handled suspense. I didn't have anything meaningful to add, so I just listened. From what Gertie had told me earlier, it might be that she didn't have anyone in her life with whom she could talk about such things. Street asked Gertie if that's the kind of movies she wanted to make.

"Maybe," Gertie said. "Mostly, I want to be able to tell stories where the problems are like real life but there's justice in the end. Which isn't like real life very much, you know? But I think that people are drawn to stories where there is justice. It's like, in telling stories, you can remake the world, make it better, make things turn out the way they should."

There was a knock at the door. I looked out Street's window and saw a sheriff's car in the lot. Then I checked the peephole. Two men in sheriff's uniforms. I opened the door.

"Hey, Mr. McKenna," Cory Denell said. "Sergeant wants us to hang here for the night." He gestured toward his partner. "This is Joe Galant."

"Owen McKenna," I said, shaking Galant's hand. "Thanks for coming. Come on in."

They came into Street's, and I introduced them all.

Spot sniffed Denell and Galant. Galant was clearly uneasy but he made a hard grin and spoke through gritted teeth, "Sergeant Martinez told me that you had a big dog. But this guy is really big." He gave Spot a pet. I took Spot's collar and pulled him away.

Gertie looked scared.

"Gertie, Street, Officers Denell and Galant are going to park outside this door tonight, just to keep an eye on things."

Gertie looked at the officers, then back at me, then at Street. For most fifteen-year-olds who haven't grown up with cops in their families, having an armed, uniformed officer in the room was unsettling.

"It's okay, Gertie," Street said. She reached over and put her hand on Gertie's shoulder. "It's just precautionary. If you'd rather, we can go and stay at one of the big hotels."

Gertie shook her head. "It's easier for bad men to move around hotels. If they come here, at least they'll stand out and be obvious."

Gertie turned to Denell. "Where will you be?"

"We'll be in the patrol unit." He pointed toward the door. "We're parked in the closest space. No one could get to this door without brushing up against our vehicle."

"Okay," Gertie finally said.

"You want me to leave Spot here?" I said to Street.

"No. I love him, but he snores worse than you."

I gave Street a kiss goodbye and said I'd be back by two a.m. I tried to make it seem casual to put Gertie at ease.

Denell and Galant and I went back outside. Spot came with, hesitating for a moment at the door, considering, no doubt, that the likelihood of treats would be greater if he stayed. I waited until I heard Street turn the deadbolt. I thanked the officers. Then Spot and I got in the Jeep to drive up the mountain to my cabin.

FIFTY-ONE

A thousand vertical feet later, the air was noticeably colder, and there was a sense of ice mist on the breeze. I took Spot for a short walk. When we were inside with the door locked, I opened a beer. The phone rang. I picked it up.

"Yeah," I said.

"Santiago here. I can't remember if you've met our deputy Rudy Marceau? Our dive enthusiast?"

"Haven't had the pleasure," I said.

"After talking to you this afternoon, I mentioned the boat that almost hit you and then collided with the moored boat. Rudy is one of the eager divers. So he popped his gear into his little skiff, and he putt-putted down to the area you described. He's got this glass thing he holds over the side so he can see the bottom. Kind of like a glass-bottom boat. Sure enough, he spotted the wreckage of boats on the bottom, and he saw some debris floating there, too. It looked too deep for his anchor line, so he went closer to shore, then dropped anchor. He pulled on his dry dive suit, put on his air tank, and went overboard."

"Alone?" I said.

"I know, going alone is a big no-no. But he had his diver flag on the float just like regulations. Anyway, he got down to just above the wreckage. It was about as far as the dive tables allow. I can't remember what. Seventy feet or something because the high altitude makes diving more risky. All he saw was a bent, charred, aluminum hull, upside down. He didn't have time to inspect it for clues as to what happened, because he could only stay down there a minute. Otherwise, he'd get the bends and all that. So I just wanted you to know that it'll be awhile, if ever, before we learn much about that collision."

"Wait. The boat that got struck was moored to a buoy. The

anchor for the buoy wouldn't be in water anywhere near that deep."

"Right. The thing is, there are valleys and ravines and all kinds of uneven territory down there where the bottom plunges off to the abyss below. It goes from twenty or thirty feet right near shore to a thousand feet or more in a short distance. Rudy said that as the wreckage went down through the water, it must've angled like a piece of cardboard falling through air. So it hit a deeper part of the bottom. Rudy said the area also looks steep, so the wreckage slid a lot deeper after it hit. It's no wonder that those treasure hunters can't find the Lucky Gold."

"What's that mean?"

"The Lucky Gold? Haven't you heard about that? Everybody's talking about it. It's just another fad, if you ask me. Sunken treasure. It's like one of those urban legends. Except, it's a rural legend. A mountain legend. But if you want to know more about it, call Rudy."

"Do you have his number?"

"Sure." Santiago read it off.

We said goodbye, and I dialed Rudy.

He answered with a six-pack slur in his speech.

"Hey, Rudy, Owen McKenna here. I talked to Sergeant Santiago about your dive today. I really appreciate your efforts. And I wanted to ask you a question if you have a sec."

"Right on, man. Let 'er rip."

"Santiago said something about the Lucky Gold," I said. "I hadn't heard about that. But after someone tried to run me over last night, I wondered if there might be a connection."

"I dunno, man. I'm a diver. Trade secrets are a diver's trade, ha, ha."

"Do you think maybe I trespassed in someone's territory? Is there something going on up by Rubicon Bay that I should know about?"

"Sounds like I should be asking you the questions. The sergeant said you were involved in some kind of child nap, but I didn't get the details. What were you doing in Rubicon Bay late last night?"

"Saving a girl. They were planning to shoot her and toss her off the mountainside."

"A drop and dump with a girl? Christ, that's rude enough on a bad-ass methhead, but a girl? That's outrageous."

He sounded genuinely mad. Maybe I could use it to my advantage.

"You'd like her, Rudy. A sweet high-school kid from Sacramento, and really smart. These guys yanked her out of her house in Sacramento and brought her to Tahoe. I found out that they had a four-wheel-drive cargo van, so I put out notices around the lake. I got a tip, found the van, and pulled her out just as they were about to execute her. They chased us, and I stuck my Jeep into a snow wall. But we got down to the lake and paddled away on a kayak. Next thing, someone tried to run us over out on the lake. The only reason we got away is the jerk hit another boat, and the wreckage you saw was from that collision. So if you know something that might connect to the motive of these guys, that girl is depending on your honor."

It was a good speech, all true. If anything could open him up, I thought that had a chance.

"Please," I added.

I heard drinking sounds. Deep breathing.

"Well, it probably won't matter what you know," Rudy said. "Not like it isn't all over the place, anyway. I always say that skill is what separates the real pros from the wannabes. Anybody can know about treasure. But only the smartest and the best can find it."

"That's the Lucky Gold?" I said.

"Yeah. Have you heard of Lucky Baldwin?"

"Sure," I said. "Wasn't he the nineteenth century guy who struck it big investing in one of those Comstock Lode mines underneath Virgina City?"

"You got it. The Ophir Mine. Turned some pennies into millions of dollars back when a million really meant something. He's the guy who created the towns of Arcadia and Baldwin Park in SoCal, built the Santa Anita Racetrack, and a bunch of other stuff. In his day, he was the largest employer and the largest tax payer in Los Angeles County. He also built the Tallac Hotel and illegal casino at the turn of the century on what we now call the Tallac Historic Site by Baldwin Beach."

"That's the hotel that burned down," I said.

"Right. So here's another history question for you. You know about the Tahoe Steamer?"

"Sort of. Turn-of-the-century boat that cruised Tahoe for years. Brought people all around the lake and delivered the mail?"

"Right," Rudy said. "It was a magnificent boat. A hundred sixty-nine feet long. As far as I know, that's still the longest boat that ever cruised our lake. It was built in eighteen ninety-six by D.L. Bliss, the guy who basically cut down all the trees in Tahoe to reinforce the hundreds of miles of mining tunnels under Virginia City."

"D.L. Bliss the lumber baron? The state park?" I said.

"That's it," Rudy said. "The park that is just north of Emerald Bay and encompasses Rubicon Point. His Tahoe Steamer was something. Leather upholstery. Twelve hundred horsepower steam engine. Electric lights, which was a big deal back then. It carried two hundred passengers in the finest accommodations of the day. And like you said, it carried the mail. But when they built the first decent road around the lake in nineteen thirty-five, that baby was no longer needed, and it lost the mail contract. The steamer's traffic dried up. D.L. Bliss's grandson scuttled it off Glenbrook back in nineteen forty.

"Anyway, a university researcher down at UC Davis was going through the archives about the Tahoe Steamer and the Tallac Hotel two months ago, and he found some correspondence between Lucky Baldwin and D.L. Bliss."

"They probably knew each other," I said. "Maybe Bliss sold lumber to Baldwin's mine.

"Yeah. Anyway, the information in those documents has created a tidal wave of lust and greed." Rudy paused. It sounded like he was drinking beer. "Can you tell I'm into this stuff? I get excited every time I talk about it. I got a copy of the main document on this, and I've studied these guys a lot, so I'm practically an expert, now."

"I can tell," I said.

I waited.

"Turns out Lucky Baldwin wrote D.L. Bliss with a proposition. Baldwin wanted a meeting with Bliss out on Bliss's Tahoe Steamer. Now Baldwin and Bliss weren't close buddies, to say the least. In fact, it's safe to say that Baldwin never had a close buddy. He was one ornery jerk and a womanizer who so angered the women he pursued that two of them shot him nearly killing him, and four separate women sued him for breach of promise of marriage. Nevertheless, Bliss agreed to a meeting out on the Steamer on September thirteenth, nineteen-oh-one, which just happened to be a Friday, in case you believe in superstitions.

"Apparently, Baldwin was putting together a land development deal and Bliss owned a small parcel that Baldwin needed to complete his package. Baldwin suspected that Bliss wouldn't like the idea of him cleaning up on the deal and as such would refuse to sell his parcel to Baldwin for any reasonable price. But Baldwin knew that it would be worth it to acquire the parcel even if he had to pay an enormous sum to Bliss.

"So Baldwin decided to ambush Bliss with a take-it-or-leave-it deal. His idea was that if he brought a small chest full of gold out on the boat along with papers that Bliss could sign, Bliss wouldn't have time to learn about the actual value of Baldwin's land development. The hope was that Bliss, while realizing that Baldwin was up to no good, would nevertheless be blinded by the gold. He would know that his parcel was worth almost nothing to anyone else, so what could be the harm in taking a fortune in gold for it?

"Well, the meeting happened as Baldwin planned it. According to an account written by a Tahoe Steamer crew member, Baldwin and Bliss sat in the saloon of the Tahoe Steamer as it steamed from Tahoe City down the West Shore. They were drinking the finest forty-year-old Scotch from the Laphroaig distillery and looking out at the most gorgeous scenery in the world. Because it was a Friday in September, the tourists were largely gone, and Bliss and Baldwin had the saloon to themselves. Baldwin made his little speech, and Bliss hesitated a strategic amount. Baldwin said, 'Well, Duane, as your good friend and fellow businessman, I understand your hesitation at selling me your little spit of land without careful research and thought. It is only through your brilliance and determination that you've accumulated such vast holdings around Lake Tahoe. But as I said, the piece I want, while a pretty lakefront lot, is but the size for an outhouse. You will also imagine, of course, that it is the final piece of a puzzle that means a great deal to me, and your speculation about that would be correct. As such, it makes sense that I would pay a great deal for it. I'm happy to admit that I own all of the adjacent land, a sizable investment for which I'm willing to pay a great deal to protect.'"

Rudy paused. "'Thus, here is my offer, simplified,' Baldwin said. 'I'm going to have my assistant wheel out a chest full of gold coins. Never mind the exact value as the rates fluctuate daily. Suffice to say it is so far in excess of the value of the land I wish to purchase that I expect you to give in to greed as well as common sense and sign these papers to make your land mine. I will give you enough time to sift through the coins, which I promise are genuine. And as you know my reputation, you know that what I'm saying is the truth. After one minute of time for inspection, my assistant will seal up the chest. You will have five minutes from that point to finish the deed and put your signature on the bill of sale. If you do not, I will never give you the opportunity again, and you will go to your grave thinking that you missed the chance of a lifetime. Realizing that you are but five years younger than me, I can state with assurance that your remaining years are few, a period of time in which, no matter what happens, no one will ever offer you even one percent of this for that land again.'"

Rudy paused.

"A great story," I said. "What was the result?"

"Bliss thought about it for a minute, then nodded. Baldwin's assistant came down the outer promenade deck of the Tahoe Steamer pushing a cart on which was a tiny chest. By the effort required to roll the cart, the chest was obviously very heavy. The man writing the account estimated the chest to be twelve inches long by eight inches deep and six inches high.

"Baldwin's assistant opened the door to the lounge and rolled the cart in, used his foot to push down a brake lever to lock the cart in place, then opened the top of the chest.

"Baldwin's assistant, his secretary, Bliss's two personal assistants, and three Tahoe Steamer employees made a collective gasp that could fill the car tires of twelve decades of future Tahoe residents. The chest was overflowing with gold coins. The account shows that as Bliss raked his hands through the coins, he picked up many of them for a closer look. At least one was revealed to be an eighteen-seventy Double Eagle, struck at the Carson City Mint. Have you heard about those, McKenna?"

"I have. Real valuable, I recall." I'd worked on an avalanche case the year before that hinged on that very coin.

"One in just fair condition recently sold at auction for three hundred thousand dollars." Rudy went silent for a moment, no doubt to let me grapple with the concept. "Even adjusting for its value over a hundred years ago, it was still an indication of the astonishing value of that chestful of gold.

"Of course, that very value reinforced Bliss's suspicion that the land deal would hold unforeseen advantages for Baldwin. Nevertheless, Bliss couldn't resist. He closed the chest and shut its latch, then picked up the papers to sign the bill of sale.

"According to the crew member's written account, what happened next is a bit confusing. I suppose that's because it shocked the writer so thoroughly that he lost all clarity of thought. But the essence is that, after Baldwin had the signed papers in hand, and Bliss and Baldwin had shaken hands, Bliss turned to his chest of gold. He used his foot to unlock the brake lever on the cart so he could wheel it away to his private office on the Tahoe Steamer. At that very moment, the Steamer's skipper blew the whistle and swung the wheel to starboard to avoid some kind of floating hazard in the water.

"The cart with its heavy chest of gold shifted, and Bliss lost his grip on it. The cart rolled to port, perfectly aimed at the doorway on the side of the lounge. It hit the door, which burst open. Without even slowing, the cart rolled across the promenade deck and struck the outside railing.

"Of course, the steamer had been built from the finest quality wood and iron, and it was maintained as if it were President Theodore Roosevelt's personal boat. But while the steamer's railing was strong enough to stop the cart in its tracks, the chest of gold slid off the cart, over the railing, and dropped into the deep waters of Lake Tahoe."

"That certainly is a story," I said, thinking about the men who kidnapped Gertie, the eccentric lady's claim that ghost boats patrolled the West Shore, and the boat that nearly killed Gertie and me the night before.

"I realize that this might be pure speculation," I said, "but has anyone connected to this story made a guess as to what the current value of that gold might be?"

"Indeed," Rudy said. "The UC Davis researcher called a numismatics expert and told him the size of the chest and asked him to produce an estimate based on the description of the coins. That man came up with a figure, but it is pure speculation as you say. Even so, are you sitting down?" Rudy was clearly something of a showman, even over the phone.

I'd been pacing my cabin. I sat down on the rocker. "Yes," I said.

"Somewhere between fifteen and twenty million. Although that includes collector value on a range of coins, which is more than their simple value as plain gold. But if the chest contained many eighteen-seventy Double Eagles, the value could be twice that."

"Enough to motivate a lot of divers," I said.

"Oui, c'est moi," Rudy said.

I recognized it as French for 'Yes, 'tis I.' "Does the account the researcher found make any estimation of the gold's location?"

"Only to say that the Steamer was going down the West Shore."

"Which gives you twenty-some miles to search," I said.

"Yeah. And most of it is at depths far beyond the reach of divers."

"But that won't stop people from looking," I said.

"People are motivated to look for treasure merely for the sport of it. Fifteen million or more brings it into a new realm. People dig substantial mines hoping to find smaller amounts. UC Davis has a submersible, but they probably wouldn't spend resources on a search unless they had a solid indication of location. The bottom of that lake is huge and very deep."

I asked Rudy if I could consult him again.

"Sure," he said.

"Thanks very much."

We said goodbye and hung up.

A second later, the phone rang.

"Owen McKenna," I said, my brain full of images of gold coins spilling out of chests.

"Glad you finally got off the phone." It was Diamond. "Sorry to tell you bad news. We got a nine-one-one from Street's neighboring condo. I'm here at her condo."

"What happened?" It felt like a grenade had gone off in my gut.

"The neighbor saw a white cargo van roll to a stop a hundred yards up the road. Two men got out. They had baseball bats. They slipped into the forest. Denell and Galant were standing outside their patrol unit, talking. The men raced out of the woods and hit Denell and Galant as they were drawing their weapons. My officers were struck on the head and chest. They are both unconscious, alive, but just barely. Then the men from the van kicked down Street's door, went in, and came out a few seconds later with Street and Gertie, both of them screaming and kicking. The men dragged them into the back of the van while a third man drove off."

FIFTY-TWO

Stunned with rage, I stood, not breathing, not talking. I dropped the phone. I couldn't move. Corrosive anger and fear for Street and Gertie shut out all other thoughts. My vision narrowed, darkness pushing in from the edges. My heart raced. A high-pitched ring pulsed in my ears. Searing pain infused my nose and head as if my sinuses had been shot with burning acid. The cabin seemed shaken by a loud roar.

Time slowed. Spot pushed his nose against my hand. I looked down. My fists were clenched as if to crush my own hand bones. Spot's ears were down, his brow creased with deep ridges of worry. His tail was between his legs. He shivered.

I raised my fists up and saw them small and distant. I stared at them, tried to make my hands open up. My throat hurt, my head throbbed. The roar got louder. I realized it was me, screaming. Terror. Fear. Torment.

Rage.

A strangling rage.

In a moment, the roar stopped. I gasped for air. But I couldn't draw in a deep breath. My breathing was short, shallow pants, quickened like those of a panting dog.

Minutes went by. I stood rigid as a board.

More minutes. I still hadn't moved.

I got my fists unlocked. Straightened my fingers in front of my eyes. I stared at them, concentrating, trying to calm without success.

My lungs finally opened up. I drew deep breaths, again and again, until I could hold a breath, until my heart rate slowed.

As I concentrated, my emotions drew together. The worry and fright and anger that turned my gut, the crushing guilt of my role in creating the frantic, despairing, tortured, ruptured world that was now Street's and Gertie's, my fury over the injuries of the cops, my ache, my desire – my need – for retribution, and most of all, my desperate hope that Street and Gertie would survive... All of these seemed to combine at that single point. My single focus.

Rage.

I noticed the time. Half an hour had gone by. Time lost. I was sitting on the floor in the corner. Knees drawn up to my chest, my back against the hard logs that joined at the corner of my cabin.

The dangling phone beeped the off-the-hook signal.

Spot sat on the wood floor near his bed. He stared at me with his ears back. When he saw me look at him, he turned away. There was a look on his face that I'd only seen once before. I couldn't place it. Then I remembered. It was a look I'd seen once when he was a puppy. I'd brought him to the vet for puppy shots. He had loved the vet, loved the other dogs, loved the people, didn't even notice the shots. Everything in life was good and fun. But on the way home, a pickup came out of a side street, didn't even slow for the stop sign, and hit us broadside, caving in the door where Spot sat. Spot looked okay, but he was shaking. It could have been deadly. I got out of the Jeep and walked around to the pickup. The driver got out. He was stumbling drunk. When he saw my puppy cowering behind the crushed door, he began laughing. Boy, lucky puppy, isn't he, he'd said with a grin on his whiskey-stench face. Lucky puppy. I grabbed the man by the throat, lifted him up, and yelled at him. My yell was a roar of anguish and anger, focused at the drunk. But when I turned to look at my Jeep, I saw that my puppy took it worse. He cowered away from me and my roar. It was Spot's first look of fear.

Spot had that look now.

I got up, walked over and sat on the edge of his bed. I reached out my arm. "C'mere, boy. It's okay. I'm sorry. I didn't mean to frighten you." Spot didn't move. I said the words again. Patted the dog bed.

Spot stood up, not tall like normal, but cowering a little. He took slow meek steps toward me. He stepped onto his bed and sat down next to me. Then he lay down, close to me but not touching, careful to have his head away from me, away from the danger of my emotions.

I pet him. Long slow strokes.

"I'm sorry boy. Something bad has happened. Real bad. But we're going to fix it. You and I."

My breaths were slow and deep. The cabin was cold. I looked down at my hands. They were pale with cold. My legs ached with cold. Feet numb. Spot shivered.

But my heart was hot. And my brain was afire.

"We're going to fix it, Spot."

Everything that mattered in the world had become one small thing. I internalized it. I'd submerged my emotions so that I could focus. I was an emotional black hole. Nothing could escape, and nothing could be seen from the outside. My purpose was simple, unfettered, uncompromised, undiluted. It was hidden from Spot, as well.

Yet it was powerful.

Rage.

FIFTY-THREE

I put Spot back into the Jeep and drove down to Street's condo. There were multiple sheriff's vehicles with lights flashing. No sirens. I pulled up to the parking lot entrance. A deputy tried to wave me away.

I got out and walked toward him.

"This is a crime scene!" he said, alarmed that I'd ignored his signal to move. "Move on!" He lifted his radio with his left hand and spoke while his right hand hovered over his sidearm.

"I'm Owen McKenna," I said in a low voice. "Diamond's expecting me."

"I'll say it one more time. Get into your car and drive away!"

I repeated myself, louder.

He spoke again into his radio. A crackle of voice came back. "Are you sure?" More crackle.

"Okay," he said to me. "You can go in." His voice was still a bark, full of frustration. Cops get jumpy, stressed, scared, and mad as hell when their own are injured in the line of duty.

I got back in the Jeep, drove over to the corner of the lot and parked. I left Spot and walked up to a group of officers who had marked off a large perimeter around the patrol unit. Bright lights had been set up. Men with evidence bags and collection kits were inspecting every inch of vehicle and pavement. Their voices were heavy with tension and anger. Try to kill a cop, you set off a firestorm among the ranks like nothing any other crime can do.

"Here to speak to Diamond," I said to a deputy.

The man turned and shouted. "Sergeant? A guy's asking for you."

Another voice murmured, "That's McKenna, her boyfriend."

Diamond came off the far side of Street's deck so he could

walk around the circle of cops.

"Sorry about this," Diamond said.

"I'm sorry for you. For Denell and Galant. They have families?"

"Galant, no. Denell, yes. His wife Sherry and his boy Jared. Jared's two years old." Diamond's eyes were wet. "They both have severe head injuries. The chopper took them to the trauma center in Reno. Let's hope they make it. And let's hope that Gertie and Street are..." Diamond stopped. He looked out toward the big black lake. In the dim light, I saw his adam's apple go up and down. "I was starting to worry when you didn't show up."

"I was... Collecting myself," I said.

Diamond looked up at my face. "You don't look good. You okay? No, of course you're not okay. I'd like you to come inside. See if you notice anything unusual."

"You think the men had reason to take anything?" I said. "Or leave anything?"

Diamond shook his head. "No, but you should look. See if anything is different." He turned me and walked me around the cops and back up the far side of the deck. We went in the slider. The place was as I had left it except for a lot of stuff on the floor, some broken. The front door was swung open, a deep crack in its middle, and the door jamb was broken with part of the frame lying on the floor. Cold air blew through the condo. The heater vents blew warm air, more vigorously than I'd noticed before.

I walked from the entry to the bedroom to the kitchen to the living room. Nothing seemed to be missing. But the place was a mess, furniture askew, stuff on the floor. Street and Gertie had obviously fought and tried to grab onto doors and tables and counters as they were dragged outside.

Street's TV screen was on, as was her computer that streamed shows onto the bigger screen. The image was a YouTube page. It looked like they'd been watching one of Gertie's videos, and it came to the end and stopped.

I took another trip through the small condo. Nothing else caught my attention. I looked at the front door and its splinters spread across the floor. The little entry mat near the door still

TODD BORG

held Street's shoes, unmolested by all of the violent activity. They sat side by side right where Street puts them when she trades them for her slippers.

Diamond was on the front step outside the broken door. I stepped out. "I don't see anything unusual. Was there anything out here?"

"Just this," Diamond said. He held up one of Street's slippers.

I stared at it, the coldness in my gut getting colder still. My sweetheart was taken prisoner in the winter, and now she didn't even have two slippers. I didn't speak. I was locked down, choked off. My vision narrowed to a tunnel.

Rage that would explode when it found its outlet.

I gestured at the broken door and spoke to Diamond. "Do you have a policy..." I stopped, something interrupting my thoughts.

"We secure crime scenes when we're done. We'll arrange for sufficient repairs to close up her condo. You can deal with it later."

"Thanks." I turned away, looked at my Jeep in the corner of the lot. Spot took up the back seat. I could see his black nose stand out from the fogged up glass.

"You okay?" Diamond said again. "You want to stay here? Come home with me? Or I could come up to your cabin."

"I need to think," I said, my mouth moving at slow speed as my thoughts raced. I was trying to find a thread of an idea that danced just below my consciousness, a thread that felt like it would lead me to something.

I walked down Street's front steps, turned to move around the perimeter tape, and walked to the Jeep.

Spot sniffed me after I climbed in. He was subdued. I knew he would be depressed at the smell of trauma. The lingering fear from my earlier screaming at the cabin affected him as well. I should have been reassuring. I should have talked to him in a sweet voice. I should have hugged him. Instead, I said, "Hang in there, largeness. I'm going to need you."

I drove away, turned up the highway heading north.

I had no plan, no destination. I just drove.

FIFTY-FOUR

Street and Gertie were out there somewhere, terrified. I wanted to race to find them. But I knew of no place to search. I had to find an idea, make some kind of connection that had eluded me.

The highway was dark with moisture condensing out of the air. Occasionally, moonlight poked through the trees. White snow at the side of the road caught the light, emphasizing the black stripe that was my path to nowhere. Then the clouds returned, and all the world seemed black.

My thoughts were non-linear, uncoordinated, disjointed.

There were only two things that mattered in the world.

Street and Gertie.

On their way to die.

Wait. The men could have just killed Street and Gertie, like they tried with the deputies. But they didn't.

Why?

When I rescued Gertie from the van, they were going to kill her. Now they had Gertie and Street, too. Why would they want them alive now? Was it only to postpone their deaths? Was it because they wanted something else before they killed the women?

The question choked off my breath.

My hands gripped the wheel as if to crush it. Only one thing kept me from imploding.

Rage.

I was driving, but I wasn't seeing the road.

I was seeing a kidnapped girl with a desperate desire to move past thoughtless parents and a cleft lip, and the perils of growing up homely in a world hyper-focused on beautiful people. I saw Street, woman of my dreams, with a passion for all living things including the insect creatures that everyone else thinks are pests. I saw a chestful of Lucky Baldwin gold. I saw an old lady who talked about seeing strange lights at night and hearing ghost boats.

But the ghost boats turned out to be real.

I remembered what I'd heard her say. He thinks he's king, hums and crows, true the crown. When I'd asked her about it later, she denied saying it.

The eccentric lady had shied away from human contact. She'd spoken in strange ways. She'd looked disheveled as a witch.

But she didn't seem like someone who'd lie.

She'd told the truth about the ghost boats. What if she had told the truth about the man who thinks he's king?

Maybe I'd just heard it wrong. She could have said something else that merely sounded like hums and crows, true the crown. Then it would make sense when she'd told me that she'd never said those words. It could be those words sounded as crazy to her as they did to me. She might never remember other words that could be confused with them.

I said it outloud to myself. "He thinks he's king, hums and crows, true the crown." I repeated it.

What did it sound like?

The only thing that came to me was almost as strange. 'He thinks he's king, comes and goes through the ground.'

I remembered that when the lady talked about Lassitor's castle, she mentioned George Whittell's famous castle across the lake, the Thunderbird Lodge. Maybe they were similar in more than just their construction material.

The Thunderbird Lodge had a secret tunnel from the castle to the boathouse. So that he could 'come and go through the ground.'

What if the architect of the Lassitor castle had replicated that design?

I thought about Lassitor's boathouse. It was made of stone and was unlike most boathouses in that it wasn't built over a pier. Instead, the foundation started ten feet back from the shore, ran to the water and continued another twenty feet into the water.

As with many boathouses, Lassitor's boat could be moored in the water, inside the boathouse. He could raise the door at the end and simply pilot his boat out onto the lake. Lassitor's boathouse also backed up onto solid ground. The ground sloped up from the lake, and the back wall of the boathouse was set into the rocky slope.

When the neighbor Craig Gower took Santiago and me inside the boathouse, I noticed that its back wall had a custom built-in cabinet and closet very similar to the built-in bookcases in the castle's entertainment room. But just how custom were they? Could they really be facades designed to hide a door?

When I'd asked Gertie about the men bringing her to the place where they held her, she said that when they put the bag over her head and first went indoors, the inside temperature wasn't very warm. She also said they walked a long way as if through a warehouse. Why such a long walk? Why wouldn't people just go in the front door or a secluded side door or back door? Could it be because they were in a tunnel that provided a way into the castle without being seen by anyone near the front of the castle? The layout of the grounds was such that someone could drive and park near the boathouse without being seen by neighbors on the opposite side of the castle.

If the Lassitor castle had a secret tunnel, did it also have a secret room where Mikhailo the Monster and his men could take Gertie and Street?

Time to find out.

FIFTY-FIVE

I thought of finding a phone, calling Agent Ramos, and telling him what I thought. But Ramos and I had a checkered relationship. Because I had no evidence, and because I had a history of sometimes being wrong before, Ramos would tell me that there was nothing he could do other than have someone stop by Lassitor's house and knock on the door and look around.

I'd already looked around, inside and out, and seen nothing.

I had a better relationship with Sergeant Santiago at Placer County. If I called him, he might put together a team based on my hunch alone. But he wouldn't be able to get a warrant. No judge signs a warrant based on a hunch. If Santiago were to help me, we'd have to hope to find some indication of distress at the castle and go in on a no-knock entry with a mission to save whomever was in distress. Legally, it was a tenuous action. Unless every aspect of a raid goes well, and it actually saves a victim, even a beginning defense lawyer can get the case thrown out on illegal-search-and-seizure grounds.

But my biggest hesitation about a hostage rescue team was that the more men that went in, the more noise and commotion. Stealth is reduced exponentially as more people are involved.

I didn't know the territory. If the castle had secret passageways, the kidnappers would have a significant advantage. As soon as they heard someone coming, they might be able to escape.

There was one more option.

Instead of assembling an official Placer County Sheriff's team and playing by the rules, I could bring my own private backup. Diamond had helped me before despite the threat to his career if he should be caught doing something outside of his jurisdiction. Once he heard my plan, he might sign on out of desire to save

Street and Gertie and catch the men who attacked his deputies.

But as I thought about it, my doubts grew. Not only did I still not have a phone to call him, I had no evidence. My past inspection of the castle revealed it to be empty.

By every measure, my idea of a secret tunnel was outlandish. But what better idea did I have?

I decided to go alone. Just me and Spot. One more inspection of the castle. I would have the advantage of stealth and surprise. And if I found nothing, I wouldn't have engaged local law enforcement on a worthless mission.

As I drove up the dark, deserted East Shore, I once again regretted my personal prohibition against guns. I wanted a gun. Multiple guns. I wanted to shoot the men who took Street and Gertie. Not kill shots. Thigh shots that would incapacitate and cause much pain. But that was the very reason why I no longer carried a gun. Because I might use it. Because I'd used it in the past with tragic consequences.

There was a small amount of traffic on Highway 50 as I headed up Spooner Summit. But after I turned north on 28, I didn't see a single vehicle until I got to Incline Village. There were a couple of cars and a few late-night delivery trucks near Incline's shopping areas. Otherwise, the highway was empty. I checked the dashboard clock. One a.m.

As I came around Crystal Bay, the wind had shifted out of the south. There was a fine layer of lake-effect snow on the highway and a frozen mist in the air as moisture, picked up from the lake, cooled off once the air came back over land. The cooling condensed the moisture molecules into micro ice particles. Occasionally, my Jeep drifted on the corners. I realized that my tension had me pushing my speed. I backed off on the gas.

From Crystal Bay, I drove through the dark, silent towns of the North Shore. Kings Beach, Tahoe Vista, and Carnelian Bay all slipped by. There was a bit more traffic as I came into the lights of Tahoe City, a few locals coming home from working late shifts as slope groomers at the ski resorts.

I turned south on 89, drove across the Truckee River on Fanny Bridge. Again, the traffic disappeared, and I had the dark highway to myself. A couple of miles south I went by Sunnyside, and a mile after that I went by the drive that led back through the trees to Lassitor's castle on Hurricane Bay.

Without slowing, I continued south then turned right into the eccentric lady's neighborhood. I drove a few blocks, turned left and parked on the narrow street. Because the snow walls were so tall, the Jeep was mostly hidden.

I grabbed the penlight from the glove box, got out, and let Spot out of the back seat.

Whenever I wanted to be incognito, walking with Spot created a challenge. Unless it was completely dark, the white splash of his coloring would catch the light. And the darkest nights always motivated people to turn on lights if they heard a sound.

My best approach when I didn't want to be seen and noticed was to go when no one was around and go alone. The middle of the night worked well except where there were other dogs. Bringing Spot would increase the chance that other dogs would bark. But if I left Spot behind, I would be leaving behind my best multi-use resource.

Spot wasn't brilliant. But like all dogs, his ears and eyes and especially his nose were much more sensitive than those of people. In a quiet situation like walking at night, Spot would alert to any human presence long before I could tell anyone was around. And in addition to standard dog abilities, Spot also had bonus characteristics. His size made him intimidating. And his weight and strength were such that no man could fight him off without a good weapon and a focused ability to use it.

We got out of the Jeep. I walked over to the snow wall and kicked at the base. In and down. Harder. Farther. I came to the shoulder of the road. Kicked more. Hit dirt. Like so much of Tahoe, the ground under all the insulating snow wasn't frozen. I scuffed some of it up and rubbed it on my face and hands. Gathered more and rubbed it over Spot's white areas of fur. He didn't protest. I'd done it before. When I was done, he was no longer a standout. The blacks spots blended into gray-brown background. I'd transformed him from a Harlequin Dane to a Merle Dane with black spots on a gray background.

We stayed next to the snow walls as we walked out to the highway. When we came to the corner, I looked out. There were no vehicles on the road.

"Let's go, Spot," I whispered. I held his collar as I ran. He trotted next to me. We went down the highway a couple of hundred yards. Instead of turning in Lassitor's drive and risking the attention of any cameras that might be mounted in the trees, I turned into Gower's drive. By using the connecting path between the houses, it was the most direct route to Lassitor's boathouse.

I slowed to a walk as we approached Gower's house. Although it wasn't as big as Lassitor's castle, it loomed in the dark, two stories high, with all its windows dark. Assuming Gower pulled his car into the garage, there was no way to tell if he was home or at his place down in Carson Valley.

Spot stopped moving and panting, something he does when he hears a faint sound.

I heard a faint sound. A low moaning in the distance.

Another ghost boat?

I listened. I couldn't place the direction. I watched Spot. His direction sensitivity is far better than mine, and he turns his head and ears toward sounds he's interested in. But so far he didn't seem interested in the moaning sound. He looked left, then right, listening, sniffing.

I cupped my hands behind my ears, increasing my sensitivity. The moaning sound seemed to rise and fall.

Then came a light in my peripheral vision. On for a moment, then off. Then twice again. Was it in the trees toward Lassitor's castle? At the castle itself? It happened so fast that I couldn't tell if it was someone with a flashlight or something else.

I turned toward the trees. Watching, listening. At the same time, I was aware of Spot's head below my own. He turned away from the castle and faced the lake.

Then Spot jerked his head toward the castle. He went rigid.

I saw nothing. Heard nothing. Spot began a low rumble in his throat. I jerked on his collar.

"Quiet," I whispered.

Then a woman screamed.

FIFTY-SIX

The scream was distant and muffled but no less terrifying for it. My heart thumped. My breaths were shallow pants. I couldn't recognize any quality to the sound that suggested that it was Street or Gertie. Screams don't reveal much about the voices that make them.

Like the moan, the scream seemed to come from everywhere at once. But the muffled quality sounded like it was deep inside a building. I couldn't sense any direction to the scream. But Spot did. He stood rigid and stared through the dark toward the castle.

We ran toward the castle. I followed the path from Gower's drive over to Lassitor's. There was a dusting of new snow that made it quiet but slippery. Still hanging onto Spot's collar, I leaned on him for extra support. With his tough claws, he had more grip than studded snow tires.

My left shoulder bumped the snow wall as we ran. Spot's right shoulder rubbed against the other snow wall.

Fifty yards down, we came to Lassitor's drive. There were no vehicles and no tracks in the recent snow. I looked toward the massive stone walls, trying to see the few small windows in the dark. With no light inside or out, they were nearly impossible to pick out. Up along one of the roof peaks was an area of darkness that looked different from the stone walls. I realized that it was the row of clerestory windows. I walked with Spot toward them. I got close to the big wall with no windows. That would be the windowless wall in the entertainment room. Or else it was the wall that people were supposed to think was the entertainment room wall. The row of clerestory windows was at the peak of the room. Regardless of whether there was one wall or two with a secret room between, if anyone turned on any light in the entertainment room, it would give a glow to the clerestory windows.

I stood in the dark, my neck cranked up, staring at the windows. Eight large panes in a row. A big enough expanse of glass that, even if someone in the house below were using a flashlight, a chance moment of reflected light would probably produce a glow visible through those high windows. But they remained dark.

I turned around to head to the boathouse when Spot jerked again. I sensed a brief glow on the snow around me. I spun around. Nothing. No glow in the clerestory windows. No glow from any of the other small windows off to the side of the big windowless wall.

Turning slowly, I scanned the forest around the castle. Looking for movement, for any light. My hand was still on Spot's collar.

Maybe I was imagining the light.

The house seemed deserted. The scream could have come from another house in the area.

My only hope was probably a fantasy. A secret tunnel that would allow me to get into the house where Street and Gertie were being held. It was a ridiculous idea that seemed more ridiculous the longer I considered it.

But even if I'd been hallucinating, I still knew that someone had screamed. Spot had heard it.

Spot and I ran to the intersection of the path that went to Lassitor's boathouse. We turned toward it and the lake.

I slowed Spot as we got closer to the shadowed building, then pulled him to a stop. We waited, both of us listening, Spot sniffing the air. He didn't alert. Which meant that no one was hiding in the shadows.

We walked up to the boathouse door. The only light was dim starlight that reflected off the snow. Spot sniffed the knob and the deadbolt and the doorjamb. It was his casual sniff. Nothing like I would have expected if he smelled scents from Street's condo.

The deadbolt looked strong, and the door looked solid. I remembered that the overhead garage door was the only other sizable opening, and it was at the end of the boathouse out in the icy, black water. The water would be deep enough to handle the draft of the average boat. Probably four feet. Spot wouldn't want to go swimming any more than I did.

"Spot, stay," I whispered, touching the palm of my hand to his nose. I put the penlight in my teeth and waded into the water.

The cold rush of ice water into my shoes and clothes, around my legs and up to my waist was nothing compared to when they'd dropped me in the lake to die. The water rose to the bottom of my ribs as I went around the boathouse corner to the overhead door. Without the light reflection off the snow, it was even darker out in the water. I reached out and felt the door. Its bottom was about two feet off the water's surface, probably to minimize damage to the door from waves. I could get underneath it without ducking my head, but not much else.

I bent forward at the waist, the front of my chest dipping down into the water as I ducked under the door. It was cave black inside. But the loss of all vision inputs was curiously made up for with audio inputs. In the enclosed space, every little water movement and wave sound was huge in my ears. My breathing was loud. The splash noises of my movements were loud.

I flipped on the penlight. It was like a searchlight, a bright blue-white LED beam that was hard on my eyes. Anyone within a mile of the boathouse would be able to see light in the windows. I cupped my hand over the beam, took three fast steps to the side door, and called Spot into the dark space.

He pushed past me, much less handicapped by darkness.

The inside of the boathouse was as I'd seen it before, a few items hanging on hooks, some other things on the shelves. There was a white rag. I could wrap it around the light beam, but that would light up the balled-up rag.

On one of the shelves, there was a dusty cardboard box with a little illustration of a kayak sinking beneath the surface of the water. I picked it up. It said, 'Kayak Repair Kit.' I opened it. Inside was a small plastic bottle of some kind of solvent, a flexible rubberized sheet, and a roll of blue tape. It looked like electrician's tape. I tore off some small strips and positioned two of the strips over the edges of the light, blocking most of the beam. There was enough light to see, but it wasn't quite so obvious.

I turned to the wooden shelving unit. It covered most of the back wall of the boathouse and went from floor to ceiling. There were three vertical sections. One was built out into a closet with doors like those on an armoire. Another had wooden dowels positioned such that water skis and kayak paddles could stand on end on the floor and be held in place by the dowels. The third vertical section had shelves for storing miscellany. I opened the closet door and looked inside. There was a rod at the top. Flotation vests and windbreakers and wetsuits hung on hangers. There was nothing behind them but the same wood panel that backed the shelves.

Nowhere on the organizer unit did I see an indication of where there might be a hidden door. I pushed and prodded at different points near the edges of the back panels, looking for some give. It was all solid. I ran my fingertips along the trim boards and down every corner and intersection, feeling for a catch of some kind. There was nothing.

I wanted to knock on the back portion of the organizer to listen for the sound of a hollow area. But I knew that would resonate like pounding on a bass drum. If anyone was around, it would give away my presence.

Standing back, I began to think my idea was just silliness, a feeble attempt to imagine that Street and Gertie were in a place where I could rescue them. The Lassitor castle had probably always been empty since the day when Ian Lassitor drowned.

Nothing stood out.

If I wanted to get into the house, it might be easier to break in the front door. Then I had an idea.

"Spot," I whispered, getting his attention, wondering how to communicate what I wanted. "Can you smell Street? Can you, boy?" I put my hands on his chest and gave him a shake, a standard way to excite a dog on a search mission. I had nothing to search him on, but maybe the concept of simply smelling people would translate.

I turned Spot's head toward the wooden organizer. "Spot,

find Street! Find!"

I made the hand motion in front of his face the same as if we were out in the forest and I was sending him on a search. My fingers pointed toward the organizer.

In a normal situation, Spot would take off running, looking for whatever smell I'd scented him on.

This time, I had nothing to scent him on, and there was nowhere to run. Nevertheless, he walked over to the armoire closet, poked his nose between the wetsuits and windbreakers and wagged. He turned around and looked at me, then looked back in the closet.

"Good boy, Spot," I said. I gave him a pet, then I pulled out all the wetsuits and windbreakers and laid them on the floor.

I pushed on the back panel. It was solid. I looked again at the side corners, the top and bottom corners. I ran my hand over the panel feeling for any irregularity.

Nothing.

I backed up from the closet unit and tried to look at it in a broader way. Never mind how thoroughly I'd inspected it. What hadn't I touched? What hadn't I really looked at?

The closet rod.

I'd moved everything that hung from the closet rod, but I hadn't studied the rod itself. I shined my light on the rod, moving from left to right. The middle of the rod appeared a bit darker than the ends.

Smudged.

I gripped the rod. Gave it a twist.

The rod rotated a half turn. The back of the closet swung out an inch. A gentle, humid breeze blew through the opening into my face.

FIFTY-SEVEN

I reached out and pushed the door farther. It opened with a gentle resistance. Maybe there was a silent alarm. If so, it made no difference

"C'mon, Spot," I whispered. I shined my dimmed penlight into a dark, narrow stone tunnel. I realized that I was possibly walking into the killer's lair and I had no weapon other than Spot. I took another look around the boathouse. There was no potential weapon but kayak paddles. But they would be too big to swing in an enclosed space. I played my penlight in another circle, finding nothing smaller except a broom, the kind with a small paddle of bristles on a wooden handle. Because I had nothing else, I picked it up. Then Spot and I stepped through into the tunnel and let the door swing shut behind us.

Spot panted, excited. He'd never been in a tunnel before. I didn't want him trotting ahead, so I held his collar with my left hand while I carried the broom and penlight with my right.

I turned around and looked at the door. It was a heavy, solid-core door with a metal handle in place of a knob. A hydraulic closer at the top held it shut. On the stone wall to the side of the door was a swing handle that no doubt operated the latching mechanism, just as the closet rod did from the other side. There was no lock. Security came from the fact that the door was hidden from the other side.

Like the rest of the castle, the tunnel was made of stone, flat pieces for the floor with more irregular pieces for the walls and ceiling. My light showed nothing in the distance ahead.

Ten feet in from the secret door, the tunnel began a slight curve to the right. It made me wonder if we'd bump into people should we come around a curve too fast. Better to anticipate if possible.

I pulled Spot to a stop, then turned off my penlight.

The darkness was as black as it gets. My eyes had already adjusted to the relative darkness, but I waited a full minute, letting my irises open fully. With one hand on Spot's collar and the other on the wall, I moved forward slowly, hoping to round a corner and see something. But after ten or fifteen feet, I still couldn't perceive the tiniest glow of light. I turned the penlight back on. Spot and I continued walking.

I counted my steps, making a crude guess that the distance from the boathouse to the house was half a football field, or 150 feet. With my steps being slow and tentative, I guessed the length of my stride to be about two feet long. Which meant the tunnel was about 75 steps from the castle. So far I'd come 25 paces.

Another curve made me stop and turn off my light so that I could once again feel my way forward in the dark and be prepared to see the slightest bit of light coming from down the tunnel. Again we moved several feet. Again there was no other light.

I turned on the penlight, and we continued.

One of my feet slipped. I shined my light down. There was moisture on the floor, seeping in from the ground, joining the lake water that was still draining from my pants. I turned my broom around, bristles up at my chest, so I could use the broom end as a safety cane in case I slipped again.

As I went farther, I began to feel two strong emotions. The thought that I might be close to Street and Gertie and that they were prisoners encouraged my rage. But the fact that I'd heard a scream, a clear indication that they were in severe distress, made me despondent. Despair was the antipode of rage, one driving a person to inaction, the other the opposite.

I focused on my rage.

Forty paces down the tunnel, Spot stopped walking. Then he stopped panting. I paused and angled my head for a clearer look. My penlight shined on something other than stone and mortar. The tunnel was blocked by another door, similar to the one we'd come through.

I stopped, turned off my penlight, and waited in the blackness for my eyes to adjust. A minute later, I could see nothing.

I turned my light back on, shining it down on the floor, and moved forward. We walked slower as we approached the door. I worried that Spot would smell something and make a noise. I put my finger across his nose, the sign for silence.

This door had a regular knob. There was no lock. There could be a deadbolt on the other side, but there was no way to tell from the tunnel side. A regular knob suggested that this tunnel entrance was not hidden from the other side. The architect must have figured that once you were in the secret chambers, there was no point in hiding the passages.

As we approached the door, I was aware of Spot's nails clicking on the stone floor. There was nothing I could do about that. Moving very slowly, I again turned off my penlight and put my ear up against the door and listened for a long minute.

Nothing. No sound, and no light escaped from the edges of the door.

I let go of Spot's collar, grabbed the doorknob, and gave it a slow, gentle twist. The knob turned without making a sound. It reached the end of its motion. There was no way to know what I was walking into.

Still holding my broom in my right hand, I pushed the door inward with my left.

I tried to ease the door open, but Spot was eager to find out what was on the other side of the door. Or maybe he smelled Street. He pushed forward next to me. I let go of the doorknob and reached for Spot's collar. I missed.

A dim light came through as Spot's nose hit the door and it opened. I took a step forward trying to understand what I was looking at. There was a wall sconce throwing off low light like that in a castle in the movies. The dim light showed a stone wall off to the left but curving to the right. A room that stretched out to the right.

There was a muffled woman's scream as I sensed a streak of movement to my left.

A baseball bat swung at my chest.

The bat came as fast and hard as the swing of a major league lefty hitting a line drive out to right field.

FIFTY-EIGHT

The bat struck the broom that I held at my chest. The blow was so intense that the plastic bristle base seemed to explode, bristles flying into the air. A chunk of the handle hit my abdomen as the broomstick broke into pieces.

The blow was hard and mean and deadly. It threw me back against the door frame. The impact blew the air out of my lungs. The shock was astonishing. But the plastic piece and the bristles probably saved me from a collapsed lung or a ruptured aorta.

At first, I didn't see the batter. My attention was on Spot, whose head was just below the bat's arc. In an instantaneous movement, Spot reached up under the batter's leading right arm and grabbed the man's left elbow. Like other dogs, Spot was quicker than a person. Unlike other dogs, Spot's jaws are bigger than a mountain lion's.

Spot's mouth fully enclosed the man's elbow. I couldn't see the details, but I knew how it worked. Spot would initially bite medium hard, enough to hold on no matter what happened. The assailant who acts subdued is held but not critically injured. The assailant who resists gets a harder bite. If an attacker is foolish and tries to throw the dog off, the bite gets serious.

I saw the man try a big jerk to pull away from Spot or maybe swing Spot into the stone wall. The crack of breaking bones came fast and loud, three or four crunching sounds. The man screamed a high yelp of pain. He dropped the bat and fell to his knees as Spot pulled him down. The bat bounced and rolled away. As the man tried to kick, Spot growled his deep guttural rumbling, not unlike a lion's roar. He shook the man's arm. The man screamed louder, terror creeping in as he realized that the huge dog was able to crush his arm and maybe rip it off.

I sucked air into my burning chest and ran towards the bat.

As I bent down to grab it and then straightened up, I saw the women.

Street and Gertie were over in a far dark corner of what looked like a windowless dungeon room. They sat back-to-back on the hard stone floor. Their arms were pulled behind their backs and down to some kind of anchor bolt in the floor, their wrists handcuffed to the bolt. Across their faces were pieces of duct tape, sealing their mouths shut. And in their eyes was a terror that nearly broke me.

My rage welled up, a searing anger. My vision narrowed.

I carried the bat over to the man.

"Spot, let go," I said. I nudged Spot with my foot. He moved away.

The man looked up at me from the floor.

"You sick, twisted bastard," I said.

"Go to hell," the man said. He pushed up onto his knees, then stood. He spat at me.

I hit him with the bat. Again. And again. He fell. My rage made my vision go dark and my ears numb to his screams. I didn't give him any deathblows as he'd tried with me, and as he and his pals had no doubt attempted with officers Denell and Galant. But I disabled him. Permanently. Elbows, wrists, knees, ankles. When he went silent, I ran to Street and Gertie. Spot was already next to them. I kissed Street's forehead and held the side of her head for a moment.

"This is going to hurt," I said as I ripped the duct tape from their faces. Each in turn gasped with shock. But they both stayed relatively quiet. Spot sniffed Street, then Gertie. Gertie shut her eyes, then leaned her face over so that her cheek was against Spot's chest.

I wanted to grab Street and hold her. Gertie, too. But there wasn't time.

"Do you know where the handcuff key is?"

"No," Street said, her voice shaky with stress and fear. "One of the other men had it."

"Where are they?"

"I don't know. I think they left. They went out that door."

She looked toward a door I hadn't seen. "An hour ago. We haven't heard anything."

"Earlier," I said, "maybe a half hour ago, I thought I heard a scream. Was that one of you?"

Street nodded. She glanced at Gertie. "After the other men left, the man you just hit groped her. He was rough and mean. She was brave. Even with the duct tape on, she screamed through her nose."

"That's why you think they left," I said. "Because he wouldn't have gone near her if the others were here."

Street nodded. I noticed that she had on just one slipper. Her other foot was bare. A little part of me broke.

I reached over to Gertie and put my hands on her shoulders. Her eyes were red. She shivered with fear. I squeezed her shoulders.

I ran back to the unconscious man and went through his pockets. I found a wallet and some keys, but no handcuff key. I put his stuff in my pocket and ran back next to Street and Gertie.

"Have you been anywhere in the house? Do you know what's on the other side of that door?"

"We've only been in this room," Street said. "They brought us through the tunnel, then locked us to the floor."

I nodded. "Spot," I said. He looked at me. I pointed to Street and Gertie. "Guard them." I grabbed Spot's head for emphasis. "Do you understand? Guard them."

I turned back to Street. "I'll be back as soon as I can."

The bat would make a good weapon. But it wasn't where I thought I'd dropped it. The man was clearly unconscious if not dead. I turned around. The bat must have rolled someplace. The tunnel door was broken and partly open. Maybe the bat bounced back down the dark tunnel. There was no time. I picked up the longest portion of the broken broomstick, walked over to the other door, opened it.

There was a stairway lit by another wall sconce. I didn't want Spot to be tempted to follow me. Street and Gertie needed his protection and presence. I shut the door behind me and walked up the stairs, out of the dungeon. There was another room. White sheetrock walls. A bed. Four doors. One of them was open.

I walked through, my little broomstick raised and ready.

The room was lit with another wall sconce.

The only furnishings in the room were a narrow mattress on the floor, a small desk, and a chair. On the desk was a computer. Sitting in the chair was a man. Attached to his ankle was a long chain that stretched to another bolt in the stone floor. The man was in his forties but hunched and wan and skinny as an emaciated 80-year-old. I recognized him from the photos that Nadia Lassitor had shown me of her husband.

The man we thought was dead.

Ian Lassitor.

FIFTY-NINE

As the man turned toward me, the terror on his face was obvious. He was severely bruised on his face and neck. A purple knot of swelling protruded an inch from his left jaw.

"I'm Owen McKenna, here to get you out," I said. "Is there a phone in this house?"

He shook his head and spoke in a small, weary voice. "No. No landline. No wifi either. They disconnected it. This computer is isolated, too."

"Who's they?"

"I don't know," he said. "Three men. Big and brutal."

"Where are they?"

"One was down in the cellar. The other two left. At least I think they left. That's their pattern." He pointed to one of the doors.

"When do you expect them back?"

"If it's like most nights, they'll be gone another two or three hours."

"How long have you been chained in this room?"

"Almost three weeks. I'm starving. My brain has mostly stopped working. Are you a cop?"

"Private. I was brought into this by Nadia."

Lassitor looked away as if it took him a moment to process the thought that Nadia might have been worried about his absence. His confusion looked genuine, although I didn't trust that to be the case.

"Why do they have you here?" I asked.

"It's a long story. I wrote a new type of facial recognition software."

"What does that have to do with you being chained here?"

"My software uses an unusual kind of algorithm that analyzes nodal points. By changing the nature of the nodal points, I can use it to recognize not just faces but objects that we can describe in general terms, even when we don't know their size or what they look like."

"So?" I said.

"Objects, for example, that are underwater. Objects that we don't have photographs of but that appear on sonar scans."

What he said didn't make any sense to me. "I don't... Oh, you're looking for the Lucky Baldwin gold. A chest of gold."

"Yes," Lassitor said. "Somehow, these men found out about what I'm doing. I don't know how because I've told almost no one about my facial recognition software."

Lassitor looked away, then back as if he'd thought of something new. "Except Nadia. I told Nadia about it." He paused. Processing. "The men came into my house and took me prisoner. They took my project from me. Now I do the same thing, looking for the Lucky Gold, but I do it for them. Somehow they knew about these secret rooms. I didn't even tell Nadia about the rooms. They put me on this chain. I'm kidnapped in my own house. They're forcing me to perfect the software so that it will recognize the gold chest. They're using my boats to make the scans. Each morning the leader brings me a hundred sonar scans loaded onto a flash drive. I analyze them. Every day I have to show him what I've done with the previous scans, and how I've adjusted the software. He knows just enough about coding that he can tell if I'm faking it or not. So I keep working on it. But if I succeed, I know they'll kill me."

"They've already killed you once," I said.

"What do you mean?"

"A man died piloting your Gar Wood when he was struck by another boat. Everyone thought the skipper was you. Including your wife."

Ian stared. He made two, slow shakes of his head. "God, what is happening?! That was... I was making a movie. A fictionalized documentary. That man was my stand-in. He looks just like me. I found him by using my software on actor databases. I hired him, trained him on the boat, then sent him out on his first rehearsal.

I'd mounted a tiny fish-eye lens camera on the bow of my Gar Wood. The guy was a method actor, and he wanted to rehearse with the camera on. But right after he drove my Gar Wood out of my boathouse, the three men turned up, brought me into this room and kept me chained here ever since. I assumed they scared off the actor."

"That's all you know?" I said.

"Yeah, but there's something else going on that I don't know about. A few days ago, I heard noises in the room next door. Then tonight I heard a scream in the cellar."

I gestured at the door. "That's what you call the room down the stairs?"

"Yeah."

"They kidnapped your stepdaughter Gertie. She's tied down there with my girlfriend."

"Why?" he was pleading. "What would that have to do with the Baldwin gold?"

"It doesn't. It has to do with ransoming the insurance payout on your death."

"Oh, Jesus," Lassitor said.

"You think the men will be gone until when?"

"It's usually three or four a.m. when they come back. I think it's because that limits the chance that anyone will see them. I only know the times because I can see the time on the computer. I pay attention because when they're gone, I try to signal with the desk light."

"What do you mean?"

"I can never be sure they're gone, so I can't make noise. They've made it clear they will kill me if they hear me try anything. The leader is sick. He says he'll use his power drill with a very long bit to drill holes all the way through my head until I die. So I'm quiet. But when I think they're gone, I shine the desk light up at the overhead windows." He pointed. I looked up.

There were two clerestory windows high above in the small room.

"Those windows are part of a long line of windows," I said.

Lassitor nodded. "There are eight in a row. Two are here. The other six are in the entertainment room on the other side of that wall." He pointed at the wall behind his desk.

"So I turn the desk light up and down, hoping that someone, somewhere will see my distress signal. Three short flashes, followed by three long flashes, then three more short. SOS. The problem is that the trees outside the windows are so thick that I don't imagine that anyone could ever see my dim light. But I kept trying in case there is a strong wind blowing the branches, making temporary openings."

"Tell me about this house," I said. "Do the men always come and go through the boathouse tunnel?"

"No. Usually they come in that door." He pointed. "There's a room through there with a bathroom and a storeroom off the bathroom. You'll see the secret door that leads to the entertainment room."

"Does that door open in the bookcase unit in the entertainment room?"

Lassitor nodded. "Yes."

"So they come and go through the front door of the house?"

"No, I don't think so. Even though this room is pretty soundproof, there's a very soft thud you can hear when the front door shuts. I've only heard it a few times since they put me in here. I've wondered if the thuds might be someone else, if I should yell and try to get their attention. But when I first tried that, the men were in the house. They came in here later and beat me nearly to death. So I didn't dare call out the next time I heard it. Anyway, I think they come and go through the landscape garage tunnel."

"Is that like the boathouse tunnel?"

"Yeah. There's another hidden door in the bookcase next to the piano in the living room. The tunnel goes out to the landscape garage on the far side of the property. There is a small drive in from the highway. The lawn-mowing tractor and the utility Cushman are in the landscape garage. It is also close to the lake, but it doesn't look like a boathouse, so that's where I hid the aluminum fishing boats that I used for my sonar scans. I assume they are still keeping the boats there. The boats are automated and run off GPS signals."

"So someone can come and go from the landscape garage tunnel, and it never looks like anyone is ever here in the house," I said.

"Right. Unless they turn on lights in the entertainment room at night. Then the glow is detectable out the clerestory windows. Of course, someone on the lake could see in the big windows on the lake side. But if you keep all the blinds closed, then the clerestory windows are the only ones in the house that let any light out."

I raised my hand to stop him talking and trotted back down the stairs into the cellar.

"I haven't found a handcuff key, but I'm making some progress," I said to Street and Gertie. Spot jumped up. "Spot, stay," I said. I pointed again at Street and Gertie. "Guard them," I said again.

Spot didn't lie down, but he stopped and stood still.

I walked over to the prostrate man on the floor.

He was still unconscious, his breathing shallow and rapid.

I ran back up the stairs to Lassitor. "Where do you keep tools?" I asked Lassitor.

Lassitor shook his head. "I'm sorry, I'm all thumbs with tools, so I don't have much. There's a drawer in the kitchen with a small screwdriver and a pliers, but that's about it. You could check the main garage. The door is next to the kitchen. There's a workbench with some stuff in drawers and cabinets, stuff that was there when I bought the place. I've never gone through them."

I picked up my broken broom handle and walked through the other door. As Lassitor described, there was a room and a bathroom. On the far side of the bathroom was an open door and a storeroom beyond. The small mattress that Gertie had described was on the storeroom floor.

I pulled down the handle on the secret door. The door swung in toward me.

In front of me was darkness. I realized I was looking at three shelves with an amplifier and CD player and turntable and wires attached to their back sides. On the far side was the back side of a cabinet door.

I ran my hand along the wood and found a brass handle that was recessed but swung out when I pulled on it. I lifted it up. The shelves and the cabinet door all swung out into the entertainment room.

The room was dark. Carrying the broomstick, I stepped through the now-open shelving unit and pulled the hidden door shut behind me. There was a dial where the closet rod had been on the boathouse door. I gave it a turn and felt the locking mechanism engage. Then I swung the cabinet with its enclosed shelves back. There was a little click as they snapped into position. I could have left it all open, but if the men were in the house or if they came back soon, I wanted to be able to hide and have them think that nothing had been disturbed in this part of the house.

I walked through the dark entertainment room, under the arch and into the grand space that contained both the living room and the kitchen and dining area.

There was a dim glow coming from under the kitchen cabinets, little hockey puck lights shining down on the granite counters. Next to the kitchen counter was the door to the garage. I opened it and walked out. I flipped on the light switch.

There were no windows. But the gap under a couple of the garage doors was at least a quarter inch. The light would be obvious from outside. I took a look around, memorized the layout and the location of the Mercedes and Porsche, and turned off the switch. I switched my penlight on and walked over to the corner where Lassitor had said there were cabinets and drawers.

I opened the cabinet doors. There were some old quart cans of paint, a partial gallon can, a roller and pan, some blue masking tape, a plastic coffee can with brushes in it. I pulled open the drawers and found a rusted utility knife with a broken blade, a bottle opener, a crescent wrench that was missing its lower jaw and was mostly covered with paint as if its primary use was to hammer shut paint lids, a plastic Ziplock bag filled with yellow electrical wire nuts, a glass jar with finishing nails, and some molly bolts.

On the wall nearby was some pegboard with hooks. There was a small coil of thin, braided nylon line, a hack saw with an old blade that was so obviously dull it probably wouldn't cut butter, six six-foot, brown extension cords still wrapped in their display cardboard.

Leaning nearby were some miscellaneous chunks of lumber left over from a building project. A couple of eight-foot 2 X 4s, a six-foot 2 X 2, some three-quarter-inch dowels, a short chunk of Glulam that someone had maybe saved to turn into a butcher block.

What was notable was what I didn't find. There were no hammers, no cold chisels, no bolt cutters, no large cross-cut saws, no large screw drivers. There was nothing that would make a good weapon. After Spot, who was on guard duty, my broken broom handle was still the only weapon I had. Worse, I found nothing that I could use to break the handcuffs that held Street and Gertie.

At least, the vehicles would have tire irons, which would be useful weapons. I turned toward the cars. Behind both windshields were little blinking red lights. Despite being in a locked castle garage, their alarms were on. Assuming they belonged to Lassitor, he didn't trust that they would be safe even inside his garage. If I bumped the cars and set off the alarms, the men would hear it if they happened to be coming back.

I went back into the house, back into the entertainment room and through the hidden door to the room where Lassitor was chained.

"Where are your car keys?" I asked.

"The men have them. I tried to resist telling them where they were, but they beat it out of me."

I nodded, then trotted back down into the cellar. "The men are gone," I said to Street and Gertie. "I'm looking for some way to cut your handcuffs."

Street made a nod that was mostly grimace. Gertie cried softly. Spot looked concerned.

"I'll be back," I said.

I ran back through the secret rooms and into the living room. I looked for the other hidden door that opened into the tunnel that led to the landscape garage. The door was like the others, hidden in a section of built-in storage cabinets. I found the release catch. The door opened.

I trotted down the tunnel, and came out into a garage that had nothing more to offer than what Lassitor had already told me about. There was a riding mower and a Cushman utility vehicle. I looked for tools but found nothing. I couldn't even remove the mower blade to use as a weapon.

Back in the house, my throat constricted as I realized that the simple act of pulling out the floor bolt that held Street and Gertie was defeating me. Panic welled up, making it hard to breathe. But I focused on my rage. I was determined to take down these murderous men, not the other way around. I stopped and looked around the house. Tried to see it anew. Even a stripped-down castle with no tools or weapons would hold formidable resources if only I was smart enough to see them.

I scanned the cavernous living room that was lit only by my penlight and the dim kitchen-counter lights. I didn't know what I was looking for. I just needed a weapon, an advantage of some kind. But nothing seemed any more useful than the broken broomstick that I already had. It was as if the men had carefully gone through the house and removed any possible tool.

I leaned the broken broomstick against the kitchen counter and went through the drawers. There was nothing sharper than a fork and butter knife.

I looked again at the room. Next to the fireplace, nearly hidden in the shadow below the mantle, was a fireplace set, a poker, ash shovel, and log gripper. I picked up the gripper. It was not designed to grip small items like the bolt that held Street and Gertie. The shovel was bendy and weak. And the poker wasn't pointed enough to wedge under the edge of anything.

It was something I could swing. Hefting it, I walked over to the side of the secret door, imagining how I could use it on anyone who came through the door.

But a poker wasn't much use against guns.

Was it possible to set some kind of trap by the hidden door? Something that would incapacitate them as they walked in?

I looked at the piano. It was a big, old upright design, and very heavy. It would be hard to move. I wondered if it would make a useful barricade. I tried to imagine how it would work.

The men would come through the tunnel from the landscape garage and open the secret door. They'd see a piano in the way. It would merely slow them down. I looked back at the piano. What else could I do with it?

I thought about Diamond's explanation of how the Paiute Deadfall trap worked.

Could it be done in a very large version? Instead of a four-pound rock, could the weight be a five hundred-pound piano?

It seemed a ludicrous notion.

But Street and Gertie and Lassitor were all held prisoner. And two men, presumably heavily armed, were going to return shortly.

Anything I could do was worth a try.

SIXTY

I went back into the garage and got the coil of line still in its package. Back in the living room, I stretched the line out and made several measurements, tying knots to mark lengths. As I made my plans, it again seemed ridiculous to think that I could trap one or more men with some cord and sticks. But as Diamond had said, the Paiute had used traps for survival for thousands of years. No reason I shouldn't take my turn.

With the line as my measuring tape, I put the 2 X 4s on the garage workbench and used the hacksaw to cut into the wood. It was slow going. Even though the blade was very dull, it gradually cut the wood. Several times I stopped to listen, wondering if the men had returned.

After much sawing, I had the basic lengths I needed, one with its end shaved to a chisel edge, and the other with a notch cut out into which the chisel edge would rest. I also cut three pieces of dowel. I carried my wood pieces into the house and set them up near the piano, checking my measurements. The notch I'd cut needed an adjustment, but I seemed to be on track.

One 2 X 4 was to be the vertical fulcrum piece, the other the seesaw that would hold up the piano, held in place by a trigger cord.

When I had everything in position, I lifted up on one end of the piano. It was very heavy, over two hundred pounds on just one end. As the end raised higher, more of the weight was supported by the side that was still on the floor. When I had the piano tipped up very high and it almost reached the balance point, I was holding very little weight.

By getting my body under the piano, I was able to balance the piano with my back and hips and let go with my hands so I could reach my wooden pieces. I held the vertical fulcrum piece with one hand, and positioned the seesaw piece with my other hand so that the short end came just under the raised end of the piano, propping it up. The long end of the seesaw and its attached piece of line angled back down toward the floor. I pulled the line over, and tied a short piece of dowel to its end.

Then I took the longer piece of dowel – my trigger twig – and gently wedged it between the angled bottom of the piano and the short dowel. I had to shift things a little here and there, but eventually I let go of the pieces and eased my way out from under the piano.

It shimmied, but stayed in place.

I now had a 500-pound Paiute Deadfall. If anything bumped the longer trigger dowel, the short dowel with its string would come loose, the seesaw would give, and the piano would come crashing down.

Of course, no one would be under the piano when it fell. But as Diamond had pointed out, the falling weight could trigger a snare.

I tied another little piece of dowel to the end of a line and tossed it up and through one of the big timber frame trusses that supported the roof. The weight of the dowel pulled the line over and back down. It stopped about twelve feet above the floor, out of my reach. I shook the line, sending waves of motion through it. Gradually, the dowel dropped farther, and I was able to reach up and grab it. I removed the little piece of dowel and pulled the line through the truss until I had enough to make a snare.

Using a slip knot, I made a loop about fifteen inches in diameter and worked it into the carpet nap in front of the hidden door. Then I pulled the back end of the line down from the truss to take the slack out of it. When it was in position, I cut off the line and tied its end to the frame at the bottom of the piano, choosing the part that was tipped highest in the air so that it would pull the line the greatest distance when the piano fell.

Now all I needed was a cord that would run to the trigger dowel and a way to stretch it in front of the door to the tunnel.

Over by one of the living room windows was a pedestal and on it an abstract bronze sculpture. It weighed about thirty pounds. I carried it over and set it on the floor to the side of the cabinet that contained the hidden door. I took another piece of line, tied it around the sculpture, and stretched it over to the Paiute Deadfall trap.

I bent down under the raised piano and, moving as carefully as a cardiac surgeon at work, gently ran the end of the line around the trigger dowel and tied a knot. My breath was short as I backed away on hands and knees. When I was clear of the piano, I stood up.

There was no way to predict if the Paiute Deadfall snare would work. But my hope was that the men would come through the tunnel and the hidden doorway and push open the cabinet door. One would step out into the snare, simultaneously hitting the trigger cord. The cord would pull the trigger dowel free, the seesaw would give way, and the piano would crash down, pulling the snare line. If it worked perfectly, the snare would close around the man's leg and lift him several feet up into the air.

With my trap in place, I made another search of the house, looking for some way to cut off Street and Gertie's handcuffs. The only tool I could find was a small scissors that would never be strong enough.

Then I saw the log rack to the side of the hearth. It held split pine. Many Tahoe residents buy their firewood split and delivered. But some like to split wood themselves.

I ran back through the entertainment room and into the room where Lassitor was chained.

"Do you split any of your own wood?"

"Huh?" he seemed startled. "Some, yes. Why?"

"How do you split it? A hydraulic splitter or what?"

"I use a splitting maul, the old-fashioned way."

"Where is it?"

"Let me think. The last I used it was probably over a year ago. But it should still be in the same place. Outside the slider near the fireplace. The far left end of the deck. There's a woodpile under the eave. In front of that is a giant slab of fir I use as a splitting base. I think the maul is just leaning up against it. It's probably all covered in snow, but it should still be there."

I nodded as I ran out.

The woodpile was as described under the eave. Where the roofline stopped, the snow rose sharply up to six feet of depth. I kicked around in the heavy snow, to the left, then to the right. I moved deeper into the snow, chopping it with my arms, knocking it down. Poked my boot in deeper. Hit something solid.

I dropped down on my knees, the snow up to my neck. Reached in and found the slab, dove in deeper, arms probing, waving. There. Something to the far side. I pushed in farther, my head under the snow. Wrapped my fingers around a handle. I had to jerk it back and forth multiple times to free the head of the maul from its frozen home. Then it came out.

The wooden handle was slippery with ice and snow, so I held on tight as I ran back inside and shut the slider behind me. I was turning toward the entertainment room when I heard a deep tone.

Men's voices.

SIXTY-ONE

I heard movement, a whoosh of weather stripping. The cabinet in front of the hidden door in the living room opened. A leg and foot stepped out. The man never had a chance.

His ankle brushed the trigger cord. The Paiute Deadfall seesawed, and the piano crashed to the floor with a tremendous gong from all of the strings. The snare jerked up, closing on the man's leg. It went tight at his knee and jerked him into the air. He fell back against the man behind him. He was suspended from his knee, which was four feet off the ground. His body draped down. He grasped at the floor and cabinet. His other leg pushed him in wild gyrations.

The man behind him saw me. He looked a bit like the Dock Artist from Carson City, but he was in the shadows of the cabinet and hidden doorway. I saw his gun as he raised it above the other man. He leaned forward to take aim. As I threw the splitting maul, light caught his face.

He was huge, but he wasn't the Dock Artist.

The man fired as I dove sideways. The shot missed me. The gun sounded like a cannon in the enclosed space.

The maul was very heavy, and the handle twirled about the maul's head as it arced through the air. The maul head hit the top of the cabinet above the second man's head. It fell down and struck the man on the shoulder. I dropped to the floor and rolled toward the hearth. The fireplace poker I'd picked up earlier was just out of reach.

The man fired again. The edge of the hearth exploded, stone chips stinging my face. I crawled over, grabbed the fireplace poker, and threw it like a javelin. It struck the man who was dangling by his knee, the dull point hitting his free leg hard enough to puncture his thigh. He screamed and flailed, his arms windmilling into the man behind him.

The second man fired again, hitting the glass front to the fireplace. The tempered glass exploded into a million diamonds. Once again, the man took aim, but this time his gun was pushed sideways by the injured man who still rotated as he hung from one knee and tried to right himself with his other foot.

I jumped up, grabbed a split of wood from the rack, and gave it a short hard throw. It hit the hanging man whose body still protected the man behind him. Running now, I grabbed the fireplace ash shovel, then turned in a short arc. The second man reached his gun out above the hanging man and took careful aim at me. I ran toward him. Just as he pulled the trigger, I slammed the shovel down on his gun and hand.

The man grunted with pain, and the gun went off as it flew out of his hand. It slid across the floor. I picked it up. The slide was bent and jammed. I tossed it aside.

I took another step toward the men and swung the shovel. It hit the shooter's forearm with a glancing blow and then slammed into the snared knee of the other man. He yelled.

The man behind pushed past him and came at me like a trained fighter. He had his arms up in a blocking position, and he made fast steps, bouncing, dodging.

I remembered what they'd said about him.

"Mikhailo the Monster," I said. "You used to kill for revenge. But now you kill for money?"

He was still dancing. I stepped forward then back, feinted with the shovel.

The man's kick came so fast that I didn't even see it. The shovel flew out of my hands and slammed into one of the big picture windows. Glass exploded and rained down at our feet. His blow to the shovel was so hard that my hands and arms stung with the shock. I jumped back and brought my fists up like his. I knew that going up against a Mixed Martial Arts champion was nearly hopeless. If only I had the broomstick that had broken at a sharp angle... But it was leaning against the kitchen island counter.

I feinted left, dodged right, grabbed the small log gripper out of the fireplace rack. I held it out with both hands, pointing it toward him. His footsteps were quick, his arms quicker. Because I had no experience with his type of fighting, I saw no telling movements.

He shot out a jab that hit my left shoulder so fast I couldn't hit him with the log gripper. A kick shot up and hit the gripper handle from underneath. The gripper flew out of my hands. Without a weapon, I was helpless. I took a fast step sideways and tried to leap over the couch.

As I went into the air, a kick hit the upper backside of my thigh hard enough to break my femur. I was moving away from him, which softened the blow just enough to spare me. But the impact threw my legs forward and out from underneath me. I was in the air, rotating backward like I'd pulled the flight control stick all the way back. I was upside down when my back slammed into the back of the couch. The couch tipped over onto its back, and I collapsed on top of it.

I was dizzy. It took too long to roll off the back of the couch. The next kick came just as I stood up. It came from my side, just behind my field of vision. The blow struck my shoulder. It felt like getting hit by a train.

My shoulder collapsed in and up, the deltoid muscle smashed. Like a train, the man's foot was not deflected by the collision. His heel continued past my shoulder and hit my upper neck and the mastoid skull bone just behind my ear. I went down and was out before I hit the floor.

SIXTY-TWO

I was a little boy on a road trip out of Boston. My favorite uncle was taking my dad and me up to his cabin in the mountains, there to teach me the manly art of lake fishing. We stopped to fill up his brand new pickup. But when he pulled the hose nozzle out of the fill pipe, gasoline dribbled down the side panel. My uncle ran to get a cloth to wipe it up. I watched as the gas left pretty, spreading rivulets of wetness on the new shiny paint. The gasoline smell was both alluring and off-putting at once. I could have moved away to the fresh breeze, but I was taken with the smell.

The smell eventually got stronger and then became overwhelming. I tried to move away, but I couldn't. My legs didn't seem to work. Then the gas gagged me. It was on my face, in my mouth. I spit and gagged and coughed and shook my head.

Mikhailo had a red five-gallon gas can and was pouring gasoline over me and the couch next to me. He held one of his hands in an awkward position as if it were broken. Despite the injury, he was still very good at pouring gas.

He moved across the living room floor to a wooden table and soaked it well. Next came the wooden storage unit where the secret door opened to the landscape garage tunnel. Mikhailo was a perfectionist and didn't miss a spot. He soaked everything with gasoline, including his pal who still hung by his knee from the snare. The man never moved as Mikhailo poured gas over his hair and face. Mikhailo must have helped his buddy into unconsciousness the same way he helped me. Mikhailo poured gas down the man's shirt, over both pant legs.

Don't forget the shoes, I thought. Mikhailo didn't.

I tried to pull away, tried to crawl. My left arm was numb. I used my right arm, gouging my fingers into the slate floor, and dragged my body at least a half an inch, maybe more.

Mikhailo moved to the piano, opened its top lid, and dribbled gas down inside. He went across one of the rugs, drawing a nice neat X pattern from corner to corner. When he got to the front door, he splashed gas up and over its surface. Then he opened the entry closet and splashed gas on the coats and the closet door. Even after all that gas, he still didn't have to tip the can very much to pour it out. Five gallons is a lot of gas.

I kept crawling. Half inch after half inch. Mikhailo was so focused on his task that he never looked over at me. Or he knew that whatever I could do, it wouldn't make any difference. At any point, he could strike a match and the entire castle, myself included, would be engulfed as he jumped outside into the snow.

Mikhailo moved to the kitchen and carefully applied his gas-splash technique to the cabinets and the bar stools that surrounded the kitchen island.

I kept crawling. One more inch. Then another. Yet another after that. It was amazing how many times I could move an inch and not seem to get anywhere. There were many inches between me and anything else.

Mikhailo moved to the dining table. Turned it into a gasoline lake. Then he focused on the dining chairs. They had upholstered seats. Great for absorbing gasoline.

I kept crawling.

Milhailo finished the chairs. He still had a lot of gas left. There was a rug under the table. Persian maybe. The table prevented him from drawing a nice X through the center of the rug. So he made little curlicue patterns around the edges.

I kept crawling.

When Mikhailo was done with the living and kitchen area, he went through the stone archway into the entertainment room. That room had lots of furniture and wooden built-ins. It would keep him busy for several minutes.

I kept crawling. I would have left a trail from the gasoline running off my body but for the fact that the floor I crawled across was already a lake of gas.

My progress was like the hour hand on a clock. If you watched me from above, you might not perceive movement. But if you looked away for a while and then looked back, I'd be in a slightly different position.

Two or three eons later I approached the kitchen counter. I rested for awhile, then summoned astonishing strength and sat up so I could lean back against the counter, my knees drawn up to my chest to help support my body. My head bounced against the granite top. But I could barely feel it. Instead, my focus was on the little man inside my skull, working with hammer and chisel to cut a hole and escape.

I heard an inhalation of breath.

With Herculean effort, I turned my head.

Mikhailo had come back into the room and seen that I was no longer lounging on the floor by the overturned, gas-soaked couch. He spun around and saw me. He had a little grin of satisfaction as he marched over, stood in front of me, and made an almost casual front-snap kick at my jaw with his right foot. It had been such a struggle to hold my head up that I only had to relax my neck muscles. My head fell to the side. The kick scraped the edge of my jawbone, but missed connecting a solid blow to my head, instead hitting the underside of the granite counter overhang.

At the same time, I made my best, wimpy, worthless effort to straighten my legs. By some miracle, my foot hit his left foot, knocking him off his balance. He didn't flail or fall over, but dropped to his knees like a professional fighter. We were now face to face, my head an easy, tempting target.

For the first time since we'd gotten up close, I sensed the telling movement in his shoulders and knew a power jab was going to finish me off.

Mikahailo said, "You were supposed to die underwater, McKenna. Now you will die again."

In one of those moments where time expands, I remembered why I crawled toward the kitchen island. The broken broomstick was still leaning against the counter, about three feet from my shoulder. I grabbed it and jerked it toward me. Just as he threw his killer punch, I swiveled the dull end of the broomstick under my armpit, jammed it against the counter behind me, and held the stick, pointed end out toward Mikhailo.

Mikhailo's twisting punch carried him forward onto the sharp end of my broomstick spear. It pierced him just below his right ribs, going in a few inches, far enough to maybe shish kebab his liver, but not pass all the way through his body.

Fortunately, getting stabbed took some of the power and all of the accuracy out of his blow, and his fist hit the counter behind me.

Mikhailo didn't make a big reaction. He looked down at the wooden spear, then sat down on the floor. He wrapped the big fingers of both his good hand and his broken hand around the broomstick as if to jerk it back out. I saw his jaw muscles bulge as he prepared for the movement.

I reached up my foot and kicked, striking the dull end of the broomstick and driving it the rest of the way through his body.

Mikhailo loosened his grip on the wood. He stared down at it and slowly tipped over sideways onto the floor, the broomstick protruding a foot from both the front and back of his body.

SIXTY-THREE

My effort had left me even weaker. I was so dizzy from gas fumes that I couldn't balance. I crawled on hands and knees over to Mikhailo. He was still breathing, short difficult breaths, his eyes clamped shut with pain. I got my hands into his pockets, feeling for the handcuff key. I found it in the little change pocket on the right front side.

With great effort and focus, I pulled myself up next to the island counter, then hand-walked myself along the counter. I half-walked/half-fell across the space between the island and the wall, then went hand-over-hand along the wall to the arch that led to the entertainment room.

The gas smell was stronger than ever. The entertainment room was smaller than the living room, and it didn't have a broken window to let in fresh air. I stopped, tried to get my head clear before I toppled to the floor. Maybe there was clearer air in the secret rooms.

But maybe he'd already been in those rooms, soaked Street and Gertie and Ian down with gasoline. My only hope was that he thought I'd entered the castle from a different direction and he hadn't bothered yet to check the hidden rooms.

I stumbled across to the entertainment cabinet, found the release lever, pulled back the shelving with the music equipment, pushed in the secret door. I tried to hang on as the gas fumes overwhelmed me. But as I stumbled ahead, I lost my grip and fell through into the next room. I crawled across the little room and through the second door.

"McKenna!" Lassitor said when he saw me enter. "I smell gas! My God, now it's really strong. We have to get out of here!"

The fresh air near the floor revived me a bit. I crawled past Lassitor, through the far door, and tumbled down the stairs and into the cellar.

"Owen!" Street shouted. "We smell gas. This entire place could blow up." Spot ran over and sniffed me up and down.

"I've got the key," I mumbled.

"You're bleeding on your jaw. And the back of your head! There's blood everywhere down your neck!"

"Hold still." I reached down to her handcuffs. Spot stuck his nose in there, too, blocking my vision. I got the key into one of Street's handcuffs. It opened.

She pulled it through the chain and was freed. She got onto her knees. "Give me the key. I can get Gertie free faster."

She took the key. They were both free in a few moments.

"You should both escape through the boathouse tunnel," I said. "Spot, too."

"You have to come!" Street said.

"I have to get Lassitor. He's chained in the next room."

"Here, you need the key."

I shook my head. The hammering man inside my head went crazy. I stopped and put my hands to my temples. "Lassitor's ankle is chained to a floor bolt. No handcuffs. But I found a splitting maul. I can use it to cut his chain."

"I can help." Street said. Given the fire danger and her chance to run, her earnest offer was gut-wrenching.

"No. Save Gertie. Go. Now."

She hesitated.

"Run!" I said.

Street took Gertie's hand, and they ran to the door that led to the boathouse tunnel. Spot hesitated.

"Spot," I said, pointing. "Go with Street. Go!"

He ran over to them. They all three stepped past the man who still lay on the floor, perhaps dead, perhaps not. Street opened the door. The tunnel was pitch dark. She looked around, found a switch, flipped it on. Lights turned on in the long passage. Street and Gertie and Spot stepped into the tunnel. My last view of them before the door shut was Spot in the lead, with Street running behind him, limping because of her bare foot, pulling Gertie along.

I turned to head back up the stairs. I remembered throwing the maul at Mikailo near the secret door to the landscape garage tunnel. It wouldn't be hard to find. I could fetch it and use it to cut the chain that held Lassitor.

The air had more gas fumes. I dropped to my hands and knees and took several breaths to store up some oxygen before I headed back into the main part of the castle. Then I crawled up the stairs and into the room where Lassitor was chained.

He was up against the wall, terror in his eyes.

Mikhailo stood in the other doorway, wavering, the broomstick spear still sticking out front and back. Blood soaked his shirt and pants. Foam frothed at his mouth. He held the splitting maul in his right hand, the gas can in his left.

He set down the can and kicked it over. A gush of gasoline flowed out across the floor, toward Ian and toward me. I wanted to charge him, but I could barely stand. Mikhailo raised the maul, both his good hand and his broken hand on the maul's handle.

I'd left him for dead, but he was like a mythical bear that couldn't be killed. I'd never seen a man who could continue his carnage with a spear through his body.

I could turn and fall back down the stairs to the cellar, but that would leave Ian helpless. Maybe I could dodge the maul. I advanced on Mikhailo. He brought the splitting maul into his back swing and then hurled it around in a sideways loop. But instead of releasing it toward me, he flung it at Lassitor. The maul flipped over in flight one complete rotation, and then struck Lassitor in the neck, cleaving deep into his flesh. Blood spurted with each heartbeat, arcing up and out.

Lassitor collapsed to the floor. It was obvious that there was no hope of saving him.

But maybe I could make certain that Mikhailo also had no chance of survival. I advanced on him, my rage overwhelming.

Mikhailo pulled out a lighter, flicked it, and dropped it.

The gas fumes were so thick from the flowing gas that the room exploded into flame before the lighter hit the floor.

I staggered back through the doorway. The last thing I saw as I shut the door was Mikhailo standing there, his feet spread wide for balance, as flames roared about and up his body. The broomstick protruding from his body was already aflame. As I shut the door, flowing, burning gas ran underneath it, nearly touching my gas-soaked boots. I jumped back and fell, rolling down the stairs. I got up and did my best trot to the tunnel door. The man lying on the stone didn't seem to be breathing. I bent down, put my fingers on his neck, and felt for his carotid artery. There was a weak pulse.

I stepped into the tunnel, dragging the broken man. My head screamed pain as I pulled him thirty feet into the tunnel, then stumbled back and shut the door to the cellar. I wasn't saving him for benevolent reasons. I wanted him to live, crippled and broken, to face his punishment. As I dropped him to the stones, he made a sound.

I bent down and spoke in his ear.

"If you bother me or anyone I know ever again, I will find you, and I'll finish the job in a way that makes you think your current injuries are mosquito bites."

I was halfway down the tunnel toward the boathouse when I heard an explosion. I kept trotting, ready to dive to the floor if a flash of fireball light came from behind. But it didn't happen.

SIXTY-FOUR

S treet and Gertie were in the boathouse.

"You're safe!" Street said as I opened the secret door. "But you are soaked in gas!" She was standing on one foot, holding her bare foot in the air. In the dim light coming from the tunnel lights, I could see that both of them were shivering.

With pounding head and screaming muscles, I took off my gas-soaked sweatshirt and undershirt and pulled on one of the boathouse windbreakers. The sleeves were six inches short, but it helped. My pants were still wet with gasoline, but I'd be a little less explosive. As I put on the jacket, Street grabbed two other windbreakers and handed one to Gertie.

We went outside. Street and Gertie ran, Street doing a kind of hop and skip to minimize how much her bare foot was down on the frozen, snowy pathway. I stumbled, my brain foggy from pain and gas fumes.

Street turned and called back to me. "Do you have your Jeep? Where should we go?"

"It's parked a good distance away. I don't know if I can make it that far. Your bare foot will freeze..." I stopped and bent over as I began to faint. Street grabbed me, trying to keep me from collapsing.

After a moment, I said, "I assume the men took your phone?"

"I never had it. It was plugged into my charger when they kicked in the door of my condo."

"We'll go to the neighbor's house. Craig Gower. It's early morning. He might be awake. If not, we'll wake him up. If he's gone, we'll break in. We can use his phone and call for help."

"How far is it?"

"Not far. There's a path through the snow."

Street kept her arm around Gertie's shoulder. I kept my hand on Spot's collar. We hurried down the path to the drive, then took the other path over to Gower's drive.

There was a flash of light followed by the deep kaboom of another explosion. We all turned to look. The distant trees were backlit by flames that were coming out of the small windows of Lassitor's castle.

At Gower's house, I knocked on the door continuously.

"Thank you for finding us," Street said while we waited.

"Thank God you're alive. They were going to kill Gertie when they had her in the van. I thought they'd kill you before I got there."

"It was Gertie's quick thinking that saved us from being killed at my condo. She told them that she took their pictures with the phone that you took from the guy in the van. She said she hid it in your cabin. One of the men was going to beat her until she told them where it's hidden. But the other man said they didn't have time and they would take us with them and force her to tell them later."

I reached over and squeezed Gertie's shoulder as I kept knocking.

"I'm coming!" a distant voice shouted.

The door opened a minute later. Gower rolled forward in his chair. He looked nearly the same as the last time I saw him. Jeans, a lap blanket, heavy sweater, a watchman's cap.

"Sorry to intrude like this," I said. "But we're in a jam."

"Good Christ! What is happening?! A few minutes ago, I saw the flames over at the Lassitor place, so I called nine-one-one and reported the fire. But it never occurred to me that you were over there. Is everyone okay? You don't look okay."

"We're alive," I said. I didn't feel like mentioning the men who were probably now dead in the fire. "This is my girlfriend Street Casey. Street, this is Craig Gower. And this is Gertie O'Leary."

"Pleased to meet you, Gertie," Gower said. He reached out his hand to shake.

Gertie slowly raised her arm.

Gower grabbed her hand, spun her around, and jerked her

down onto his lap. His other hand came out from under the lap blanket. He held a gun. He wrapped the hand with the gun around Gertie's waist and angled it up toward her chest.

"No, not again," Gertie pleaded, her voice high and tiny.

"Do exactly as I say," Gower said. "Any sudden moves, she's dead. Both of you turn around and go down the ramp. Slowly. I'm following. McKenna, you keep your hand on your dog's collar."

I took Street's hand, and we slowly turned and walked down the ramp. Street limped and skipped, trying to hold her bare foot up off the ice and snow. She gripped my hand as if to cut my skin with her fingernails. I heard the motor of Gower's wheelchair.

"Stay calm, Gertie," I said over my shoulder as we walked. "I'm sure we can convince Mr. Gower to let you go."

"That's rich," Gower said. "Have you considered the investment I've got into this little operation? No, McKenna, you won't talk me out of this. Either I succeed or it's a suicide mission."

Street and I got to the bottom of the wheelchair ramp, Street still skipping.

"Turn down the path to my dock," Gower said.

Street and I turned. Like all the other paths, the snow had been cleared with a big blower. The sound of Gower's chair followed us. We came around a curve and had a straight shot to the dock. The lower part of Gower's boat was visible under the canopy.

I studied the boat hull as we approached. It looked to be a custom-built yacht, about 50 feet long with a large aft deck, a gunnel-to-gunnel cabin with saloon on the main level and forward cockpit, which was part of the saloon. The galley and staterooms and head would be down below. How Gower would get to them in his wheelchair, I didn't know.

There was a gangplank entrance wide enough for Gower's wheelchair. There was no walkaround deck, upper level bridge, or any other rigging that would require a non-disabled skipper.

Gower rolled up next to the gangplank and pointed.

"Street, you go on board first, Gertie will follow, and then I will board. Don't get any ideas about what you might find on the boat. There's nothing more dangerous than a towel. And I'm not afraid to use this gun."

He lifted it up and gestured with it. In the darkness of night, all I could tell was that it looked like a small, semi-auto pistol.

Gower pointed to the bow line. "McKenna, you man the bow lines. I'll let you know when we're ready to cast off. And don't take your hand off your dog."

We all did as told.

Gower kept his eyes on me as he drove across the gangplank.

The boat had large windows. I could see Gower usher Street and Gertie through the rear door into the saloon. He motioned for them to sit on the rear settee. Then he rolled over to the front of the saloon, rising as he went, moving up an unseen ramp to the cockpit. He flipped some switches. I heard a bilge exhaust fan turn on. After a minute, he hit the starter, and the big diesel below the aft deck rumbled to life. More lights came on in the saloon.

Gower opened a window. "You can cast off. Spring line first, then stern, then bow. Swing the fenders onboard."

I did what he said.

He called out, "Now bring your hound aboard."

We walked up the gangplank. I flipped the electric winch button to draw in the telescoping gangplank.

Gower motioned for me to come inside. I opened the saloon door.

"Leave your dog on the aft deck."

"Spot, stay." I gave him a pet, went inside, and shut the door behind me. Spot could see all of us through the windows.

The boat rumbled and started to move as Gower shifted into Forward.

"You stink of gas, so you stand there, behind the port-side captain's chair," he said, pointing. It was the easiest place for him to keep an eye on me. "I don't want you touching anything. You can hold onto the back of the chair. And crack that window."

I squeezed Gertie's shoulder as I walked by her and Street. I was dizzy. I held onto the back of the left captain's chair, facing a bit sideways toward Gower.

Gower's gun was on his lap, close for quick grasping. No matter how fast I moved, he would have enough time to shoot me. In the light, it looked to be an older Walther PPK. Probably only seven rounds in the magazine, but that was enough to kill three people and one dog and still have three shots left over. With all of us sunk in the lake, Gower could drop his gun overboard. It would be hard for the police to bring a case against him.

I looked around the boat's interior. It was tidy and clean with not even a loose map on the chart table. The only visual warmth and comfort came from a big bowl that seemed attached to the center of the dining table. Just like the bowls in Gower's house, this one was filled with oranges.

When we were a hundred yards out from shore, Gower eased the throttle forward, and we sped up a bit. The bounce of the boat as it cut through the swell set the hammer in my head pounding at double time.

"I'm surprised you figured out that the Lassitor castle was where the women were held," Gower said.

"Your elderly neighbor lady gave me the information about how you can come and go through the ground and that the castle was like the Thunderbird Castle. Finding the tunnels was easy enough. And Mikhailo wasn't the tough guy you thought. You should have been more careful choosing your men."

Gower looked at me. "You know about Mikhailo?"

I wanted to unnerve Gower, get him tense. I didn't think he would shoot us until we were well out into the lake. But maybe I could anger him enough to get him to make a mistake.

"Yeah. Mikailo and I have met a couple of times."

"I figured he'd do something foolish," Gower said. "So you followed him to Lassitor's."

"Yeah. He even tried to fool me for a minute with a lot of talk about being a martial arts wizard. He put on a little dance trying to make it believable. Of course, I didn't buy it. But these talkers, they can fool an old guy like you. What is it about age that makes you oldsters so gullible?"

Gower tensed his hands. I'd found a sensitive point.

I said, "Too bad he poured gasoline on everything and then set it afire, himself included."

Gower's jaw clenched.

In my peripheral vision I saw the flames from the Lassitor castle shooting into the sky. There were still no flashing lights from fire trucks. Gower hadn't called 911 as he'd said.

I was thinking about what Diamond said about the ghost boats. A device that works as a negative feedback loop, always correcting when the inputs went one way or another.

"Your thermostat company makes a nice little cover for you. But you should have known that being in the business of manufacturing what is essentially a negative feedback loop device made you our prime suspect for the ghost boat assault. I called Sergeant Santiago a bit ago and told him that he could probably come and pick you up at your house. I also said that if your boat was gone when he got there, that you would have us out on the lake trying to put us on the bottom. He said he has access to a speedboat and will be out on the water in a bit."

Gower made an angry little motion of his head. His teeth were clenched. His lower lip was pushed up making both lips bulge.

"The ghost boat concept was brilliant," I said. "You must have provided the tracking mechanisms to Lassitor before you took over his operation."

"Ghost boat," he said, his tone derisive.

"That's your neighbor lady's name for what you do. She's been keeping track of you. She knew you were evil. She told me how your ghost boats run all night, slow and relatively quiet. No lights, so no one can find them. Most people don't know that they're out there. And the ones who do never know that there's no skipper, just a bit of electronics and a motorized steering mechanism. It was a good idea for how to gradually map the entire lake bottom near the West Shore in your search for the Lucky Baldwin gold."

Gower held his head at an angle as if trying to keep a hard wind from blowing in his ear.

"So you had Mikhailo and his men put the boats out every night and bring them in before dawn, downloading the scans onto flash drives to bring to Lassitor."

Gower stared ahead at the black lake. Light from the burning castle behind us flickered on the inside of the windshield.

"Lassitor tweaked his facial recognition software to look for the shape of a small chest," I said. "It was a great idea, and it yielded the results you wanted over a week ago."

Gower looked crazed.

"But of course, Lassitor kept that secret from Mikhailo. Lassitor put the location on the flash drive, which is now in my pocket."

Gower turned toward me. He lifted up his gun. Even with the dim cabin lights, I saw his finger tighten on the trigger.

"Give it to me," he said.

SIXTY-FIVE

"I won't give you the flash drive. You can shoot me dead, but you'll have to roll back down your ramp and come get it out of my pocket yourself. In the meantime, my blood will be making a big mess all over your nice boat. How are you going to explain that to the police? And if you don't shoot me, I go and find the chest and keep the gold for myself."

I saw movement in my peripheral vision. I turned just the smallest amount. Street was shaking her head in a way that was minimal, almost unnoticeable, but also frantic. She sensed that I was pushing Gower too far.

Gower took a deep breath and spoke, his own rage just beneath the surface.

"Lassitor died in the fire, right?" he said.

I didn't know what Gower knew. Maybe Gower had a hidden webcam in Lassitor's room so he could keep an eye on him. Maybe he saw the whole thing. I decided the truth might be the best distraction from his mission.

"Yeah. I tried to save him, but Mikhailo killed him with a splitting maul."

"I'm so glad to hear that," Gower said. "I hope he suffered. Tell me that he really suffered. I can die in peace."

"Yeah, he suffered."

"Lassitor was the worst person I've ever known," Gower said. "A natural predator. One of the first patent trolls. I was one of his first victims. He sued me for patent infringement, citing obscure aspects of one of the patents he bought cheap. He had no case, but he didn't choose me based on the merits of the case. He chose me based on my business assets."

Gower turned and looked at me. On his face was pure hatred.

"At the time he sued me, I had invested nearly all of my money in my business. It was a big risk that many entrepreneurs take, trying to grow their sales. I could have brought in outside investors and spread the risk, but I didn't want to lose control of the company I'd started. I even mortgaged my Tahoe house, which has been in my family for three generations.

"Along comes Lassitor suing me for twenty million for infringement damages. I had about about eight million in cash, and two million of that came from the mortgage I'd taken out on my house. Every cell in my brain was screaming that it was an illegitimate suit, that I would win in court. Even my lawyer told me that I could possibly win in court, but that the litigation might cost twenty million and many years. Lassitor said that he would settle the case for eight million. How he knew that was the amount I had, I have no idea.

"My lawyer said it was a no-brainer. That I should give that thief the money because it would be less costly in the end. He said that settling would leave me solvent. Not settling would bankrupt me. It was the most revolting money grab, the most audacious theft that I'd ever heard of. And it was all legal. Legal theft. It's hundreds of times more lucrative than robbing a bank, and it's legal! And Lassitor chose me not because my thermostats really infringed on his patents, but because I didn't have enough funds to fight the lawsuit! He knew I'd settle!"

Gower was breathing as if he'd just sprinted a quarter mile.

"So I paid. It was the hardest thing I've ever done. I still had my company, but I was broke, and I still owed two million on my mortgage." Gower's eyes looked demonic, the lower lids raised up over the bottoms of his irises.

"Nasty business," I said.

"That's just the beginning. Two months after the settlement, I found out that Lassitor bought the castle next door to me. He used my money to buy that castle! When I told him he was scum, he just grinned and said, 'Hey, buddy, no hard feelings. Lawsuits are just business. We can still be personal friends.' I almost killed him right then and there. I remember, I was holding a tree-trimming saw, and I wanted take his head off with it."

"I understand," I said.

"It gets even worse. A thousand times worse." Gower was shaking. "I had a wife and daughter. They were both sweethearts. They were everything in the world to me, all I ever wanted, all I ever really cared about. It was for them that I settled the lawsuit. It was because of them that I couldn't bear to lose everything fighting the lawsuit."

"I heard they died in the car accident," I said. "And you were paralyzed."

"Go ahead and say the rest," Gower said. "That I was driving. Say it."

"I didn't know that," I said. "I just heard about the result."

Gower's hands were white-knuckled on the yacht's wheel. I wondered if this would be a good time to make a grab for the gun. I might have risked it had I been alone. But I couldn't with Street and Gertie in the mix.

"I was driving," Gower said. "When we left home, I pulled out of our driveway and turned toward Lassitor's. I accelerated normally. I wasn't going fast. I was only at the speed limit. Maybe a little more. As we approached the entrance to Lassitor's, he came flying out from his driveway. Lassitor was always a lead foot. He must have been going forty or fifty down his own driveway. He didn't appear to slow down at all. In the past, I'd seen him skid out onto the highway without stopping and almost without slowing. This looked like one of those times. It scared me so much that I swerved away. At the last moment, Lassitor slammed on his brakes. He came to a stop right before the highway."

Gower's voice was loud, almost a plaintive whine.

"But it was too late for us. As I swerved, it made our car skid. We veered into the oncoming lane. We were struck head-on by a bus-sized RV."

Gower went silent. The only sound was the rumble of the big engine below us.

"I told the cops what happened," he continued. "I told my lawyer. They all agreed that there was likely no law that Lassitor broke. They didn't think reckless driving applied on his own property. My lawyer said I could sue Lassitor in civil court, but he didn't think I'd win. After all, Lassitor had stopped. Even I admitted that. And I'm the one who swerved. My lawyer pointed out that Lassitor had the funds to defend against such a suit, while I did not have the funds to pursue it."

"You had lots of reasons to hate Lassitor," I said. "It must have been crushing."

"No one understands! When a sociopath destroys you, takes away everything that ever mattered, and does it with a grin, no one will ever understand what that's like."

Gower stopped to catch his breath. His chest heaved.

"This wasn't about getting money for me," he continued. "This was about taking from Lassitor. This was about revenge. Justice. Payback. This was about making him work for my gain instead of him stealing everything I had."

"So you found Mikhailo to exact your revenge?"

Gower nodded, his breath slowing a bit.

"It was so easy," he said. "You post on certain Internet sites. You work through emails, always changing the email address and signing in through a virtual private network, which makes them impossible to trace. After arranging a couple of substantial, anonymous payments, you can get a psycho like Mikhailo to do anything in the world just on your request.

"Of course, Mikhailo never knew my real name even though I'd learned his. We never even met. He thinks he was hired by a guy in Montana, an ex-business associate of Lassitor's. He thinks I'm just the old guy neighbor who runs a thermostat business in Carson Valley and is sometimes up at the lake house. I even told him through email where to steal the boat to use to drown you."

"But that's no reason to take it out on us. Gertie and Street had nothing to do with Lassitor's actions. You've already tried to have Gertie killed. For what purpose? She never hurt you."

"I came through the secret door once when Mikhailo and his men were gone. She was in a different room than I anticipated. I thought she saw me through the door. I couldn't risk her identifying me later." Gower focused on the black lake ahead. He made a steering adjustment.

"My wife and daughter were everything!" Gower was panting.

He shouted, "Do you hear me?! Lassitor took them away! Nothing matters anymore!"

Gower picked up the gun from his lap, raised it up and aimed it at me.

"No!" Street shouted.

I slowly raised my hand toward Street and Gertie, palm out. I spoke in low tones.

"Think before you pull the trigger, Gower. You'll make a mess. Go back to your plan and you might pull this off."

Gower's hand and gun shook. Not with the stress of holding up a gun, but from anger and rage.

I said, "I've got a friend who talks about the value of a plan. She's a softball pitcher. She says that you can pull off nearly anything if you have a plan and follow it. But if you ignore your plan, you'll mess it all up. Her plan made her a great pitcher. It's amazing what she can do with a softball."

"Shut up!" Gower shouted. "Don't talk mush-brain psychobabble with me! The only thing worse than losing Jeanette and Marianne is when someone like you tries to soften it with gushy nonsense. I'm done with you, McKenna!" He reached up his other hand and gripped the gun with both hands, steadying it on my face. His right finger was tensing when an orange blur cut a horizontal line from the back of the boat's saloon.

The orange struck Gower's hands so hard that the gun flew out of his grip in an explosion of orange pulp and crashed on the instrument panel. Nearly grinning because Gertie had taken my cue, I rushed Gower, but he was faster. He leaned and was grabbing the gun when another orange struck it, bouncing it out of his reach. Like a practiced soldier, Gower didn't slow down. He pulled a knife out of his pocket. But he never got a chance to raise it up as a third orange exploded against his temple, knocking him forward in his wheelchair.

I got to Gower, jammed my right elbow into his chest, pinning him back against the wheelchair. I pulled the knife from his grip and threw it over to the other side of the boat. I pushed him and the chair back and got in front of him so that I could grab both arms. He fought like a young man, slugging me. A fourth orange hit the back of his head so hard, his face slammed into my chest.

He was stunned. His head lolled.

A fifth orange hit the lower back of his neck. It was like a shot from a cannon, faster than I could imagine a ball being pitched. The impact on his neck was savage. It snapped Gower's neck forward, leaving his head to jerk back in whiplash. The blow turned him a bit.

The next orange was harder still, hitting him behind his ear so hard that his body flew forward and sideways, pitching him out of his wheelchair where he collapsed on the floor.

I bent down.

"Make it stop," he cried in a weak voice. "I give up. I'm finished." He was crying. "Make it stop. Please." He was pleading. Whimpering defeat. "Tell your pitcher she has won."

EPILOGUE

"I was pleased to read that both Denell and Galant are going to make it," I said. "The Herald said over eight hundred people attended the fundraiser."

Diamond nodded. "Good men. They brought Denell out of induced coma three days ago, and Galant just yesterday. Denell is already saying a few words, and Galant won't be far behind. Doc Lee told me that it's even possible they'll both make complete recoveries, although it might take a year or three and a whole lotta therapy."

We'd driven up to Incline Village and were in the main room of the Sierra Nevada College Library, a beautiful and warm dramatic space with lots of wooden architectural components.

"Is Denell's wife holding together?"

"Hard to know," he said. "Having to be strong for their kid will help."

"The paper also said that in addition to the account for medical expenses, the boy's college scholarship fund was already up to thirty thousand."

Another nod. Diamond looked around the library. "Nice crowd assembling," he said, obviously wanting to change the subject.

The people coming in the door ranged from college kids in jeans and ski jackets to adults in jeans and ski jackets. Through the various groups trotted Spot, moving quickly, causing a few gasps, as he explored the space. Following him was the school employee who was trying tentatively and without success to get him to go outside.

"Lot of people in jeans and ski jackets," I said.

"Number one ski racing school in the country," Diamond said. He pointed to a distinguished-looking older couple. The woman wore a floor-length black coat. Black leather boots with heels poked out beneath the coat. She had silver hair and gold earrings with inset obsidian jewels as black as the coat. Her partner wore a matching black trench coat. The collar was open revealing a white shirt, black bow tie, and black suit jacket.

"Heading for the San Francisco Opera and made a wrong turn," Diamond said.

"Looks like it," I said. I saw Gertie at the other end of the room. She stood with her mother Nadia on one side and Street on the other. Nadia was wearing jeans and a simple blouse. Even from a distance, I could see that she didn't have her standard layer of heavy makeup. I'd never seen her looking so ordinary.

Sergeant Santiago walked in, stomped snow off his shoes, saw us, came over.

"So something good came out of the kidnapping," he said.

"Sí," Diamond said.

Santiago looked around. "Is this a dry event? I'm not on duty."

Diamond turned to an elegant woman who was wearing a long red dress and carrying a glass of red wine.

"Excusez-moi, madame," he said, "s'il vous plaît pouvez-vous me dire où trouver le vin rouge?"

She grinned. "A noble attempt," she said. "If you weren't wearing a Douglas County Sheriff's jacket, and if your syntax weren't a bit scrambled, I would have been taken in. Come to think of it, I'm taken in anyway." She pointed to a table in the corner with a plethora of wine bottles and glasses, then grinned again before she walked away.

"What was that?" Santiago said. "French? It sure made that lady smile. Nice teeth, too."

"If you'd gotten your syntax right," I said, "she probably would have handed you a perfumed note with her phone number."

"I better practice some more," Diamond said.

We walked over and got wine.

"On duty?" I said, pointing at Diamond's jacket.

"Nope. Just needed the warmth. Helps get attention from les femmes, too. I'll disrobe before anyone infers an association between wine and the sheriff's office."

"Any news on the survivor?" I said to Santiago.

"You mean the guy who dragged his ass into the tunnel of the Lassitor castle before it was gutted by fire?"

I nodded.

"He pretty much confirmed everything Craig Gower said. Mikhailo the Monster found Gower's posting on one of those Internet bulletin boards where dirtballs hang out looking for somebody who is willing to pay for a hit."

"Like, 'Assassin Wanted'?" I said.

"Something like that. Only they use colorful euphemisms. 'Job involves travel and discretion. Must be accomplished at cleaning skills.' Like that. Then they communicate with email through those networks where everything is scrambled."

"Hard to trace," Diamond said.

Santiago nodded. "I talked to Agent Ramos. He said that anticipating this stuff is nearly impossible."

Diamond said, "So Mikhailo brings in Amanda Horner to follow Nadia. When Amanda screws up and gets caught by Owen, Mikhailo kills her by drowning because he thinks that will send an intimidating message to Nadia and encourage her to pay up."

"And besides, he likes drowning people," I said.

"Then when Owen intervenes, Mikhailo tries to kill him the same way," Diamond said.

"Except that McKenna is hard to kill," Santiago said.

Diamond sipped wine, smacked his lips. "Mikhailo writes 'The American Dream' because he wants to taunt cops, 'Hey, I'm the guy who did the other murders, and you still can't find me.' But in the end, Owen kicked his butt." Diamond looked at me. "Right?"

"Not really," I said. "Truth is, Mikhailo mostly kicked mine."

"Any idea how the fire started?" Santiago said.

I thought about how to phrase it. "He was pouring gas over everything, planning to torch the place. But he accidentally lit himself on fire. I barely escaped."

After a pause, Santiago said, "Which brings up another question. The Medical Examiner found a wooden dowel stuck through the abdomen of Mikhailo's burnt corpse. The dowel was burnt at both ends right up to the charred flesh. So it appeared that Mikhailo had been skewered all the way through before the fire. You wouldn't know anything about that, would you?"

"Maybe he fell on his sword as soon as he realized he was going to be toast," I said.

Santiago made the tiniest of nods.

"The ME said the dowel was painted yellow. The paint was chipped. He thought it was once an old broomstick."

"A broomstick sword," I said. "That might be a first."

"What I don't get is how the man we found in the tunnel got so banged up. Nearly all his bones were broken, and his insides were busted up like a train crushed him. When I talked to him in the hospital, I repeatedly asked him what happened, but he just said he fell when he ran for the tunnel. He also had large puncture wounds on his left elbow, and those bones were crushed. The doc said it looked like he'd been bit by a mountain lion."

"Spot came in through the tunnel with me," I said. "He must have grabbed that guy in the commotion."

"The docs say it'll be another month before he can even sit up in bed and that he'll never walk again or even be able to brush his teeth. Not that I mind that he got hurt. He and Gower will spend the rest of their lives in prison for helping to kill Ian Lassitor's actor-standin and Amanda Horner. And it's almost a certainty that they'll be convicted of attempted murder in the attack on Denell and Galant."

I saw Diamond's jaw muscles bulge.

"I also saw Gower in court," Santiago said. "His head is still dark with bruises. And he's wearing a neck brace. You must have smacked him around."

"Nope. Gertie's a fastpitch softballer. She can fire an orange like it was shot out of a cannon."

"The girl did that to him? With oranges? Whoa."

The elegant woman in the red dress came back, walking past us. I saw her slip a piece of purple paper into Diamond's hand, which he then slipped into his pocket. She continued on and went up to the front of the room, held her wine glass up and began tapping a pen against the rim. The room gradually quieted. I realized that she was the emcee. The woman looked over at Gertie who was now sitting in the front row of seats.

Sergeant Santiago pointed. "I see Street on Gertie's right. Is that the girl's mom on her left?"

"Yeah," I said. "Nadia Lassitor. Probably the first time she's been willing to be seen with Gertie in public."

"Why is that?"

"She's embarrassed by the girl's cleft lip scar."

Santiago shook his head. "No wonder Gertie wants Street there, too."

"She said she needed Street nearby to keep her from freaking out. But from the looks of it, maybe Nadia is changing her perception of her daughter."

"Did Gower and Mikhailo ever collect on the blackmail? Or is the woman now rich?"

"Neither. Turns out the insurance was a 'Key Man' business policy payable to Ian Lassitor's company Symphony TechNation. But because the company had already gone bankrupt and was dissolved, the policy was void."

"So you're sure she never had anything to do with Lassitor's murder," Santiago said.

"Gower's confession was clear. He planned the whole thing. He knew that Lassitor had hired a lookalike actor to play himself in the movie he wanted to make. So Gower put a GPS unit and an avalanche beacon on Lassitor's boat. The two electronic devices use different systems and combining them makes for amazing accuracy. When the actor was killed by the ghost boat, his face was banged up enough that even Nadia thought it was her husband. That allowed Gower and Mikhailo to keep the real Lassitor as their software engineer prisoner, and no one would look for him because everyone thought he was dead. Gower's company also created the GPS and avalanche beacon zipper fob to put on clothes. They used one on the hoodie that Mikhailo had Gertie wear so that they could find her in case she ever got away."

The emcee grinned as she began talking.

"Thank you all for coming. We're here tonight to celebrate a fifteen-year-old artist named Gertie O'Leary who's recently made something of a splash in the film world.

"This event is made possible by one of our patrons, a man who wishes no focus on him. This man is what some people have called a merit angel, a near mythical benefactor who drops out of the sky on unsuspecting but worthy artists who've worked very hard against difficult odds. This angel provides those artists with opportunities they would not otherwise have." She made a very quick glance over toward the distinguished couple in black coats. "But while he shall remain nameless at his request, a short explanation is appropriate.

"Suffice it to say that our patron went to this college some years back and subsequntly went off to USC Film School. Since then, he has made many films, some of which you are all familiar with.

"A month ago, one of his colleagues contacted him and explained that he'd read an article about a girl who had recently been a crime victim, and the article said she'd made some videos. So our alum-patron watched them on YouTube and liked them. After viewing the three videos that you are about to see – videos written, filmed, and produced by our young guest – our patron contacted Gertie.

"He told her he was impressed and that he wanted to talk to her about a potential future in filmmaking. He also called USC Film School and asked that they consider Gertie for admission to their summer program. The school accepted, and our patron agreed to provide a scholarship for her tuition and expenses."

The emcee paused and grinned at Gertie. Behind the emcee appeared Spot. He looked out at the crowd, wagged once, then moved over toward the wine table.

The emcee said, "So we asked Gertie O'Leary to come up from Sacramento today to be with us for a celebration of filmmaking. Please welcome filmmaker Gertie O'Leary!"

There was polite applause. Then the four large flat screen

monitors at the outside of the room began playing Gertie's videos.

They were filmed in black and white and told a gritty, noirish, crime saga in three parts, a tense, rushed tale of a teenaged girl involved with a drug gang. The girl decided to become an informant for the police. But the gang leaders discovered what she was doing, and they determined to kill her.

The story was filmed from a first-person point of view, and the videos were presented as if the viewer were seeing what the protagonist saw. The only voice track was a voice-over narration by the main character with some tense, creepy music in the background.

Each of the first two videos ended in a cliffhanger and left the audience short of breath waiting for the next segment to begin.

At the end of the trilogy, the audience cheered and gave her a standing ovation. I could tell that it wasn't just because the filmmaker was so young, but that they thought it was pro-level stuff. Next to Gertie, Nadia beamed.

When the audience calmed, the emcee walked back out in front and said, "Gertie, it looks like you have a film career waiting for you. Would you be willing to say a few words and answer questions?"

Gertie hesitated. She looked left and right as if to see if she could run and hide. Slowly, she stood and turned to face the crowd.

Her voice betrayed a little nervousness, but was otherwise strong. "I'm glad you like my videos. I asked my mom and dad if I could go to USC, and it turns out mom is selling her house. She's getting an apartment down by the USC campus so I'll have a place to live. I don't know what else to say except thank you all for your interest."

Several people raised their hands and asked questions about where Gertie got her ideas and such, to which Gertie gave thoughtful answers. At one point, she saw Spot and patted her thigh. Spot walked up next to her. Gertie rested her hand on his back the way someone might lean on a table. Spot wagged. His ear stud glittered.

At the end, I raised my hand. Gertie saw me and grinned.

"One last question from the gentleman in the back of the room," she said.

"I heard that you admire accomplished artists who acquired their skills on their own without benefit of school. Does that mean you might drop out of USC?"

Gertie beamed. "I suppose it depends on how good their softball team is."

Gertie thanked everyone again. They clapped. As she made a little bow, I saw for the first time the flash of a silver necklace and a pendant that hung from it. It was the wax fir tree I'd made her on the sailboat, the Celtic symbol of Friendship, Honesty, Resilience, and Strength. The stuff of real beauty.

TAHOE GHOST BOAT

About the Author

Todd Borg and his wife live in Lake Tahoe, where they write and paint. To contact Todd or learn more about the Owen McKenna mysteries, please visit toddborg.com